Keeper of the Magic

Trena VanHoff

Trena VanHoff

❀ Created with Vellum

Untitled

Dear Reader,

Thank you!

You have no idea that you are making my every dream come true right now as you are reading my book! I have dreamed of this day since I was a kid, and I cannot believe that it is finally here. I have dreamed of being an author since I read Rachel Higginson's, *Reckless Magic*. It was the first book that I got to read and discuss with my mom, which is something I will always hold dear to my heart, as well as opened my eyes to the world of self-publishing and that I could achieve my dreams.

Never did I think that anyone would be reading my book (anyone other than my family and close friends) so the fact that you picked it up means the world to me!

I hope that you fall in love with these characters in the way that I have and that you enjoy every part of their story as it's filled with so many parts of myself and the people that I love!

Love,
Trena

PS:

Check out my Instagram for book updates and behind the scenes information! @trenavanhoffbooks

Check out my website for a way to subscribe for email updates about the next book in the series & all that is next to come for the Bradbury witches! www.trenavanhoff-books.com

Untitled

<u>Table of Contents</u>

Preface

There was an overwhelming opinion in our towns that I was different, or at least, that the women in my family were different.

It was that sixth sense that told one to be cautious. That is what caused the hair on their necks to rise when they saw us nearby; it was a warning to be aware that has been ingrained in the human body since the beginning of time.

It was the way that trivial things always went our way that caused people to start looking twice in our direction. It was the way that neither of my sisters ever had to fix their hair in the mornings. My mom never worried about any meal that had to be prepared or the house getting cleaned. I suppose that it might be the way that my grandma always had the right answer instantly with the tools to go along with it. I had come to realize that the trivial things that had always seemed to go our way were not a happy accident or a stroke of good luck, but instead, it was that each moment was choreographed in our own way to keep everyone else in the dark of all that we were truly capable of.

While the world thought my family had just a little bit more luck than the family next door, it was actually that they were witches with a bloodline from Salem.

Descendants of the witches they couldn't burn.

And I had that magic in myself as well.

Chapter One

"There is one important thing to remember, Blair Marie, and that is that this is your destiny, but it does not come to any of us naturally. This will not come to you without putting in a lot of hard work."

My sisters and I always knew Grandma was being serious when she decided to use our middle names during one of her lectures. By taking that small second, she let us know the berating was made only for us, as was the disappointment that rang through her words. Thankfully, this was something that all three of us were used to. She often took over the role of disciplinarian during our growing up years and we knew when that line was drawn and when she would draw it.

I tried to be as calm as possible, but her words really were starting to dig in the more she droned on, especially because this had become a regular conversation as my training progressed. She had grown tired of the time this was taking me, just as I had grown tired of spending that time with her; our relationship was beginning to strain the more it fell into the teacher/student role, compared to the normal grandmother/granddaughter role that we were used to.

"I am willing to put in the hard work. I have been putting in the work," I tried to overly emphasize my words to show how sincere I was. "I know that this will not come naturally, I have been putting in the effort and I will continue to try for this."

"You need more than effort. It is sacrifice that brings greatness, and you must constantly be pushing forward with that in mind, or you are never going to get anywhere," she responded. She had lifted her tanned, wrinkled finger and waved it in my face with the intent of driving the point home,

She continued, "I need you to put your entire focus into this and you haven't done that yet." The disappointment she had for us was worse than if she had been mad. I would rather hear her scream than tell me that she was disappointed.

"I understand that," I retorted, "I promise that I do study and work on these, it's just a little harder for me to catch up to the rest of you when I am this far behind."

I wanted her to see my side of it and how hard I really was pushing for this; maybe even have her feel bad for me so that she would give me a break. This was not the first time we had this conversation, and it wouldn't be the last if I continued to be behind the rest of our Coven. My sisters also started at the bottom, but they weren't the last witch of their line. Our Coven can't cast as powerful of spells until I have mastered my magic.

"I don't think you know how much I have put into this," I finished.

She didn't change the expression on her face, it was as tight as ever and full of frustration that she wasn't even trying to hide from me like she had done in the beginning: "I do not want to hear excuses. What I want is results."

"I truly have been studying every night, putting in that time whenever I can around my shifts at the shop," I tried to explain to her why it was taking so long. Explain that I was struggling with keeping my attention on our lesson, the magic still felt too foreign to me, and she was clearly getting frustrated with the lack of results.

"There is still so much that I need to learn and that is a little overwhelming."

She kept going as if I hadn't said anything either time, which wasn't uncommon when it came to her lectures. She had a one-track mind, and she was not going to stop talking until you at least felt the minimum level of her disappointment.

"You must put in the effort if you want the reward, and I can see that you want it. What I can't see is how hard you are willing to work for it and that is the part that I need to see the most!"

If I couldn't manage to get it together for at least this spell before the day was over, then I didn't know what I was going to do or, even worse, what they were going to do to me. Being exiled from our Coven seemed like a possibility if she continued to look at me like that.

My mother was at her wits end when it came to training me after days of endless lessons that didn't seem to go anywhere. It didn't help that magic was the only thing that we discussed when we were together, and my lack of progression was frustrating her with each passing day. Living together meant that the lectures never ended, even if she tried to. It was hard for her to switch off between her role as mother and the one she was forced to have as my teacher. I could tell that Grandma was close to her breaking point as well, as I had been handed over to her and had become her responsibility to deal with the last few weeks.

Grandma did not wait for my response, instead just continued with her lecture. It was as if she had a goal to say a minimum word count every minute and tried to use as many as possible while she was with me.

"So let us break this down further. The word *otium* and *pax* might, in theory, have a similar meaning. Because it is in Latin you have to ensure that you are using the right one. You have to understand that Latin uses many different words to communicate the same message, but that is the way to turn a precious house cat into a ferocious lion. At one point they can both be considered tame and at peace; there is a chance that one of them will change their attitude and now you are chasing a large lion through the town and calling it fluffy. That is not a battle that you would win, I can confidently tell you that one," Grandma explained firmly.

She held up the spell book so that I could read it while I cast the spell. She had a hope that I would have the words memorized before the next time that we came together to practice (it was yet to happen) but the hope was still there, nonetheless.

At least I could say that she had faith in me.

"I understand that." I repeated the words once more, trying to put as much sincerity in my voice as possible. Although, her tone made me feel very discouraged about the entire conversation and my ability to do this.

This was not the first time she had tried to get me to understand the importance of using all the words correctly in a spell even if I were yet to see anything wrong happen. She claimed that was only because I do not hold the power yet to do any real damage and that I had to learn this lesson before I was that strong. It was like learning how to walk before you learned how to run, frustrating, but more useful than I wanted to admit, especially to her.

Grandmother was right about one other thing and that was my need to study the books more and to get the language to the point of, at least, what could be considered a general understanding, which was the part I continued to struggle with. Latin was a *complicated* language, and it was easy to get confused when you add in the element of magic — it intensifies the need to get it right, which only made me more nervous. I had spent *endless* hours studying the language already and it was barely coming together to make any sense at all.

"While it does not matter as much right now because you are still copying the spells of our ancestry and your Coven members, it is going to matter when you are creating your own spells. Now why don't we go again from the top once more." Grandma might have been frustrated with me, but she did believe in me, and I was going to have to ride on that blind faith until I had that same faith in myself.

"You got it this time; I can feel it."

I could feel a shake in my hands and my heart was beating a little faster than it should. Fingering my amethyst amulet, to calm myself down I took a long, deep breath and began to try the spell once more, with a small prayer that it would finally go right.

My poor dog sat in the middle of the table staring back at me, thankfully blissfully unaware of what she was being put through. Grandmother had put her there in replacement of the normal witch's Cat like the one that the spell was created for. I do not know if my dog, Jinx, would turn into a ferocious lion or closer to a dangerous wolf if I mixed up the words, but I also did not want to be the one to find out.

The spell I was trying to master today was one that accompanied training an animal, getting them to calm down so they could focus. Grandma was the one who suggested using the spell on my puppy who was not taking to the potty-training idea despite the last few months that I had tried to enforce it. I personally did not feel like this was a chance I was willing to take on my baby and by the look in Jinx's eyes I could tell that she felt the same way about the situation, her anxiety levels rising to the state that mine were.

"My pet is sweet and deserves a treat, make my pet pax for she runs at her max."

I repeated the words slowly and carefully, trying to remember the rhyme I had studied so diligently last night before bed, refraining from looking down at the book my grandma was holding in her hands— mostly to prove to myself that I could do it. I tried to focus on Jinx while I moved my wand around her head.

The tip of my wand had a faint golden glow that came off it as I cast a spell on the small white puppy. Thankfully, the only physical reaction that she gave was the slight tilt of her tiny head, probably in wonder of what I was doing to her.

"Does every spell have to rhyme like that? I know that I haven't written any of my own yet, but all the rhymes seem like they would get old fast and that you would run out of words to use," I had initially been encouraged to ask questions, but sometimes the look on Grandma's face said otherwise, this being one of those times.

"Your sister, Penelope, created this spell when it came to a sweet calico that ran around your grandparent's farm so that she could catch it. Her goal was to convince your parents that she could have it as a pet," Grandmother smiled softly before quickly removing the expression on her face, moving forward as fast as possible from her comment about my father as if it was something that burned her tongue. This was never talked about, so the fact that she casually brought him up surprised me even if it was *just* in passing.

"Not every spell has to rhyme, but it does help you remember it when it does," She explained, "When you make your own spells, you don't have to use them unless you want to. Most do it as a way to remember the spell, just like a nursery rhyme; the cadence helps it stick."

"It doesn't help me remember it!" The rules of witchcraft were exhausting to say the least and it seemed like every time I turned around there was a new one that I had to follow, "It almost makes it harder for me to remember what word is supposed to come next."

"Honey, your concentration must stay with the spell or else it will not ever work." She even went as far as to reach up, grab my chin, and move my head down to where my eyes would be put on Jinx who sat in front of me, "You must be able to put your entire attention on your spell, having it memorized because one day you will have to say these in your head instead of having a book there to read off of."

"Okay, I understand that."

When the women of my family sat me down on my eighteenth birthday to share our family legacy with me, each of them moved forward to give me a part of the magic I had patiently waited years for. It was also then that I was able to become one with the curse that had a hold over each member of my Coven.

The curse started during the Salem Witch Trials. It was

then that the women of the Bradbury family, the witches, came together and decided that the only way to protect their family was to freeze the magic that the women held. They hoped that by doing that it would protect it from being taken by someone's death as the villagers were willing to go after anyone in search of the witches they feared. Their desperation caused them to turn on those they had previously considered friends. The witches in my Coven protected themselves by only allowing one woman in the family to hold the magic until she felt that the next members of the family were ready for the gift. This is why, to this day, we were only given the magic once we were old enough to handle the responsibilities that had to come with it. It was a lot easier to hide the magic when only one person was having to be careful with it and even easier than that when it was hidden in the oldest women who could easily keep it away from the eyes of others even when they were looking closely.

This witch, the one who held all the magic, became the matriarch of our family and was known from then on as the Keeper of the Magic. As she was the oldest and the wisest, the Keeper of the Magic was tasked with raising up the next line of witches and the secret was to only be kept within their family. It was an especially critical position that came with great power.

The first Keeper of the Magic, Andromeda, was able to keep her family safe by keeping the magic within her control until she felt ready to share it. Andromeda slowly started giving back to her daughters as the villagers stopped coming after them. Her mistake being that she gave it to her youngest daughter, Annabelle, too early. She had a plan to add her to their Coven of witches so that they would be more powerful as the threat of the Salem Witch Trials was towering over their heads with many of the young women in town being sentenced to death.

Annabelle was born a simple girl with big dreams of much more than what her modest life held for her. Her father was long gone before she knew him, a sickness later known as smallpox causing his death. This was long before the witches understood recovery magic: when they would be able to save those from worldly illnesses and afflictions; in their world, there was nothing that could be done. His untimely death left her mother, Andromeda, alone with her three young daughters to raise on a small farm where they kept their modest horses and a few lanes of vegetables that helped them make it through the long winter seasons. They all relied on their human skills far more than their magic, since everyone was watching for magic during this time.

All Annabelle wanted was to impress and marry the mayor's son, Henry. She had a theory that if she were to marry the mayor's son, then the magic would not have to be hidden anymore. They could be free to wield their magic whenever and however they wanted. She would be powerful in her social stature as well as in her magic so they would not have to hide from the people who feared the witches, those who hunted them, because she would rule over them all. She saw the power she was given by her mother as an opportunity to do this.

The young girl used the magic she had been given to her advantage, running the town rampant as fast as she could. She was set out to ensure that none of the other girls in the town would get the chance to get to Henry while she worked on getting him to pick her. Annabelle caused mischief and mayhem everywhere she went, terrorizing everyone that stood in the way of her goals. She started roaring fires, caused great winds, massive floods. All these casualties forced the other families to flee the town for the sake of their crops and harvests, farmers needing to protect their livelihood from the town they lived in. The young witch even went as far as to have the other young women become uncontrollable within their actions, or had things mysteriously happen to their physical appearance such as having their noses grow, lose their hair or it turn grey, or even gain large amounts of weight.

Henry was a very vain man and by doing these things to the other women in their small town, the ones she couldn't manage to send their entire families away, she ensured that no other unwed woman would ever match her beauty or catch his eye in the way that she could.

Andromeda saw the problem within this and what it was going to be for their community. The mother tried to pull her daughter back in, tried to get her to see that damage that she was causing and the danger that it would bring to their family and their Coven. She even went as far as to encourage their Coven of witches to take her magic away from Annabelle, but they all chose against it.

Annabelle's fault was becoming too powerful and too strong, letting her vanity propel her forward. Her actions causing all these things to happen to the other women made the townsfolk become worried for their safety, especially the safety of their daughters, who were obviously the target. It became too much, that even Henry made the decision to run away to sea. He told the town that he would return days before he was to name his bride, as he was convinced that his indecisiveness was what had caused all these things to happen, taking the blame unto himself.

Andromeda was concerned about what the town was going to do to the youngest of her family, as she was the only young woman unaffected by the "bad luck" Henry thought he had brought to their town. As a mother, she worried that they would also find out that her daughter was the reason they were now in search of the mayor's son and why their town was falling to pieces. If they were to discover that she was the cause, it would only be a short amount of time before they were bringing a worn-down rope noose around her neck or building a stake to burn her at as they had done to all the witches they had found before.

As the Keeper of the Magic and the most powerful of them all, Andromeda did the only thing that she thought would protect her family. She cursed her daughter and the remaining unmarried women in our family.

She placed a powerful hex over them that the men in their lives would leave once they had served their purpose, so that they would never get in the way of the magic ever again. A man could never cause another Witch to put their magic in danger for his affection or admiration. She rained this curse down through the generations, casting each woman to be affected by it until a man was worthy of being joined into the Coven, of being trusted with the magic. Only then would the curse be lifted.

This was what caused our uncles, fathers, and grandfather to all disappear long before I came to know of them, only staying long enough to propel the magic to the next generation.

My father was one of the great loves that had left due to the consequences of the curse. He had been a small-town farmer before he met my mother and moved with her to the city. He farmed pigs, cows, even sheep. Every time I asked my mother to tell the story, the details changed. I think this was in a small part so that my sisters and I never had the opportunity to go looking for any other information about him since all our minds were curious and she only was willing to share so much. She worried about who we would find if we went looking. He had a family out there some-where that she was afraid we would contact and that would only make it messy. It is hard to have a relationship with someone who cannot know the biggest part of you.

The way my father was sent away was like how most of them left, telling my mother that it had all become to much for him. Just as the curse predicted, he was gone before the month was over and my mom was left broken hearted with a family of three young girls to then raise on her own. My mother had thought *somehow* that she had been the one to break the curse, that she had found the one man who was worthy of the curse breaking.

Although I think all the women since the curse had been cast had that very same idea as they met their great loves, she did have a good reason for believing it when the others had not. My father did not disappear the moment my sister Celeste was born and not even four years later when Penelope was born. It was unusual for there to be any more than two daughters born into the Bradbury family and even more unusual for the man to stay after he had produced two daughters. My parents had done this without my father having to leave so my mother thought that the curse was broken, that somehow my father got to stay with them forever.

The day she found that she was to give birth to another Bradbury witch, she sobbed to our ancestors begging for my father to be allowed to stay with them. She cried to the Coven, cried to Andromeda to take the curse from her love and from our family, but I completed the reason my father was sent to her, and he was gone just as quicky as he had come. My mother never fully recovered after that day, just as I imagine none of the Bradbury women before her had.

Agatha, my grandmother, was the current Keeper of the Magic and she was the leader over our Coven, controlling the magic just as the first witch, Andromeda, did centuries before.

She had trained my mother, Endora, and her younger sister, Mira, how to be a witch and the three of them together instructed my sisters, Celeste and Penelope, when they came into their full magic. The five of them were the ones tasked with teaching me of our magic and to bring our family to its full strength of the Coven.

"Now try again," My grandmother coaxed, "Try saying the spell slowly this time around. Remembering to stay as calm as possible, take a deep breath, and now go once more."

It has been taught that we are to use a wand while in training as it has magic from our ancestors and is a way to help produce the spell at a stronger level than what our own magic could do. Then once a witch-in-training was at full power, it was a clever idea to still use one for the harder spells so that it once again could help conduct that power to its strongest form. So, the wand had been attached to my hand throughout all my training with the hopes that one day soon I would be able to leave it behind with the rest of my spell books.

Jinx gave me a scared look, but I felt confident enough to keep on going. I raised the wand and spoke with a strong, steady voice, "My pet is sweet and deserves a treat, make my pet pax for she runs at her max."

There was a shiver that went down my spine as I watched my sweet puppy jump down from the table and walk herself through the back door, out onto the patch of grass outside.

Grandmother dropped the spell book onto the table and

reached out for my hands, clasping them in hers; I could see the look of pride on her face now that I had carried out the spell, "See, I knew that you could do it!"

"Thank you, Grandma for all your help today. I couldn't have done it without you."

"You are right about that, although it was you who did it. I just helped you to focus on the spell."

I didn't know if she meant to be comforting or if she was implying that she had spelled me, but either way I felt successful now that I had done a spell.

"I tell you," She continued, "Your sister Celeste took only a few minutes to accomplish this task, but that could be due to her using an actual cat and, of course, not having their cellphones going off in their back pocket the whole time that they were supposed to be studying their spells."

She was shockingly right, and despite her slight dig at my expense, I knew that I could do this. I would just have to learn how to master the patience needed for the job and remember to silence my cellphone before doing anymore spell casting when Grandma was around.

Grandma gave me her tight twisted smile and I realized that she was not yet done with her proclamation despite the soft pause she gave: "I know that the modern world is compelling, but you need to be willing to put your everything into this. This is it; this is your family destiny, and you need to be willing to step up to it all."

What I did next did not show her that I was truly listening even if I was, because I jumped up out of my seat and proceeded to gather all the spell books up into my hands. I did a quick spell on them to mask their look so that they appeared like math and chemistry textbooks instead of their weathered old covers with Latin scripts.

"That's great, Grandma, it really is! I appreciate you are helping me study and for training Jinx."

"You're leaving so soon?"

"I just must go meet Aunt Mira at the store," I tried to explain, but the look on her face told me that it was falling to deaf ears. She was disappointed in me for leaving so soon after we were done.

"I need you to practice your studies more. You are only going to get out what you are willing to put into this. That means reading over your spells, writing down some of your own, doing some potions or charms in your free time," she tried to emphasize her point by wagging her weathered finger in my face, "You are still treating your magic like it's something you are worried will disappear. It is yours; the magic is in your blood. It is supposed to be another part of you, it should be fluid within your actions."

"I can do that!" I could just barely see the fleeting look of disappointment cross her face as I raced for the backyard, collecting Jinx with me as I hurried out the garden gate, already going to be painfully late for my shift at work even if I ran.

Aunt Mira owned a shop along Palmer Cove where we all lived. It was a small store with an even smaller room in the back where she could take the time to master her craft. In the front of the store, she sold everything from the lavender that helps people to sleep, to the cilantro that we eat.

Her store is called the Corner Shop because it actually is on the corner of the boardwalk, within its obvious cliché it was beautiful at the same time. It is the perfect location for a lot of foot traffic, both for locals and for all the tourists that love the idea of walking along the water. The window displays do wonders to pull people in when there is free time within their day.

Every woman in our family had a very similar look that tied us all together. We all had long black hair, tall slender bodies with olive skin to match. There was a wicked competition between good genetics and the magic that flowed through our veins, but it was probably the magic that helped my aunt and mother to still look like they were in their early thirties.

In a town this small there was not much worry for troublemakers and as a witch, we had a very dependable security system that outdid anything that you would be able to buy at the store. The small bell above the door was alarm enough for Aunt Mira that someone was coming inside.

I found Aunt Mira standing in the middle of the room stirring a large wooden bowl. She was using her magic to mix the ingredients together. The strong fragrance of lavender and rosemary hit me as soon as I turned the corner, and my eyes caught the large bottle of salt sitting on the table beside her, along with half a dozen wooden boxes, glass vials, and jars that held more ingredients for the potion she was mixing.

Grandmother had told me when I received my magic that none of them had found a love potion yet that would combat the curse — even though they had all tried at least once in their youth. Apparently, it was often the first potion that the Bradbury witches made their mission to master on their own. Love is what all young girls hope for, especially when told that they will never get to have it, much less get to keep it. Many gave up after a few tries, but my Aunt Mira was different and more resilient in her pursuit for happiness. She still tried about once a month just in case she cracked the code on a new one, one that would work to bring her love to her and maybe more than that, help her keep him.

Herbs are special, their capabilities depending on how they are used and paired with other ingredients. Aunt Mira was an expert at mixing different herbs together and had an amazing way to find a cure for anything that someone might be looking for: colds, flu, stomach aches and even broken hearts; just not a cure for the curse that hung over all our heads. Rosemary is said to make new things grow, lavender comes with good luck and salt is to be thrown over one's left shoulder to keep out bad luck especially when trying to master a spell of this power; a potion this strong could only come from strong magic. I could only guess the hundreds of other ingredients that she would have added to her potion in hopes of getting it to bring her all that she wanted. There were enough open wooden boxes, mason jars and glass vials beside her that I could throw out a name of any herb and it would be one of them.

While there were negative comments about some of the more interesting beverages she created, there were also rave reviews of the teas that we served. What she was really doing was practicing her love potions on the other sad, single women in our town who were also hoping to find the one. The goal was to find a spell or a potion that worked and when it did, she would take it upon herself — praying that it was strong enough on a witch to break the curse. While she had found a few potions that worked on the women in our town, finding them their true love, none of the potions were ever strong enough to break the Bradbury curse.

She had the opportunity to watch my mom fall in love while young and mournfully watched her raise her babies with the man she loved. It was tremendously hard to watch everything she had ever wanted to be taunted in front of her when she knew how far away from her reach it truly was or even that once she got it, she would not have the chance to keep it. My sisters had both looked for a way to break it, as they were old enough to know my father and to watch the way our mother went through his loss, feeling within themselves what it was like to lose someone in that way. But I do not think that they would break it for themselves even if they were given the chance.

Celeste had gone through the curse herself, been gifted her daughters, and had moved on like it was something of the past. Choosing to focus on the blessing of her daughters and the gift that they were instead of looking backward, saying once that it only held sorrow for everyone. The world is full of single mothers and Celeste saw her role no differently, figuring that magic gave her an edge over the rest and she was confident she was going to be fine.

My other sister, Penelope, had yet to find a love that was strong enough to give her heart to and I often wondered which of my sisters I would take after. If I would be like Celeste and take what was handed to me then quickly move on or if I would act as Penelope does and try to pave my own path with the intention of never getting hurt by never putting my heart out there.

I had always been told that my mother had a softer personality when she was younger, that she was different from the overprotective woman I now knew. That she was wild, fun, and had a way of independent freedom running through her. Losing our dad had changed that in her, took her hope away.

Aunt Mira was unique in a way that no one would ever match. She had hope brewing inside of her so strong that it was overwhelming, it could even make me sick when I had too much exposure. She believed without any doubt in her mind that she was going to find her person one day, that she was going to fall in love and that he would be the one worthy of staying. That does not mean that she was going to be patient about it either, which was something I could relate to.

Aunt Mira would be best categorized as a hippie if I had to choose. While we all had the same pitch-black hair, she wore hers in a long curly mess that had an overwhelming amount of volume, which she often paired with satin head-bands woven through the tangles to bring bright colors to the look. She was never seen without a long dress or pants that had enough fabric to put parachutes to shame. Her arms were always adorned with metal bangles that made noise whenever she moved. Aunt Mira was made of something bigger than the stars and she carried herself with that confidence.

"You're here! Do you want to try the new drink that I made up today?" She prompted as she held up a cup as if it were peppermint tea, not that of a potion. "It smells really good, and the extra sugar I mixed in should make it really sweet."

I laughed and quickly shook my head, not even slightly tempted to partake in the drink she was offering, "Not a chance."

Jinx jumped out of my arms and headed for the break room in the back where I had a dog bed waiting for her with an abundance of food and toys to keep her occupied while I was at work. It was a good place for her to run around when I was here with Aunt Mira working so that she wasn't stuck at home.

Lately Aunt Mira had been changing the narrative and coined her herb shop that of a tea store as an easier way to promote the products, get more people in the door, and give herself an alibi for all the teas she was handing out to those hopeless women who came around looking for answers. Aunt Mira figured that with any potion that doesn't work for her, at least it works for the woman in our town, giving her an opportunity to bring that light unto their lives. She had started to make a good name for herself now that she had become more willing to hand out some of the potions within the teas, especially when she gave them a little bit of luck within the leaves. She only worked small magic for it to only seem as if it was good, home-grown ingredients that were helping someone feel better instead of the magic that she infused.

"Grab a kettle from the shelf and start boiling some water for me, please." She continued, "I'm a little behind, I didn't realize how long I had been working."

She was moving even faster than when I first walked into the room. My apron was hanging up on the hook we had on the wall beside the door where I had left it from my shift the day before. I threw it over my head and tied it tight around my waist.

"We need to get started on the Blueberry Sunrise so that there's a lot when the high school lets out. We ran out at noon yesterday and you were not here to help me make more like the slacker that you are," she teased.

Aunt Mira let me use her store as an excuse to earn some extra money, but also a back room where I could study my spells without being interrupted. In a family as large as mine, this meant that there was never a moment alone. It is nice to have Aunt Mira as the other designated black sheep of the family out there watching my back and willing to study with me, especially since she didn't get annoyed when I pestered her with hundreds of questions.

"You could have yelled for me," I retorted, "I would

have run out from the back if you were really slammed and helped you." I would hate for her to be taking all the blame as for why I am busy all the time, but then not having the help that she needs to go with it, especially now that the business is growing with each new tea that she puts on the menu.

She just brushed me off with a smile, showing that she was taking the opportunity to tease me, and got back to work on her potion. I watched as she would slowly add the ingredients. She had all of them laying out beside her within reach for when she felt another pinch needed to be added. There was a method to potion making, and while I was not ready for it yet, that did not mean that I did not take the opportunity to watch. Aunt Mira took her time, mixing it slowly to help the flavors blend into a calming combination. She had told me once that if you rush the flavors, the magic of each element would not blend the way they are supposed to.

I got to work putting the tea together. The large pot was on the counter, so I sat it on the stove, turned the burner on, and added water in the hopes that I could quickly get it to boil. I picked up my herbs and spell-books, even taking a moment to study the ones that were laid on the table in person since they were all sitting back there with me. I had to fully go over this specific herbal book and master it before I would be able to make powerful potions like the ones Aunt Mira makes here at the shop. I had learned a lot from studying where there was such exposure to magic. I learned here that a poppy flower is very pretty, but if I added it to a potion, then it could be used to put someone into a gentle sleep. Such as the potion, or what we referred to as tea to the humans, called "Sweet Sleep" that Aunt Mira sold each day.

I heard Aunt Mira exclaim with delight from the front of the store, "This should be a good one! I have got it this time."

"Goodness, Jinx," I whispered to my sweet white puppy who had been curled up at my feet, having fallen fast asleep the second she laid down. She had jumped up at the commotion of Aunt Mira's shouting and was now on guard for whatever was going to happen next, acting like a fierce guard dog despite weighing less than ten pounds. "Do you think she's got it this time? She sounds confident."

Jinx just stared back at me without much to go on in terms of understanding the situation other than a lick of her tongue against my hand. She then silently went back to laying down, easily falling sleep as she had before.

While most witches have a cat, especially a black one when they want to follow the traditions, Jinx had been an unintentional gift from my sister Celeste. My little puppy had been incredibly slim, skin and bones, and was in desperate need of a home, so Celeste had brought her to me thinking I could take the puppy to school with me. She hoped that I could find someone who wanted her, but as soon as she was with me there was no way that I could have given her up to anyone else. It was truly a blessing to have her come into my life, even if my mom did not always appreciate her in the way that I did. She had even threatened to turn her into a statue once or twice upon finding treasures she had brought in from digging holes in the backyard. Jinx had managed to stay on her good side for four years now and I stopped worrying it was going to happen.

I went back to the front room in time to see a whirlwind of wooden boxes and glass vials floating around me as Aunt Mira used magic to send them all back to their places on the shelves. I stood there with the tea bags in hand to see her twirling around like a little girl, holding the newest potion in a pot above her head like a winner with a trophy.

"You really think that you did it this time?" I asked her, interrupting her little dance party. Her smile was overwhelming. "Careful, you might spill it all over yourself if you keep jumping around like that."

"I did this time! I know that I did. This feels more than right," She jumped up and down with excitement, "I can feel it! The magic just feels right this time." Aunt Mira secured the pot over the spout and poured the potion into a skinny glass vial. The potion she created had an iridescent purple color that seemed to shine when the glass enveloped it. Then I watched her scribble onto the label a quick title, even going so far as to draw a heart to go with it like she did with most of the love potions that she had made. That way they would be able to be found again once she put them up on the shelf. When they didn't work to break the curse, she would cross it out and give it a new title reflecting whatever purpose they served and move on.

"Are you going to give it to someone?" I inquired, as I had often been curious about Mira's potions and her willingness to try so hard for something that seemed impossible.

I know that we all feel it, even if it is just a little part of us. It was the longing when we see a couple who had been together for over 50 years, the ones who still hold hands walking down the street and who have a look of love struck in their eyes. The old couples who discuss their children with strangers in the lines at the grocery store because they are so proud of them. There was a very small chance that I would ever take a sip of any of the potions Aunt Mira made. It didn't matter how much I wanted to understand love or at least the idea of love, there was no way that I could put my faith into something with so much uncertainty.

The door swung open, the bell above sending off a ring as the first customer of the day came in. I took that opportunity to send myself back behind the counter before the young girl had a chance to see me standing beside Aunt Mira signaling that I was ready to do any sales.

It was dangerous to use our magic in front of people, but sometimes the temptation was too hard to handle when it felt so second nature to us all, especially to those like Aunt Mira who used their magic as often as they could. Thankfully most of the time the person who was supposed to be watching would just assume that they hadn't really seen what they thought they had. Humans wanted to believe in normal, which is why they typically ignored the things that should catch their eye.

"Welcome to the Corner Shop. What can I help you find today?" Aunt Mira chimed out with her welcoming smile. I felt a burst of magic in the room as the vial Aunt Mira was holding in her hand landed securely in the pocket of the apron I was wearing.

I think her name was Ninnie, but most people had just talked about her family as a whole, not choosing to single any of them out. Many of the people in our city had started calling them a silly name that had been made up when we were in elementary school. The townspeople called them the Weird Walkers, as all her family sat in the back row of the church, never attended public school, and only went into the town monthly. Their house was found on the very edge of the city, near the woods where few would be willing to venture out of fear of the things that were held there.

There was something to be said about keeping to oneself and their family. A family like mine was often together, excluding those who were different. Many of the people in town tried to stay away after they started feeling that something was strange about us. Grandmother always said that it was nothing about us, rather the other people, that they often had a sixth sense about things like us. That helped them stay safe, just as they were weary of a tiger or bear, knowing that even at their most tame, they were still dangerous. That advice hadn't really made me feel any better when I was a teenager, wondering why no one took me to prom or let me be a part of their social group. This girl, Ninnie, did not seem like she was a part of that crowd. She had not a single part of her that was nervous to approach either one of us, but she was nervous about something else —evidenced by the way her eyes bounced from object to object within our store.

I sent out a little magic, using a spell Grandmother had taught me last week. It helps us to know the intentions of someone's actions before they approach, looking to gain perception from the situation. It was helpful when I managed to get it to work for me, but my magic was uncertain of her intentions because it came back to me without a purpose to expose. Because of this, I made sure to stay within their circle to be able to hear their conversation just in case Aunt Mira needed anything.

The young girl seemed as though she was getting ready to say something several times, she opened her mouth to then close it quickly. I watched the nervous way she wrung her hands together and how her eyebrows pinched together in distress, bringing out some wrinkle that showed years of intense thinking and worry despite her young age.

"What is it that you are looking for? I could make a few suggestions of our items on sale or show you things we have on display?" Aunt Mira asked her softly, gesturing around the room. She grabbed a straw basket and went to give it to her; I could tell that she was also growing tired with anticipation as well. "With our fall line out now, there are plenty of autumn inspired smells to go around. We just updated our displays this weekend so even if you have been in before, it is a completely new store, and we are both more than happy to point some things out for you if you are looking for something specific today."

Ninnie took a deep breath, pulling her confidence together before continuing to speak to us. "I know you are a witch."

Chapter Two

Aunt Mira and I both just stared back at her with matching blank expressions on our faces as we tried to make sense of what she was saying. I flustered around for a second before my thoughts started to come together enough that I could speak in a fluid sentence. "What do you mean?"

Ninnie seemed to have gained the confidence that she was missing when she first walked into our little store because she spoke louder this time. "I was born a witch and I know that you were too."

"How do you know that we are witches?" Aunt Mira asked her in a gentle and soothing tone. My head spun around to look over at her with only shock on my face. I could tell that Aunt Mira was afraid to say the words out loud. Admitting that we were witches outside of our Coven or to other witches that we already knew was a very dangerous thing. The Salem Witch Trials were evidence enough of what could happen if we started to share our secret with humans. They never seem to take it very well; despite the benefits it could bring to their lives.

"I can sense your magic just standing here now. And if that wasn't enough, the magic of your ancestors is very strong here. Anyone with even a little magic in their blood would be able to feel it. The Bradbury magic is well known by all the witches in a hundred-mile radius. It radiates off you in waves." My head was spinning as I listened to Ninnie speak of such a forbidden topic in the open with two complete strangers in an area that was not protected. There was probably nothing more forbidden than that — or dangerous. "It's a well talked about subject in conversations when it comes to nomads who wander through Salem."

I tried to put together what Ninnie was saying, but there was too much of it that didn't match. "Nomads feel it? How often do nomads come through Salem?"

Aunt Mira had a guilty look written clear on her face that let me know she also knew about the nomads and that maybe I was the only person who didn't. "Yes. They often come to find their ancestors' magic since it is so strong here."

I understood our magic and how we were able to keep it within the bloodline, but there were many witches who were not so lucky. "How can someone find their magic?" I asked.

"You can feel it in the ground. Magic is fluid with the earth and even more so if it has been passed through death. When magic is lost to the earth, it fuels the growth of nature around it." Aunt Mira quickly rattled off an explanation without seeming to think about the words. "There is a reason why the colonists who came after our people thought they were cleansing the earth of evil. When a witch was laid to rest, a tree formed in its place, so their thought process made sense."

My influx of questions made me feel foolish as they kept coming out of my mouth. It was obvious how little I knew in comparison to either one of them. "You can feel magic in the earth?"

"Somehow it's kept there to protect it," Ninnie nodded along with the words, scrunching her nose as she decided how she wanted to finish her sentence. Her hands fussed with her blonde hair, showing her personal battle. "It's a lifeforce in a way I could never understand or be able to describe in words, but it's there."

"So, what are you going to do about it?" Aunt Mira enquired. "Now that you know our secret, we have done nothing to disobey or disrespect the Council, so there is nothing that you could take to them," she probed, trying to pull the information from Ninnie. I could tell that she was afraid and extremely weary of what was going to come next from this girl since we had so much to lose.

Ninnie shook her head quickly. She looked like she was trying not to fall apart, her deep blue eyes welling up with tears that threatened to fall in trails down her cheeks. Whatever she was going to say next had obviously been weighing on her mind. "I don't want to be different anymore! I don't want my magic, and more than anything I don't want to be a witch. I just can't do this; it has become too hard." She got louder with each word that left her mouth. "I want this to be done."

I might have also hated the secret a few times, it was an unbelievably huge secret to keep, and it alienated us from the crowd, which was hard enough to deal with as a normal teenager. All that aside, I also knew that our magic was what kept us together. It was what kept our family strong and connected us to our ancestors, also within our Coven. It would be an incredibly hard thing to give up, if that was ever even an option.

"I understand what you are asking of us, but I am in no

way strong enough to do that on my own or even with the help of Blair," Aunt Mira responded with empathy. The expression on her face showed just how remorseful she felt about her inability to help. That was probably one of her biggest things, not being able to help those who needed it — whether it was a sore throat or something as big as this.

I could tell by the ripples in my aunt's magic that she was trying to keep it contained, not let it overtake the situation. Our magic reacted to our emotions, the stronger the emotion, the stronger our magic reacted.

Ninnie's face had a clear look of anguish. "I understand that. That is why I am coming to ask your entire Coven to do it for me. I have done my research on the spell, and I know that it requires a lot of magic and a combined power to complete it." Her eyes threatened to shed tears once more. "Please, I know that this is asking a lot. I wouldn't be coming to you unless I felt it was extremely necessary."

"I wish we could help you, but only an extremely powerful Coven of witches would ever be able to take magic away from someone. Even if we could, it's typically done by that of your own Coven, at least, that was how it was done in the past," Aunt Mira tried to explain to the emotional Ninnie. "That is the only way to take magic from you and leave you alive."

Her voice sounded like a child's, defeated and frustrated. "My Coven would never do this."

In hopes of protecting our secret now that we were talking about it, I focused on the door handle and locked the shop door, then turned my focus to the windows. I managed to flip the open sign over to closed as well, taking the blinds down with it to make the building dark. At best that would keep any humans out if they came to the door trying to come inside. The last thing any of us needed was for someone to overhear our conversation and come to understand that the broomsticks they used in their kitchen could potentially be used for something else.

"I don't think that it has been done in over a hundred years, if not longer than that," Aunt Mira pushed on like Ninnie hadn't responded. I could almost see the rapid collection of her thoughts as she continued to speak to the young girl. "You do realize that we could be accused of treason if your Coven didn't agree with your choices? In addition, it is also an excessively painful process to go through and it is usually only done as a punishment for extreme actions."

I could only think about how my ancestors chose not to do it to Annabelle all those years ago, even after she had betrayed her entire Coven and all the witches in Salem. It truly was an action that was seldom used if they chose not to do it when it was needed so desperately.

Ninnie seemed put off by what was said because of the way that she seemed to retreat within herself. Despite that she kept talking, it was obvious that she would feel very strongly about this if she wasn't going to back down. "I can't continue on like this."

"Where did you hear about it being done? Has your Coven removed someone's magic before? I don't think our Coven has done anything like that since the time of the Trials and even then, it was only the transfer of magic between Coven members the full removal of their magic. Things like that are just not done anymore," Aunt Mira rushed the words out in fear of Ninnie acting irrationally.

"My Coven has never removed someone's magic before, but I figured if anyone would have done it before then it would be your Coven since it has been around longer than the Council." Ninnie explained it slowly, taking her time as if we were missing something important that should be obvious.

I shrugged, taking a second to think over what she was saying before I responded. I knew our magic was old, but it was not as strong as it once was. Our magic isn't used like it once was. "Just because our Coven is old doesn't mean that any of us have done anything like it."

"I understand that, but my Coven is much newer than yours. Our numbers are extremely small, the smallest they have ever been."

"Why is your Coven so small? Have you not continued to have children and families? I thought with your sons marrying witches it made your Coven numbers larger than others."

"That may have been true once, but we also have a lot of our females marrying out of our Coven. That has made us much weaker, far weaker than your Coven where the women never leave." Ninnie's voice almost had a negative tone beneath it, with feelings tied to losing her sisters, cousins, aunts, and more to marriages or other Covens. She know about the curse and the power it held over the women of the Bradbury Coven causing our men to leave even if we wanted them to stay. Our women don't leave our Coven because with magic comes the problem of any man with magic in their veins being repelled from us. They don't come near us, let alone get so close as to love one of us enough to break the spell. Only human boys fall for the Bradbury witches, which was a good and a bad thing.

"You are right," Aunt Mira responded. "Our women never leave our Coven, but that isn't what makes our magic strong. Our magic is strong because we always work on it, constantly trying to push it further so that we know we can always use it. We can't risk losing our magic, it is who we are. To our very core we are the granddaughters of the witches they couldn't burn and there is nothing more powerful than that," Aunt Mira tried to explain what our Coven meant, all without giving her any information about the curse.

The problem with having a curse over our heads was the power that it gave other Covens. Placing a curse on a family like ours was incredibly hard, but adding onto it? That was child's play if someone got enough witches together.

"We don't have the magic of history or the strength that is needed for such a powerful spell," Ninnie insisted, "There is no way that my Coven would be able to even cast a spell of protection, let alone take my magic away from me."

That magic isn't used by anyone anymore, but that doesn't mean that it couldn't be retaught. Studying spell books is the same whether it be current reads or the ones of the past.

Aunt Mira stood tall and braced herself as one would do before a fight. There was so much uncertainty in both of us about what Ninnie's intentions were, especially since our magic couldn't tell us. She tried to keep her words contained within a normal tone. "Just because it's in our history doesn't mean that we would have the ability to do it anymore. Our magic isn't strong enough for it."

"Do you fear of being a witch and the secret getting out?" I asked her as softly as I could, presenting the question mostly out of curiosity. It was like trying to approach a wild animal, slow and cautious or else she would make a run for it. "Doesn't that feel rash? You could choose not to use it instead. Just let it stay inside of you and be dormant until you need it."

Ninnie started to quickly pace up and down the aisle, ready to walk her way through her thoughts and words. Ninnie was a runner; when it came to the fight or flight, it was obvious which side of the line she fell on. "My family has been hearing some rumors about the extinction of witches — that there is something, or more accurately, some*one* coming. They call themselves the Cabals. Someone or something that has been going around, stealing the magic of the witches, and then killing them before they have a chance to scream. I can't imagine having to go through something like that!"

The thought made my stomach turn a full rotation and Aunt Mira looked like she was going to be sick from the news. I tried to get to the root of the problem, "Where did you hear of this if they are killing everyone?"

"I suppose that it was more than just a rumor," She gave us a hesitant smile; it was obvious that she was hoping to keep this part to herself even if she trusted us enough to talk about our magic out in the open.

"And that means?" The ripple of Aunt Mira's magic made my magic react as well; it moved me with the anticipation of what was to come. I had never had my magic react so much at one time. I had never had it try to warn me, protect me, like it was trying to do now.

"One of the girls they tried to kill was able to escape. She ran to our Coven for safety when she got the chance. She has been living here with us for over a week now," She explained in a quiet tone. Her eyes started getting shifty with fear once more. While she had said a lot of things tonight that could be considered a treason against her Coven witches everywhere, that one was the worst of them all. Admitting that she had been hiding someone that the Council was potentially looking for was the worst of her crimes. "She called them the Cabals. She said that they were fierce looking and ready to kill anything that crossed their path."

Joining another Coven would only come from something that extreme, and I wondered if there was a connection between the two Coven if Ninnie's was just the first one the girl found. I would much rather be on my own than to give someone outside of my Coven access to my magic.

When witches are within a Coven, not only do we have others to build us up, teach us, or help us learn our craft and magic, but we also have a stronger connection to our ancestor's magic as it flows through the generations and within each other. We will only be as strong as our Coven the witches that we surround ourselves with.

Aunt Mira continued with her questions now that she would be able to get some answers from Ninnie. The words shot out of her mouth faster than it seemed they were coming to her mind, as if she worried Ninnie would return to her quiet, evasive ways before we could get the information that we sought. "What is your family's plan? They *must* have a plan if they are going to keep her!"

Ninnie shrugged. Her eyes danced around the room again instead of staying on either one of us. "Their plan is not really in place yet. I cannot say what they are going to do, I think they are trying to figure out what to do with her."

"What are they going to do with this witch? They can't hide her forever; the Council is going to have to be informed about her staying with you, especially if it's going to be long term." Aunt Mira only got more animated as she continued talking, her hands waving in the air with enthusiasm.

"They plan to hide from it until it passes, at least that is what they want to do right now. But I can't do that anymore; I have lived my entire life in the shadows, and I can't do that anymore," Ninnie exclaimed with a determination I hadn't imagined her to ever have. Suddenly the quiet girl I had observed for years, who avoided the world, had blossomed into a fierce warrior ready to put on a fight of her life. It was really something amazing to watch. "I am going to find someone to remove my magic so that I can live my life without being terrified of someone trying to take it away from me. If I am going to lose it, then I want it to be on my terms. I would rather lose it to become a human than to lose it and die."

Aunt Mira clearly wasn't loving Ninnie's Coven and their plan, especially the way that Ninnie wanted to deal with it, that was written clear as day on her face. Having her magic taken away would mean being human, being more vulnerable, and that could only be more dangerous, not to mention she would be released from her Coven on her own. Not being with my family would be the hardest thing in the world, far worse than being turned into a human.

"You *aren't* going to get your magic extracted."

Ninnie got a look of determination across her face, ready to ignore anything I said. "I will find a way to, even if you are not going to do it."

"You are not. You are going to join with us, and we are going to fight this together." Aunt Mira was made of the same fighting spirit as all the witches from the Salem Witch Trials. The ones who made sure to keep our magic strong and survived extinction. Their fight is the reason that our magic is still alive today. Mira Bradbury was amazing in every way!

"I'm not sure if my Coven would ever be willing to do that. They don't *want* to fight and even if they did, we don't have that kind of magic. We especially don't have enough strength to fight against anyone who is that powerful,"

Ninnie explained, the fear returning. I had witnessed first-hand that her family was more comfortable with hiding in the background as that was how their magic had gone undetected.

Aunt Mira got a sharp look of perseverance across her face. Her voice got stronger with each word that left her mouth. "That doesn't matter, we have a sister Coven. The two of our Coven nether should be strong enough to get through this, especially if we could get yours to join us. That much magic combined would be stronger than anything they bring forward."

Sister Covens are extremely rare, especially since the Council was created. It meant that within a family line, the magic was strong enough to split in two and produce twice as many witches all without losing any of the magic along the way. It was something that happened before the Salem Witch Trials since there were so many of us, but after that time and the executions, there weren't sufficient witches to keep the magic strong enough. Now, within our modern times, as a witch married into a family with magic, then she would join their Coven her magic would fuse with theirs. It's in the same way that a human would take the last name of their spouse after marriage.

Grandma has a younger sister, Edna. It was only a few years ago when Aunt Edna and Grandma made the split of our Coven. Due to our family only producing women, it kept our magic strong and larger than most Coven splitting into Sister Covens, it contained the magic and kept it safe. Aunt Edna took over her own Coven when her daughters had come of age into their full magic so that there was not too much magic under one matriarch. Splitting a Coven also meant that it would not become too large. It wouldn't look good to have a Coven that was bigger that of the Council.

We never want to look like something that could potentially be a threat to them and all that they have created. They are what has given our world order when it had been in such madness during the time of the Trials.

"I have never heard of witches fighting for their magic on their own before, but I can tell you that it would be a hard sell for my family. They would rather take a gentler approach to the whole thing or not approach it at all, if possible," Ninnie continued, although extremely hesitant. I could understand where she was coming from. When she had walked into our shop, she was prepared to never be a witch again, yet here we were trying to convince her that we were going to be her saving grace, planning on keeping her magic forever.

I tried to reason with her in a different way, "That doesn't mean that we can't be the first ones to fight for our magic. We must be strong and brave if we are going to get through this."

"I will let you know that my mother spoke about calling the Guardians and asking them for help in this situation. Her belief is that they would be the best option for us all. She thinks that they could take care of us and get rid of the problem," Ninnie explained with a strong note of hesitancy, the same one I had heard before when we proposed the idea of fighting back against the Cabals. "I think she is going to do it too. She hasn't been willing to entertain another idea." She did not seem very confident in that call, which I could understand as well. I would also be hesitant with the idea of calling for someone else to join our cause. My Coven had enough magic to stand on their own within our number of witches and the power that each of us held.

The Guardians were the sons of witches. These were men coming together to make their own "group" or their own Coven. In some folktales, the Guardians have been called Warlocks, but that didn't do justice to what they are or even give an accurate title to all that they do. The part of the Guardians that makes them different from a warlock or any other complicated title is that only half of them were blessed with magic, where every daughter of a witch is born with magic.

If they are given magic, then the boys are trained and raised up with the understanding of how to wield their magic for the protection of witches, an honorable cause if there ever was one. They were taught protective spells and spells to cause harm to others, something that was rare to be found in normal spell books. When a Guardian is born without magic, then they are trained to be powerful, using their physical strength and extreme wit to protect those of the world. These men were often given a blessing from their Covens to make them stronger, smarter, or even braver than that of an average man — as if being from a Coven witches didn't already give them an advantage over the humans.

A group of Guardians are chosen to work for the Council, being their personal bodyguards in the most traditional sense, swearing to protect them through the end. Many of the others come together to work as mercenaries on their own, making it their job to ensure good and balance within our world. They are usually tasked with protecting the women in their own Covens.

The Council stood over all witches and oversaw any one that stepped out of line. It did raise the question on why they hadn't stepped in yet to deal with this issue. There was no way that they did not know about it, especially if anyone had the thought of calling on the Guardians.

"They are going to *call* in the Guardians! How do they know how to get to them? Or are they just hoping they can find someone who knows them well enough to get ahold of them?" Aunt Mira pushed forward once more, and I could tell that her passion to be involved in this cause had changed to a new purpose altogether. Aunt Mira had been infatuated with the Guardians since the moment she learned they existed.

The only issue with getting ahold of them or calling on them was that a witch had to have a direct link to get in touch with them. Our issue was that because our family only produced women, we had no link to them. If our cause were great enough then they might be willing to overlook that issue or at least think about it, but their argument was often that a Coven had to add to their army if it was going to be protected by them. I don't know what we would say to convince them to help us.

"My family has a connection to the Guardians," Ninnie smiled with some pride in her eyes as she talked about her family. "We have sent our men there since the Guardians were founded. My Aunt Lydia's son, Seth, is a current Guardian."

"That's amazing!" Aunt Mira gave an excited shriek. It was the kind that could shatter glass if she wasn't careful. "Do you think they would help us?"

"My Aunt Lydia says that Seth would be willing to come if we asked him to and I believe that we could convince him to protect your Coven as well," Ninnie explained softly, the earlier smiles dropping from her face. I could tell that her bravo was gone, she had used it all to come in here and confront us. I could also tell that she was a little nervous about whether their case was strong enough to get the Guardian army here and not just Seth. "So, your answer is final? You aren't going to help me take my magic away then?"

I saw Aunt Mira shake her head quickly at Ninnie's question. There was no way that we were going to take her magic away, especially not if there was an army of Guardians that we could convince to protect us all.

"It's not that we are not going to help you," I assured her, "but we cannot take your magic away from you. The two of us would not be powerful enough to do it and there is not a chance that our Coven would do it either. Our family would not go behind the backs of yours to do that." I realized that I was speaking for everyone, but I was in too far not to keep going at this point. "If we do have to fight them, I would be honored if you chose to join us and fight them as well."

* * *

The rest of the day after Ninnie left was calm. There was a small stream of customers that came in. I could tell that the news that Ninnie had brought to us was weighing heavily on Aunt Mira's mind throughout the day, especially as she moved through our tasks. On a normal day, she would have wanted to chat as she did them, but today she stayed silent.

When work was done, Aunt Mira sent out a few waves of magic to close and lock up the shop, ensure all the bins were tightly closed, and that we would be ready tomorrow to open the store back up. She informed me that she had decided to call a Coven meeting so that we could discuss what Ninnie had brought to us. I knew that none of the women in my Coven would be willing to lose their magic, but what I didn't know was how hard they would be willing to fight to keep it when hiding was such an easy choice.

I left my aunt with a promise to see her tonight and let her finish closing the store. I could feel my hair standing on its ends as I walked home. The playground of the local park was on my left as I rounded the corner to my street, and I could see a group of small children playing on the swings. There were even a few little boys who were playing on the cement top with a ball that seemed a little too big for their hands. The little group was trying to play basketball, but their legs weren't quite long enough, and the basket seemed too high for them to even come close to making any points. If it had been a normal night, I would have sent a little magic their way. Taking the chance to lower the basket, only by a few inches, so that they would be able to at least get it a few times and make them feel like they were playing the game in the way that they wanted to.

Tonight, I didn't take the risk of exposing my magic. While the humans would have never taken the time to notice the basket suddenly getting closer to the ground, a witch could see it just as it was happening and be able to easily spot where it was coming from.

There was a quickness in my step as my house came into my view, Jinx being right on my heels as if she could feel something was off as well. It was probably my anxiety being pushed onto her. I bounded up the steps into the home I shared with my sisters and mother. They were all standing in the kitchen waiting, quite possibly for me, as they knew I would have been at the Shop with Aunt Mira today when Ninnie came inside. Even my nieces were sitting patiently in the chairs at the kitchen table, both coloring a picture.

My frantic mother swept up her arms for a hug. "I am so glad that you are home now. I feel better when you are all home with me." She tucked me into her side before disposing me to the table where she sat beside me. I could tell that she was nervous by the way she kept patting my hand. "What happened today? Mira sounded frantic on the phone."

"It's more Aunt Mira's news than mine," I tried to explain quickly as well as give myself an out. I used magic to take the leash off Jinx once I was in the kitchen, sending it away to the coat closet along with my jacket. Jinx took the opportunity to jump up into my lap, resting her head on my forearm and falling asleep with soft snores.

My Mom jumped from the table and started to nervously pace the room from one wall to another. "Your aunt knows that mystery is intriguing, that must be why she was so vague on the phone. Sometimes I think she does it just to get under my skin."

"Mom, I think that Blair is having us wait for Aunt Mira so that they can share the story without any interruptions," Penelope shut down Mom's suggestion. She didn't say it, but I knew she wanted to wait for Aunt Mira because she wanted to watch the end of the football game without being interrupted.

Mom agreed to wait for Aunt Mira with only a mild complaint about her younger sister and her inability to be on time even when she was the one to make the plan. While we waited for our aunt to arrive, my eldest sister, Celeste, made polite conversation by asking about the shop, how sales were going, and if people were enjoying the new flavors, we had recently added to the tea menu. Aunt Mira and I had decided to put out some seasonal favors at the beginning of September to run through November such as pumpkin, cinnamon, apples, and more. Just because we didn't need the profits didn't mean that we didn't want to give Starbucks a run for their money.

Once the game was over, Penelope joined Celeste and I at the table. My sisters quickly trailed off in their own conversation in the way that they often did when we all sat together to talk. The two of them had the most in common out of our small group of three, being in their late twenties and me barely entering mine. Celeste brought up her girls, how well they were doing in their classes at school, and Penelope brought up her music, her practicing schedule, or her job at the local middle school teaching music lessons. I couldn't help being born so much later; my life wasn't nearly as established as theirs so there wasn't much I could add to the conversation.

From where I sat, I could see that Aunt Edna, and my cousins Grace and Cassandra were in the living room talking with Grandma, but it wasn't a surprise since their magic had already let me know they were near when I first came through the door.

I got up to let Jinx into my bedroom so that she would be out of the way and took that opportunity to put my bag away. I tucked my spell books onto their shelves so that they were ready for tomorrow's lessons. It's an everyday thing now where I sit down with Grandma, Mom, or Aunt Mira for some lessons, but I also had the independent studying I had tasked myself with. Suddenly, I felt the same feeling of being watched again, as if there were eyes on me, a feeling I had never felt before today. I sent a wave of magic to close the blinds as tight as they would go. Even if I wasn't going to stay in there it still made me feel better knowing that no one would be peaking in.

There was so much that had happened today, so I wanted to take a moment to digest it while there was no one watching or waiting for something from me. That included processing the feelings that the shadows in the dark had been giving me today. There was so much danger in the world for humans, but that wasn't always necessarily the case for us.

I could hear the door swing open as my cousin Piper arrived and I felt the shift of magic in our house as Celeste sent her girls upstairs to play. There was a flurry of conversation as they were all waiting to see what was going to happen next, comparing stories, what they had heard, and theories that they had created during their wait. I imagine that Aunt Mira only gave a small description of what had happened today since it wasn't safe to discuss it over the phone as it could be charmed.

I felt Aunt Mira come inside the house as her magic joined ours and I came out in just enough time to see her walk into the kitchen to approach the others. A silence covered the room as all the women in the kitchen came to sit in the dining room.

Once we were all seated, Grandma propositioned our group to open the meeting with a spell. Grandmother lit a large black flame candle, sitting it on a plate in the middle of the table so that we could all be surrounded by its light and grace. The spell was one Grandma picked often since it was used to promote the truth told by everyone involved.

Wicked Eyes, tell no lies
The truth shall set you free,
It is the only way to be,
Devil tongue tell no tales,
By witch's hand spare no honest details,
Choke on air each time you try,
Never again will you tell me a lie

Once the spell was cast over the room, Grandma then opened the floor for Aunt Mira and I to talk. The two of us stood simultaneously bringing the attention of the room over to us. Aunt Mira started talking, slowly at first, taking her time while she gauged the reactions of everyone in the room. "I guess that I will just come out and say it."

I reached out a hand to hers to give her some silent support. I could tell that she was nervous to talk to them about what we went through today. "You got this," I whispered under my breath.

"We were approached at the store today by Ninnie Walker, the youngest daughter from the Walker family that lives on Vine," Aunt Mira kept talking. A few nodded their heads, showing that they knew who she was talking about, which in a town this small it was hard not to know everyone who lived here. Especially when our entire lives revolved around a secret and our ability to keep it.

"She had a proposition for us, and it wasn't a normal one. She requested that we take her magic away from her. She was hoping that Blair and I would be able to do it or get our Coven to help us."

I jumped into the conversation and the rest of the room responded with a few gasps of distress, "She's a witch! They are all witches."

"That just isn't right," whoever spoke, her voice broke clear through the silence while everyone else tried to collect their thoughts.

Grandmother threw her hand to her chest. This was her clear sign of distress, her way of showing that she couldn't fathom the situation she was put in. "Doesn't she know that just isn't done? We could be accused of treason by the Council for even thinking about removing magic from a member of another Coven."

Aunt Edna and some of the other older witches chimed in with their agreement of what a terrible idea that would be. The Council would come in and only bring problems with them. It was in our best interest to stay as far away from them as possible if we could manage it.

"You don't have to worry about that," I spoke up, "We told her that it was not something that we would be able to do for her and that shouldn't be something she should even be thinking about."

"But I will let you know that she also came to inform us of the dangers that her family had come to be aware of," Aunt Mira interjected. "They were told that some witches, who call themselves the Cabals, have decided they want power over all the witches. They have started going around taking magic from the witches that they find, then killing them to ensure that there will be no one finding out about it until it's too late." Aunt Mira addressed the real issue that brought us here today for our Coven meeting, "that is why she wants her magic removed. They wouldn't be able to take anything from a human and she can continue her life without this threat hanging over her head."

Casandra spoke in a whisper with a very similar look of despair written across her face as the others, "How does she know about this happening? Are they coming for all of us?"

"The Walker family is giving sanctuary to one of the witches that managed to get away. She was able to warn them about the Cabals coming," I said, feeling like I was betraying the trust of Ninnie by sharing that, even if I was sharing it with my Coven, the people I trusted the most.

Mom gave us a concerned look and I could feel the way that her fear overcame her magic, ready to unleash as it was needed to protect her family. "What do you mean witches that want more power?"

Celeste reached out to hold Mom's hand, adding to her strength as she was almost shivering in her seat. I could tell that she was nervous too, glancing to the stairs where her daughters were upstairs playing.

"They are taking magic by force and the Walker family wants to hide out and wait for them to stop the search," Aunt Mira explained, "Actually, they decided to call the Guardians and then they are going to hide out while the Guardians take care of any issues that might come up." Her voice raising to match the magnitude in which she felt the cause.

Celeste sat forward, her eyebrows piercing together in concern. "What will happen if the Guardians are called? Will they even know we are here?" Her body shook with fear, her magic pulsing with the desire to act out. "Will they protect us as well? Or are they just going to let us die here?" I knew she was thinking of her daughters who sat upstairs and had not received their magic yet or be able to protect themselves if anything was going to happen to our Coven.

I could see the other women of our Coven all nod in agreement, as that was also going through their heads.

My great aunt Edna finally spoke up, "They will only help if we ask them to and only if we promote a persuasive enough argument to convince them to help us. They won't just be able to do it on their own regard. They have a code to uphold." Her voice was shaking with age. "There must be what could be called a bonded connection for them to come and do their duty. They do not just protect every witch that they see, it has to be from a sense of duty and that of a responsibility."

"Don't they have a duty to all the witches?" Grace proposed the question to her grandma.

"The Walker family has a history of having connections

to the Guardians due to immediately sending their sons away for training as soon as they turn twelve, with having produced quite a few sons within each generation," Aunt Edna continued with her explanation. She obviously knew and understood the Guardians. "Our family no longer produces sons, so we have never sent a son there."

"That means that the Guardians don't feel like we have given a contribution to their cause. Which opens the question on why they would protect us?" Grandmother finished her sister's thoughts. "We would need to figure out a way to get them to help us if that is the way that we want to go forward with this. Convince them that we are an ally that they need instead of a burden."

Would the Guardians really be able to sit on the sidelines and let us die? That wasn't a thought I had time to process yet and it was one that I couldn't fathom being true. How could they not do anything?

Aunt Mira seemed impatient once more, jumping back into the conversation. "What do we want to do?" She waited for everyone to agree, even disagree, or at least have them talking instead of mulling over their thoughts. "I vote that we fight. We fight for our magic, and we fight for our family."

"You said the Walker family as if you knew of them. Did you know that there was another Coven here?" I directed my question to Aunt Edna. I had no idea that they were witches until today and I could tell that Aunt Mira had no idea either when Ninnie walked into the store with her announcement.

My great aunt nodded slowly; her lips puckered together while she decided how much she wanted to share. "We have always been aware of their existence, but they had no problem living with the existence of us and we never had a problem with them being so close. Their family has been in the area since the Witch Trials as ours has been, but they have moved in and out of the city limits a few times as the size of their Coven changed. Their magic is very weak, which is why I think they have never contacted us before."

"Why did I not know that they were here then? I had no idea that there was another Coven of witches anywhere near us," I pushed once more for the details that were under the surface. If I could just get her to open up, then maybe the words would just start flowing. "Why did she act like coming to us was such an act of treason? Coven live with each other, work together, cast magic together, and even mix with families all the time. Isn't that how the magic continues through the generations and stays strong? With witches marrying those with magic?"

I have never even felt their magic before today. A Coven of any size would have been felt even if they barely had any magic in them.

"Mixing Covens isn't something that you can do easily when your Covens large as ours," Penelope laughed, acting like this was all one big joke.

"It might appear that we are trying to make our own Council or trying to become powerful enough to overtake them," Mom explained in a hurry, her words almost seeming to stack on top of each other. When she got nervous, her words always flew out of her mouth, a trait all three of her daughters inherited. "We don't have any men to offer to anyone for a spouse and we don't want to lose any of our girls to another Coven either, which poses the problem of any of us marrying a man a part of a Coven is own."

The older women in the Coven nodded in agreement as if this was something they had already thought of. We all know to be aware of the Council. They were too powerful to risk upsetting.

"Even the threat of creating a new Council is something that could cause the downfall of our world," Grandma had a grave look on her face as she spoke. "You know that the Council was formed of the families of the fallen witches. They took over this job so that none of the magic was lost. As the people of Salem came forward and slaughtered our kind, others hid in the shadows and collected the fallen bits of magic to keep it from entering back into the ground. If a Coven was down to one witch left, then they would take the magic to ensure that it wasn't lost forever. Some brave witches who felt that they could not survive the Trials even sacrificed their magic to the cause. This is what the Council is trying to do and what they are trying to protect."

"I understand the sacrifice the first witches made for us, but what are we going to do for the future witches?" I asked my Coven. "What about the girls upstairs who don't have their magic yet and can't protect themselves? Is it not our job to protect them? Is it not our job to ensure that the magic lives on?" I took note of what these comments did to each of the women in my family, my Coven way that they interacted with it and what it meant to them.

Mom proposed the question that had been going through everyone's mind, "Why hasn't the Council stepped in yet? They should stop this! The Cabals should not be taking advantage of their power or the power of other witches. The Council is in place for a reason, and this is part of why they were created," Mom got animated as her exclamation grew. The magic within her rose as well — it was ready for a fight to protect her family. "There is no possible way that they don't know what is going on. If they have the power to do it, then why would they let this go on?"

I wondered why no one mentioned the whispers of a traitor among the Council and how this could be connected. There had been a scattering of conversations about it for a while, and this was only pointing to it being true. Although, I knew that Grandma was in denial.

"Maybe there is too much at risk for them to step in? These Cabals are dangerous, they can't risk themselves even at the expense of the rest of us," Cassandra suggested.

While her comment did have some merit to it, what would the rulers of all the magic have to be afraid of when it comes to facing off against these witches? They were supposed to be all powerful and with the Guardians backing them, then there should be no reason for them to not take these people on. And what did the Council have to fear if they did not have a secret? They were the ones who were in charge. Without them our world could only descend into chaos. Had they not come to realize that their power of guidance was needed even when other witches don't follow the rules?

Aunt Edna scoffed at the idea of a risk. She was obviously not afraid of whatever the outcome was going to be. "They are more powerful than any group of nomad witches, even ones set out to only inflict mass destruction on our world. The Council is waiting until they're stronger and then is going to make an example out of them. This would be an opportunity to show the people that they will never be stronger than the Council. It would fit their history to do it that way."

"They are just fine with losing a few Covens now that Sybil is in charge. When Hawisia was the one in charge, she would have cared for her people and put an end to this before it hurt anyone else," Mom looked disappointed. The change of power had happened ten years ago. I didn't remember any of it, but the other members of my Coven did. This wasn't the first time that the women of our Coven had hoped for the return of Hawisia even after she had left.

She had been the leader of the Council for centuries and had been fair and just within all her decisions. Her daughter decided to suppress her own magic, choosing to go against the ways of her magical upbringing to live a human life, and it broke her mother's heart. Hawisia stepped down from her position, following her daughter to the life of a human so as not to lose her forever. Our magic can keep us alive for a very long time, far past that of a human's lifespan, but we lose that ability if we don't use it.

"So, what are we going to do now?" Grace asked beside me.

That pulled everyone to a still since we didn't really know what we were going to do. What *was* there to do in a situation like this one?

Chapter Three

Mom pulled out a cedar smug stick from the cabinet, and after lighting the end, she walked circles around our house to ward off the negative energy that she believed our intense discussions had brought into our house.

She had made the decision to charm our house years ago. Charming it meant it was protected from any magic inflictions and stopped anyone from coming into our home unless invited. Even after having done this, she was constantly worried about what might enter our house, including negative energy that might come in and take part of our lives. This meant that our house was subjected to weekly smugging.

Mom had told my sisters and I since we were young that negative energy in our home causes issues for all of us. It causes people to fight with each other —which might have just been a way to blame something for having three daughters constantly fighting over the bathroom.

Everyone had left once we called an end to our meeting, the last witch finally walking out our doors just after nine.

The final decision was to send everybody home to get some rest and reconvene here two nights from now. That would hopefully give everyone some time to think about what we had talked about and decide how they wanted to move forward.

Celeste had taken off upstairs as soon as we were finished, putting her girls in the bath before getting them off to their beds. They both had school in the morning, and this was already getting to be a late night, much later than she usually allowed them to stay up. My sister was somewhat obsessed with keeping them on a schedule, especially now that they were old enough to be in elementary school. Celeste felt that with them being surrounded by humans whose lives also revolve around a proper schedule, it would only benefit her daughters when it came to helping them blend in with the other children.

Celeste was always the one who kept her life closest to that of a human, so her intensifying that habit once she became a mom only made sense. My eldest sister had decided to raise her daughters on a different path than the one we had been raised on. This was to protect them from the magic for as long as she could. Maybe then they would get a chance to avoid the curse or at least not have the threat of it looming over them for the eighteen years they had to wait before they got their magic.

I could hear Celeste upstairs singing in a soft tone. It was a spell she was casting over her girls to put them to bed. Her voice gave a lovely sound as it floated down to where I was sitting. To an unsuspecting human's ears, it would be a typical mother's lullaby, but we knew it as a spell to grant her girls a good night of sleep and to help them fall asleep faster.

Trena VanHoff

By this candle they do sleep,
Hidden from the day, in the night so deep
O lady moon,
Guide their dreams
Cover them with your
Beautiful beams
As the candle flame dies,
Please close their eyes
Allow them to awake with
the warmth of the sun

It was the same spell our mother would cast over us each night before we went to bed. Even now with Celeste casting it in another room, I could still feel the pull of the spell as it tried to get me to fall asleep too. If the spell worked for them as well as it worked for my sisters and I, the girls would be asleep before Celeste could finish it.

It has been said that magic is stronger when it has pure intentions and a mother's wish for her children to sleep well was probably the purest intention that any spell could have.

"So, now that we are alone, why don't we talk about what just happened in that meeting?" Penelope winked at me, because her and I both know that we are never truly alone in a house full of witches. There was no way to get a moment of privacy around here, as all the women in our family loved to overshare. It was a blessing and a curse. "How do you feel about everything? I could see your face almost twitching with every word that was said."

There was something about sisters that is hard to explain, it's something that people who don't have sisters will never be able to understand. No matter what the occasion, they were in tune to what I was feeling.

"A little bit." I hated the confrontation that Ninnie's appearance in the store had created and what would happen next. "I hate that she came to me and Aunt Mira. If she went to anyone else, then I wouldn't be in the middle of this."

It was hard to resist the call to tell her all my secrets and fears now that we were sitting here at the kitchen table. While I was made to be the rebel of our family, and Celeste the perfect one, Penelope was made to be the secret keeper. She could pull the truth out of anyone without hardly trying, one of her given gifts. Even still, she was never the first to produce any information, even when provoked. It was something I could only envy. Unlike hers, my face displayed every thought that crossed my mind before I could stop it.

Penelope nodded along to what I was saying. I could tell that she was trying to be as compassionate as possible even if she didn't understand what I was trying to communicate. "She *did* come to you though, and that means having to make some of the big decisions. One of those being if you were going to come to the Coven with what she came to you with. So, you have already done at least one thing for the cause and that was without having to get help. I am proud of you."

"Aunt Mira made the call on sharing the news with everyone. I was slow on the draw." I think Aunt Mira used a little magic to practically float over to the phone. She was there, dialing the numbers, before the door closed behind Ninnie.

Penelope rubbed her hands down her pants, a nervous

tick that our mother had passed on to each of her girls. "Is there a reason why you didn't hurry to the phone?"

"It's hard because her words reignited something within me. I have worried about magic and if it's something I can handle for the rest of my life. I can understand why she would be willing to part with it if it would release the stress and burden that it carries. Not to mention the fact that there is an actual threat hanging over our heads right now." I tried to explain my side, but the way that Penelope was shaking her head let me know that she did not agree.

"Blair! I promise that you will feel better once you have finished your training. The magic will feel foreign until you make it a part of you instead of letting it work against you. Once you do that, then you won't be willing to part with it," she looked sincere. One thing about her was that once she had her mind made up, it didn't waver.

I didn't know if I would get that feeling of comfort, or even to the point where my magic didn't feel like I was wearing an itchy sweater.

Celeste came down the stairs to join us. The steps were old and they creaked as she walked down. Our house, around since colonial times, came with creaky stairs, which in a way, was its own kind of magic.

"I agree with Penelope, it is worth it in the end. Your magic will feel better when you are more comfortable with it," Celeste chimed into the conversation without missing a beat.

I was shocked when she agreed so quickly with Penelope. While the two of them were the most alike, they also were the ones who bumped heads the most —especially when we were growing up.

"Keep working on your magic. It sounds like a cliché, but it will feel better," Penelope reached over and rubbed my back gently in a motherly way. A small infusion of magic was pushed through to me with each movement, helping me fall into a state of calm.

"It's just like riding a bike! Once you get on then everything feels normal even if you haven't done it in years." Celeste waved her hand in excitement, resembling her girls when they were offered a treat. Mom always had them wave their arms to show how much they wanted it before she was willing to hand it over. "Remember how it sucked at first?" Celeste continued, "You fall off, skin your knee a few times and then finally, one day, it works!"

I giggled a little. That would be a great comparison if that had been the case for my learning to ride a bike. "My experience was definitely not like that. Do you not remember how Aunt Mira charmed the bike when she was trying to help me learn? She was tired of being outside in the heat for hours."

"Oh yeah... I guess you are right," Celeste pursed her lips, sat back on the couch, and pondered deeply. "I will keep thinking for another example."

Mom finished her cedar ritual and walked into the room to find us all huddled together. "Wow, look at this sight. It is like you are little girls again." She hurried over to sit at our feet, her grin completely overtaking her entire face. She was infectious in her joy. "What are we chatting about?"

She was right, it did feel like we were little kids again, taking on a problem together. It was like when my sisters sat me down to talk about high school, boys, and even like the night before I received my magic when they explained to me what the ceremony was going to consist of.

"We were just sitting here discussing Ninnie coming to see Blair and what that meant," Celeste, as the oldest, chimed in first just as she would have done when we were kids. Always the ringleader.

"There was more," Penelope bumped Celeste's arm with her fist, "We were talking to Blair about magic and the training she's had with Grandma. But I am now moving the conversation to the plans we have for the Cabals." Penelope prompted. I knew she would eventually lead into that; she was biting at the bit to discuss it and had finally found the opportunity to present it.

I was sick to my stomach again.

Mom grinned and I could see the fire in her eyes that had been missing since our dad died. "I want to do this. I can't imagine a day in my life without any of my girls, so if we must fight for this then we will fight."

"Mom!" Celeste's voice got louder, and her face got more animated with each word that left our mother's mouth. "How can you say that? It is so much safer if we hide. My plan is to suppress our magic so they can't feel it and bunker down until they have made their way to some other city. If they don't feel us here, they won't stay long."

Penelope and I bounced our eyes between the two of them waiting to see the way they were going to end this conversation. Mom was usually on the same side as Celeste, taking the side of caution instead of anything resembling danger. Never had we seen them go against each other before for something even as small as dinner. I figured they would have had the same opinion on this situation as well.

"What if they circle back around? We might not know the next time they come through," Mom prompted her to go over it in a new way. I could tell that she had been thinking about this for a while. "Right now, we have the warning that they are on their way. We won't know anything next time and they might be quick to take us by surprise."

Celeste started to cry, tightening her arms around herself. "What about my girls!" Her voice wavered as she cried out the words. "They can't be left alone if I go off to fight, and what if something happens to me? They will be all alone."

"Blair, I am asking you to meet with Ninnie again," Mom bypassed Celeste and her cries, but that is not to say she didn't care. "Tell her that we want to help, that we would like to get help from the Guardians, and that we are willing to do anything that we can for the safety of us all. Maybe see if you can convince her to talk to her family. See if she could get them to help the group. They might be more willing to fight if they know that we are going to be there as well." Mom finished off with a pointed look on her face that didn't leave any room for discussion.

I tried anyway, "I don't know if I can do that." I shook my head quickly; I was not someone who was typically willing to step out of my comfort zone, and she was proving that *she* was willing to overlook that for the cause. "It was hard enough carrying on a conversation with her today and that was in my environment."

I didn't know where I could even find Ninnie, let alone if she wanted to meet me or have another open discussion like the one we had today. It was obviously a scary topic, and I could see that it put her in a vulnerable position.

"You can do this," She gave me an encouraging look that only a mother could manage to show that the conversation was over, and she wouldn't be willing to hear my complaints.

Penelope reached over to punch my arm. She was hoping to lighten the situation with humor. "You got this."

Mom turned to my sisters, completely ignoring what had come out of Penelope's mouth. "Once we have those answers, we will be able to move forward with a clear and rational head."

The only place I would know where to look for her would be her house and with her mother around I didn't know if that was the best option. Her mother was not someone that I would ever want to come face to face with, even in the terms of a normal conversation. She scared me, and I got the impression she scared Ninnie too.

I got up from our conversation, deciding that I needed a break from my family. Plus, I wanted an opportunity to go over everything myself before I went searching for Ninnie Walker. I walked down the hall and used my magic to quickly open the door to the basement.

Without using magic to open the door, it was the stereotypical basement of any home, but Mom had used her talents to transform it years ago. The basement was a large room with a couch against one wall and a TV on another, a good place to watch movies — which was a good escape from our large family. Mom had gone forward with casting a few spells on our home to help with the expansion of our family, thus providing large bedrooms, enough bathrooms for all the women, and a kitchen with plenty of counter space. It was a spell even more useful than charming Jinx to stay at my side or to potty outside.

The greatest thing about the basement was that with a wave of my hand, it opened to a huge room — a library full of spell books and anything we could ever need to make a potion or a hex. There was even a large cauldron in the middle that Mom had used just yesterday to make a remedy for the sore throat she had been dealing with.

The spell book I had been studying was still up at the front of the shelf, the worn pages open to the potion I had been reading up on. Behind that book there was another, that one full of herbs and their uses. I had been using the room the most out of our family, using it to catch up to everyone. Thankfully no one else had felt the need to move my messy pile around so I could pick up right where I left off.

I grabbed the books from the shelf, then sent some magic upstairs to let Jinx out of my bedroom so that she could join me. I settled into the large recliner that sat next to the fireplace. The likes of which, with a little magic, easily roared to life. My sweet puppy was quick to run down the stairs to me, knowing our normal routine well enough that she was able to easily maneuver around the obstacles that stood in her way. Jinx laid down on my lap, snoring softly in a patterned way, but shifting about every two minutes which only continued to pull my already strained attention span.

A wave of magic brought a blanket to cover my legs, and Jinx seemed happy with that decision as she finally settled down enough that I could concentrate. I had been studying the use of typical garden herbs for a week straight and had managed to memorize about half of them. If I was willing to sit down for at least three hours every night to read them over, I knew I could have them all memorized by the end of the week. The only issue was how boring the book was. It made it painful to read, especially to keep my eyes concentrated on the words on the page.

There was a short while of peaceful, silent reading before I heard the soft patter of graceful footsteps coming down the stairs to join me.

"Blair," Mom's voice followed the sound of her steps. It was obvious that she didn't like the way our conversation upstairs had finished, and she was coming to remedy it. "How is the studying going? I know that you have been working hard all week. The dedication you have put in is very impressive and something that we have all seen and appreciate." She obviously wanted something big; she was buttering me up too good for it to just be something small. That only made me more nervous.

I sat the book down in my lap, leaving my study notes inside to hold my place, and felt Jinx move to lay down against my leg. "I think that it's going well. I have been struggling a little with understanding the measurement of the magic in the herbs. Although, I do think working with Aunt Mira at the stop has definitely helped a lot with getting comfortable with them. I have gotten a lot better at identifying them." The words weren't worth anything. I was just passing the time until she told me what she was thinking.

"It truly is amazing that for a simple human, it means one thing, yet to us, it's another." She was getting excited again, this topic pulling her away from the one she came down to talk to me about. "Take lavender as an example. Lavender has the ability to soothe and calm, even helps humans to sleep peacefully at night. For us it can do all of that, but also bring peace and happiness if put in the right potion."

While Aunt Mira might appear to be the herb and spice queen of our family with her shop, it was actually my mother who held that title proudly. Her garden stretched out through the entire yard and even extended to the windowsills of our kitchen where they were conveniently placed for cooking.

"I have been studying the history of hibiscus most recently and the uses that it will have for potions. I had no idea that it could do so much. Has it really been put into love potions before?" I held up my book to show her that was in fact what I was reading, feeling like I was a kid proving I was doing my homework. The book might have been boring, but the pictures were pretty. While I struggled reading it, it was Aunt Mira's favorite book, taking the opportunity to read it over at least once a year to refresh her knowledge.

She gave me a tender smile that every loving mother masters during their lifetime, especially for conversations with their daughters about matters of the heart. "I've never tried it on myself, but it's been known to work on a few unsuspecting humans. Maybe you would want to try it on yourself one day."

I shook my head, moving it down to look over the page again. Taking the opportunity to reread its uses and the information underneath it, mostly going over how it could be best prepared to use in a potion. "I don't think love or lust would be the results I would be looking for from the first potion I decided to do on my own." I would leave the love potions to Aunt Mira. "I did hear that it can be made into a delicious tea, maybe come summer I should try making it for the Corner Shop. That might help get some people in the door."

"Aunt Mira would be able to give you the best advice about love potions if you ever wanted to use one on anyone, although I do agree with you. I was never tempted to use it for either of those purposes. Tea sounds nice. Herbs are such a wonder, aren't we just so lucky to have them at our disposal." Mom was right. We were lucky to have them available, especially now when I was still so new. She continued, "I think we all appreciate how much effort that you have been putting into this and all the extra studying that you have done."

Although Aunt Mira didn't always go over the ingredients of her love potions with me, mostly because I didn't ask, I did know that she was the reigning expert on them all. She tried to make a new love potion at least once a week, but lately it seemed like she was doing a new one each day, her search for love intensified by her impending fortieth birthday.

"I don't like being behind everyone else," I murmured softly, "It's extremely frustrating needing to have everything explained to me instead of just understanding it," my thumb flicking the corner of the page. I wanted to equal the ancient witches, how their magic flowed through them like blood in their veins. Living in modern day Salem, that wasn't an option. To many people were weary of witches, some of them remembering the old stories about what we were capable of. "I figure that if I could just study a little more each day, then I can bridge the gap and catch up."

"You are not behind anyone! You have got to get out of that mindset!" She pushed against my shoulder with a chuckle. "You are just new at this; we all understand that. Trust me when I say that we have all been there before. You aren't the first one to turn eighteen and finally get into your magic." Mom was obviously trying to make me feel better, the same way that Aunt Mira did whenever I talked about studying.

I could only smile at her reaction. "Mom, I appreciate that you are trying to help, but no matter what you say, I will still worry."

"It's a new experience when you finally get your magic. Even if you had read over the books and tried to memorize them before that day, it is still a whole different thing when you finally get the magic into your own hands. I know that your sisters were trying to explain it to you and the way that they felt about it." Their words had started to run dry from how many times we had gone over it. "Your grandma warned me about the same thing when I got my magic and worried about being able to keep up. She had to have that conversation with Mira too."

Nodding, I raised the book back up to keep reading. I was slightly hoping that it would end the conversation. I wanted to get back to studying the material, the faster I went through the book then the faster I could go to bed. "You're right. I am new at this, but I do need to catch up to everyone now that we are contemplating taking on a group of witches." Even saying those words out loud sounded crazy, just like the idea we would be taking on an actual fight. "That doesn't make sense, yesterday I was worried about getting to work on time. My magic needs to be ready and strong enough to do that, and I can't say that it is there yet."

"If it's okay, I do have a small favor to ask of you," Mom hedged the conversation softly, choosing to change the topic instead of letting the conversation end the way that I desperately wanted it too. I was ready to resume my studying and be alone for a while, wanting a moment to think over what we were getting ourselves into.

But I knew I couldn't get out of this, so I cautiously approached the conversation she was presenting, knowing that there could be a double-edged sword awaiting me on the other side of whatever gentle request she was ready to offer. "What do you need?"

"I really would like for you to go talk to Ninnie Walker. I do think that she knows more than she let on. I also think having a clear picture before we make a decision is the best course of action."

My anxiety rose, "I can't do that! You know that I can't do that."

Mom reached out to grab onto my hand, whether it was to comfort me or to trap me, I would never know. "I think that she trusts you, that must be why she came to you today instead of anyone else."

"She came to me because I was accessible. That was the only reason she came to the store today." I was confident that was the only reason that she found me now that I had a moment to think over her actions.

She gave a hesitant smile like she was waiting for me to blow up on her. I imagine that the wrinkles in my eyebrows only proceeded to deepen as she continued to speak. "No, Ninnie came to you because she knew she could trust you. She discussed deep secrets with you when she could have been charged with treason for doing so. I think that really means something."

"How am I supposed to talk to her? I had never heard her say anything before today, now you expect us to get along like old friends? I think you are setting your sights of this working too high."

"You are being dramatic, and you know it. I am not asking you to suddenly be her best friend, but being friendly would be nice, especially given the situation that we are in now." Mom gave me a stern look that put a little fear in me. She was not going to take no for an answer. "Ask her questions about her plans, the plans that her family has. If you get an extra second, maybe get some information about the Guardians and what they have to offer to either one of those plans. I just need you to get a little bit more intel from her before any of us decide to commit to anything. I think that we all need to go into this with our eyes wide open, and Ninnie is the one with the answers."

It was hard for me to fully process her words. I was nervous enough about the chance that Ninnie was going to try to find me again, let alone Mom forcing me to go find her. It was like walking into a haunted house afraid of my own shadow. "Mom, I don't know if I can do that. I don't know if I can go to her! What if she doesn't want to talk to me?"

"She did talk to you once; I think that she will confide in you again. She proved that today when she sought you out at the store. I am asking you to do this for your family." Mom gave me such an earnest look that it was hard to say no to. "Do it for me. What about your nieces?" She was laying on the guilt thick.

"What would I even say to her?" I might have sounded like a little kid, but the question was real and so was the whining that I laced through it.

Mom cocked her head, giving me an intensely maternal look. "The most important thing is probably the Guardians. Start with that."

"Guardians. Okay, I got it. I will go talk to her tomorrow." Although, even as I said the words out loud, I wasn't completely sure I could, in fact, do that.

The steps I took to Ninnie's door felt like the actual steps into Hell. I would even say that they burned a little from how the nerves were shooting through my body, and the physical response was making my hands shake. I still didn't know what I was going to say to her. This was not something I had ever done before, not that I think anyone had marched up to a stranger's door to discuss the witching world. Anyone with common sense usually wouldn't do something forbidden.

The Walker's front door was a deep red color and

weathered on the sides, with chipping paint that showcased the raw wood behind it. I reached out for the bronze apple door knocker that had a light shine despite the wear on it. It gave a hollow sound against the door as the knocker dropped back down.

My magic let out a gentle ripple of awareness as it felt my anxiety spike along with the adrenaline of meeting the Walker family. I had seen her family over the years, always hiding in the shadows, not wanting to be the center of attention anywhere, and their house matched the sentiment. It was a small home on the outskirts of town near the forest line with brown walls, a black roof, and an ominous red door. It was not a house that anyone would give a second glance walking by on the street, which was probably intentional. I had never been there before, but in a town as small as ours, everyone knew, at least to some degree, where everything was. Just as I knew they lived out here, they had always known where we were too, even if we had never crossed paths before yesterday.

An older woman answered the door. She had a hardened look on her face that didn't shift even after I tried to soften it with my own reassuring smile. Melinda Walker, Ninnie's mother, was a terrifying woman, and the look she gave me sent a shiver that went down my spine. "Blair Bradbury. What brings you here?"

"I'm here to speak to Ninnie." I could hear my voice shake as I spoke to her, which only trembled a little more than my hands. "If that's okay with you. I would only need a moment of her time."

I could see Ninnie walking out behind her, coming fully into the light and walking up to the door. She seemed almost more hesitant today than she was the first time we spoke. "Blair? What are you doing here?"

"I am here to see you. I was hoping to get a second to talk." It was obvious from my tone that I was petrified to be here.

Ninnie looked up at her mom and then back to me. It seemed like a silent signal that her mom didn't know about our meeting and that it needed to stay that way. "Why are you here to talk to me?" She said it in such a surprised way, like I was a random person from town just stopping by. It was almost believable that she hadn't changed my entire world yesterday by walking into the Corner Shop.

"I was hoping to get a moment to talk to you. *Alone,*" I tried not to over enunciate the word too much, but enough to still inform Ninnie what I was talking about. The look her mom gave me then made me even more nervous to be standing there. It was like I was sinning by wanting a moment with her daughter.

Ninnie reached up behind the door to grab the same coat she wore yesterday, despite the lack of chill in the autumn air. "We can go for a walk around the block and talk then. Get some exercise for a little bit." She paused for a second, peering up at her mom with a pleading look in her eyes. "If that's okay with you, Mom?"

The older Walker woman gave me a threatening look, one that carried a lot of weight, "Be back soon."

Their exchange was strange for me to watch, especially how, despite being an adult, Ninnie had to ask permission to go for a walk. I could only imagine the lie she had to spin to be able to come see us yesterday.

Ninnie took her mother's words as an opportunity to join me at the bottom of the stairs, and we started down the pavement side by side, moving toward the city and away from her house. It was probably best to move away from there if we were going to have a deep conversation.

"So, I'm guessing that this is about yesterday?" Her voice was just as soft and unsure as it had been the day before.

"You're right, this is." I didn't know how to start the conversation now that it had been opened, that much was clear to her as the silence plagued each step that we took. "I guess my Coven was hoping for a little more information about what you brought to us yesterday. I think we are worried about what it means for us. There is no way that we can't get involved now that we know that they are on their way."

She nodded slowly; I think even contemplating if she could make a run for it by the way she looked behind her toward the street that would take her back home. "I don't know what answers you are looking for, and even if I did... I don't know how much more I can really share about the situation." Ninnie's eyes bounced around, looking in the shadows as if something was going to pop up and get her.

"Why don't we find somewhere more private to talk," I gestured with a tilt of my head up at the Corner Shop sign, hoping that since she thought it was fine to talk there yesterday, it would also be an acceptable location today. I had steered our walk in that direction on purpose and was grateful I did. Upon her agreement, we crossed the street quickly and carried our conversation into the Corner Shop. It was a safe place to talk without anyone overhearing anything, especially after Aunt Mira had come through this morning to verify that it was not charmed by anything but the magic of a Bradbury witch.

"Okay, I guess we can talk about it now that we are here, but it will have to be quickly. She already started a stopwatch to keep track of the time that I am away," Ninnie started, the look on her face letting me know that she wasn't making a joke. "I don't think you understand. My mom is very overprotective of our guest, especially considering the situation and what the Council would do if they figured out she is hiding here. Treason is a hard thing to escape."

"You really think they would deem it treason considering the circumstances surrounding it?" I tried to picture our leaders and what their reaction would be if they found out she had been taken in by another Coven. I unlocked the door and let us into the shop. It hadn't opened yet, so it was empty inside. Aunt Mira was struggling with the meeting still and decided to take a break from the store today so that she could have time to process.

Ninnie lifted her shoulders ready to shrug the questions away like she did the day before until she saw the look on my face. She was not one who willingly overshared and I think she realized that wasn't going to fly in this conversation if we were going to get anywhere. "Our ancestors came from the same original Coven and that was why she came to stay with us. Since our magic started in the same place, the rules of the Council wouldn't be able to stand anything against us if we did decide to share our magic with her. We are all hoping the Council wouldn't have as big of a problem with her staying here with us as custom typically dictates."

"Is your mom worried about that?"

"Trust me, if there was any way for us to get into serious trouble, then she wouldn't have allowed it. She is very aware of the rules and the justice that the Council will inflict if they feel we aren't obeying them." Ninnie didn't have to over express that point, it was obvious enough from meeting her mother that structure and rules were essential to her everyday life.

"Okay, so matched magic makes sense as to why she came to stay with you, and I can appreciate your mom's protective nature. My family is the same way, we take care of each other over anything else." My own mother was more subtle than hers in her protective nature, but that wasn't something I was going to mention to Ninnie. I could tell that her mother being overbearing was a sore subject.

Ninnie scoffed, averting her eyes away from me until they were trained on the ground. "I doubt that."

I let her comment pass without adding to it, I really didn't know how to converse with her even though I was trying. She was shy and had been conditioned to stay out of the spotlight; my pushing for information was not going to change that.

She took a quick glance at the watch on her wrist. The white face was in sharp contrast to the solid black band. I couldn't remember the last time I had seen someone my age wearing a watch, and I took note that it probably had something to do with her mom and the aforementioned stopwatch. "Are we done? I really should be getting back."

"Almost. I have a few more questions for you." I could tell that she was nervous about her mom's reaction if she took longer than was expected by how intensely she was staring down at the quickly ticking hands. "I have to ask what the plan is for the Guardians? Has your mom already called them?" I had practiced all the questions in my head on the walk over to her house, but now that I was working my way through them, I could tell I was losing my confidence.

"Yes, my mom called them last night to ask if they would help us, and they agreed to come." I sighed a large sigh of relief; I could tell that Ninnie agreed that was an overwhelming blessing. The Guardians coming to Salem would help with everyone's anxiety, especially Celeste's. Ninnie gave me a tight smile when she finally looked up from her watch. "My cousin Seth is going to be here this week and is bringing Tate with him. They did ask a few Guardians if they would come as well."

"And Tate is?" I pushed a little more, which seemed to be the only way that I was going to get the information outside of her that I wanted. She would be able to beat out Penelope for a winning poker face.

"Tate Bishop." The way her eyes glazed over the name gave a lot more information than she intended. "Seth and Tate graduated in the same class at the Academy and have been friends ever since." Ninnie had a small blush that floated across her cheeks when the word Academy came out of her mouth. A few more questions sprang to mind about why that would give her such a reaction, especially to something that should have just been a statement. "That doesn't matter, what matters is that he is another Guardian who is willing to protect our Coven. The others that they asked might join later depending on if anything was to happen closer to us and if the danger becomes a larger threat. I think Seth is waiting to see how real this is."

"They were just allowed to leave? I thought that it was a very structured program with rules to ensure their training would continue to progress." I had no idea how the Guardians worked; I only knew what Aunt Mira had talked about when she fawned over the idea of them coming to Salem. I don't even think she had ever seen one in real life before, rather dreamed about them often.

Ninnie seemed to think about how to respond for a minute before coming to an answer. She was making me work for any intel. "Both of them are out of their initial training, which puts them in a different position. After a Guardian graduates from the Academy, they are allowed to come and go as they please. Both are one of the few who choose to stay on campus to continue studying to obtain more training. They are both trying to qualify for the Council's Guardians."

"And the other ones you mentioned? Would they be willing to help my family too?" I could only wonder how many Guardians there were out there and how many of them would be willing to help with something like this. Their code was very strict about who they can help, which was starting to feel like a sick joke against the Bradbury women. "We haven't sent them any men since the Trials. We don't have anyone out there."

Ninnie picked at her nails, yet another way of avoiding eye contact in this difficult conversation. "I don't know about that one. I suppose that answer would have to come when they get here."

"I have to tell you that my Coven really needs them and would be willing to do anything to convince them to help us." Those were probably the worst words that were said in this room, and I was only making it worse by letting her know how vulnerable we are without their help. "I know that it is a lot to ask of them."

Ninnie didn't give much to go on by her expression. It was unwavering, finally giving away the family resemblance to her very serious mother. "Seth promised that he would, but Tate will need to be convinced to do it. It is technically against their code and that is the potential issue, although the honor code to do what was right is always held above it."

"Okay, I just need to convince Tate to help us, and everything else will fall into place. Got it." That brought some calm to the room as my stress lessened. Even if I didn't get all the answers that I was looking for, I could at least report that back to Celeste. She would be very happy that there would be at least one Guardian that would help protect her girls, maybe a few additional Guardians on our side if I could figure out how to convince Tate to join our cause.

"Good luck," Ninnie said pointedly. I couldn't tell if she was being genuine or sarcastic, although her straight expression pointed towards the latter.

"Would your Coven be willing to join ours if we decide to fight? This isn't something that we would be able to do on our own, especially if they are as powerful as you say they are." Delving into my next set of questions, I could feel my magic start to pulse under my skin, eager to match the anxiety I felt coursing through the same veins. Any sense of calm left just as quickly as it came. "My Coven is of the opinion that the only way that we would be able to win is if we go forward as a complete team: Bradbury's, Walkers, and any Guardians that we can get."

"I can't speak for everyone, but I will tell you that we are having a Coven meeting tomorrow to discuss everything once Seth and Tate get here." She did her signature pause, where she decided how much to tell me. "I think that I can convince Tate to join you, but only if I get a chance to speak to him alone first."

Her comment raised some alarm in me. "Alone? Why would it have to be alone?"

"I don't think approaching him during the discussion would go over as well with my mother being there. She is not as okay with this being outsourced and wants Seth to handle it all."

"I have to admit that we are all a little worried about not having Guardians in our Coven to help take on this fight." I didn't know how to explain the way that we all felt, especially Celeste. "Having Seth in our corner as protection, even if it is just over those in town, is a relief, and if we could get Tate to help us, then I think everyone would start feeling better about the situation."

Ninnie gave me a small, very genuine smile that I wasn't expecting to come from her, especially for it to be directed at me. "I think you would be able to hold your own. I am really impressed with you and your magic. Your entire Coven is completely different than mine and I have been envious of how close you seem to be with each other."

"Our Coven is very close, which I am grateful for. I don't have to tell you how hard it is to grow up in a town where everyone treats you like a bad omen." I had never taken a second to contemplate how different Coven ated each other. One would think we all got along and tried to be friends since no one else could ever understand. "What is your Coven dynamic? I know that it is a lot smaller than mine, which I imagine contributes to a lot of differences."

She gauged my reaction before proceeding. I seemed to pass the test, because she continued talking. "Our Coven relies more on our men than our magic, especially since we have produced more men in the last few generations than we have women. Our own magic isn't very strong. My mom doesn't even use hers anymore and didn't put much effort into teaching me about mine."

"I can't believe you weren't trained to use your magic. Does your family wait until you are eighteen to give it to you?" I knew that other families, Covens of witches, did it the typical way, choosing not to wait like my family does and having it flow into new witches since the time of their birth.

She acknowledged my question with a nod of her head. "For the girls, they wait until we are eighteen. For the boys, it's an immediate thing. How else would they know if the boys had magic? Whether they have magic or not dictates which training camp they are then sent to."

"Is it weird to send your boys away so young? I think that would be weird for me, especially when they return so different than when they left. Ours don't return after they leave." That was probably a lot more information than a starter friendship needed, but I was dying for answers.

Ninnie seemed to feel awkward about the conversation we were having so she quickly changed the topic, acting as if my last question wasn't asked. Instead, she grabbed a flower from the table and started playing with it in her hand avoiding eye contact. "I love that you use herbs in your magic enough that you feel comfortable going forward to sell them to the public. I wouldn't know what to do with any of them even if they were laid out with detailed instructions on what to do." She paid specific attention to the texture of the petals. "I certainly don't know enough about their uses to feel comfortable using them on my own or on myself."

"We all have a backyard garden at our houses where we grow it ourselves. That is what produces supplies for the store and where I learned a lot about each of the plants." They were all huge gardens and had been charmed to produce all year. It was important to my Coven to always have plenty of herbs on hand. "I won't deny that the women in my family often give the garden a few extra spells before spring to ensure that the items grow to their full potential, but for the most part, it comes from understanding how to take care of them."

"I wouldn't be able to do that."

I got up and grabbed two cups from the cupboards where we kept the kettle, then used my magic to heat up some water to the perfect sipping temperature. "Do you want to have some tea? I don't know if you are a tea drinker, but we have blueberry tea that is really good. We also have apple cider if you want something that tastes like fall."

I could tell that it was a weird conversation for her and that my offer was something she wasn't expecting. Although, her eyes lit up when I mentioned apple cider. Even as she reached for the cup, it was obviously with a hesitant hand that had a small tremble.

"Thank you for making it for me." She took a cautious sip from the mug. "This is really good. Best I have ever had."

I made my own cup so that we could sit together. "I have always loved this part of our store."

"Is this something that you normally sell here then? I must admit that yesterday was the first time that I had been in here, despite walking past it every week on my way into town."

I jumped up to my feet, leaving my cup on the table, already forgetting about it now that a new opportunity for conversation was opened. "Since this is only your second time in the store, do you want a tour of the place? I could take you around and show you what we have on the shelves for the fall."

It felt like a weird olive branch of friendship was being extended, even as she refused, taking one last glance at the ticking clock on her wrist and racing towards the closed door.

Chapter Four

Using my key to unlock the old, weathered front door, I opened the Corner Shop for the day. It was just after seven in the morning, but the sun was already shining, rising from the east, making the crystals in the windows cast rainbows around the room. It was a special type of magic that had everything to do with the human world and our place in it.

Aunt Mira had spent more than a few restless nights followed by stressful days and was finally asking for help, which in this case meant asking for a break from the store. The stress of these mysterious, dangerous witches coming our way had been getting to her, even if she didn't want to admit it, and the impending doom feeling of our Coven discussion was getting to be overwhelming.

It was beginning to feel that way for me as well, although, that feeling had diminished a little since I had the opportunity to talk to Ninnie yesterday — not that any of the questions she reluctantly answered were of much use.

I was kind of glad that Aunt Mira wanted me to open the store today, even if it was rare. It gave me the opportunity to be alone, which in a family as large as mine was a rare occurrence and a blessing. To be alone also meant that I could study, allowed to go from book to book, leaving pages open to compare without feeling the weight of someone looking over my shoulder with a disapproving glance. Grandmother says that was not how I should study witchcraft or spells, at the risk of getting them confused.

Studying witchcraft felt like I was constantly cramming for my midterms all over again, the downside being that the study of witchcraft was never going to end. Even if I caught up to my sisters, there would always be new spells to practice, or all the ones I could make my own. I still had potions that I could make, use them to do anything I wanted, which was enticing at least. My list of things to study was long enough without mentioning all the hexes I could do or the charming of objects, which I had still not tried.

The back light of the shop was on, which sometimes happened because we left out the front door the night before, and it had been light enough outside it didn't stand out enough to catch it. The backdoor had gotten stuck years ago, so only the dog door was in use now. Even that was only since I had adopted Jinx and taken the time to ensure that it was working so she could come and go as needed.

I flipped all the lights on in the front, the bright light being its own announcement that we were open for the day as people walked by out front on the pavement. Although, we didn't have a ton of people come in throughout the morning, since that was within normal working hours for most people. We really hit our busy hours when the middle school and high school got out, then those kids would stop in on their way home to look around or buy some tea. It had become a daily activity for some of the kids, there wasn't much else to do in a small town like Salem, and our little store became a great place to pass time on their walk home.

I went ahead to mess with the cash register and start it up for when customers were here. Since it was so old, it needed plenty of time before we could start using it. The ancient cash drawer had a little rust on it and would often stick when we tried to open it after it sat in one place all night. The buttons would sometimes need to be pressed down a few times for it to register that we were using it. If the old machine took a while to get to work, the customers would start to get impatient.

I reached up and flipped the closed sign to open. While I was there, I sent a small amount of magic out to open the containers at the front of the store to save me some prep time. I had walked in the door a few minutes later than I had wanted, that being the result of hitting the wrong button and turning the alarm off instead of hitting snooze as intended. I walked to the back room to grab the fresh produce to put out at the cashier counter. Going through the checklist in my head, I needed to put my bag away, since my hands were already reaching up to put my apron around my neck as I walked through the short, narrow hallway.

A strange man stood in the kitchenette, which had become a makeshift breakroom for Aunt Mira and me. With his back to me, I pulled back behind the wall as silently as possible. All I could see from my position tucked in the small doorway was his dark brown hair, his broad shoulders, and a strong wall of back muscles, even if they were supposed to be concealed beneath his black T-shirt.

I tucked my amulet into my top and pulled my wand from my knee-high boots as quietly as possible and braced myself for the fight that was inevitably going to take place here in the store. Before I could cast any spell of protection for myself or do anything to harm him, the man turned with a knife pointing back at me. He had somehow managed to move at a speed faster than my eyes could catch, the blade seamlessly positioned at the bottom of my throat. It was extremely sharp and obviously ready to kill or at least do some serious damage to whoever was on the other side. His smirk came quick and strong to match the weapon in his hand. "Well, well, well, what do we have here?"

"I believe that we have someone here who is about to learn what real pain is," I choked out. As far as threats go, it wasn't very good. I sounded enough like a cartoon villain that even I had to roll my eyes at the idea I could ever sound dangerous. Even if it was a poor threat, I could only hope that he didn't see how hard I was shaking beneath the surface or hear that my voice was wavering with each word that came out of my mouth. "Who are you?"

He looked dangerous. His mannerisms matched someone who was trained for something more, each movement was calculated and precise like a panther waiting to strike. Whoever he was, he was obviously not from Salem.

"Why do you need my name?" His eyes danced over my face, not landing on anything long enough to show that he cared. This man did not see me as an equal, that was clear. "Will that alter the treatment I then receive by your mighty hand?"

He was most definitely mocking me, the tone of his voice full of disbelief that I was going to do anything. I hadn't realized that the Cabals were going to come here so fast, or that they were going to come one by one. His arched eyebrow suggested that he did not think me to be that scary, despite the fact that I was trying very hard to appear that way.

"I want to know your name because it would be terrible

to not know the name of the person I am about to turn into a frog." I could tell that comment surprised him by the further arching of his eyebrow, so I kept going. I could feel my magic as it fluttered beneath the surface, ready to join the conversation whenever I was willing to invite it in, but I held it back. Whoever he was, he was far more powerful than me, and it would be better if I waited until I could take him by surprise. "I figured that it would be great to have a proper name for you before I sell you as a house pet. It would really add to the marketing value as I try to make more than a buck."

"I think I might be your worst nightmare as said by the look on your face." The mystery man baited me a little bit more. He wanted me to give a reaction, to show the cards in my hand before he offered up his own. Taking a step back he dropped his hand to his side and as a result so went the knife. I could think clearly now that it wasn't so critically near me.

I tried to keep my face as straight as possible, not willing myself to fall into the trap he had set. "I think I am *your* worst nightmare because I know that you aren't mine." The magic inside of me made me feel powerful in a way that I had never felt before. It almost seemed to bubble within me. The magic being this strong was something I wanted to keep with me even after the intensity of this moment had passed.

"I imagine that must have been a real surprise to find me here by the way you are trembling. Although, I must give you props because the flourish of insults and thinly veiled threats were a nice touch for you to add to the outfitted sparkly boots." He smirked back at me, advancing forward slowly this time with the knife pointed towards my heart instead of the normal handshake most would have offered with the introduction he was headed for. He was doing it purely for the threat. He had already proven he was capable of killing me. "My name is Bishop."

"Bishop? What kind of name is that?" I didn't think that the Cabals were going to be introducing themselves, especially if the plan was to kill me — then it seemed like an unnecessary step.

His smirk sent a flutter through my body that I wasn't expecting. "Tate Bishop if you want to be formal. Now you, Wicked Witch, it's time for you to be gone. I have things I have to do."

"Wait!" I exclaimed loudly to stop him as I held my wand tight, still ready to act as needed, but I was also slowly putting the conversation pieces together. His introduction took away, at the very least, a small amount of my fear of him, enough that I could finally take a full breath, the first since I had entered the room. "The Tate who came down with Seth Walker? You're one of the Guardians! Aren't you?"

I let my body relax as I took him in. The muscles in his shoulders that had first appeared dangerous, then became powerful in my mind as I realized he was on my team. His deep scowl went from angry to determined, although he still seemed frustrated no matter which team he was on.

Tate also seemed offput by how excited I was to see him. He gave me another raised eyebrow and seemed skeptical; the combination appeared to be a permeant fixture when it came to addressing me. He obviously didn't seem to know what to do with me or even what to say. "Oh yeah, you think so? What's it to you?"

His lips slipped into a smirk. The threat was still there as his hands twirled that same knife, doing it in such a casual way that I almost forgot it was a sharp weapon. Tate even went as far as to start tossing it into the air and catching it again with the opposite hand. He did it in a minacious manner that was alluring, like a moth to a flame.

"Would you drop the freaking knife? I am not a threat to you!" I scolded as he then took another step forward, advancing once again toward me with the tip of his blade still pointed at my heart. Weapons that weren't being wielded with the advantage of magic were not something I was accustomed to, especially when they were that sharp and even more so when they were pointed at me.

"Why don't you drop the attitude first, sweetheart? Then I might be willing to negotiate the use of weapons."

"This is not an attitude! But if I did happen to have a single ounce of attitude in me, I would ask that you remember that you are in *my* store. Obviously, with you having broken in — considering that the front door was locked when I opened the shop this morning and I know that I locked it before I left last night." I crossed my arms firmly across my chest and set a stern expression on my face.

He lifted his shirt, showing delicious muscular cravats that created a washboard of abs which I tried not to stare at, and casually slipped the knife back into the black case that was attached to the waistband of his dark washed jeans. I had truly never seen a man so captivating before. Tate Bishop was doing something funny to my heart.

"The front door was indeed locked, but the back door was not. That says a lot about the faith you have in the people of your little town." His overconfident expression only grew as he spoke, sarcasm thick in his tone showing just how little he thought of me and my desire to be the alpha of this futile conversation. "Even if it was, neither door had a complicated enough lock to make it hard to break into if I had needed to come in that way."

"You're such a liar! It was broken." There was absolutely no way that he would have been able to open that door on his own. Massive muscles aside, the amount of force necessary to open it would have alerted the neighbors in the apartment building behind our shop. There was a few of the older women who watched our store, ready to strike if they saw anything concerning. They were always cautious of us even if they didn't know why they should be.

Tate walked to the back door and demonstrated opening it in an obviously mocking manner. The door did, in fact, open without the expected creaking sound. "See, it opens." Written across his face was the implied 'I told you so,' but he was gracious enough not to add it.

"That door has not opened in years. How did you get it to open?" I walked forward to test it myself, not believing him. Sure enough, I could push it without any issue at all. It barely took any effort on my part, at least no more than any normal door would have needed.

"I put my hand on the knob and twisted it all the way to the right... like you would with any door." I could tell that he gave the pause purely for my benefit, as if expecting me to over speak and finish the sentence for him. The very same way a character in a children's cartoon does when they want the child to take part in the storyline.

I was frustrated enough by finding him in here, but this felt like I was ready to break — and a small part of me, for the first time ever, thought strongly about hitting something just to get the feeling to pour out of me. "I raise the question again, what are you doing here in my shop? Because I imagine that it was not to knock items off my honey-do-list."

"Although the honey-do-list was tempting to tackle, you are right," Tate was mocking me again. His arm learned to hang on the doorframe, the casual manner going against the blade that I knew he was hiding on his person. The way his shadow overtook my body sparked a fire inside that I had never experienced before. "That is not why I am here. Ninnie took me aside and mentioned your family name and the predicament that this threat has put you in."

I rolled my eyes at how small he was painting this problem, when to me, it had flipped my entire world. "Predicament is putting it lightly."

"She said that you might need a little help and that I should reach out to you about that." As he spoke, he walked away from the door over to the counter and grabbed some lavender from a vase, taking a second to play with the flower petals, that I knew from experience, were extremely soft to the touch. It was a weird nonchalance, as if he was already completely comfortable in the room, even though he had never been in there before — especially since it compared so closely to what Ninnie had done. "I had never heard your name before. That *is* to say the Bradbury name. Not that the name Blair is not a fun twist on the Blair Witch Project and the cliché of your magical powers that go with it, although that was a notable film."

"My family has never sent a man to the Guardians. The Bradbury family hasn't had a son in a while." I imagine that itself set our family apart from others, especially a Coven of our magnitude. It felt weird to have this conversation with someone who had threatened me just a moment before. "That is also why Ninnie took the opportunity to talk to you for me. We have a lack of manpower, and you were coming. You served up the very thing we were searching for."

He gave a deep throaty chuckle at my expense. "You wanted me solely for my muscles?" Tate seemed to be enjoying our conversation more than he had expected to. His eyes lit up with each word that came out of his mouth in a devious way that showed how handsome he was when he dropped the thick coat of aggression. "You have a lack of manpower? I would have never used those words to describe the mystifying Bradbury Coven. I understand you all to be very 'powerful' witches, not ones that need the addition of Guardians to hold their own."

He said that almost to the note of knowing us, not having only heard of us from Ninnie. Like maybe he had done some research of his own before coming into the store today; I cannot imagine she would have shared anything more about us to him given the way our conversation was going. I tried to hold my head high and prove that I knew what I was talking about, even as I felt flustered by the way he was looking at me. His light brown eyes seemed to stare into mine, like he was reading something there.

"Maybe it's less about your physical strength, maybe you just make for a bigger target for when this does turn into a fight." I couldn't tell if I was trying to flirt with him or if I was trying to hurt his feelings. I jokingly place my hands out to show the width of his shoulders. "You would be a good person to hide behind."

"I think you can hold your own quite well." There was a fire in his eyes that I was trying hard not to melt into. I was coming to the realization that we were almost playing a cat and mouse game — I being the defenseless mouse. He would burn me if I gave him the chance. It felt like I was sitting there in a complete trance, captivated by his presence. It was addicting.

"I can." My voice sounded meek in comparison to the conversation we were having. Tate had a way of making me feel like I was behind the conversation instead of a part of it.

"I bet those boots help a lot with that," Tate taunted me with another glance down. When I had left my house, they complimented my rich black coat very nicely, but now under his scrutiny, they made me feel like a little girl playing dress-up and they certainly did not look as good on me as his jeans and snug T-shirt looked on him. "So, you didn't get Ninnie to ask me for help?"

My entire face twitched as I tried to get my earlier aggression back. I stomped my foot, and the ripple of magic gave me the small amount of satisfaction I was looking for, a reminder that I could have the upper hand if I wanted to. "For the record, I had absolutely no idea that she was going to talk to you for me. I was going to come find you myself. Ninnie basically told me that I had to do it, she wasn't going to."

"The record will therefore state that you did not seek me out or send someone after me." I could tell that he was continuing to make fun of me as he said the words with a sinister smile that only went along with his voice, dripping in clear, thick sarcasm. It appeared that was his favorite way to converse once he was comfortable, or maybe once he realized that he had the advantage in the situation and didn't need to treat me as a threat.

My voice sounded smaller than I wanted it to, so I tried to pull it together, clearing my throat before I proceeded. "The reason she spoke to you is because of the Cabals coming to town and your part in it. You came with Seth to protect the Walker family if it does turn into a fight. Although we have a large Coven, we will also be in need of your help if that does happen." I didn't want to add that we had no idea how to conduct ourselves in a fight since that would probably only further his idea that we were defenseless.

"I did seek *you* out to talk about it," Tate's energy seemed to shift, which made my magic react even stronger than it had before. It was a tango of his physical dominance forcing my magic to be ready to protect me.

I nodded, wondering where he was going with this conversation that he had danced circles around more than once now. "And why is that? Why are you here to talk to me?" It took me a second to remember that he had broken into the store and that we were not old friends taking the opportunity to chat, even if a conversation with him felt comfortable, yet somehow just as dangerous in a way I didn't want to understand. "You have got to have better things to be doing today rather than trespassing on *my* property."

"Could one be accused of trespassing if you didn't lock the door? Especially of that of a place of business like this one. Is it not that an open door promotes customers to come inside?" He was snarky in a way I wouldn't have been able to predict, which might be why it was continuing to pull me in.

"If something requires magic to open that which is considered locked in the human world, then it is trespassing! A world that I could bring the police to if I chose. You do realize that they don't allow you to walk into a stranger's home in that world. Therefore, this is, by definition, trespassing." I could tell that he was going to continue no matter what I said, but I was too fired up to stop now, the words were coming out at a speed I could no longer control.

Tate's eyes lit up in response, which only fueled my anger further; I could tell that he thought our entire encounter was a joke. He bowed his head, bringing his brown eyes softly down to the floor, adding the words in a softer tone, "It didn't require any magic to get it open."

The bell on the front door rang out to announce that a customer had come into the store, which meant that I would have to leave our conversation, even if it was for a minute. I felt instantly conflicted, my job required me to go out there to the customer, but I desperately wanted to stay here with him, even if he was a problem.

"I have to go take care of that." I got to the doorway and hastily turned around to look at him once more, still surprised to have someone in the back room with me, especially a man who looked like him, abs and all. "Don't go anywhere. Okay? Just stay right here and I will be right back."

Tate gave me a sarcastic salute and followed it with, "Yes ma'am. I shall man my post."

He even went so far as to take a seat at the table, although not in a comfortable manner. Tate Bishop was rigid with his back straight against the chair, somehow it showed his entire disciplined personality. His hands continued playing with the flower, pulling on the petals until they were close to falling off. It was like he was teasing destruction, if he was only given the chance. Even without knowing him, I could tell that he enjoyed destruction, but it was the unpredictable side of him that he played into the most.

In the front of the store, there was a returning customer standing at the large bins that lined the west wall, but her head barely picked up when she heard me enter. She was pouring the thyme buds from a large wooden barrel into our signature brown paper bags. The woman gave me a happy, carefree smile and continued along, filling different bags with things that she needed and tucking them into the wire basket she had hanging from her arm.

Our fresh mint leaves always seemed to fly off the shelves as quickly as we put them up and were our best seller throughout the year, so I was not surprised that she reached for that next.

I was ready at the register whenever she was ready to pay, finally taking the time to actually tie the string of the apron I still had hanging from my neck. I forgot to knot it when I found Tate in the back room. I tried not to be embarrassed that I hadn't done it before she saw me, my mind still lingering on the mysterious man in the back room. "Did you find everything that you needed?"

She gave me an enthusiastic grin. This woman was contagiously happy in an infectious way, if my mind wasn't elsewhere, it would have made me feel better. "Everything was as perfect as ever."

"That's wonderful!" I tried to give the same level of interest to the conversation, but the prickling feeling on my neck reminded me that someone was still sitting in the back and how desperate I was to get back to him.

"You always have such an amazing selection of fresh items. Even the farmers market doesn't have anything like this, and believe me, I have looked at them all without any luck. They don't even come close to as good, although they try their best." The woman clamored on, not waiting for me to respond to her or supply any input to the conversation.

Her words flew in a way that was hard to concentrate on, so I sent some magic through my body to keep my focus on her and the conversation she was trying to have with me. I attempted to produce a smile, but it felt forced. "I am so glad that you have enjoyed your time at our store today."

She grinned on, totally willing to take point in our exchange, which I appreciated, since for the last two days, it had been my responsibility to carry them. My mind was elsewhere, but she didn't seem to mind or even really take notice of it and just kept talking. "So, what is the damage to my card today? Should I be worried about it?"

"It will be fifteen twenty-five today." I patiently took the card from her hand and swiped it through our machine — silently using my magic to speed up the processing time. Once the transaction was approved, I handed her card back to her and quickly threw the items into a bag. "Thank you so much for coming into the Corner Shop today. Please come again soon!"

I tried to appear as calm as possible to not alarm her, but as soon as the front door closed behind her, I rushed to the back room. I started talking as I walked down the short hall-way. "Tate, I hope you don't plan on going anywhere for a hot minute. I have about a million more questions for you."

Instead of his gravelly voice meeting mine, I saw my notebook sitting open on the table where he had previously been sitting, yet the flower that had been in his hands was nowhere to be seen.

Wicked Witch,

Had to run. I will catch you another time.

T.B.

***(P.S. You might want to find a lock for that door
of yours, it might help make your trespassing
argument better the next time we meet)***

I was embarrassed by how fascinated with his masculine
handwriting I was and how it promised that we would see
each other again. I felt drawn in by the comment at the end,
almost like he had written it as an afterthought — if I left the
door unlocked, he would try to sneak back in.

His note did pose an interesting question: could I be
considered the Wicked Witch? I ripped the page his
message was on out of the notebook, and after folding it into
a small square with the words on the inside to protect them,
I slipped it into the back pocket of my jeans. I was choosing
not to put much thought into why I did it as I returned to
work.

Even without using my magic on the tasks, they only
took up an hour of my time, and I was desperate for some-

thing else to occupy my mind. I went to the back to grab my book, deciding that if it was going to be slow, I would take advantage of that. I used magic to conceal the cover of my spell book and sat down behind the cash register to study. The spell book was one for emotional issues; I was hoping to find the solution for my anxiety.

The first spell of the book looked promising, so I took one of the vanilla candles off the nearest shelf. I used a little magic to light it, deciding not to waste my time on finding the matches we had somewhere in the kitchen, and started to read the weathered pages. The words were a little worse for wear and had turned a stained brown.

Vanilla chases this
mess away,
Keep it far
away today.

The instructions in the spell book read that I needed to light the vanilla candle, and once the flame went out and the wick was gone, my anxiety would be too.

I charmed the plate the candle sat on to ensure that the flame wouldn't go out if a burst of wind from the door came in and went back to reading pages of the spell book; there were a few more options for an anxiety reliever within the first few pages.

The book was interesting enough to read on its own. It was one that I had looked over a few times but hadn't paid much attention to until now. When I found it, there was about an inch of dust on it, and it was at the back of the shelf. Neither one of my sisters had ever reached for it, and I suppose neither had my mom or Aunt Mira. None of them felt the same stress that life gives me, or at least not enough that they were desperate for a solution.

"Hey, you." The bell on the front door rang as my cousin, Grace, walked in. Her appearance in the shop was complete with a brown wicker picnic basket on her arm. The matching red coat made her look like a version of Little Red Riding Hood. "Mira asked me to work with you today since she's still not feeling well."

"She's not coming in today? At all?" I was officially worried about her. Aunt Mira saw this store as her baby; she might trust Grace and me, but only for a few short hours. It was very unlike her to leave it in someone else's hands for the entire day, especially without calling the store ten times to ensure everything was okay in her absence.

Grace shook her head, not seeming concerned about the situation like I was, setting the basket on the counter with a thud that only emphasized how full it was. "She called me this morning and asked if I could cover for her. She didn't feel up to coming into the store." She pulled the top of the basket, and the smell of chocolate and sugar drifted through the room, making my mouth water. "Mom sent some treats with me for us to sell."

The sight of the pumpkin chocolate chip cookies she lifted from the basket made me smile; those were my favorite. Grace's mom, Cassandra, was amazing in the kitchen, even without the added benefit of a few dashes of magic to sweeten the treats without the added calories. Quickly, Grace and I put the plates on the counter and then took our seats behind it. Only then did she decide to speak up, "My mom told me that you were going to talk to Ninnie. How did that go?"

"Scary, awful, terrifying. Those were just a few of the emotions I faced while walking to her house. Her mom is even scarier in person than she is from twenty feet away." I still wanted to throw up, even a day later, after the way the older Walker looked down at me. "The actual conversation with Ninnie went well. She was forthcoming with information about what her Coven was thinking and went into detail about Seth. She said that he would be willing to offer protection for us as well."

"That's great news! Have you seen Seth? Is he hot?" She almost jumped out of her chair with excitement. Grace was overwhelmingly enthusiastic about anything, especially if it involved boys. "Any other sexy Guardians on their way to Salem? I am hoping he will bring a few with him."

I should have told her about Tate. I could feel his name burning the tip of my tongue. I wanted to tell her about our interaction and how he said he would wait for me, then left out the back door with only his close-to-cryptic note as a reason for his disappearance.

The note in the back pocket of my jeans pulsed, reminding me that it was back there and that I was keeping it from her.

"She mentioned another Guardian possibly coming with him. I'm not sure if that was a positive answer or if maybe she thought he could convince someone else to come." The ancestors would strike me down where I stood for the lies I told a member of my Coven.

Grace was content with that answer, giving a smile and a shrug since she had no reason not to trust me. She leaned forward to pick up the spell book I had been studying before she got there. "Here's hoping he brings ten. We need something good to look at." She trailed off as she became engrossed in the words she was reading.

* * *

100

The energy in the room was never as calm as I needed it to be when we had our Coven meetings, but even more so tonight, because I was nervous about what everyone else would say now that they had the opportunity to think it over. All the women came to sit at the table, each filling an empty seat. We all took the opportunity to join our magic by putting our hands together and saying our opening spell to promote truth and honesty from us all since what we were talking about was so important.

Wicked Eyes, tell no lies
The truth shall set you free,
It is the only way to be,
Devil tongue tell no tales,
By witch's hand spare no honest details,
Choke on air each time you try,
Never again will you tell me a lie

Grandma took the opportunity to speak to our group first, "I trust that you have all had time to collect your thoughts and have come to your answer. I will take this time to remind you that we will move forward together as a group." She stood at the head of the table with Edna beside her, serious expressions on their faces.

Edna started us off. Her voice broke through the silence, "I think that we need to do this. I can't imagine our magic not moving forward for the next generation."

Aunt Mira and my mom agreed to move forward with this war, which didn't feel like a surprise; neither was it that Piper and Penelope were siding with them or that Grace liked the idea of a fight.

Celeste had already pointed out that she was against this, so her answer was also unsurprising. "I don't want to put my girls in a dangerous situation. I think hiding and waiting this out is better than putting ourselves in the middle of this." Grace's mom, Cassandra, agreed with Celeste. She didn't want to put anyone in danger and didn't think that our taking on the Cabals was a good decision for our Coven.

I was the only one left. "I think that we should do it. I no longer want to be scared of tomorrow, and this is a way to ensure we *have* a tomorrow."

The Cabals had the Bradbury witches coming for them.

Chapter Five

There was almost a hum in the air, similar to the sound of the static radio channels make out of tune. It had the same crackling that made my skin crawl when I heard it, starting quiet and growing louder with every second that passed.

The noise caused me to open my eyes, and I was frozen in place by something more powerful than myself. I was suddenly standing still in a deep field of the greenest grass I had ever seen. My body was positioned next to a stream of fresh blue water, I stood at the bank with cold mud squished between my toes. I had not woken up in my bed, where I had been when I closed my eyes.

I was in an Astral Projection.

An Astral Projection is a spell that casts the person from their dream state into a world of their choosing. It is rare that an Astral Projection is ever anything pleasant, which meant that unless one had control of their magic, it was futile. The bewitched would just have to wait it out until the Keeper of the Dream decided that the Astral Projection was over, and they released them from their spell. But once they found someone's location, they could do it as often as they pleased.

The Keeper of the Dream could be anywhere, and they would seek out thoughts, using that as a way to insert their target into whatever dream world they wanted to create — the greatest dream or worst nightmare.

A forest to my left was thick with trees that echoed toe-curling screeches from the animals that I could only guess were lurking there. They were ready to strike whenever the Keeper of the Dream used them against me. Each growl or crunch of leaves beneath their massive feet made my body tense. My thin pajamas did nothing to keep me warm against the cold chill from the strong winds. I tried to send my magic through my body to heat it back up, but there was a block on it.

There was no movement within my magic, as if I had lost any ability to use it. The Keeper of the Dream, the creator of the Astral Projection, was in total control, and I was helpless until they were finished with me. It was impossible to avoid an Astral Projection. If someone knows where their target will be when they're asleep, it can be easy for them to creep into their dreams and hold them in a spell there.

"You need to stop and get out of this now while you still can." The Keeper of the Dream sent their voice out from the treeline, letting me know where they were, and it was clear that they were watching me even if I couldn't see them. There was power in their position, and I was defenseless against them even before they froze my magic. "This fight does not concern you."

I turned my attention to the treeline, but nothing could be seen there. The owner of the voice was too far back for me to view them, so I called out, hoping that my voice would carry itself through the wind to their ears. They didn't start with pleasantries, nor did I. "Why did you bring me here?"

"I *brought* you here to stop you from getting further involved in this mess of a fight."

"The Cabals are a threat to my family; I believe that means this is a fight for me to participate in." I sounded meek compared to their booming voice and even more so in contrast to the animal growl that rang out as I spoke. "I have to protect them."

The earth under me shook. "You need to be done with it. Wash your hands and walk away; this fight isn't yours!" The voice shouted out to me once more. Whoever stood out there, their voice rang with an anger I had never received from anyone before, especially someone I didn't know. "You are getting in the way, which will only result in you getting hurt. You are smarter than this; get out of it now while you still can."

"How could I walk away from this? This is about my family."

Their voice hit me in almost a whisper. I knew they did it to make me focus on their words after I ignored their shouting. "You have to know the value your life has to them."

I tried to take a step toward the noise of their presence, ignoring their words, and took the opportunity to search for some of the answers I desperately wanted. "What do you want with me?"

My feet were frozen in place, trapped within the spell. I was a prisoner to this person and all their magic could do. It was different from anything I had ever encountered; their magic felt heavy as it was cast over me, hinting that they came from a darker background.

"You are not a part of this!" Almost a scream came from the forest walls, and I heard a few of the animals react to the sound, readying for their master's call.

I knew better than to feed into what they were saying, as it would only add to their argument, but the temptation was too strong to resist. "I *am* this war. You are the one who doesn't get a say in this."

"It's time that you step down from the fight. I have continued to warn you of the danger that you will bring to yourself and your family if you keep going after this and you are not listening to me." The Keeper of the Dream barked, the vibrations in their voice strong, matching their magic. "You are only going to get yourself hurt. Heed my warnings and get out now before it's too late."

My eyes danced around the dream. I was trying to take in all the details surrounding us. The trees had a typical green color, lush and thick between each of the branches, that made it hard to look through to the other side, the perfect place for someone to hide. That part of the Astral Projection almost made me believe that everything was as expected, but it was the sky that tipped me off that something was different. Instead of the typical blues of the night, the sky almost seemed purple, a light lavender that made the stars look like they were ready to jump out of the sky. Those clues told me I wasn't home in the forests of Salem, but there was nothing to say about who it was that brought me here.

I tried to be as confident as possible, holding firm against what they had to say. I had never been in an Astral Projection before, but I knew from my studies that the owner of the dream would be able to do anything they wanted within the world they had created. They could kill me right here, and I would be powerless to stop them, especially as my magic seemed caught in a chokehold. "I am stronger than you know," I hollered back, "No matter what, I will get through this, and I advise that you stand back to watch."

"You are still very weak compared to the battle before you, and you don't have enough time to catch up." Their hiss came out strong, causing the animals to start up again. If I looked deeply, I could almost see the glowing eyes.

I tried to remember any of the spells I had memorized to bring peace; even if my magic was frozen, maybe the repetition and familiarity of the words would do something for my racing heart. "Worries be gone. I need you no more. Worries be gone, out of the door. Stresses and strains-"

Their voice interrupted my words with a deafening bang, and I heard the animal's howl. "You are barely a witch, newly coming into your magic. It is pointless for you to try and use your magic now."

Their comment stung like a swift slap across the face. It hit right where my insecurities lie, making them seem real when I could previously sweep them all away for another time to justify them. I started the spell once more, starting small and working louder.

Worries be gone. I need you no more.
Worries be gone, out of the door.
Stresses and strains, worries and strife.
Leave now, be gone from my life.

"You will lose your abilities and even your Coven. You will lose your magic and all you hold dear if you continue playing this dangerous game against someone far more powerful than you."

I focused on the sound of the stream beside me. While the water didn't make much noise, it made just enough that

I could hear the soft pattern of the waves hitting the rocks that lined the sides when one path of the water overtook another. Their voice was still in the background, softly drifting to my ears as I tried to force my thoughts only onto the wind in my ears as a slight breeze went through the trees.

Focusing on the nature around me, I started my magic in my hands, pulling the power through my arms, chest, and torso. I pushed the magic down my legs and into my feet where I could harness it. I could only smirk as I felt the push of one foot moving toward the voice; I felt the strength of my magic within me like a match was lit, ready to start a large fire if given a chance. I propelled my magic through my body until the other foot followed along. I kept my body moving, pushing it towards the voice in the trees and anything else hiding there.

"Stop! You shouldn't be able to do that," shrieks of distress came from the treeline where the owner of the Astral Projection stood watching me. I could feel their magic come closer to mine, as if they stepped forward to get a clear look at what I was doing. I felt ripples of magic as they tried to push back against me, trying to keep me frozen now that I had found a hole in their magic. It was the one place where I could fight back. "Your magic should not be able to do this!"

"I told you that I was stronger than you realized," I had barely moved a few small steps, but it was enough to shake them. They knew that their magic was struggling against what mine could do, and this was only the beginning. A noise came from the treeline, and then there was only darkness.

* * *

With a sharp intake of breath, my eyes opened. I was back in bed with the blankets wrapped around my legs. The only reminder of my night activities was the dried mud on the soles of my feet, caked on from standing still so long on the stream's banks.

I sat up, swung my legs out of bed, and threw a sweatshirt over my head to fight the chill in the air. I left my room, but all the darkness lingered in the air. Jinx was on my heels as we skipped down the familiar creaking stairs. There was only one fix for my distress: a mug of hot chocolate. It was just after four, so our house was quiet, everyone would still be sleeping for a few more hours.

The kitchen was dark, so I turned on the light above the oven. I sent magic out to get the items from the cupboard while I turned the stove on. My magic finished the job by pouring the milk into the pot and adding the chunks of chocolate. I reached up to stir the two together, the whisk in my hand making the white milk a creamy brown. I felt relief that my magic seemed unaffected by the Astral Projection.

"I like your shorts," his voice shot out in the silence, startling me. The noise caused my mouth to open agape and my entire body to jump. To my surprise, it felt like I had jumped out of my skin for a second, and everything around the room was starting to fizz with the magic I sent out around me. "I would have figured you to be a nightgown girl, or maybe that was just what I pictured in my mind."

I spun around to face him, the look of clear shock written across my face that he was in my kitchen. "What are you doing here?"

Tate's lips curled up into a tantalizing smirk; the small light of the kitchen made him appear larger than normal. "Did you miss me, Wicked Witch?" Tate leaned against the wall in a way that seemed far too casual for his sudden appearance. "Or maybe it was me that missed you?"

His comment flustered me. He could not have missed me, but my heart jumped at the thought. "You do know that this is my house, right? And that when people come to visit, most knock on a door to announce themselves, and arrive during what would be considered reasonable visiting hours." I sent my magic out to finish mixing my drink and walked toward him, taking the opportunity to stand close to him. I welcomed the chance to simply be near him. It felt like I was missing something since he had walked away from me at the store, and I had been craving his closeness ever since. If he was a drug, I was already addicted. "How did you get in here?"

We would have felt it in our bodies when he breached the barrier. There would have been a clear sign that the line had been broken. Everyone had been on high alert since Ninnie told us about the Cabals, and one of us would have felt the sizzle of magic that the charm used to announce someone nearby.

Tate stepped closer to me; the only thing I could see was his irresistible brown eyes. He was wearing a similar outfit to what he wore the day before, only trading out one dark shirt for another, the rest stayed the same except the addition of mud covering the soles of the his bulky combat boots. "I was passing by on a run and decided to check on you."

"And now that you have?" I could hear the tremble in my voice as his eyes clocked mine. It was like he was looking right through me and waiting for me to call him out on his lie. I couldn't function appropriately around him; he could throw me off my game with a glance.

Tate's expression changed quickly into one of exhaustion. I don't think he was expecting me to question him. "You are intriguing. You can't blame me for wanting to know more."

Something about how this stranger looked at me made everything okay, even if it meant not feeling like myself. Being around him made me feel like I was the strongest I had ever been. "I wasn't planning on blaming you."

He avoided my eyes, choosing instead to look around the kitchen. His eyes appeared to be looking for something specific, but I hadn't the faintest clue what it was. The vault of his mind was sealed tight. "I just came to see you, and now that I see that you are okay, it's a good time for me to take my leave."

I tried to send my magic out for some perception, but his mind was protected from anything my magic could do, which only made me question his level of power. "Tate. You're just going to leave again."

His head tilted to the side, and he seemed to contemplate what he would have to say to finish the conversation. "Didn't you get my note?"

"Your vague note that gave no information on why you had to leave and when you would return?" I was trying not to display my frustration as that would probably not help shift the conversation to where I wanted it. "Yeah, I got your note. It was *really* helpful."

He didn't say anything. Instead, Tate came closer. He pressed his lips against my forehead and then was gone. The door was silent as it closed behind him. It was as if he had never even been there at all.

Jinx stared up at me, her expression as blank as mine. Especially after I realized that, once again, he had left without answering any of the questions I had asked nor explaining why he was there in the first place.

I ignored the boiling pot on the stove and grabbed a tall candle from the cupboard, sending my magic to light the wick, and reached up to hold my amulet. Once in my hand, I rubbed my thumb against the rich purple e amethyst gemstone. Celeste gave me this amulet to bring me peace, but it didn't seem to be helping much, so I opened one of my favorite spell books. I repeated the spell that I had studied the night before.

Day and night,
safe and sound.
I am protected by
Divine Light

"Sneaking boys into the house now?" Celeste came down the rest of the stairs, her feet making a soft patter with each step she descended. She had learned long ago which steps to avoid when keeping the house quiet, sneaking down so as not to wake the girls.

"That was Tate Bishop." I sat down at the kitchen island with a groan, putting my head in my hands, although it seemed more appropriate to slam it down onto the marble countertops.

Celeste raised her eyebrow at me. She went over to the stove and poured us a large mug of the hot chocolate I had forgotten.

"Should I know who Tate Bishop is?" She chuckled to herself. She said his full name in the way one would say a celebrity's name. "I guess I should phrase it this way, do I want to know who Tate Bishop is?"

"He is a Guardian. He came down with Seth Walker." I had yet to see Seth, but if Tate was here, he had to be too.

She handed me my mug with a tight smile, sat beside

me, and put her arm around my shoulders in a comforting manner. Celeste would never demand answers, but I knew she wanted them. "How do you know him? He seemed like he was comfortable with you."

"Yeah, comfortable enough to break in."

She gasped, "He broke into our house to see you?"

"Ninnie talked to him about us, so he came by to ask why he should help us." I didn't want to overthink the thrill his reckless habit of breaking and entering sent through me.

Celeste nodded slowly in a rhythmic way; it was her way of helping a story continue so that she got all the details she sought. It was a trick she had picked up from Penelope a while ago, and it did wonders against her young girls. "What did he decide? Is he going to help us?"

I was grateful that she didn't seem mad. I hadn't told them about the Guardians being here, about Tate, or our earlier conversations. "I think he really will help us if it comes to a fight, although he was hesitant to believe it was going to turn into that." I tried not to think of his note that I had tucked into a spell book in my room. "Once I got him to realize I was not a threat, he was willing to share some things. Although when I went to the front to work with a customer, he left even after he promised to stay."

Celeste gushed in the same way that Aunt Mira did when the subject of Guardians came up. She was excited, the most enthusiastic I had seen in her in a long time; her eyes lit up and her cheeks flushed bright red. "Based on your conversation, maybe he doesn't understand why you have a pull on him and is trying to figure it out."

I raked my hands through my hair, wanting to yank on the roots and tear it out. Just three days ago, my life was easy. "My pull on him?"

"The things that drive you crazy might be for a good

reason." She was acting strangely calm considering a stranger just broken through the charms on our house and had been standing just a few feet away from where her daughters were sleeping.

I started reiterating my frustrations, hoping she would understand why it bothered me. "His disappearing act being one, and that's small compared to his inability to finish a proper conversation or answer any of the questions I have for him."

"I noticed that he had a talent for that," she responded to all the thoughts I had brought up while I sipped from my mug. "Let's start small first, and later we can work on the harder questions. Why do you think he was here?"

Now, that was a loaded question that even I didn't understand. I stared out the window at the rising sun. The sun's yellow mixed nicely with the colors left over from the night, such a difference from the Astral Projection I had experienced.

"He said that he wanted to check on me." The slight raise of her eyebrow confirmed my suspicion that this was an odd comment for him to make. "It seems strange that he would know where we lived." I was trying to piece together everything he said. Some parts were missing, keeping me in the dark, which I think was his intention. It was almost like he tried not to tell me something, waiting for me to fill in the gaps he was leaving open.

Her fingers tapped the top of her mug, almost like she had trouble finding the words she sought. "Was everything okay, though? It is four in the morning, and you are awake making yourself a drink."

I tried to open my mind, letting my magic flow out to share the story with her in a way that she could watch it in her mind. "I was in an Astral Projection. Someone brought me there and tried to get me back off the fight. They don't want us to move forward against the Cabals." Even if she hadn't gone through one herself, I knew she would be willing to talk me through it and help me process.

Once she had seen everything from the Astral Projection, Celeste mumbled under her breath, "I wonder... It seems like-" before stopping suddenly. She twisted the mug in her hands a few times after stopping tapping. Her fidgeting was making me nervous. "I think that you should speak to Grandma about that. I don't know if I can share."

"No, Celeste!" I could tell by her pursed lips that she would not start sharing, yet it was sitting there on her lips, ready to be said. Her inability to keep secrets could be used against her if I was persistent enough, and this was information that I was willing to fight for. "Don't you dare just pause there. I need to know what you were going to say."

Her face started turning a particularly nasty shade of green, "I have to stop there; this isn't mine to say. You really need to speak with Grandma. She needs to be the one to explain all of this."

There is no way that I could possibly be expected to wait until this afternoon when what Celeste had to say was pulling her to pieces. "What were you going to say? Celeste, I need to know." I went over my point again, hoping that she would see the look on my face and know how desperate I was for this secret.

She mulled it over, almost struggling to find the words to explain what she meant. "I'm not going to say a word, but I will tell you that I think this is a sign that we shouldn't do this."

"A sign! You have got to be kidding me! I think this is the *biggest* sign that we need to do this," I could feel the magic in my body start to fizz like it did when I was frustrated. "If we weren't the only thing standing in their way, they wouldn't have come after me to try and scare me off."

A long pause sat between the two of us. Her voice came out meek, matching the consistent wringing of her hands. "We could still run, and I will mention once more that hiding is still an acceptable option."

"This was a warning that they are coming, and we need to be ready. They obviously fear us, our magic, and our power, but that isn't going to be enough."

Celeste looked distressed, but instead of lashing out like Penelope or I would have, she sat there calmly and accepted my answer even though it was not what she wanted to do. Celeste asked the one question I was hoping to avoid having to come back to. "What about Tate?"

I brought more hot chocolate through the air, using my magic to levitate it until it landed in my mug with a satisfying plop. "What about him?"

She wondered aloud, baiting me further, hoping I would keep talking. "Do you think he was the one who was in the Astral Projection?"

I hadn't thought of anything close to that, but suddenly my mind was rolling over itself in waves, each thought messing with the one before, forcing my imagination to go farther into the extreme. "I have been around him long enough that his magic wouldn't have felt as foreign as whoever was in the Astral Projection." Even though I knew Tate Bishop was dangerous, I couldn't imagine an evil spirit attached to him.

"Maybe he suppresses his magic when he's around you so that you don't feel it. He would give a different feeling than when he does something malicious." She was fueled by this idea and kept going, each thought balanced on the one before it. "His closeness would make sense as for why he knew you were sleeping, plus the access to your mind, and the mud on his boots would match the forest of the Astral Projection."

The thought of Tate having hostile intentions toward me forced a feeling of miserableness to come upon me, and the butterflies he had given me before he disappeared again formed into a rock sitting in the bottomless and dark pit that was now my stomach. Suddenly, him having a thing for me seemed even more like a joke.

"If we entertain this ridiculous thought that he was in control of the Astral Projection, why would he come here to check on me?" I was clinging to my ideas even if her theories started coming together. Tate stayed the hero in mine, and I preferred him that way.

"How did he know something was wrong if he was not the one to put you in a dangerous position? I was two rooms away from you and did not know anything was wrong." Her words put a shiver down my spine. Tate could have killed me, and my family would have had no idea. "He could have been here to finish you off but was thrown off his game when you were awake and aware of him being here."

Celeste sent her magic over to refill our mugs and bring down some cookies from the cupboard. I happily accepted the endorphins from the chocolate and mass amounts of sugar. "Wouldn't he have surprised me if he wanted to kill me? Instead, he made me aware of his presence by announcing his arrival and conversing with me. That doesn't seem like a good idea for an assassin attempting *murder*."

"Not if he changed his mind when he got here." She almost seemed excited by the idea of Tate coming to kill me, which, if it was anyone but my sister, would have made me worry about their intentions. "Maybe he was ready to kill you, but when he got here, you made him hesitate, and he didn't want you to find him with a weapon in his hand, so the best option would be to engage with you. It could be a romance novel; he came with the intention to kill you but was overcome with your beauty and couldn't help but to engage in conversation with you."

He *is* trained to be a ruthless killer when needed. There would be nothing I could do to stop him from going forward with it if that was his mission. "Both of those are good theories. That works well, but I still think you are wrong."

She got up from the counter and started to pace the kitchen. "Okay, let's change gears briefly and go with another thought process." She tapped her finger against her lips to help her think. "Maybe he is the one who is going to break the curse?"

That was it. I was done; now Celeste was just talking nonsense. I know my face went deadpan at her words. I was sick of this curse being a part of every conversation. It was hanging over all of our heads and had caused enough fear and worry for my sisters to make me sick. "What would the curse have to do with him being a stalker with a pension for breaking and entering? Especially when seconds ago, you were under the impression that he might have been here to kill me, but now you think that there is a chance that he might be my soulmate. You do know how crazy you sound, right?"

My sister paused her pacing and started going in the opposite direction. She twisted her hair between her fingers until each twirl matched the dropping of each foot. "The curse says that it will end when there is a man worthy of knowing our secrets, but what if the thing that makes him worthy is that he is your protector?"

"You have watched too many princess love story movies

with your girls. True love doesn't work like that, and you know it. The chances of the curse ending because of Tate are ridiculous." I was past the point of frustration with her and the theories she was willing to develop.

"The curse started because a man was forcing our magic to become exposed, therefore putting it at risk, but in this situation, it would be the opposite. His entire purpose in being here is to take care of us and *protect* the actual magic." Her pacing was making me nauseous. I could tell she was getting more excited by this thought, and with each patter of her foot, my heart about jumped out of my chest. "What if this is it? What if this is what breaks the curse, and everything becomes right again?"

"While I can appreciate your excitement, I doubt that is how this will end."

Celeste dropped not only her face, but her voice as well, until her words came out in nothing more than a whisper. "Everything in this life is a risk." A small tear fell from her eye, proof of how strongly she felt about what she was saying. "I can see that you are worried about putting your heart out there, but if you break the curse, think about your nieces and the lives that they will then have because you were willing to run the risk of getting your heart broken."

"I want what is good for the girls, but that is also putting all our eggs in the Tate-was-sent-to-break –the-curse basket." She had to know that I would do anything for my nieces, but this one was out of my control.

I heard another person come down the stairs, and Celeste and I turned to see Penelope join us. She did not care about keeping quiet; each of her feet fell heavily down the steps. Celeste quickly wiped the tears from her cheeks and gave our sister a cheeky smile, brushing off any emotion. "You're up early."

Penelope shot Celeste a snide look that only meant sarcasm would pour from her mouth. "I could feel the two of you having sister time without me." She couldn't stay serious for long, and suddenly she was giggling in an infectious way that had Celeste and me joining in. "It was that I couldn't sleep. I am anxious about the Cabals coming. I even had a weird dream about them showing up."

"Was it an Astral Projection?" I couldn't contain the surprise that we might have had a shared experience.

Her alarm answered before her mouth could, with her eyebrows shooting up to meet the dark shadow of her hair-line. "No. Why would your mind go there?"

Astral Projections were so rare that it should not be the first thing to come to someone's mind when the topic of weird dreams came up. This was the first one I had been to, and none of the other members of my Coven had gone through one to my knowledge. We had all only read about them in our studies. This was all uncharted territory, which only made it worse. If this person decided to come after me again, I would be powerless to stop them, especially if they continued to freeze my magic.

"I was pulled into one tonight. That's what we were in here talking about. I had someone in the trees talking to me, and what they were saying didn't make any sense," I sent out my magic and let her into my mind to watch the Astral Projection the same way I had done with Celeste.

I saw shock and awe on her face at what she saw me go through. "That is incredibly creepy! Who do you think it was that brought you there?"

"I think it was the Guardian that met with Blair." Celeste piped up. She had used Penelope's arrival as the cue to start her usual morning routine. She opened the blinds and started on the girls' lunches; even with her movement, she was still very focused on us and our conversation.

Our other sister shot her head back to face me once more. She had millions of things to say on the tip of her tongue, but only a name came out, "Seth?"

"Tate. He is *her* sexy Guardian." Celeste chimed in with a smirk. "The very one who snuck in to see her this morning."

"What?" The noise that came out of our middle sister could only be classified as a shriek — which Celeste and I quickly tried to hush. "You have got to be kidding me! And you were just going to let me sleep through all of this? Shame on you, shame on both of you."

It was rare for Penelope to display this level of erratic reaction, and she was showing no signs of slowing down. This might have outranked the Cabals on the week's exciting information list.

"Tate is not my Guardian; he is *a* Guardian that I just happen to have met," I tried to enunciate my point as best as possible, not taking ownership of the frustrating Tate Bishop. "He was standing in the back room when I opened the store, and I tried to get answers out of him, but that proved ineffective. Tate had supposedly been running nearby and came to check on me."

Tate Bishop became more of a mystery every time I interacted with him.

"Give me a few more details. Let's see if we can piece this together before everyone else wakes up." Penelope felt the need for the answers just as desperately as we did, and all I could give her for a response was a shrug.

When frustrated, I felt an overwhelming need to pace the room like Celeste did. I pushed that urge down, and instead, I raked my hands through my ebony hair and took in staggered breaths. "He did come in with mud on his boots which matched the forest of the Astral Projection, but there are also trees outside of our house, and there was a lot of rain last night, so the mud could have come from there too."

"Good point. How would he know you were in trouble if he wasn't the one who put you there?" Now that was the question that had plagued me and Celeste as well. "Is this why you think he was the Keeper of the Dream?"

"I am under the impression that he is the one to break the curse," Celeste spoke up from her position at the sink, her hands rinsing apples for the girls' lunches. She was committed to that thought process, maybe because that was the safer of the two options we could think to choose from.

I knew that if I said yes to that, it would only come from a place of hope, so I tried to suppress that one. "Even if he is my person, what makes you think he won't leave like the rest? Then I have a broken heart and we are down a Guardian. Neither of those things will help us against the Cabals." My sisters mulled over what I had said, taking their time to process it before responding. I could tell that they had different opinions on that thought. I knew my sisters wanted me to be happy, but we all learned a lot was on the line.

Penelope walked to the bookshelf on the side of the kitchen, pulling down a spell book that had been read so many times the hardbound cover was worn to pieces and the pages were falling out. The cover had been masked to look like a cookbook, but when her hand touched it, the truth of the contents came through. "How about we do a spell for emotions? It will keep your mind at peace and keep you positive while we figure it out."

She filled my mug with hot chocolate to the brim and

pulled a spoon from the drawer. "You need to start stirring it clockwise," She ordered me, then moved the spell book in front of my face so I could read the words while I facilitated the magic.

I started stirring the liquid like the spell directed. "Bring me happiness, bring me joy. Let not my sorrow use me as a toy." I repeated the words three times as I continued to stir the chocolate in the cup, ensuring that each time around, the speed was consistent.

Sometimes magic sends a rush through me, and this was one of those times. I felt my entire body shift as it shot out me, even the flutter of my hair as the magic picked it up and settled back down.

"Did that make you feel any better?" Celeste came over from her position at the counter, put her arm around my shoulders, and hugged me tightly.

I nodded slowly, concentrating on how the spell made me feel and ignoring the rush of old emotions threatening to return if I didn't stay calm. "This last week has gotten very complicated." Magic only worked when the recipient believed in it, so I had to learn how to trust myself. "More so after Tate showed up today."

"I do think that we should cast another charm onto the house. Just in case he does come with impure intentions," Penelope suggested. She almost seemed to be walking around my feelings on the matter. "With the Cabals on their way, it is a good idea to ensure that it is secure and strong."

Celeste agreed that it was necessary, especially now that she knew how easily it could be broken and its failure to warn us someone was on their way. She sent her magic to the candle on the counter to ensure it stayed lit for the spell, and the three of us joined hands. The spell flew from our lips. Our magic blended to strengthen the spell further.

> We call on powers far and near
> to banish what is not welcome here.
> By this candle, with this charm,
> We banish all that would cause us harm.
> This we ask, these charges we lay,
> Send unwanted things away.
> This is our will, so mote it be.

I could feel bricks made of our magic start building a wall around the house, each word of the spell making another layer of strength and protection.

Looking at the two of them, I could see that it made them both feel better, even if it was for different reasons; Penelope, in knowing that she did her part for her family, and Celeste, feeling secure that her girls were safe again. But for me, it made me a little sad that Tate would no longer be able to sneak in.

"Now, who wants to wake up the girls, and who wants to start scrambling some eggs?" Celeste questioned. I could tell she was trying to get our minds off the Cabals, the curse, and, for myself, the alluring Tate Bishop.

I quickly volunteered to get my nieces and went up the stairs to their bedroom. They were bundled up in their beds, eyes closed tight, and I knew from experience, they would be grumpy to wake up.

Morning was not their time of day, much like their Aunt Penelope.

"Girls, it's time to wake up. You have to get ready for

school." I sat on Kira's bed, shaking her shoulders gently. Her dark hair was spread across her satin, pink, princess pillow, and she even had a little drool coming down her cheek. Her sister, Lucy, lay in the adjacent bed; the purple sheets had curled around her legs, resembling how I had woken up, although her face was peaceful.

"Aunt Blair, it's too early," Lucy grumbled, turning over in her bed so that she was no longer facing me or the light coming through the door behind me.

I walked over to her bed and gently ran my nails across her back in what she called back tickles. I could only imagine Celeste and the yelling it would take to get them in the car with their shoes on in the next forty-five minutes.

"Lucy, you have to get up. You have school today." I watched her little eyes flutter open to peek at me, then quickly close again in hopes that if she stayed sleeping, I would let them stay home — something that my mother would do if she had been the one to wake them up. "Your momma is downstairs making breakfast, and the longer you wait, the more Aunt Penelope will be eating. She might just eat it all if you don't hurry."

"Pancakes?" The voice of Kira piqued out from under her sheets. She had apparently woken up to the idea of breakfast being her favorite meal. Kira loved to pour her sugary syrup until there was more of that than there was of the actual pancake. "Is Mommy making pancakes?"

"Yes, pancakes. But you will only get to eat them if you hurry up and get ready." With those words, both girls jumped out of bed and hurried to their closet, where their school clothes awaited them.

Once they were dressed, they raced in the direction of the kitchen. I followed behind them, using my magic to make their beds. They jumped into their seats at the counter where my sisters had a plate of pancakes made and their packed lunches sitting off to the side, ready to take to school.

"Do you want syrup on your pancakes?" Penelope smiled at their enthusiastic reactions, taking it as a yes, and poured it on their pancakes.

Celeste planted a kiss on both of their heads. "How did you sleep?"

"I didn't want to wake up, but Aunt Blair said there were pancakes, and my stomach was excited to eat them," Kira told Celeste in her sweet little voice, which only brought out a smile from the rest of us.

While the girls ate their breakfast, Celeste held firm to the idea that the only acceptable choice was to tell our Coven about Tate's break in, but Penelope and I had our hesitations. "We can't keep this from them, especially Mom. She would be so mad that he broke in and we didn't tell her."

Penelope quickly disagreed, "We handled it. The house is safe. There is no reason to worry her."

I nodded along, siding with Penelope. Mom had a pension for surprising us, but I knew she would not handle this well.

The girls announced that they were done eating, and Celeste ushered them upstairs to help them finish getting ready. Penelope and I took over cleaning up the mess in the kitchen, taking advantage of the leftover pancakes for our breakfast.

I picked up the trash bag from the container and went to take it outside, but when I opened the kitchen door, I froze in place. "Penelope, you're going to want to see this."

On the doormat sat a white envelope with my new nickname embossed across the top and another vague note.

Wicked Witch,

The Corner Shop. 4 pm.

We need to talk.
T.B.

Chapter Six

Ninnie's meek nature stood out against the chaos that was The Corner Shop —especially the overwhelming mess in the back room.

The two large Guardians made the room seem even smaller than it already was, which wasn't helping the tense situation. The room seemed to shrink further in size each time a person shifted their weight from one foot to another. No one was willing to speak up, our eyes bouncing around the room, avoiding each other. I rapidly became more unsettled with anticipation.

Penelope placed her body in front of mine, my personal bodyguard. Her muscles were tense and ready for deployment when needed. Her position conveyed that she was confident and strong, just as she intended. She surveyed the Guardians and waited for them to make the first move.

"Penelope. It's so nice to see you again," Seth Walker broke out. He had a similar look to Ninnie, further proof that they were related, but his was the more assertive personality.

My sister had already masked her face when she walked

in. I knew her mind must be trying to figure out what his words meant and how they would have known each other before today. There was a slight chance he was just saying that to get a reaction out of her, which wouldn't happen if she could help it. She didn't like not being in control, especially when she was unaware of what was coming next. "Again? I don't believe we have met before today."

"I'm Seth Walker," He chuckled; I doubt that he had to introduce himself very often, or at all, considering the field he works in. The job usually goes with animosity. Seth gave off the impression that he would not hide in the shadows like the rest of the Walker family.

Her haughty response was quick, "So?"

"We did grow up together in the same town; although, you didn't seem to know I existed, that is to be expected from an amazing Bradbury witch," He retorted with an attitude that she wasn't expecting and smirked at her reaction. I could tell he was getting to her as her eyelid did a subtle twitch. That was a sign her exterior was starting to crack.

"I suppose you are right; I hadn't needed to know your about existence until today." Her superior response was meant to sting him, but instead, it only fueled him more, according to how he reacted.

Seth laughed methodically. He knew he had gotten under Penelope's skin, and that was something that he could work with. "In my defense, we ran in different crowds, so overlap didn't happen often."

"Why did you bring us here? We don't have all day just to stand around," I tried to converse with Tate, but he didn't bother looking me in the eye.

"The intention was for you to arrive alone, but I suppose basic instructions fail you," He looked down at me, forcing me to feel small.

I didn't know Tate and wasn't sure I wanted to if he was going to act like this. I was right to be weary when it came to the Guardians. Rolling my shoulders back, I kept myself as squared as possible. I was done having to do these stupid meetings alone, and she was the best backup I could have. "You turned this into a group activity. Why couldn't I?"

He rolled his eyes, taking a moment to show how ridiculous he thought my answer was. "I am here to figure out who you are and what we are going to have to do with you," Tate said in a way that insinuated that we didn't know each other; I knew better than to go against him, so I played along.

"And what are you going to do with me? Is your plan to tie me to a cross and watch me burn?" Although I knew that he wouldn't ever take it that far, it was tempting to play with him.

"That might be a better plan than leaving you to deal with this on your own; you've only proven to be incompetent thus far." He gave me a snarl of his lips, finally taking a second to look me in the eye, and they were ice cold, frozen from any emotion. "At least then I will know you would be out of my way instead of under my feet the entire time."

I spit out my response in hopes that my words would sting, "You *asked* me to come here! Not the other way around, and I think it's about time you realized that and stopped taking every opportunity to talk down on me. It's not very polite!"

He scoffed at me. The way his arms crossed his chest made his stature bigger, obviously an intimidation tactic. When his elbow knocked against an overcrowded shelf, it made me feel less nervous about being in his presence. "I asked you here to know what you were going to do. It's clear that you aren't going to stay out of this."

"Tate!" I lost it faster than I could contain myself. Stomping my foot let out a small amount of magic, and it gave a ripple to the room's energy that caused both Walker cousins to take a visible step back, giving me some satisfaction. "You must realize that we *need* your help. It's not that we want to be a part of this; there is no way we could avoid being part of it."

"You need more than help; you need something closer to a miracle," Tate snarked right back at me. Miracles were in short supply, but he was right. I did need one of those.

I felt my hands shake; the anger was becoming overwhelming in a way I hadn't faced before. My magic started to bubble beneath the surface; while stomping my foot would release it, the shelves were filled with enough glass that it wasn't the way to go.

"We are doing this with or without your help, but I will tell you how much easier this will be if you are there to help us." I hated to admit it, but we needed him. Despite his ridiculous attitude, there wasn't that long of a list we could go to for help. "You have two options: help or get out of the way while we find someone who will."

Tate sighed in notable exhaustion. "Why are we entertaining the idea of helping these strange witches? We don't have a connection to their Coven. This is a waste of our time." He spun away from me and spoke only to Seth, which was frustrating when the conversation had started between the two of us. It only further proved that he thought less of the rest of us, as if his nose that was pointed to the sky wasn't already sending that message.

He continued to imply that we had never met before, which only alluded to his mystery. What edge was that going to give him?

Ninnie looked ready to respond, but Penelope stepped in

first. "Could you really stand there while someone hunts innocent people? Do you have no remorse for the innocent witches? They have done nothing wrong. They are getting killed; it's bad enough that we have to suppress who we are." She mirrored Tate with her own crossed arms. She was surprisingly rational; only her face gave away how she felt. Her reaction was very different from how I acted — my own magic going off whenever given the opportunity, more proof that she had more self-control than me. "Now we are being hunted for it too!"

Her words resonated with me by sinking into the pit of my stomach. This feeling seemed like it was going to stay.

"You have to understand the position that we are in. I can only protect so many people. It won't do anyone good if I end up dead while trying to save you," Seth tried to explain to us calmly and reasonably, and that was a dangerous combination. The more he talked, the more I could see him easily playing both the hero and the villain, charming in an almost sinister way.

"You don't strike me as a professional killer." I realized that these were the first words I had spoken to Seth, and being a slight insult was not the best idea if I wanted his help.

Although both Guardians were similar in many ways, Seth was smaller than Tate. The latter was large in height and wide in stature. Tate stood out in a crowd. Seth was the opposite; he was of a reasonable height and size. He could wear a suit, slip into a group, and never be seen again. His only distinguishing feature was the auburn color of his hair. It was different from the light brunette color that Ninnie had, but their eyes shared the same grey-washed blue that was unique to the Walker family.

His head swirled around to look at me, surprisingly

without the look of distaste I was anticipating. "I imagine you expected someone who matches the mighty and huge Tate here? Every team must be diverse if it's going to be successful, which is why if we do move forward with this partnership, I can see it being very successful." Seth seemed to be okay with the difference between the two of them, at least to the point where the conversation didn't bother him. "The two of you would add a lot to our up-and-coming team if we decide to move forward with this."

He was more enthusiastic than his fellow Guardian about teaming up. I figured he would continue with the calm approach that Tate was sticking with.

"What makes you think that our team would work? You have no idea what any of us are capable of. We would probably surprise you with what we can do." I would have questioned him further about his knowledge of us and our capabilities, but Tate had been smart enough to stake us out. It wouldn't have taken much for Seth to have done that too, especially in a town he knew.

Their training would have told them it would be best to be prepared before approaching someone new, although Tate breaking into the store and my house was possibly going a bit too far. He was ready for whatever I would bring out.

"I know that your Coven has a lot to lose, which puts a desperation into people to come out on top, forces them to work harder and show up for the battle at hand." Seth proposed it like a physiatrist, knowing how people think before the thought can go through them. "But I can also see from the interaction between the two of you that the bond of your sisterhood is stronger than anything else. That being taken away would make you feel *weaker* than anything else.

Imagine if you were taken away from your sister. That would hurt quite a bit, wouldn't it?"

The mocking was evident in his tone, but I had to give him credit, he was more intuitive than I would have given him credit for. He appeared to be the brain behind this partnership, Tate obviously being the muscle as Seth pointed out earlier.

He couldn't be that buff of a man and not be the power behind the operation. Those very muscles were sticking out of the sleeves of his shirt even now in a way that made it apparent he was packing some serious heat that had nothing to do with the gun and knives. Something that, from our first interaction, I knew he had with him.

"Blair went through something similar to that this morning. Isn't it weird when you are pulled somewhere without your control? Magic has a funny way of making you lose your sense of security, especially when someone else freezes it." Penelope supplied information in a way that didn't make the conversation flow naturally. Instead, it drew everyone's attention to her, just as she had hoped.

"What did you go through?" Ninnie asked comfortingly, having finally joined the conversation. I could tell she was putting in the effort, but it felt somewhat foreign since we were still far from that. I would not have thought for her to reach out first after our initial interaction at the shop, especially since she was terrified of her mom, and it didn't take a genius to know that her mom disapproved of me.

I couldn't figure out my sister's angle by sharing those details, but I would listen if she felt I should tell them. Her mind could strategize much faster than mine. "Someone put me into an Astral Projection, but I don't know who." I took a second to pause, thinking over the Astral Projection and the position that I was put in. "They never walked out of the trees to reveal themselves and used magic to conceal their voice."

Penelope was using this opportunity to survey the room and the reactions that this news would bring from people. The boys kept their faces blank, not showing how they felt about the information, something their training set them up for, but Ninnie looked shocked. The sincerity behind her words seemed genuine. "People still do that? I didn't realize that anyone still called people into Astral Projections. I thought the Council banned them from being used after the massacre at the end of the Salem Witch Trials."

She was chatty now that she was around Seth. His presence seemed to make her brave. Ninnie was right about how rare Astral Projections were. When the Witch Trials were over, the remaining witches decided to take their revenge on some of the villagers. Bringing them into their dreams and torturing them to make up for what they put their mothers and daughters through. The Council banned Astral Projections after that, not wanting us to use our powers for the destruction of men.

"Which is probably why they were hiding in the trees," Tate snarked out like I was missing something obvious from the Projection. I didn't have enough time to worry about what his reaction meant.

"Didn't you recognize their magic? If they were that close, it would have to be someone near you, or they would have been around you a few times to find you in your dreams," Seth pushed for more information, raising his hand to stroke his chin. The Academy taught him to use his magic as a weapon while Ninnie had been taught to subdue hers. I could feel from his energy that this was something he had interacted with before, even if his cousin hadn't.

I had heard a rumor that the Guardians still used Astral

Projections when the Council directed them, but that didn't seem to be common knowledge based on Ninnie's reaction.

My attitude became strong as I whipped my head around to face him. My head bob went too far, the motion matching the jut of my hips to make a combination that has occasionally been considered dramatic. "Have you ever been taken into an Astral Projection before? I will tell you how bad it sucks! Your magic is taken under complete control, and you can't do anything even when you force it. At best, you manage to move your feet as I did, but you're unable to move them fast enough to do anything, and then they pull you out before you can do any damage. Forcing your body back into real life only leaves you feeling alone."

"You could always use your tarot cards on her?" Seth threw the suggestion out to Ninnie, which had her giving us all a deer-in-the-headlights look. He was more willing to be the center of attention than she was. "See if you can get a reading on what the intention behind the Astral Projection was. It might even help us to know what we are getting ourselves into before we fully commit."

I was not sure how happy I would be at the fact that I was the one we were testing this theory on, especially when it came to something Seth was suggesting.

Ninnie reached into her bag and brought out a pack of red and purple cards, the colors representing blood and royalty; I knew that the writing on the cards was supposed to promote truth and light from them. I wouldn't have expected her to carry them with her, especially after she told me how her family treated their magic, how they were unwilling to touch it with a twenty-foot pole even when needed. "I haven't done them in a while. I don't know how powerful the magic will be if I do them on her. I can't control the answers even if you ask a specific question."

"It is worth a shot," My sister said behind me, her voice not leaving it open for debate, "Just try." She knew me well enough to know that I was ready to take off now that I had been put in the hot seat, but I also knew her well enough to know that she wanted answers. Penelope was willing to do anything to get them, which put me in a difficult position — something that Ninnie and I had in common.

We were pawns in the games of others.

"I thought your family was against you using your magic." I didn't mean to throw that back in her face. It had become a nasty habit I needed to get a hold of. I could only imagine that it would happen again, and it would get me in more trouble than the looks I had just gotten. "And doesn't this classify as magic?"

Ninnie took her cards out of their pack and explained she was shuffling the deck to cleanse the cards of any earlier questions they had been asked. No one I knew used cards, but there was enough information in my spell books to learn the basics. The necessary intuition, however, is only something that can be done after lots of practice. "It's kind of like what they call a gateway drug. It's not the whole thing, so it's considered okay in some doses, especially when you can keep it under the radar."

"Are we going to have to check you into a rehab facility for this small-dose drug problem?" I heard Tate question her from behind me. He didn't think this would work even if Seth did, although he was calm enough to make a joke; even through our small interactions, I could say that this was the Tate I liked the most.

"Sometimes you must justify your actions to get your way. I'm not hurting anyone, and they will find out how useful this is one day." Ninnie was cunning and artful in her lies, unlike the girl who behaved so tightly under her mother's eye and avoided direct eye contact with anyone else. Maybe I didn't know her as well as I thought I did.

Ninnie walked forward to the table, took a seat, and directed me to do the same. She shuffled the cards absent-mindedly while she spoke, "Something to remember when it comes to tarot is that everything could be taken subjectively depending on how you want to interpret the results."

Tate took his place behind me. The heat of his body was close enough that I could feel it and the rush it inflicted on my heart. I heard him scoff as he surveyed the situation and her responses. "So, what, she gets the answer to her question here, and that is it? No changing it? That doesn't seem right," He cross-examined her like she was sitting on a witness stand. Even if he disagreed with using tarot cards for answers, Penelope was right when she pointed out how desperate we were — any answers the cards gave us would help us know where we were going next. "If this becomes a battle, there are far too many variables for the cards to tell us who will win."

"You have just about as much personality as a dead slug, yet you have captured the eye of someone special. The cards would have never been able to predict that one, yet here we are." Penelope took Ninnie's side, and in doing that, she divulged some of the information I was hoping to keep close to the vest as she gave Tate a pointed look. "It's worth a shot if it means opening the door for necessary answers."

Ninnie passed the cards across the table to me, her smile an open invitation to keep going. "Think of your question while you shuffle the cards; only think of your question so that they will read it from your mind, and the cards will be ready to find the answer."

"Here's hoping that it works," The muttered words slipped as I shuffled, trying to go through what I wanted. I asked the cards what the results of our battle would be and if we were going to win, desperately trying to contain my questions that involved Tate. Her cards must, at the very least, know that answer.

She took them back from me and started to shuffle them once more, taking the ones that flew out of her hands and laying them flat onto the table face down so the coordinated backing was shown. That part seemed like it was only for theatrics, but I wasn't going to risk interrupting the moment by voicing my thoughts. "Okay, are you ready for some answers?"

"I'm ready even if you aren't," Penelope said while sitting at the table beside me and directing her attention to the cards that were laid out there. "I am banking that it will give us some answers."

Ninnie explained the order, the cards, and how the reading needed to go. Then she reached out and flipped the first of the cards. "Your first card is the Chariot. This means that you will have to have discipline and courage. A departure will happen, which will push you to develop that discipline and courage throughout your life. This is probably also hinting at the battle that we are going toward."

Even without seeing the other cards, I knew that one to be accurate, and the boys had already made it known that we needed to step up our training. "Okay. That is a good place to start," I encouraged.

"The Hanged Man." Dread started to set in just as she flipped it over to show the picture drawn on the front, and the image on this card was possibly more concerning than the name. "It's telling you that a large change and a release will have to come after that as a response. Everything you are going through now will lead you to that end."

My stomach flipped with anticipation for all she had to

say. I might not have believed it when we started, but I was beginning to believe it now.

"Does it know when that will be? Or what would be being released?" I could only imagine what that meant to a family who had already lost their husbands and fathers regularly. Maybe Seth's earlier comments were correct; perhaps I would lose one of my sisters when this was over.

She declined to answer that part and kept going with the reading. "Upside down Judgment. This means that there will be much destruction in your path." I knew from my brief studies that the chances of upside-down cards were rare, making it more evident that this was built only for me.

"So, this will turn into a battle," Seth almost seemed excited at the idea that we would get into something danger-ous. It was like a little kid being told they could play with firecrackers, everyone else knowing what a bad idea it was.

"The Fool card, this means a new beginning and inno-cence," She explained without pausing, then grabbed the second to last card, and my stomach sank even further as I saw what it was. "The Lover's card. You will have a blos-somed love come through your life at this time; it will be filled with passion, and a union will come from it."

I could feel Tate tense behind me. For someone who didn't believe in this type of magic, he was paying close attention.

Penelope reached under the table and took my hand. She knew what the sacrifice would mean. "Could that be breaking free of the Cabals? That we win this and no longer have them hanging over our head?"

My sister suggested it as the option she was looking for and a solution to our problem. It gave the room something to grab onto, but we thought about the curse over our family and the chance it would be broken.

"The last card represents your ending answer, kind of the conclusion to everything we have discussed," Ninnie held my fate in her hands but didn't seem worried about what the cards told us. "Interesting, it's the Wheel of Fortune card."

Everyone knew what that card meant even before she explained it, and I wanted to burst at the seams; even Penelope gripped my hand tighter to remind me to be calm, although it did nothing to stop me from exploding a little. "The answer I am getting from the cards is that 'we will see!' You have got to be kidding me."

Tate leaned away from the table, taking the opportunity to step away from the situation, and nudged Seth to come with him to the side of the room. "I knew this was a joke," He mumbled as he stepped away, quiet enough under his breath that I knew he wasn't saying it to anyone else, even if I had heard him. Little did he know that the cards had given me more information than I expected.

"Okay, that was fun, but now we must discuss this," Penelope stood up and marched over to the boys. I could tell her patience was over; the boys had exhausted it all from her. "Tate, it sounds like Seth is all in. Are you?"

I don't think he was used to someone going against him. Tate stood tense, surveying her and deciding what he would do with us. "We will help you only if this continues to be a situation we will benefit from."

I tried to control the little dance of excitement that almost escaped me, "See, you do care what happens to us."

Tate gave me a look of pure exhaustion, his eyes dropping to frustration before they bounced over to my sister. She was starting to bother him. "Just because I'm helping you doesn't mean I care," He spoke something closer to a growl, "Your death would be a minor inconvenience. That's all."

Seth was excited at the prospects of a battle; I could see it in his eyes even if he tried to contain it. "Now that Tate and I are on board, we must discuss the training you need. I imagine that you only have magic training." We both nodded our heads. I didn't even know that there was any other training I would need or that existed. "We need to get up your physical strength. We don't know what they are going to come out with, and we need to be ready. Tonight, we will need to meet and start your training before we get any more behind."

"We have two other Guardians on their way to aid in this battle. They will be here tomorrow, but we need to start now. You are behind where we need you to be, and training needs to start now." Tate was already coming out like the soldier he had been trained to be. "How many members of your Coven can physically fight and hold their own?"

Realistically that number was tiny.

We were confident that Penelope, Celeste, Grace, Piper, and I could join in a physical fight. Aunt Mira was a strong possibility as she would do it if asked, and Mom would be willing to do anything for her family and the cause, but anyone else would only be magic wielders. Not to mention that Celeste would argue being with her girls so that she knew they were taken care of.

"Probably five, maybe more, depending on their training level," I spoke up, which didn't spark any confidence in him. "How many would the Walker family be able to bring?"

"Me."

Penelope and I must have given Ninnie a surprised look. And I heard my sister whisper under her breath, "Well... That's not good."

Ninnie kept going, her bravery coming through her words. "I guess it would be Seth and I from my Coven, but everyone else has decided not to move forward with this." Suddenly our small numbers seemed enormous compared to the Walker Coven what they were bringing to the table.

"Now you know why we will send for more Guardians," Seth seemed frustrated at that. The number of people we would have for this was almost a joke. I imagine, just like his lack for wanting to reintroduce himself, he hated having to ask anyone for help.

I tried to judge Tate's facial expression, but like always, it was void of emotions. He had pulled out his knife and flipped it between his hands. It was the same way he had done the day we met, but I wasn't scared this time.

"Tonight, we need to meet up and start our training. We need to start getting you ready for a fight." Tate commandeered the room like a general getting his troops ready for war. "Bring your people and be ready."

* * *

Aunt Mira's house matched the Corner Shop; chaotic and complicated. Thankfully, she liked it that way.

She was standing in her kitchen with her focus on the kitchen island, but instead of food, half a million spell books and ingredients were sitting up in piles that somehow made sense in her brain. To her left, there was a pile of plants that looked like she had just pulled them up from the garden; the traces of dirt trailed in from the back door. The cherry on top was the altar in the middle, made up of crystals and the sweet perfume of lavender candles.

"Hey Hun, what are you doing here?" She was so casual about my walking in, hinting that she knew I was coming.

"I just needed someone to talk to."

I tried not to show my intention immediately, but it was seen despite my effort. She raised her head from the altar in a way that made it seem like she already knew why I was there. "Blair, I am worried about you." She came around the counter in a flash. Once she got to me, she reached out and started picking at the air around my head. "Oh no, your aura is awful. Come here and let me see you. I need to fix this."

I reached up and tried to fluff her away, but she persisted in picking at me like we were chimpanzees. "Stop, I am fine, and my aura is fine."

"It is swirled in red and yellow. Destructive and irritable don't look good on you. You must clean up if you hope to have a good day." She tried to grab at the end of my aura once more, but I moved out of the way before she got the chance. "It even has black around the edges. You are full of blocked energy and distrust. Who wronged you?"

"I will let you cleanse me only if you let me tell you everything wrong in my life," I conceded, knowing it was like dealing with a toddler, and sometimes they just had to get their way. I could only hope she would treat me that way, letting me get my way while I let her get hers.

She shook my hand, sealing the deal with a grin, happy she was finally getting what she wanted. "I would have let you talk anyway, but I am glad we could come to a proper compromise." I finally let her grab onto my aura and pull at the pieces she disagreed with as she led me to the couch, or at least what was the couch, before she dumped out her entire closet onto the cushions. She made a quick motion to push it onto the floor or the adjacent overflowing chair. "What are you struggling with? There is a waxing crescent moon tonight. Have you sent your hopes and desires into the world yet? I can help you."

I shook my head. I knew better than to assume we could jump straight to the topic. "No. We can do that too."

"Why are you here then?"

"I am completely uninterested in a life without magic. That is why I am here." It was vague, but I didn't know how to describe what I was feeling. I flipped around on the couch so my head was in her lap and she could start cleansing without the rest of me getting in her way. She was a woman on a mission, furiously pulling at the colors surrounding me.

Aunt Mira laughed but finished pulling the bad parts of my aura off before she would talk to me. "Okay, I fixed you as best as possible, but you still need a lot of work before we can officially call you saved."

I couldn't help but take the opportunity to tease her about her obsession with making sure we were clean, a craft only she cared about. She wanted to see all our auras and be able to cleanse us when needed, which only added to her bohemian look. "Doctor? Am I going to come out of this alive? I am quite worried."

"You are finally clean, but only on the surface. We will have to work hard to keep it that way. So yes, you will live." Since she had my head in her lap, and she was done with my aura, her hands started playing with my hair. "Pink is a good color, very feminine. And this red is the one I want to see; it's an interesting combination of love and power."

I hated the way that her words made me feel. "It follows me like a ghost over my shoulder, right? I didn't want you to see that."

"I am rather fond of ghosts and spirits, it's the living that never fail to frustrate me." Aunt Mira showed me a new side of her personality; this darker side went much further than I expected, casting a shadow over her eyes. "It's like when the sky thunders, it makes me feel better that the sky needs to scream sometimes too. It makes me feel less alone."

"I agree with you, but that doesn't mean those living people aren't the problem," I was trying to figure out how to bring up that I had come to talk about Tate. Him breaking into our store was one thing, but everything had been just as much of a mess after that.

"One does not need the size of the dragon to have the soul of the dragon," Aunt Mira said in a calming tone that had the opposite effect.

"Are you on drugs? I need you to talk to me and give me advice that isn't from a fortune cookie. I need some real help! You only sound crazy." My head shot out of her lap, and I spun around to face her, ready for whatever she would say next and if it would sound as ridiculous as that comment about the dragons. If it was, I wasn't sure if I could sit around with only the hope of some advice.

She just giggled at my frustration, reaching over and pushing my shoulder to make me almost fall back onto the couch. "I'm not acting crazy, and I'm not on drugs. It's a quote from Robin Hood; it means you don't have to be big to be mighty, but I think you knew that. Why else would you be willing to take on the world right now?"

"I am willing to take on the world because someone has to. You should have been there today! I don't know what I expected, but that was not it." There was such a high chance of something going wrong. "Aren't you worried that we are going to die?" I could hear the meekness in my voice.

Aunt Mira giggled again, abruptly stopping the tears from coming out of me. Her hands motioned through the air and, with a swift flick of her wrist, caused the tea on the counter to float over to us, the sugar cubes following in a neat row behind it. "I wouldn't worry too much about that.

We're good at surviving," She said it so casually, like she didn't worry at all.

"Our ancestors were. I believe you and I both have dead fathers that prove our genetic lines have gotten a little messed up since then." It was cryptic, but that had been going through my mind lately. We were made of the same chemical makeup, but many things had changed since the day the witches survived.

"You have a lot going on in your little head. You've been down for days, and you're lucky you haven't brought the group's energy down. Forget your aura, we've got to fix your soul while we still can." Her bangles knocked against each other like a melody of wind chimes as she moved her arms. "Tell me everything that happened today."

Thankfully I had good news. "Penelope and I had that meeting with the Guardians. There was some back and forth, but they will help us." I could see the relief cross her face, but I kept going. That relief would only last so long once I explained everything. "We got there, and they were so rude! You would not believe the words that came out of Tate's mouth! They almost made me feel silly for being concerned."

"Give him the benefit of the doubt; how often did he come into contact with women in his training? Maybe he forgot how to say anything without it coming out aggressively."

I let out a surprised laugh. "You have never met him before! How do you know how he talks?"

She waved me off. "Don't you dare ruin the fantasy for me! It's all I have right now."

"They want us to start training." My muscles were already sore just thinking about it. I can only imagine the hours of training that went into getting to Tate's size. "I can't imagine it will be a good experience. You should have seen the evil look in their eyes. I don't think they are going to be gentle on us."

She gave me a strained look, anticipating the worst. "How did that go? They want to start training in what?" Her rapid-fire questions almost made me dizzy, especially when she failed to take a single breath in between each one. She was probably the only person more excited than Grace. "I thought you were just going there to talk? That's why we closed the shop early. It sounds like there was more than that going on by the way you came running here."

I felt the shudder of my magic. "Well, we told them that we were worried about the Cabals, and as a response, Seth had Ninnie use her tarot cards on me in hopes of finding an answer."

My head was still trying to wrap around what the cards told me. Aunt Mira responded with even more excitement than before. "Tarot cards! I have always wanted to learn! What did you ask? What did you get as your answer? How did it make you feel?"

"Aunt Mira! You need to slow down!"

She shoved her hand against my shoulder again, this time almost causing me to tumble onto the floor. "You need to talk faster! You are dragging this out on purpose."

Ignoring her, I continued. "Do you know the Wheel of Fortune card? That was the ending answer." It felt even more ridiculous the second time, saying it out loud to someone who fully believed the cards to be valid. "My answer was to be patient and see what the future will hold."

I was flustered when I left the shop, so I was here. Aunt Mira did give the best advice, it just took her a second to focus and stop speaking in riddles, but once she got there, it was pure gold.

"That doesn't sound too bad. Imagine if you had gotten the answer that everyone would die and that we would lose. Would you still go forward with the fight? Or would you give up now and decide to hide?" She reached her hand out, her magic bringing an old wooden box off her bookshelf. Inside was a set of tarot cards, random scraps of torn paper, and a strange metal bracelet. "Imagine if it had gone the other way for a second? What would you do if the cards told you would live through this, winning without a problem? I can tell you that if it were me, I wouldn't keep training, I would trust that the cards would be right no matter what and allow myself to slip up. The cards not giving you a direct answer opened your mind to the chance of winning, but that losing is still an option. Because of this, you will continue to train daily, building your strength with the idea that the Cabals will be stronger than you, and you must match them."

Pure gold. She thumbed through the box's contents before settling on the cards at the bottom. She started shuffling the tarot cards in her hand, almost to keep herself in the moment; it was the same thing she did with a pen at the shop.

I wanted to pretend that she wasn't right, but that was futile, and judging by the look in her eyes, she knew that too. It didn't make me feel better about the situation. "Okay, so the lack of an exact answer will encourage us to fight and keep moving. I'm glad I came to talk to you about this, but that's not the big one." She folded her arms in my direction, and that was the only thing that kept me talking, if she had interrupted, it would have only caused me to shut down. "The Wheel of Fortune card was not the card that bothered me, and that drives me crazy. That should have made me want to tear my hair out, but I am so deeply fixated on another card that I can't turn my brain off."

"And what card was it?" She didn't even have to question my inability to turn my brain off or why I wanted to.

"It was the Lovers card. Ninnie said I would find love. It pulled me in even if I wanted to pretend I didn't know what she was talking about. I can't get my mind off of it. Only a few outcomes can come from that card, and I have to keep that in mind, but even then, you have to understand what is going through my head. You know the curse, there isn't a chance that I can get through that and the Cabals coming at the same time. The combination would break me, and I can-"

Her loud gasp interrupted my sentence. "It's Tate! I knew it! I could feel it the minute after you met him at the store! Your entire energy has been changed since that moment."

"It can't be Tate. I won't allow it to be Tate." I took a deep breath, trying to calm myself before speaking, knowing that whatever I said wouldn't change her opinion. I stared at the green color she had painted the kitchen door. It made it easier to talk to her when I wasn't looking at her. "Tate makes me sick. My heart feels like it will explode when I'm near him. In one second, he is right there, sneaking into my house to flirt with me, kissing my forehead, and the next thing I know, he is snarking at me and lashing out at something as simple as trying to have a conversation. You should have seen him at this meeting. Why does he act one way when we are alone and another way when we are around anyone else?"

Aunt Mira started to break it back down to basics. "Would you say that you at least like him?"

"I don't want to."

"But you do? Don't you?" She pushed further; it was apparent that she was anxiously sitting on the edge of her seat. I imagine that this had to be better than her reality television some days. She *wanted* me to have a crush on him.

"I do."

Aunt Mira cracked a huge smile, and I was sure she would have broken out into song and dance if this were a movie. "Why do you look so disappointed? That's a good thing. This is so exciting! I bet your sisters are having a field day with this one."

"You did hear me say that he bounced back and forth, being nice to me one moment, making me fall for him more and more. The next, he is mean, sarcastic, and ugly." I was going crazy, that had to be the only answer. The push-and-pull he had created was awful, and it confused me about what would happen next, or what he would say; Tate was devilishly taking over my mind. "I have no idea what is going on anymore. I think he wants me, but then he turns around and does something rude! I don't know how to interact with him. You shouldn't feel that way around your person."

"How do you want to interact with him?" I should have known that coming to her for advice would come with hoops to jump through before I could get anywhere. "How you interact with him might help him understand how he's supposed to act around you. Lead by example whenever possible."

I stood up to pace the room, carefully stepping over the piles of clothes on the floor and the stack of spell books next to them. My sisters thought I was the messy one of our family, but when it came to Aunt Mira, I was the loser in that competition. I took a second to contemplate her question in a rare moment of clarity.

How did I want him to treat me? Did I want him to treat me like a friend and maybe someday a lover? I needed to figure out how to accept him treating me like a soldier in this war. He made it very apparent that there was no way for anything to happen between us until the war was over.

"I want him to want me." I hadn't known those words were coming, but as soon as they came out, I knew that was how I felt — whether he was my person or not; I wanted him to want me. "Is that silly? It sounds ridiculous to want that from him, especially with everything happening, but I have never felt this way."

"Do you really think that he could be your person?" She was shocked out of her mind but now even more excited than she was before. I had filled in enough gaps to make her feel confident about her previous guess about Tate, now she was just waiting for me to accept it. She resembled a golden retriever with a ball, not letting it go until she got what she wanted.

I paced the room some more, hoping it would get my brain together enough to make sense of everything I had said.

Aunt Mira didn't look concerned, which only fueled my emotions further. "Breaking the curse is an option, and you must remember that. Especially if Ninnie's tarot card reading is true."

"But if he is my person, he will have to leave. I can't let that happen. I like him, and if I go through with this, it means I will have to fulfill the curse." There was way too much to lose and only a small amount to gain.

Aunt Mira seemed ridiculously calm about this while my world turned in circles. "You still need to love and be loved. You can't avoid it forever."

"But I can try."

"Do you think that his father is available?" She tried to break the tension with a joke, but it didn't improve how I felt as she had hoped it would.

I took a deep breath and went along with her joke, letting it do its magic. I remembered why I came here to talk to her. "No, but I will ask if he has a much older brother for you. You look young, we could convince him that you are twenty-five."

Aunt Mira reached over and hit my arm; her giggles echoed through the room as she shifted her body around the couch. She often laughed with her entire body, and this was one of those times. "You know that you are my favorite, right?"

"I better be if you're going to keep hitting me like that." At this rate, she was lucky that I hadn't started hitting back; those boys had me wanting to go off and beat anyone who even dared give me a look.

* * *

Ninnie's presence was somehow calming. I knew it was because she was more anxious than I was. It pushed me to calm down, knowing that if something happened, I would have to be the one to handle it since she would be unable to do so.

The presence of her companion did the opposite. Harriet was the girl Ninnie mentioned the first day she entered the store. Harriet was the one who brought knowledge of the Cabals to the Salem Covens; her family's death resulted in her running to the Walker Coven for safety, their bond making them a safe place for her to run to. She had almost felt like a rumor until today, talked about but never seen.

I convinced Ninnie and Harriet to come to the store for lunch; it was the most neutral location. Neither seemed happy when they arrived, although Harriet was somehow more anxious than Ninnie, which I didn't know was possible. Ninnie hadn't been kidding when she shared Harriet's background and how she had to run from the Cabals after they had murdered her family.

Harriet had a mousy look with the contrast of bright red hair, which fit her personality — or at least her attitude. Nonetheless, I could confidently say that Grace and I were sincerely trying to welcome her, but Harriet didn't take to it. The second she walked into the store, she quickly made it known how she felt about us and her situation by greeting Aunt Mira. "Did you get this place right before foreclosure? Or is this your personal touch?"

Despite Harriet's rude question, Aunt Mira supported my efforts. Before they got there, she helped me set up lunch in our backroom. I covered the table with a tablecloth and laid out small decorative plates for our tiny sandwiches. It was basically the adult version of a tea party... Something that Harriet was quick to point out once she arrived and realized what I had put together.

I continued with my plan by believing that her negative attitude was just a feature of her personality and not an explicit choice to shoot me down, even if it was. "Harriet, I'm glad you could make it! Ninnie, great to see you," I tried to be as welcoming as possible, considering all that she had gone through. I even went as far as to welcome them in with tight hugs, with Harriet turning her nose up in disgust.

When I invited the girls, Ninnie mentioned that Harriet was feisty under the surface and willing to dish it out when she felt it was needed, apologizing in advance for anything she would say. Something about her scared

Ninnie: she knew what Harriet was capable of. The entire Walker family welcomed her with open arms, but Harriet remained unpleasant.

Grace wasn't happy to be here, but there was no way I would throw myself to the wolves alone, so she was out of luck. She was very vocal that her excitement would have changed by adding the Guardians. I didn't think we needed bodyguards, but the glares Harriet was shooting around the room had me second-guessing that decision.

Ninnie was also hoping that Harriet would be willing to join our ranks and support our forces, channeling the anger inside of her toward the very enemy who caused her pain. I never thought Ninnie would try recruiting others to our team, but she was working hard on Harriet, and I suspected that Seth was too.

"Did you steal the plate sets from a child?" Harriet asked as she yanked her chair out and sat at the table in a huff. She had at least dressed up for me, wearing her most excellent pair of jeans and a sweatshirt; apparently, a step up from the sweats Ninnie said she never got out of. "Or just the teacups?"

I plastered a large, fake smile on my face, trying to keep a positive attitude about the situation. "No, but I will keep that in mind next time. My nieces might have nicer stuff than what I found in the back closet. It's been a while since we had any celebration here."

Ninnie sat down beside her, but shifted her chair so that it was closer to where Grace and I stood, either joining our ranks or trying to hide in our shadows.

"Why did you bring me here?" Harriet wasn't beating around the bush, something that I appreciated. She had an interesting way of being bold and brave when alone with us girls, but I imagine that if anyone else had entered the room, she would have quickly changed her personality back to the quiet one. It made sense as a defense mechanism, but not for a budding friendship. "I know it wasn't so we could all share a meal, even if it does fulfill a childhood fantasy of yours."

"No, but I'm trying to create common ground, and a meal is always a great way to do that," I tried again.

She scoffed at me, "You were just hoping to have an opportunity to butter me up and get me to join your stupid battle." She avoided my eyes, instead choosing to pick at a hangnail. "Well, you are wasting your time. I'm not doing this."

"I'm not here to convince you of anything. I figured you needed a support system, and we were willing to be it. So here we are, trying to come to your side." It felt like I was baiting a bear, hoping it wouldn't bite me. Especially she had managed to go through hard stuff without batting an eye, a survival instinct more like that of a serial killer than a twenty-year-old girl. "I am just hoping that you will meet us halfway. I also hope you want this, so I don't feel so alone."

She sat up a little in her chair and squared her face, making up her mind before hearing whatever I said next. "You don't feel like I am trying hard enough to build this friendship with you? And that must be just crushing your feelings." Harriet seemed to be reading right through me. I had no idea I was so transparent. "I guess that means boo on you."

I ensured the smile was still plastered in place, knowing that was the only thing keeping me together, even if it was fake. "I was hoping we could sit down and get to know each other better. I don't know what you are trying to read into me, but everything here is innocent."

"You don't want to get to know me at my speed, though,

you want to get to know me only when I fit into one of your little boxes." She crossed her arms and gave me an unsettling glare. The perspiration that hit the back of my neck sent a shiver down my spine. "Doesn't that sound right?"

I realized I was doing this alone; Grace and Ninnie were not saying anything despite the way their eyes bounced back and forth between us like they were watching a game of tennis. "No, I was trying to meet you in the middle, and since you weren't putting any effort into this, it was up to me to start where you were and try to build from there."

"You think you care more about this than me. That is why you are pushing so hard for this."

"I don't think you care at all. I am trying to add support to your life. You have often said that you want family and people in your life, yet you are pushing us away," It came out harsher than I meant to, but the words were out. I had to accept it and stand by them, hoping Grace and Ninnie would too. "I know you have just been given lumps on lumps the last month, but what about our future? Don't you want to have one of those?"

She shrugged in response, choosing instead to reach out for a sandwich and add it to her plate. Grace and Ninnie followed suit, deciding to go through with the meal instead of picking up the conversation. We sat in a painful silence.

Chapter Seven

Meeting at the high school football field to practice combat strategies was not how I had used it in high school, not that I had often been out to the field when I attended. However, it looked the same as it did before, which made me wonder how the boys would use the space for their training.

Celeste, Grace, and Piper hung toward the back of our group, but they were all present, which meant a lot to Penelope since she was *very* enthusiastic about being here and getting this experience.

I was more shocked than anything else at the turnout. I didn't think Celeste or Piper were going to come. I was still waiting for either of them to make a break for it or, at the very least, devise a lousy excuse to leave early.

Harriet decided against coming, so Seth brought up the rear with Ninnie. It didn't take a genius to see that being together made her feel better. I could also tell she was nervous about being here; her eyes bounced between the Bradbury women individually.

I imagine that she also noticed she was the only woman

in the group not wearing a pair of black leggings. However, that does say something about her individuality, something that the Bradbury women were missing, especially regarding our wardrobe.

Tate was the apparent leader of our ragtag group, taking the field by stomping his way across until he got to the middle, where he dropped down his weathered red duffle bag with a loud thump. The shape of his bag resembled a dead body, so it was strangely reassuring when hundreds of weapons came falling out instead when he pulled the zipper.

I didn't realize how close I was trailing behind him until we were alone in the middle of the field while the rest of our group was still at the start of the grass, the white yardage lines tracking how far they still had to go until they met us there. I quickly realized how much alone time we were going to be allowed to have.

"I didn't realize you had brought so many weapons with you. Is this the carry-on luggage you brought on the plane?" I reached out to touch the handle of the one closest to me, trying to appear as calm as possible, even if it made me nervous. The metal was cold to the touch and felt forbidden, a weapon of man rather than the magic I was born with.

"Wait until you see my gun collection. It's even bigger," Tate's wink sent a thrill through me. It was an even brighter look than the one he gave the weapons. His eyes sparkled; even if he had seen them a million times before, they would always be exciting. "Is there one that you want to try first? We need to get you comfortable with them if we do this."

I sat on the cold, wet grass and stretched my legs out in front of me while he inventoried his supplies. I worked hard to refrain from looking at the muscles in his arms as they flexed with every movement. He did it without knowing, which made it even worse. He was just that good-looking and didn't understand how it affected me. "Do you have a pink one in there?"

He paused, taking a second to give me a long look to see if I was joking, but came up short, so he took the comment literally. "No, I don't have a *pink* one."

I reached out for my toes, stretching out the muscles in my legs for whatever he was going to bring out next from his bag. It was so full of surprises; I was far from being able to expect anything. My body felt stiff with anticipation. I was already completely prepared that nothing happening today would be expected. The man full of mystery was in complete control of the situation, and that thought scared me more than it should. "That's a shame. I hoped you had something in there that would match my outfit."

I reached into the neckline of my black jacket and pulled the strap of my tank top underneath to show that it was a bright pink color, just in case he didn't know what I was talking about, but to my dismay, he didn't glance down. He didn't care to look at me as I wanted him to. How dare he not objectify me like I wanted him to! I liked flirting with him even if he didn't give me the slightest bit of encouragement.

His face twisted in confusion since he never looked down at my tank top. His eyes had been on mine since we started talking. I could see that he still couldn't tell if I was joking, but at the very least, he continued the conversation, and that was not always something I could count on, so I was grateful. That would be his way of dealing with me, ignoring my sarcastic little comments despite how entertaining they might be. "What do you want to try first?" He repeated.

My cute, black running shoes looked funny next to his. Their large size made mine look even smaller by comparison. "Did you miss that I wanted one to match my outfit? Come on, pull out a pink one from your bag, Mary Poppins."

His face told me it was still not funny, obviously not appreciating my brilliant sense of humor.

"Why don't we start you off with a light dagger? We can set a target, and I will teach you to throw them." He took a small dagger from the side pocket of the duffle bag. It had a red braided handle close to pink, so I would give him at least a few points for the effort, even if I was sure that it wasn't intentional on his part. "You can conceal it in the waistband of your pants or even tucked into your sparkly boots if you want to carry it as an everyday weapon."

I don't know why he had this fascination with those sparkly boots, but he commented on them often enough that I knew they were somehow burned into his brain.

"You brought a target with you?" I looked at his half-emptied duffle bag, but there wasn't anything left in it that could open into a target that I could throw knives at unless they were small enough to fit in the outside pockets.

Maybe a blow-up version like you would get at an arcade with matching rubber hatchets? That thought made me giggle. The colorful picture so far from Tate and the dangerous persona he gave off that they didn't seem like they could exist in the same universe.

The rest of our group finally joined us. Seth pulled a small leatherbound notebook from the back pocket of his jeans, not pausing to make any casual conversation before he started our training. "He didn't, but you did."

Penelope had a snark remark at the tip of her tongue, "Yes, let me just pull it from my backpack." She pretended to reach over her shoulder into an imaginary bag, moving them around for a second before returning her empty hands and faking surprise at their lack of target. "Oh, sorry, my bad. I left it in my other 'battle-to-the-end-of –the-world' bag. That is just so embarrassing for both of us."

"Throughout your training, we will teach you how to push your magic further than you have ever taken it before." Seth started commandeering the group, taking point over Tate and directing us, ignoring Penelope's sarcasm. "Piper, Penelope, and Celeste. You are in group one; we will have you start with your physical strength training here with Tate."

Celeste gave me a hinting look about my being placed in the wrong group, as she was apparently on the same page as Aunt Mira about the connection between me and Tate. She was very outspoken about it when we were at home, but I knew she would say nothing now that he was here in front of us. She did not want to stand out in the crowd, especially this one where we were subject to punishment. Penelope was the opposite, and she was willing to provoke either of the boys in any way she could.

"Sounds good to me," My middle sister stepped forward and shoulder-checked Tate as she walked past him to get a slight reaction from him that didn't come. His face stayed just as flat as it had been moments before. She was much smaller than his large stature, but that didn't stop her from going against him. She was an avid gym goer, but she was still not going to come close to what training Tate had gone through. "Let's see what you bring to the table, muscle man."

"Ninnie, Grace, and Blair, you will make up group two. I want you to come with me, and we will practice your spellcasting." Seth started walking away from the larger group, and we followed quickly behind. While the Bradbury women had all worn matching black leggings, the two Guardians also matched each other in their navy sweatpants and grey t-shirts and a complicated logo on the front. It looked like the tip of an arrow with a red gemstone at the bottom. I could only guess it was from their Academy, possibly their school emblem. I would have never put down Tate as someone wearing a uniform and conforming to something, but he looked terrific in the tight shirt, and maybe that was why he went along with it. "We will use your magic to create a target for them to practice with."

I studied my spell books for hours every day, but I was yet to find one to create something out of thin air. It didn't seem possible, yet so many things from this last week were impossible, so I was willing to roll with it. It seemed interesting to teach Grandma the next time we had our lesson. "I haven't found any spell books for anything like that in our library. Where did you the find spells for that?" That was a type of magic I didn't know existed, but he seemed comfortable with it, so the questions shot out of my mouth in rapid-fire progression. "How long have you been practicing this magic?"

"That's because you are a garden witch, although I imagine that your magic goes into the practice of kitchen witch skills, and they are often interchangeable." He flipped through the book in his hand, trying to find the spell he was talking about. It surprised me that he was doing it as a human, flipping each page instead of using his magic to find the one he was looking for. "A million other spell books can teach you so much more when you are willing to look for it. You need to branch your magic out further. The ability to create is going to be vital in this war."

"Is that supposed to be an insult?" As far as I was

concerned, it felt very much like a 'women in the kitchen' mindset. I felt a flash of heat come over me, my arms crossing my chest, my cheeks getting hot, turning red, and my foot ready to send out a shift of magic almost as a warning, although there was no way that my magic stood a chance against his if he decided to act as a response.

Seth turned his head back to face me; no longer looking away while talking made the conversation more personal, but that was not his intention. His expression was just as neutral as ever. "Your magic involves a lot of cleansings and protection spells. I know that you own a shop that pushes the concept of using plants to heal parts of yourself or to fix things in your life. Based on that, you use your magic to heal and soothe those around you, which sounds like a kitchen and garden witch to me."

"So, what type of witch can create something like a target?"

"That is a new blend of magic all of its own." Seth's confidence bubbled up higher than I was expecting, as did the expression on his face, finally having some life come back to it. This seemed to be the type of conversation where he thrived, speaking in the way of a teacher to those in need of teaching. I could see the resemblance between the cousins once they both stopped scowling. "Maybe we could call it being a gray witch? A witch who has taken the time to learn all the magics and can use them at their will when needed."

I tried to make sense of what he was saying; now that he had opened my eyes to the diversification of our world, I had only a few million questions at the tip of my tongue. A small part of me thought it was clever to classify something not quite black or white into an entirely new category, mixing the two into a gray. "Where does this magic come from?"

Seth thought about it before answering, shifting his face to the side and pursing his lips. "When the wars of magic first started, our people needed a way to protect themselves. As such, when the Salem Witch Trials happened here, those with magic fled to safer grounds. When the civil wars started within our people, those under the guidance of the Council wanted to be the stronger than the independents, and in doing so, that meant teaching each other the magic that they knew."

"How would you learn all the magics? Isn't the Walker family also made up of kitchen witches?"

Seth was not expecting to talk this long or that his comment would turn into a lesson. His face only displayed annoyance; it didn't matter that he enjoyed having the opportunity to talk down to us, it was cutting into his training time. "What do you think we learn at the Academy? It's not all about mastering the art of fighting and weaponry. There is so much more that goes on to get someone ready for war. Hence the reason that we are all here now."

He redirected the question back to me and made me realize how foolish it was of me to ask. He had been sent to a private school where all they learned was how to protect themselves and others. That was very different from Victor Hills High School and my education here.

"Where did you learn about the different names for the classifications of magic? Is this something that everyone else knows?" Grace raised the question that had been on my mind as well, although I did have the fleeting thought that it had come from the same place as his training.

He didn't seem to think of it as strange when he put witches and their abilities into different boxes as we did. "Every Coven of witches practices their version of magic. With Guardians coming together to train, we have gotten the opportunity to learn about each and the magic that they hold." He pursed his lips once more, that apparently being his thinking face. I could tell he was contemplating how much to share with the three girls before him. "When we take the opportunity to teach each other, it helps to be able to label what each person has. It helps to track what you want to learn; the classifications aren't meant badly. They are the same as saying you have brown hair and I have red. You can dye your hair to get the color to change, but at your core, you will always be a brunette."

"But what about-" Ninnie finally started to speak up and join the conversation when Seth interrupted her mid-sentence. Her lips pursed as it shut her down. She would not come back from that. I didn't have to know her well to know that much.

"Okay, no more talking. It's time for you all to listen to me." He even seemed to puff up his chest as he shouted to prove that he meant business, a mix of little man syndrome and having to prove himself. Seth resembled a drill sergeant coming into position the more intense the expression on his face got.

I glanced over to where Tate was training with my sisters and cousin. Tate was sparring against Penelope while the other two stood to the side and watched as Penelope desperately tried to come out on top.

Even from this distance, I could see Tate going easy on her, letting her put her all into it without doing much to fight back, although it was evident that it would not last much longer. Despite their sweaty mess, I still wished I had been put in their group. Getting punched in the stomach seemed at least a bit better than getting another lecture from Seth.

My ears were on the verge of bleeding between him and my grandma, all of their training flowing to my ears.

Seth cleared his throat in my direction as a reminder to pay attention to him. He put the spell book in front of us and directed us to read what it said. The basic instructions written told us that we had to say the words while we pictured the item we were trying to create. The bottom of the page had the words the spell used.

I need it now so
mote it be
Find me this item
or rescue me

The spell looked easy enough, but Seth explained once more that changing our magic was not quickly done. It would not happen instantly, which the three of us would need to prepare for, and that constant practice between our training sessions was required to succeed.

He had us practice saying the words a few times, almost to get used to the terms on our tongues before we went to do the real thing. "You need to get used to saying the spells in your head instead of out loud. It won't help if your enemy hears what you are doing and what you will create. You want to use your magic to surprise them, or else they will figure out a way to stop you."

Ninnie went first, speaking the words calmly, nailing every word, even including the dramatic pauses necessary for the spell. Grace and I followed suit, saying the words while trying to emulate the most successful of our trio.

"Blair, I will have you go first for the real thing. Say the words as calmly as possible, look out on the field away from any of us, and picture a target in your mind." Seth was a better teacher than I expected from our first meeting or even today's conversations. Once he lost his intensity, he became someone you could actually talk to and potentially learn from, which gave me a little more hope for our situation and all that we were getting ourselves into.

He did a quick demonstration by making himself a comfortable chair to sit in, giving himself the opportunity to judge our progress with a haughty look on his face. The combination made my stomach turn. Seth explained that if I wanted something to appear, I needed to picture the item and imagine it as if it were before me. As if it was already in the room when I got there, and it would appear before my eyes.

I used my magic in the way he had explained. I turned my body away from either group and closed my eyes, trying to picture a target in front of me the way he directed me to.

"Well, that was a good first try." His voice broke, though, causing me to open my eyes to look at where he was sitting, off to the side and out of danger. "Maybe next time we can get one out of you that can be used."

He walked forward to where I had created the target, picking it up. In his hand sat a one-inch target that looked like it had walked out of medieval times. That was not what we were looking for. The hay it was made from had nothing compared to the thin wood that looked as long as toothpicks.

"Well, that's disappointing." Grace somehow managed to become my inner monologue, speaking out about the things racing through my mind, which gave my mouth a second to rest. Although she did miss my thought about hoping Tate didn't see my epic fail since that was probably flashing across my cheeks as a giant, neon-red sign.

Which says a lot about where my mind indeed was. Darn, Aunt Mira was right! I *did* have a crush on him.

"Grace, why don't you step up and give it a try?" Seth moved his attention from me and over to my cousin.

I think a small part of him was worried about what I could bring to the table since he was taking his time to repeat his instructions, explaining that she had to imagine the item at its full size. A point at the miniature target that was my creation, which was now sitting next to his chair.

She did the same as I did, turning her body away from us, closing her eyes, and trying to picture it as if it was already in front of us.

The target he had hoped to get out of me appeared before us. It was bright yellow, resembling a highlighter, which was probably not exactly what Seth wanted, but it was closer than what I had brought to the field. The look on her face told us how proud she was of herself, and nothing he said would bring her down from that high, evidence of her self-confidence.

"That is close enough. Good job, Grace." Seth seemed okay with what we had created but was ready to continue. I felt he would not be satisfied until he got greatness out of us. "When it comes down to it, what color you create things doesn't matter, but you eventually want to start getting it right so that it's not distracting for you during the battle. Although that might become a good tactic for confusing your enemy. Either way, for a first try, that was great!"

I tried not to be jealous of the praise he was giving her *or* that she managed to do it right when I failed the task.

"How much experience do you have in battles?" Grace

pushed the idea open that I hadn't had a chance to review in my head yet. "You have a lot of stories and knowledge on the matter, but how much of that is after actually going through it? I have never heard of a battle in the history of magic; even during the Trials, no one acted out in exchange, especially since the creation of the Council."

Seth was exhausted with the two of us and our ability to run him through circles before we were willing to do anything important. The questions piled up, coming out of us at what could only be considered an alarming rate. I doubt Penelope, Piper, and Celeste were making Tate jump through this many hoops to get their training done, although I think he would be much quicker at shutting them down than Seth was with us. "Just because you haven't heard of it doesn't mean it doesn't happen. You are a witch, but your neighbors don't know that. Isn't that the same?"

He had a point there. There was so much that the world didn't know, but it still seemed strange to think that great battles were fought when we were unaware of them, especially since it seemed the Council was not directly involved with the Academy. I thought they would be further intertwined, especially since there were the Guardians of the Council, the men who swore themselves to the sole protection of our leaders.

Ninnie was next up. Seth directed her just as he had done to us. She stood to the outside, eloquently using her magic with complete control, and suddenly a target appeared just as he asked for. I tried not to be jealous as she stepped back to the edge of our group, as if what she did was not a big deal. So much for her never getting to use her magic.

"Great job Ninnie!" He celebrated her accomplishment with a huge smile on his face, even bigger than the reaction he had given to Grace, especially since this time he could go on without the added criticism that he pointed out to Grace. "That was perfect."

Grace and I shared a nasty look between us, the green-eyed monster coming out strong since we hadn't gotten a reaction like that, even if Grace had gotten close. Grace bravely mumbled under her breath, just loud enough for me to hear her, "Well, that is just great."

"Let's go through it again, and then we will switch groups. Give you all the opportunity to learn some tactile skills while they learn some magic. Taking a break between activities helps reset your mind." Seth abandoned his chair and was standing in complete focus, that drill sergeant coming back to life with his directions. "We are going to go again."

Grace volunteered to go first, taking a second to close her eyes, and stood ready to make the next target appear.

"That's it!" I shouted as loud as I could at the target, one of the proper sizes, that appeared before our eyes in a black color instead of the bright one she had gotten the first time she did it. I was ready to do cartwheels in celebration of her success. "You did it! Grace, you did it."

Grace had been worried about her skills and how she measured up to the rest of us as she was also the youngest of our Coven; she had talked about it our entire walk over to the high school and only stopped when she saw my tongue wagging in the direction of Tate. That was when Grace respectfully let me follow after him like a lost puppy. I don't think she was expecting to be better at it than me, but I tried as hard as I could not to be jealous of how good she was doing.

Seth gave us half of what could be considered a smile, the first one we had gotten all day. "You did well. That is exactly what we are looking for. Now, Blair… why don't you go again and let us see what you can do."

I tried to focus, turning my ears off, trying to contain myself, and put my mind in the moment as I closed my eyes. I tried to put my full attention onto the target I was supposed to make appear.

I pictured the grass being indented with the target's weight, the metal being a dark brass color, with the target standing proudly, facing us, ready to be impaled with the knives we would throw.

"That looks like the dopey little sister of the one Grace did." Tate's voice broke through the silence I had tried so hard to focus on, forcing me to open my eyes to see what I had created. "Good try, though."

He was right, which was annoying in every way possible. I was beginning to hate it when he was right.

My newest venture was standing at just over four feet tall, an entire foot shorter than the one Grace created, and it even looked a little uneven. One of the legs seemed longer than another, which didn't feel fair to the effort I had put into it comparable to the action she had.

"You did it; it looks great. I'm going to have the three of you switch groups, and then when you come back to me, we will give it another run and see how it goes." Seth gave out more directions, telling the other women to switch over to where he was standing, and directed Grace, Ninnie, and myself to walk closer to Tate. He was sinister in a way that seemed something close to dangerous, but that's the way he always managed to be. I tried not to notice that Ninnie did so well the first time that she wasn't required to go twice.

We walked over to our separate grouping, following Tate to the side of the field he was working at, and waited for him to direct us to the next stage of our training.

"Now that we have some targets on the floor, we will start with spear-throwing." He picked up a spear from the pile, which looked like it was straight from medieval times. It matched the target I had created, which seemed kind of fitting, although a little unfair how my misstep had matched up so perfectly. "Use your magic to put the target at the back of the field."

Grace thrust her hand out, with a small amount of aggression, and had the target move under the field goal post. However slowly it ran itself across the grass, at least it made it there, which had her giving us a very enthusiastic smile. She was very proud of herself; the confidence in her eyes showed her pride more than anything else she would say. "I just thought it, and it did it! My magic did what I wanted it to!"

This was a new way of conducting our magic that I knew Grandma had never done before let alone had even known about or approved of us doing. She much preferred for us all to stay in our own lane. The Guardians were bringing something new to our lives, and I knew we would never be able to go back.

Tate didn't acknowledge Grace's excitement, but I did. I was proud of her in every way possible, subtly taking the opportunity to fist bump her while Tate turned his back away from us since that was not something he would approve of.

"I want you to take this spear and throw it as hard as you can in the direction of the target." He used the opportunity to educate me on the objective as if I hadn't been paying attention to the conversation so far. He was probably not doing it to make me feel bad, but it did either way. "You put all your force into it at the last second. As you move to put your hand back over your shoulder, you need to start the throw."

His instructions were smooth, butter on his lips as he spoke. He had taught someone before, gone through the words enough times that he didn't have to think about them as they left his mouth.

Tate handed the spear over to me, the weight forcing me to take another step that wasn't planned. He reached for my shoulders and spun me toward the target. It was similar to playing Pin the Tail on the Donkey, although this was a high-stakes version. "Now, go. Throw it as hard as you can; once you get to that point where you feel like you have put as much energy as possible, I need you to release it. This is usually done once it crosses over your shoulder."

His directions were clear, but it didn't go far once I lifted the spear above my shoulder. It landed about a yard and a half down from where the three of us stood and somehow managed to land flat on the ground without damage to the grass underneath, which was not the intention. I probably could have heard his frustrated sigh from a million miles away, even if he tried to conceal it.

"That was a good first try." Honestly, he was probably as sincere as he could have made his voice sound. "Next time, maybe add your magic to it? It might help it go just a bit further," Tate said like I was missing something; it shouldn't have to be explained in his mind, although it needed to be presented to me.

"I didn't realize that was needed." I was willing to try that, and I would have done that first if he had explained it. Maybe it was something that I should have automatically done since that was the entire objective here.

"Grace, why don't you give it a try?" Tate opted out of going after my spear and grabbed a fresh one from the pile inside the bag. No matter where she got, it would be compared to mine, which would not make me look good, once again. It made me feel better when it seemed a little too heavy for her too, as she had to shift around for a second to get used to the weight.

"So, when it crosses over my shoulder, I release it?" She asked for clarification once more but looked confident, especially after seeing how I failed the first time. Once she got the nod of approval from Tate, she was ready to go for her turn. "Okay, I can do that."

Grace went for it, and it seemed like a breeze for her, just as creating the target was. While she didn't hit the exact center, it was close enough, and far better than what I had been able to do on my turn.

Both boys, our self-appointed trainers, had this amazing skill of conveniently forgetting to inform me of all the details until after I had tried something once. A habit that had started to become very annoying now that we had gone through it twice, me coming out as a failure both times, while the other girls in my group came out on top.

Tate seemed happy with her results; he went forward with his own fist bump to Grace to share in her success, meaning he had seen the one we tried to hide behind his back. "Good job."

Ninnie seemed more hesitant to try this one, accepting a new spear from Tate and turning it around so that she was ready to throw it at the target. Suddenly I could see that her lack of experience with magic would be a disadvantage, even in this training category. The spear she threw flew through the air, much further than mine, but still managed to stop before the target, despite all the magic we could tell she put into it.

"Do I get to go again? Give it another go?" I asked, wanting to show Tate that I was just as capable as Grace —

since this was now the second time they had allowed her to show me up. I hated that I needed to prove to him that I was just as capable as the rest of our group. I shouldn't care, yet I did. "I have to at least get more shots at this."

"I will have you do the opposite as yours didn't get as far as the others." He pointed to the spear I had thrown onto the grass after a blatant dig at my expense. "Use your magic and draw it back to you."

I was tempted to stomp my foot, but even I knew how immature that was, so I exercised using my words instead. "Do you mind telling me how I am supposed to do that? Instead of just waiting for me to make a fool out of myself?" I was not above forcing him into coaching me since he wouldn't just give me that information willingly.

"Just as with the target. You put your hand out and imagine yourself pulling it toward you. Imagine that your magic is another arm reaching out for it, extending further than your body physically could." He explained it like it was simple, and when I reached my hand out, I was surprised that it was. The spear almost seemed to float back to my hand without any issues.

"I did it!" I exclaimed, but the expression on Tate's face took all the satisfaction away from me.

He nodded slowly like I was missing something, probably referring to my inability to keep up with the rest of our group, which I was also hyperaware of. "Great. I'm glad you were able to do that," his tone that of a condescending schoolteacher.

This time I did stomp my foot. The energy shift in the grass wasn't what I was going for when I did it, but there was still a tiny amount of satisfaction from forcing Tate to take a step to stabilize himself.

He didn't acknowledge my success or the power I put

out with my stomp, and quickly moved on to a new task. "How about some hands-on fighting?" He had us drop the weapons. He talked with his hands and demonstrated some basic fighting movements that he wanted us to emulate. "The worst thing would be for your weapon to be taken away from you; if you keep your hands available, it forces them to attack you with a hands-on approach."

Tate put Grace and Ninnie against each other, choosing to go against me himself instead of making me wait it out since we had an uneven number. He dodged another one of my fists as it flew toward his stomach. He shouted out guidance to the others and then started shouting something else at me. "Stop fighting like a girl! Go harder. You need to put more into it. How will you protect yourself if you can't even get your hands free?" He swung his leg underneath mine, throwing me to the floor.

I could feel my face go red. I was so far past stomping my foot. "You have got to be kidding me; if I were fighting like a girl, I would pull your hair and dig my nails into your skin." I reached out and pinched his hand so he would let me go. His other hand, still holding me down, was tempting to sink my teeth into. "You're lucky I haven't started biting yet."

* * *

We trained for a week straight before the other Guardians could show up, their previous mission having kept them occupied longer than expected, but I knew that we were all grateful for the extra time it gave us to train. It allowed us Bradbury women to prove ourselves to the Guardians who were already here and allowed us to improve their opinions of us.

Throughout our training, I desperately attempted to improve how Tate saw me. In my free time, I bumped up my training, running to work and studying my spell books once I got there. Despite all my additional effort, nothing in his opinion changed.

Tate and Seth were willing to plan their training around our schedules, taking us back to the high school football field every night when we finished work. They had us run through the training they taught us the first night while adding additional exercises each day. They had turned us into their brand of little warriors, complete with neon sports bras and black leggings—the unofficial uniform of their soldiers.

Tate liked making us do whatever he wanted day after day; you could tell by the distinctive smirk on his lips. His favorite punishment was having us run multiple laps around the track while the two Guardians ran beside us, barking orders when they wanted us to sprint or keep it to a light jog. They barely broke a sweat, which was slightly more annoying than if they had opted out of the exercise. However, their sideline comments as they ran beside us were a different brand of torture than any of us expected.

Apparently, Tate *could* be funny when he wanted to; it just came in the form of sarcasm.

The new Guardians, Huxley and Fabian were different than I expected, not just because they were brothers with matching, obnoxiously attractive faces, but because of how they carried themselves with our ragtag group to fight the enemy. I could tell that they were novices compared to Seth and Tate. The older ones were willing to bring them here to not only train us but to help train the two of them too.

Seth put it best when he told us, "You are not a master of something until you are willing and able to teach it to someone else." This seemed to be why they invited the younger boys to come with them: to experience a real battle on a scale they had never seen before.

Tate retorted sarcastically that there was not a big enough chance of death for either of the younger Guardians for them to be worried.

* * *

"Did you package her bag with the new samples for acne?" Aunt Mira asked as she walked out of the back room. The clipboard in her hand was covered in marks from checking inventory, her least favorite activity — one she is usually willing to pass on to me or Grace. I was surprised that she hadn't done that this month. "She seemed to have a few on her cheek that looked like they had been there a while. The green ones with pus." That visual made my stomach turn over.

The same back room had become somewhat of an office for the Guardians as Seth and Tate had commandeered it the day before. The compelling Seth Walker and his ability to successfully woo a woman found easy prey in Aunt Mira's ability to fall for wildly attractive men with an impressively white smile. It had been so easy for him to convince her that they needed a place to command their army.

It was stressful to think about his powers if he could convince my poor aunt to give up half of her store, even if it was the half that she didn't like. It was hard for me to work with them back there; Seth hadn't been able to woo me like Aunt Mira. Not only was it annoying not to have a break room, but they had also made it their own by adding a whiteboard and lots of storage containers for their weapons.

In the process, they also swapped out our teapot in the kitchen for a coffee maker, which was a cardinal sin in a store that only sells tea.

"Yeah, I threw some of the samples in her bag," I responded to Aunt Mira. I grabbed a rag from the drawer and used it to wipe down the main table we used as our checkout counter, refreshing it for the next customer. "That new tea tree sample smells good. I'm glad that you put some together to give out."

Aunt Mira had me drop samples into their bags as our customers checked out, depending on their needs. The shelf under the counter was full of them, even a few of the old love potions that Aunt Mira decided to part with since they hadn't worked on her despite her constant efforts. My favorite sample was the one labeled Lucky Girl, it promoted good luck as soon as it was taken, and it was a definite favorite once someone got the chance to use it. Our sample size of Lucky Girl did a great job of taking care of people and adding something unique to their day. Still, the tea tree was an excellent solution for acne, which sometimes worked more miracles than actual magic on those terrible breakout days.

I could hear the mumble of the boys talking in the backroom. It was distracting in a way that felt dangerous to the hearts of innocent women nearby, like how sirens lure pirates to their death. Faint hearts are dangerous to those searching hard for their desires to be fulfilled.

Aunt Mira wasn't affected in the same way that I was by their presence. She only got involved when they made direct eye contact, so now she stood there at the counter casually flipping through a fashion magazine without a care in the world despite the noise from the boys in the room behind us. "I'm glad we decided to make the potions as our samples this month instead of outsourcing like we normally do, especially the tea tree one. The change in weather has done hard things to these young girls; it's not fair they can't just fix it on their own as we can."

"I think it will be good for her," Grace agreed, "It worked on mine when I had that bad breakout last year. Fall is so unfair; even if it is still August, it's already started hitting hard. There has been such a shift in the weather the last few weeks." Grace was thankfully listening more to the conversation than I was and could respond to Aunt Mira. I could say that I did not want to partake in a discussion involving the weather, even if I was listening. "I was thinking about making a love potion for the girl that does my nails. She's had a little bad luck when it comes to love lately and was complaining about it the other day when I was in there. Could you spare a moment to help me make one up? I still haven't done one on my own yet, and I don't want to get anything wrong with the measurements, especially if it's with the intent of love."

The idea of any potion put Aunt Mira in a good mood, so she jumped on the suggestion and was willing to help her with the project.

"Let's do it as soon as we close. We can break out the bowls in the backroom and mix!" She grabbed her spell book and used her magic to make a pen appear, a trick the boys had taught her after they taught it to us. I think they just taught her that to sweeten the deal of possession over the back room. "We should add some honeysuckle so some wealth can come her way. I think that would be a sweet surprise in addition to some love. Of course, we must put in some rose oil and a lot of hibiscus for it to be a perfect love potion."

"Oh! Honeysuckle would be great! She does well, but

their shop doesn't get much traffic because of its location. I think many people don't know that it's there, and I just wish she knew how great she is!" Grace had such a big heart for the people around her. "Will we have time to do it after the shop closes? We have our training tonight as soon as we close. The boys are very intense with their punishment when we are late."

She would be willing to skip the training if that was presented as a choice. While some of us had felt great strength through our intense training with the boys, she had only felt annoyed and frustrated with the endless hours we had to put in each day for something that she doubted would end up happening. She was also weirdly obsessed with the idea that one of her arms would become larger than the other and that she would start looking lopsided, something that had not gone through my mind until she said it.

I knew what she was hinting at. We were too close for me to miss the blimp of a sign that she was sending out. "Why don't the two of you go to the backroom, and I will watch the store?"

"Are you sure? I don't want to ask that of you." She was being sincere, but I also knew what she wanted, and if there were a chance to work on this potion, she would take it. Grace cared a lot more about mastering potions, much more than I did. I would rather cast a spell than throw a bunch of herbs in a bowl and make someone drink it.

I brushed her off, letting her know that it was okay for her to go since the front could be managed by one person, especially today with our low traffic flow; there was no need for all three of us to be sitting here killing time by reading magazines and studying our spell books.

The two of them had only been back there mere seconds when a voice spoke from behind me. "You didn't want to take part in potion making? I thought that was your way of breaking loose and having fun?"

Tate.

His voice was gruff, and that somehow matched his constant stony demeanor. Even after knowing each other for some time, his personality still hadn't softened like I wanted.

"They wanted to make one, but I didn't. It's pretty simple when you think about it." I didn't know the polite way to brush him off, but that wasn't it, as he didn't walk away. "Besides that, someone has to watch the store if they are back there. We could potentially have customers hoping to buy something."

"You think someone is going to come in?"

"Typically, that is what people do at a store. We weren't always a hub for a military operation." It was dangerous to stand this close to him, especially with how his heathered grey shirt fit his shoulders like a glove, and his tan skin glowed off it to create a combination that shook me to my knees.

"Are you not a mixer like the other two back there?" He reached out for the spell book I was studying, stealing it from my hands with the disrespect he was famous for.

I fought the urge to reach for the book, steal it back from his hands, and instead opted to use my words in place of my fists, especially now that I knew how to use them. "That could be considered derogatory; you do realize what calling me a mixer sounds like? Or at least realize that an apology would be considerate at this point now that I have pointed it out to you."

Whether he realized it or not, it was clear that he didn't care. He just kept talking as if I hadn't said anything at all, which seemed to be an uncomfortable theme with the people in my life — way to feel insignificant.

"I figured that was how all of you wielded your magic. Isn't that what you do while the rest of the world fills their hours by watching reality TV?" Tate studied the words in the book with an intensity that I wasn't expecting as he moved past our current conversation into the one that he wanted to have. "What does this mean? Why would you need a pinch of rosemary for a spell? Aren't items like that only used for hexes and potions? I thought that spells were words only."

"Spells use a lot of things in addition to the words you use." I could only raise my eyebrow that he didn't know what witches did in their free time or how we did it.

He reached over and showed me the page I had been looking at before he had taken the book from me, except this time, his finger was on it, pointing out the detailed ingredient list and the title at the top that declared it a spell for lovers, something I wasn't sure he was expecting by the raise of his eyebrow. "You need something tangible for this spell? That doesn't seem like how it would work."

"It's completely normal, especially when you move onto harder spells, because it helps with the room and fuels the magic. Some witches have their own specific item they always keep on them that helps with their magic. It is filled with the magic of their ancestors and helps them channel their energy in their spells." I loved my amulet and its magic and would never be willing to part with it. To keep it that way, it was essential to never divulge what I kept my ancestors' magic in, so I restrained myself from going into any more details despite my desire to share with him. Something about how he looked at me just had me desperate to share every part of myself with him, but that could get me into a lot of trouble if I wasn't careful. "Here's an example, I did a spell with a vanilla candle the other day, and it helped relax the room while I did the spell, which can be extremely useful when you are somewhere that doesn't have calm. Don't you learn about these things at school?"

It felt weird to have to explain something like this to him, and it only furthered my curiosity about what they learned at their school. He was constantly adding to my list of questions without knocking any of them off. At least now the version of training that Seth, Tate, and the new Guardians were putting us through made a little bit more sense.

"We don't have someone who sits down with us and goes over everything word for word as your little group of women does with you. We learn more from failing first, and then they fill in the gaps where they see fit. Usually, that is how people learn best, and it helps prepare them for the moments in a war when you must react without thinking." His explanation was far less informative than what I was looking for —something that I would have to expect from him at this point.

Tate Bishop operated under the assumption that if I didn't directly ask the question, then it wasn't necessary to answer it, which was frustrating when I was the type of person who divulged everything that went through my mind, even if it was a passing thought. The contrast between the two meant that I was the one dominating every conversation.

"Your family must have given you at least a little training or even some information about spell casting before you went to the Academy." I was hoping that if I started making accusations, he would be willing to give answers to prevent that thought from going further down the wrong road.

"Family is subjective to some people; we don't all have the ability to trace our family line all the way back to the first families."

"Don't you have roots somewhere? Somewhere that you called *home* before your entire job was searching the world for bad guys to beat up?" I asked the question, realizing I didn't know anything about this person despite my connection. However, the more he treated me like a burden, the more he forced me to second guess those apparent feelings.

"I am topsoil, babe," He said, like the only concept of a life I understood meant nothing to him. I realized that he never put his life down somewhere in the same way that I did, in the only way I understood, which made sense as to why the life of a Guardian seemed to work so well for him. "I don't have roots anywhere, although there was a lot of appeal to the idea."

The only thing going through my mind was whether it still appealed to him to have roots somewhere now that he was free from the Academy with the ability to live wherever and do whatever he wanted. Possibly, even though the idea scared me, putting down those roots near me. I also got a thrill at that idea, but I was rational enough to realize that even entertaining those thoughts would only lead me down a path of disappointment. And the reaction he would have was not one I could handle.

Chapter Eight

"What book are you studying?"

I held it up for Mom to read the title. "Aunt Mira suggested this one; it's been a good read so far."

"Oh, that is a good book; I've read that a few times," she gave me a hesitant smile as she slowly approached my position at the counter. "I noticed that you have been studying many new books lately. Have you found a favorite spell yet? We all find one that sticks with us more than others, making it a 'favorite.' Mine is probably the one that helps you make food faster; it makes my life so much easier, especially on our busy days when you and your sisters were younger. Or maybe the one to help my garden grow. It's great when you can find a spell that does something to help smooth out your day." She spoke rapidly, the same way my sisters and I were prone to do ourselves when we were nervous, but with enough enthusiasm to try and cover it up.

I had studied my way through the list of spell books over the last week; studying this one for over an hour every night when I came home from training with the boys, and the two activities together had exhausted me to a breaking point that I had never reached before. It's a good thing that I worked for a boss that knew what was happening in my life and was willing to work with my lack of energy; even more, I appreciated that she was willing to accommodate what had become a hectic schedule.

My life had changed significantly since the day Ninnie had walked into the Corner Shop, but I couldn't find it in myself to be disappointed in that now that I understood how boring my life had been.

I couldn't say that I was reading my spell book now, despite trying. Thankfully the book I had beneath the spell book was my own. It was the one I was supposed to use to practice creating my own spells, so the drawings I had put in the margins would only be seen by me.

My doodling kept me awake, but I could only guess the conversation I would have with Grandma if she saw them hidden there. She would lecture me on how unprofessional it was, and how I wasn't putting my mind in the right direction for spellcasting if I was more worried about the symmetry of the flowers I had drawn.

"It's good. I was just about to go to bed. I figured I needed as much sleep as possible to do it all again tomorrow," I meant to end the conversation as early as possible. My life had become *Groundhog Day*. It just repeats itself day after day without much change in the activities. No matter what, sleep was necessary, even if tomorrow would be the same as today.

Mom nodded her head slowly, running her hand over the white granite countertop, scratching at stains that weren't there in an absentminded way. I had seen her hedging all night for a chance to talk to me alone, but my sisters and nieces had been in her way. That was why I decided to study in the kitchen instead of in the basement or my bedroom, to get some privacy. However, I knew that if I sat anywhere comfortable, there was a huge chance I would fall asleep, just as I had done the last three nights.

Jinx opted out of being with me in the kitchen and was asleep at the foot of my bed, taking advantage of the additional space she was allowed to occupy while I was away.

"So, I have been thinking a lot about this war my girls are signing up for," Mom started," And I think you are in over your head. You will get hurt or possibly killed if you keep going with this, and that's not something I want to risk." Mom was predictable in that way, presenting herself so that we were prepared for whatever intense conversation she wanted. There was never a part of me that didn't think she would worry, but it was concerning that she hadn't considered this a possibility before today. "I have tried to get through to your sisters about this, but I also know that you are the operation's ringleader, and they have put their faith in your lap until this is over."

Calling me the ringleader over Penelope almost felt like an insult since she was pushing the hardest for this to go forward, something I was not doing out of my fears about the situation. I understood that she was our mom and would worry about us no matter our problems. Still, I was probably more nervous than she was, considering my life constantly felt like it was being put on the line. I also was far too aware that there was no backing out of it now that the Guardians had put in the hours to train us. Now that we knew the Cabals were on their way, we couldn't avoid the issue like we wanted.

Pandora's Box had been opened, and there was no chance of putting the lid back on.

"We are going at this the best way we know how," I was

anxious to hear her thoughts, especially what she had thought about all day when there was no one to stop her. She often took a little idea and turned it into an avalanche by overthinking when there was too much time in her day without distractions. She was a minefield just waiting to explode. "I know you are worried, but *you must* understand that we have to do this. And even if this doesn't turn into anything, we, at the very least, have to be ready for what *might* be coming. We have to be ready for so many unknowns, and this is one of them," I tried to reassure her.

"I was okay with it when it seemed like it wasn't going to happen, but now it's become genuine. Those boys have put you all through a lot, day after day. I can say that they have put you through a lot more than I was expecting initially," I knew that she agreed with why we were doing this, but I also knew that she might just need a reminder of what would happen if we backed out now and how much was at stake if we didn't at least try. "You girls are coming home sore, over-tired, and with large bruises. I thought this would only be about your magic, but now you are getting hurt. That was never discussed with me and something I was unprepared for."

She wasn't the only one unaware it would become a physical battle. Celeste had also not been happy to find out that part of the situation, but as it turns out, she was a little intense when it came to fighting. She became more ferocious when she was reminded that she was doing this to protect her girls. I avoided being partnered with her for our training. Celeste showed no mercy.

I reached for my mom's hand lying on the counter and chose not to acknowledge how fast it was quivering for her daughters and what we had signed up for. I tried to explain why we were doing this in a new way, hoping that saying the words in a new sequence would get her to understand me and why I was doing this to myself or why my sisters signed up for this. "What would you do in my situation? Our Coven needs magic to keep going; we can't stop now. We need to think of the girls and what they will need. This was the entire conversation that started it all, and we can't let it be taken away now that we have come this far."

She looked ready to cry as her words sputtered out. "I was doing good, keeping a low level of worry until Penelope came home with a black eye! My little girl was obviously hurt, and it was only time before the rest of you came back with similar markings that I would have to worry about."

I didn't know how to explain that the rest of us had been smart enough to wear clothes to hide the bruises on our extremities and use makeup on the ones we couldn't hide until we could get to the potion Aunt Mira had created, it was for good health and would take the bruises away as well as any pains.

To Penelope's defense, none of us realized that our mom was planning on waiting for us last night when we got home and that she would be sitting in the front room to witness the shiny addition to my sister's face before the evidence could be hidden.

"Our training with the Guardians is what will protect us from that. Every moment we are out there with them sets us up for success. Sadly, bruising is the consequence." It also set me up for exhaustion, which wouldn't help my argument with my overprotective mother.

She sat beside me, finally looking like she had found at least a second of calm before the worry storm reappeared. "I also wanted to talk to you about these Guardians. I worry about them being around my sweet girls and the influence that they are having on you." She made it sound like they were the devil in disguise and going to tempt her innocent girls to the wild side that they lived on instead of the actual situation we were in, the one where the boys shouted at us to run faster, hit harder, and go for just one more lap around the track.

Penelope would rather rip one of their heads off, mostly Seth's, before she would follow them anywhere, especially away from our family and our Coven.

"I promise that everything will be fine. We got this," I tried to keep my voice as calm as possible. Getting her to relax was hard; everything after that was easy. "Have a little faith in us and our abilities."

Her eyes softened greatly; reaching her hand out, she played with the piece of my hair that had slipped out from my braid. The hairstyle was my messy attempt to keep it out of my face, which bothered her. Despite her girls' love for it, she didn't think the messy look was appropriate. "You know, you remind me of your dad more and more every day, especially now that you're having to take on this new challenge in your life. You amaze me." Her hazel eyes got a soft mist over them as they often did when our dad was brought into the conversation. "I love when I get to see small parts of him in each of you girls."

I wanted to ask her about him, but I knew she wouldn't answer, so I chose a safer option that wouldn't make her sadder than she already was. "I am tired, and I think it's time for me to go to bed since I have to do this hard day all again tomorrow."

She finally accepted my answers and gave my hair one last smooth down to the rest of the flyways that had slipped out. "Okay, don't be shocked when we have to have this conversation again in a few days, especially if another one of you comes home with more bruises." She walked to the old farmhouse door that led to the backyard and twisted the lock, ensuring it was locked up for the night. "When you are done down here, just turn the lights out before you go up. I will lock the front door before I go upstairs for bed."

I heard her steps as she went to the front door, then the lock slid into place, followed by the soft creaks of the wooden steps as she walked up to her bedroom. Our old house had its way of announcing where we were at any time.

"You might want to sound more confident when getting someone to join our cause. You would have never made it as a girl scout; those cookies would have stayed in your wagon until the end of the season."

At this point, I needed to stop being surprised at Tate and his ability, as it seemed, to walk through walls because the locks on the door didn't slow him down. Even the spell my sisters and I cast over the house didn't do anything to keep him out, which I would have to take to my grave. Celeste would not be able to handle it if she knew how easy it was for someone to break in, not to mention someone who could be considered dangerous. She would never be able to get a good night's sleep ever again.

"You realize how rude it is to break into someone's house, right? It's almost like it's a crime or something." I sounded ridiculous even to my ears, but I was past the point of exhaustion, and he certainly wasn't helping the headache that was starting to form, the combination causing my usually polite nature to fall away. "I already see you at my place of work and at night to train. Do I have to see you at my house too?"

He stepped forward despite my attitude, coming to the counter, and I noted the fresh mud attached to his shoes and the bottom of his pants. Sadly, that was another thing that raised questions about Tate and all the mystery he was, but I knew it wouldn't change the outcome for me to ask him about it, so I refrained from doing so. Tate gave me his famous smirk, and the lift in his mouth made my knees weak. "Is it breaking in if the person wants you to be there? And I would say that you want me here."

"Tate, what are you doing here?" I scrunched my nose up, trying to contain the irritation and the need to lash out as a reaction. The magic in my body was starting to bubble with anticipation at what he would say or do next. I usually stomped my foot to release some of the magic, but that wasn't an option. I knew there was too much glass in the room, so I tightened my body as I tried to hold it together before it slipped out more than it already did. My magic always seemed to struggle around him in ways I hadn't experienced before his arrival. Salem was safer before Tate came to it, and I knew my mother and sisters would agree with that. "I am tired of you just stepping in and out whenever you want without dealing with consequences. What if I didn't want you here? Then would it constitute breaking and entering?"

He gestured for me to be quiet by holding a finger to his lips. It only frustrated me further since he was in my house, yet somehow still in control of the situation and over me. I don't know where he got the nerve to act in such a way, but he continued to do so even when I fought it to where it was almost not worth it. "Ah, but I didn't break anything. I will admit to entering, but only because I am standing here with you."

"What is wrong with you?"

Tate's smile only broke out larger than it had the first time. He knew that he was driving me crazy. I could only imagine the satisfaction that he was receiving from this.

"Yeah, you aren't allowed to ask that question in this situation."

That only fueled me more, and I struggled to contain my magic. "Why do I have to be quiet in my own home? Will you just explain to me why you are here?"

"You can't ask that question either." His proximity was dangerous when it came to the way of my heart. I felt a rush of perspiration hit the back of my neck as goosebumps covered the back of my arms.

I felt my magic slip out into the room. The water in my glass rippled as a result; I was out of control when he was near me. "So, what am I allowed to ask? Since you know all the rules and I know none of them, why don't you walk me through how this interaction is supposed to go?"

Tate stepped in closer, only the empty barstool between us now, but with his height, he still managed to tower over me. It was meant to be intimidating, yet somehow it sent a different type of flutter to go through me. "You're right; I know all the rules, which is another reason I shouldn't be here. You do know that, right? I am breaking all the rules to be here with you right now."

"I'd curse you, but you aren't worth the herbs," I told Tate with a sting of threat in my voice, my voice shaking, which only proved that I wasn't going to do it even if I *desperately* wanted to.

He chuckled to mock me further, "Sorry Wicked Witch, but that threat has nothing that will hold up. I've seen your magic skills and haven't had a reason to worry yet."

"Ugh! I can't believe you!" I felt my face flush with a deep red as the anger went through me, and a thick haze went over my eyes. "How dare you come into my house and insult me in such a way! Get out! I want you out, now."

He came as close as the chair between us would allow, and this time he put his finger to my lips. "Do you ever stop talking?"

Suddenly his lips were coming down, which had my heart ready to go out of my chest when I heard the door to the kitchen open quietly and then swiftly closed with the entrant making a soft squeak noise, causing us to quickly pull away from each other much faster than we had been coming together.

Our almost kiss sadly turned into a near miss.

"I am going to pretend I didn't see that," Aunt Mira called through the door to apologize for interrupting our moment. "I didn't know you would be here tonight!"

Neither did I, but that wasn't stopping me from enjoying every tortuous minute. My eyes danced from Tate's face to the kitchen door, unsure how to proceed. I felt my cheeks become crimson, and I couldn't help but mutter. "Oh, my goodness, not now," I wanted to say a lot more than that, but I was afraid of ruining the moment further by saying the wrong thing.

"Just keep going!" She yelled back through the door, her voice stifling the moment further. "Wait, that sounds like I am pimping my niece out. Just do what you think is best, and I support your decision."

I hadn't had a lot of embarrassing moments in my life, but this one was ranked high on the list. I knew she regretted interrupting, probably because she hoped we were each other's true love. She wanted me to have that experience, even if only for a short time.

"Suddenly, I feel like I am in middle school. Just trying to get a second alone with my crush," I tried to lighten the moment with humor, but I could do nothing to make this any less uncomfortable, and he wouldn't do anything to help it. Tate had no problem sitting in what I considered painful silence.

He had pulled back when the door opened, and it was clear that he would not lean back in. Tate already had a look in his eyes that I was getting used to. It was the one that was always there right before he had to say goodbye, so I was ready for it this time, even before the words left his mouth.

"I have to go." He was leaving again, and there was nothing I could do to stop him, even though I desperately wanted to — an emotion I realized I would often feel around him.

The words stayed stuck in my throat as he leaned down, put a pitiful kiss on my forehead, and walked out the back door.

Waking up in the field was a strange experience the first time. It was nothing more than *annoying* the second time. The music was an interesting touch to the scenery they had created. The Keeper of the Dream was upping the ante much higher than they had the last time they brought me here. It was the soft tune of Ludwig van Beethoven's "Sonata No. 17;" the music could only be considered sad, even to those who didn't know his symphonies. The tune made my eyes teary like it did every time I heard it because it was my father's favorite song, but there was no way that the Keeper of the Dream could have known that.

Usually, music played through the forest could only be considered a bad sign. Still, it was also my favorite tune, so I was willing to fall into the magic it held, knowing that it would potentially be the only enjoyable moment I would ever have here in this world created only for me. Somehow the Keeper of the Dream knew what my favorite symphony was. They were in my head, much deeper than I had realized the first time they were in there.

I could hear the voice sneak out from the treeline, the person choosing to hide like they did last time, which only frustrated me further and caused me to question why they should get to know my innermost thoughts if I couldn't even see them. However, the cadence of their voice did cause me to pause. "I *need* you to walk away from this before you get hurt. You are not going to make it through this alive."

Goodbye to the Blair that was willing to hold in her magic and present a happy, calm exterior. The gloves were off, and I was ready for the consequences.

"For some reason, you think you are allowed to have an opinion on my life. I am the *only* one who can decide my life's path." I was so frustrated with the way this person continued to treat me, and that only resulted in me acting out, even when I knew it would be better to stay on their good side. "Not to mention *your* unwillingness to step out from the shadows. That is a huge problem for me if you want to continue this conversation." I was louder than I needed to be, but I only hoped that would prove to them how serious I felt about the situation.

I realized one thing as I went to bed earlier. My magic was something I could fight or accept, it had gotten to the point where I could only fear it or control it as it continued to grow stronger every day. The latter was starting to sound very good as I couldn't see an end to my constant need to be strong, mainly because I was never put in that situation before when I had my Coven for any backup. I felt it bubble within me, and I didn't do anything to contain it like I would have usually done.

"I can only protect you if you keep your mind safe.

Until you can put a lock on your mind, I can't reveal who I am to you. That will only give you leverage over me, and I can't let that happen," The voice called from the trees once more. This was the first time they tried to be pleasant instead of immediately yelling at me or being aggressive. I knew it would only stay that way for a short time; they had proven to have a short temper. "You need to keep your mind safe before anyone else finds their way here."

I could tell they were trying to present themselves as soft and small as possible, hoping to act as an ally — a trick I would not fall for despite how much they wanted me to. I tried to bring back a sense of calm to myself, hoping that would assist me in getting the answers I wanted.

"I wouldn't need to keep my mind safe if you stayed out of it. I'm unsure if you noticed, but you are the only one trying to find your way into it. There is no one else here." I tried to move my body but was still just as frozen as the last time they pulled me into the Projection. I realized that might be the next lesson I wanted the boys to teach me, how to control my body in an Astral Projection since this was becoming a regular thing. I was never going to get a good night's sleep again!

I didn't need to see their face to recognize the sound of their snort. I had heard it enough throughout the last week from the Guardians. Boys who thought they were better than the rest of us. "I am not the only one trying to break through. You almost have enough people to warrant a line and a bouncer to get in." They amused themselves with that one. That slip finally showed a small part of their personality, the arrogance that they held about themselves. "I must hold up a barrier to even get this time alone with you."

"So why do you want this time alone with me? Do I get that information?" I tried to present myself as strong as possible, losing the battle balancing being a threat and a victim. Still, the tightening of their invisible restraints around me worried me about the real reason they had brought me here. I didn't think they had brought me here to kill me, especially considering they weren't being as aggressive this time. However, there was still a significant possibility of that switch happening, and I needed to be aware of it when it did because that would be when I needed to react.

"No. You don't. I can't trust that you will keep that part to yourself," The voice boomed, hitting my ears, letting the monstrous noises of the animals they had threatened to pounce last time hit me simultaneously. They were subtly letting me know they still completely controlled the situation. "I will tell you that your only hope of surviving this is to back out now while you still can," they growled.

"I hear you, but I want to know why you keep bringing me here if you aren't going to help me?" That question had been on my mind since they called me into the Astral Projection, separate from how they knew such a random fact about me and my love of music.

Just looking around the world they created for me, I realized how the Keeper of the Dream was far more aware of me than I had given them credit for the first time that they had brought me here. Even something as specific as the flowers by the stream were there to show how well they knew me. The flowers were black dahlias, my favorite. They weren't flowers known by many or even loved by those who did know of them. The meaning behind them was betrayal and sadness, not a sentiment of romance. It was very different from what most wanted their flowers to represent. The Keeper of the Dream knew that roses wouldn't sway me like they would for most. The black dahlias weren't genuinely black, but rather an intense shade of crimson, which the Keeper of the Dream took the time to emulate perfectly. I questioned who would pay that close attention to the details that would be important to me.

I could feel the Keeper of the Dream watching me, how they sat there on the edge of the trees, just watching me, and that part was unnerving.

"I tell you again that I didn't bring you here to help you but to warn you of what you are getting yourself into. Will your Coven be able to protect themselves?" Their voice started to shake with anger, the vibrations of it causing the water in the stream to ripple almost like an aftershock of an earthquake in the same way the glass of water in my kitchen did when Tate was near me. Although this time, it was not my magic causing the problem.

"I can't back down from this. I've come too far to dare walk away from it now, something I explained to you the first time you brought me here."

I could almost hear their sinister smile cross their stony face, a chill went down my spine, and the combination made my stomach turn. "Don't you understand how powerful they will be against you? How much stronger they are than you? You are nothing in comparison!" The noises changed in a flash, their voice changing from a neutral melody to a sound that matched the screeching of birds. I tried to reach up and use my hands to cover my ears, but my arms were still frozen to my sides by their magic. I was at their complete mercy to be tortured.

The sounds of the birds the Keeper of the Dream brought forth echoed inside my head, feeling as if that was where the noise originated; the sounds bouncing off the walls made it almost feel hollow inside, and it was about to bring me to my knees.

"Do you feel how I can completely bend you to my will?" Their voice broke through the noise only to taunt me further, showing me how quickly they could affect my surroundings. "How can I make you feel things without being near you? I don't have to touch you for you to be weak beneath me. Don't you know that they can do this too? But they will only take it further. This is a lesson; they will do it with the intent to kill you."

The itching feeling that started next began at my feet, raising my legs with a nervous twitch. The sensation was the same as the crawling of spiders.

Without looking down, I knew that there would be nothing there. It was only the feeling of hundreds of spiders. Each took their time climbing up my body, traveling from the inside to the outside of my clothes.

The sense, combined with the noise, caused my skin to crawl even more than it had before. I wanted to scream, tell them that I couldn't do this and give in to their will, tell them that I give up and have them stop their actions against me. I also knew that was what they wanted me to do, so stubbornly, I held on, reminding myself that it was fake. Only in this dream world were their spiders and the noises.

I refrained from forcing myself out of their magic like I had done the time before. Somehow, I knew that was also what they wanted: to show them my cards and all that my magic could do. If I restrained myself and held onto my control, it would be the only thing saving them genuinely knowing me.

They weren't finished with their assault; I didn't need to see them to know they were getting satisfaction from all of this. Their hold on me began to tighten, constricting me further until my breath caught in my throat. The magic pulled even further, my face turning red from the lack of oxygen, and my eyes felt ready to pop out of my head.

Next came the weather, of course they were able to play with the elements in the world they created just for me. The sun seemed to shift until it was directly above my head and beat down on my skin, the heat causing me to sweat, and that only angered the spiders, causing them to run up and down me at a faster pace. The birds screeched louder in my head. It was an overload of my senses.

I tried to remember the spell my sisters and I had done on our house, building the wall to keep out those we didn't want to come into our lives and onto our property. That seemed like the only way that I would be able to protect my brain from the person in the trees and their continued assault on my senses.

My body would be fine; it was still safe in my bed. There was only so much they could do from this far away, even if they could take me this close to death in this world they created.

As I heard them fully release the beasts from their cages, their claws scraped against the rocks and snarls escaped their teeth, but their threatening noises felt like nothing compared to the birds in my head. As I looked to the treeline where they stood, I could see the eyes of the monsters staring back at me, ready to rip me to shreds at their master's discretion.

I started to build a wall around my mind. Starting at the very bottom, I imagined stacking brick by brick until a small barrier was built. I could feel my magic's weakness, but it was my only hope.

A rush of wind hit the sides of my body, shifting me back and forth, and the pressure caused me to lose focus on the wall I was trying to build. I had never been through a tornado, but I knew this was what the initial winds felt like.

The birds continued to screech, and the heat came down, matching the wind's intensity. The spiders continued to crawl up and down my body as I desperately tried to build the wall around my mind until it would at least be large enough to keep out the birds.

Finally, with a huge push to put the last brick in the row, I felt some relief. The bird noises became quieter, and I could finally take a deep breath when their hold on me lessened. I could feel the Keeper of the Dream trying to intensify the sensations they had placed on me, but I had already found a way to keep them out.

"I would be careful if I was you," The voice called out to me, the threat clear. "Other witches were burned at the stake for less."

"Ah, but to burn the witch is to admit that the magic inside of me is there, and I doubt that you are willing to do that. It would reveal too much about what you know." I was playing with fire, working with their threats and a fleeting hope that they wouldn't be willing to follow through.

In what resembled a shift of the winds, I was proved right.

They were gone.

Chapter Nine

"Are you ready to go?" Ninnie walked into the shop with a surprisingly large smile that I was still not used to seeing despite all the time we had spent together throughout this last week. It had become a ritual for her to pick me up on her way to training every day. "Or maybe not. I can see that you are busy. I can wait outside if you need me to or meet you there if that's easier."

"No, I'm not busy," I was trying to fix the cash drawer on the register, refraining from using my magic since the last customer was still in the store, and I couldn't risk getting caught. I can only imagine the reaction Tate would give me if he knew we had to wipe the mind of a human. "But a few more things must be done before we can officially close."

"Do you have anything else that I can help you with before we go?" Her question was sincere in a way that I wasn't expecting. Oddly enough, she had become somewhat of a friend in the last week. It felt weird since I had never spoken a word to her before she had come crashing into the store, and upon our first meeting, it was apparent that she was terrified of talking to me — or maybe it was Aunt Mira that scared her. The latter of the two is much more plausible.

"First, I need to wipe down the counter, then I have to figure out how to close out the cash register, it's stuck here, and then I think we will be able to leave." The store had been slow enough today that leaving right on time would be easy, especially since Aunt Mira was willing to finish everything else while I took off. She felt that was her only way to support the cause since the boys told her she had to stay home. They weren't as confident as she was in handling the physical training they put the rest of us through.

I was surprised when Ninnie walked over to the counter where we kept the wipes and then proceeded to tackle that chore, so I didn't have to. Her selfless action softened my heart.

The boys had been in the back room 'strategizing' all day, which seemed to be code for a lot of discussions. They went in at the start of the workday and didn't come out until ready for our training at night. The worst part was that the door shut firmly, and we weren't allowed in.

Even now, I could hear them talking, not letting their planning slow down even as the day came to a close. Their voices were getting louder the closer we got to closing time, a little bit because they were finally allowed to. Grace had suggested adding soundproof padding to the back room to muffle the sounds, but I don't think that would fix the problem.

Penelope had been allowed to crash their meetings occasionally, given the privilege to add to their planning. I was grateful that she quickly divulged to me what happened there. However, it wasn't as interesting as I wanted it to be.

With Ninnie's help, we quickly made it through the last

few chores, and I was finally able to use my magic to fix the cash register once Aunt Mira closed the door behind the final customer. Once the cash register was closed, Ninnie and I said a quick goodbye over our shoulders as we hurried out the door. We aimed to make our way to the field before the boys arrived. It only took a few steps outside the Corner Shop for me to realize that we would walk over there in complete silence if I didn't start talking. Usually, we had one of my sisters or even a cousin flanking our side as a buffer. We would be sitting in long silence once we got there if we didn't figure out how to keep a conversation going further than small talk, something we hadn't been able to do yet.

I tried to break the ice with some empty chit chat, hoping it would branch into something substantial. "Are you having a good day so far? Anything exciting happening in your life?"

She chuckled, bobbing her head to the side and giving me an abnormal look. Her definition of small talk differed from mine, but I was willing to roll with it. "Well, someone or something is hunting me and my family. Other than that, I am doing just great!"

It was a firm slap back to the reality that I was *maybe* not paying as much attention to the big picture as I should be. While I was playing games with Tate and wondering if he likes me, Ninnie seemed aware of how close the prospect of death was — that it could be minutes away if we weren't careful. It was apparent she was not so subtly telling me that I needed to stop treating things like a social activity, although that was probably the only way I could get through this without losing my mind. High-stress environments didn't sit well with my personality.

The rest of our walk was silent in a way that felt cryptic.

The progress of our short friendship was hanging by a fragile thread which I only seemed to make worse every time I opened my mouth. I didn't know how to get even close to a conversation now that she had shot down my first approach, so I did the hard thing and stayed silent.

The boys weren't anywhere near the field yet, they were taking their time finishing up in their little war room, but my sisters were already there. They had started their warmup stretches, sitting in the grass with their legs thrown out in front of them, and I could see they were casually talking.

My sisters were wearing long-sleeved shirts as the weather had turned colder the last few days. Celeste had put the girls into our mom's capable hands, and Penelope had finished her day at the school, leaving them both with extra time to train. Only one of them was excited about that.

As we approached my sisters, I noticed a quick shift in their conversation; each time one of them spoke, they got more expressive and more heated. Ninnie and I had just barely crossed over the beginning of the white lines on the field when their innocent conversation turned into something more. They faced each other and started getting louder.

"You're pimping her out! You do see why that is wrong?" Penelope screamed at Celeste, more annoyed with our older sister than I had seen her in years. I knew her well enough to know that whatever they were fighting about had been festering within her all day, and it had finally burst now that they were sitting in the same proximity. This wasn't the first time it had happened and wouldn't be the last; there were parts of her temper that could be predictable. "I cannot believe you would be willing to do something like that! Where are your morals?"

Celeste jumped to her feet. She looked ready to run in the way we were all getting used to. This was probably on the edge of what she could handle. "I am trying to do what is best for all of us, and this is a good solution to our problems. She seems more than willing to do her part. Why can't you see that? Or be understanding of how it would benefit us all?"

"You have got to be kidding me." Even from this distance, I could see her eye roll and the dramatic bobbing of her head, similar to the one I had given Tate. "She has no idea what she wants. Even so, there is no way that she is on board with that plan."

We were only about thirty feet away when I saw their argument had turned ugly. They were one mean word away from hair pulling and maybe even some biting if the angle was right; Celeste had proven to us all that she could be deadly when she felt there was a chance that she was going to lose, while Penelope had gotten a hit of some intense internal strength during our training with the Guardians. She was also unwilling to bend or risk losing whatever they were fighting over. I could see that look in her eyes from here.

"So, we put you with Seth, and you can play the game," Celeste looked devilish, obviously baiting our sister.

Penelope gave her a pointed look; she was analyzing the situation and had already figured out how to control our sister. She had been playing mind games on her since she was born, and it was not going to end here. "Can't you see that you are just disappointed that you can't do it alone and need to ask your sisters for help?"

Suddenly, a flash of fists and flying hands as my sisters went after each other — the wailing of their arms as they both tried to strike the other. Ninnie and I took off, racing across the field to pull them off each other. Our feet flew across the white lines and green grass at a speed the Guardians would have been proud of if they had witnessed it.

"Knock it off! Both of you," I shouted at the top of my lungs, hoping it would shock them and remind them what they were doing was wrong. Sadly, it did nothing to interrupt them, and I had to watch Celeste reach out and yank a first full of Penelope's dark hair while the other returned it with a slap across her face. I went for Penelope since she was the closest to me, grabbing her arm and pulling her off our sister before she caused any more damage. Penelope was vicious when we were kids. I can only imagine how dangerous she would be now that we were all adults, especially now that she had gotten some training. If her words were anything to prove how rotten she could be, that was nothing compared to her fists.

While I managed to grab onto Penelope, Ninnie got a hold of Celeste. My oldest sister was usually a very calm person. Still, today she was the aggressor, and neither of us was confident she wouldn't go for another shot if the opportunity arose, especially if she could get her hands free.

I could see that the boys had arrived, and they approached quickly after having caught sight of what had happened. They did not look pleased with the situation. Tate especially had a sharp expression crossing his face. The four of them picked up their pace and made it to us in record time.

Tate stopped his run standing before Celeste, looking down at her until she cowered, lowering her eyes from his. He turned his attention to Penelope. "When there is so much on the line, we cannot have you acting out against each other or throwing a fit in the corner for not winning the fight." He had a hard-set line between his eyebrows that matched the tone of his voice. He was unhappy about this, not that he was pleased often. "I don't know what the two of you said to each other to start this, but I am ending it right here before it goes any further."

Seth seemed just as disappointed in all of us, not just the two fighting sisters. There was something else to note. The light in his eyes showed something hidden beneath the surface of the exterior he was trying so hard to present. He was almost enlightened by the fire from the girls' altercation — probably about what that would mean when this turned into an actual war.

The others, Huxley and Fabian, slinked toward the back of the Guardians. They had learned it was better to let Tate and Seth take the lead. Huxley avoided eye contact with anyone who looked his way, but Fabian squared his shoulders and looked directly at us, matching Tate and Seth's demeanor. Neither of my sisters looked thrilled to be talked to in such a manner. They hadn't been spoken to in this way since we were kids and had our mom getting after us. Penelope took a similar approach to Fabian, stiffening up while Celeste's lip quivered softly.

Tate took on a somber expression. I didn't think he was expecting this from us, nor did I think his training had prepared him for it.

"You must understand that this war will not determine who is right. It only determines who is left when the dust settles."

Ninnie had a sharp intake of breath and a soft mutter, "No."

Tate continued his lecture. This wasn't the first time I had seen this side of him, but it was for the rest of the women in our group. Based on the looks on their faces, it was a lot more than they were expecting. "The better you train, the higher chance you will leave behind a legacy, not a corpse."

Seth jumped in to start reprimanding us. He would not let up and miss his chance now that Tate had opened that door. It wasn't the first time Seth spoke to us this way and it was clear from the look on the surrounding women's faces that his words struck a nerve. That sinking feeling in my stomach was starting to become a permanent fixture of speaking with a Guardian"

Thankfully, Grace and Piper made their way down the field, breaking the tension my sister's fighting had created and how the boys reacted to it.

Tate wasn't letting us get out of this, even when the girls came to join our group. I could tell by their faces that they were confused, and even more so when Tate turned to Grace and asked her a starting question that would later make its way around the circle. "You need to decide. What are you fighting for? And if you are willing to lose it."

Piper gave a snort for a response that sparked something serious from someone surprising in our group.

His voice was raised louder than I had heard it before. "You need to understand that your mindset is everything. If you walk in thinking there is a chance that you will die, then you increase your chances of that happening. You have already decided that you will give up when faced with a difficulty, and it will only be worse if the enemy gets the upper hand," Fabian continued as he came forward from where he had tucked behind Tate and Seth, suddenly becoming more significant before our eyes as his words rang out for Piper, "You will walk into this with only the mindset that you will win. You will come out of this alive with your head held high."

Fabian showed some personality, and its sudden arrival took all of us back. Huxley had been the one of their pair to talk to us, while Fabian always stayed near the back and seemed to avoid us like the plague.

Tate had a look of pride on his face for the first time. He also wasn't expecting either one of the younger boys to step up and be assertive in that manner, but he looked incredibly proud of him for doing it. "He's right. If you go in with a mindset like that, you will lose every single time."

"How about when someone is trying to get into your mind?" I thought back to the Keeper of the Dream and how they kept telling me my mind wasn't safe. That had to mean that someone was trying to read into it. "Then what mindset am I supposed to have?"

My sisters raised their eyebrows in my direction, silently asking me what I was talking about. My cousins were quick to give me similar reactions. Ninnie managed to keep a very neutral expression. At the same time, the Guardians ignored me altogether, Fabian exhausting all the effort he was willing to give us. Huxley's blank expression proved that he didn't care, and Seth focused on Penelope, ready to tear into her again.

Tate was the only one who responded to my comment. The only sign that he was surprised was the subtle raise of his left eyebrow before it returned to its previous position. "You have a talent for causing problems. Maybe they're trying to keep you from getting hurt. Isn't that why I am here? To prevent you from getting hurt."

"I thought you were here to stand around and look pretty." It was a cheap shot aimed at changing the subject and not giving him enough credit for everything he had taught us.

Tate gave me a long look which only seemed to belittle

me further. He didn't think that my comment was as funny as I did. His reaction did nothing but send a wave of frustration through me, a typical emotion in the presence of any Guardian. He didn't care to let me further our conversation, instead he moved his attention to Celeste and asked her the question he had openly asked the group. "What about you? You show up only because you have to but keep coming around. Why do you do that? If you are here, then you must be all in. So, what are you fighting for?"

"For my babies. I am so unbelievably worried about the chances of someone ever hurting them. I know that our house is not safe anymore. There are too many ways that someone can come in and hurt them. That's not to mention the Astral Projection that Blair went through. What if someone decided to bring one of my girls into one? How will I protect them?" It was a genuine fear that I knew Celeste had been thinking about since this started, but this was the first time she voiced it to the Guardians. They knew she was a mom, but I don't think they understood how much everything fell onto her shoulders. She was so nervous she had started sleeping on the floor of her girls' room every night to ensure she was close enough to protect them. "I know something bad will happen, and that feeling only worsens daily."

Celeste had a unique skill that not many witches in our lifetime possessed. She could feel within the earth when darkness was near. The one stipulation was that it had to be something she was looking out for, but once she was locked onto it, she could know when it was coming closer. Since the news came out, she had been on high alert for the darkness that was the Cabals. She felt it strengthen every day, proving they were getting closer.

Her ability was not one that Penelope or I possessed, so

we could only go off of her explanation of the darkness and how it affected the earth. We all learned the validity of her power when Tate and Seth shared a weighted look, knowing that what she was saying was outside of the norm but being smart enough to avoid asking any questions.

Seth jumped over the lectures, letting that tension die. He started directing us, finally getting to the plan they had already decided on for today's training. He took his role as the main mastermind to an entirely different level when he turned to Tate, the very man who looked like a lion waiting to strike if let out of his cage, and gave him orders. He was brave to start giving Tate directions. I wouldn't dare be that bold. "Celeste is right about that part. We need to step this up. I need you to guard their house while we figure out what is happening. They can't be alone without any protection."

Tate looked over to Seth, even glancing at Huxley and Fabian for a second. The two young brothers looked scared of his wrath and what he would do to them if they dared speak up for or against him. "Can someone please explain to me why I am the person being assigned to this task? Or what I did to deserve this punishment because I seem to be missing it."

"You are the only one of us who is deadly alone. The rest of us are your backup; even then, we are mostly there to offer a show," Seth tried to appease Tate's vanity, hoping that would get him to agree to his plan. It only opened my mind to why he would be trying to segregate Tate away from the rest of them. Or why he was putting him in our home. "I need to get the boys up to speed, and I know that you don't want to have to sit through that much talking. You couldn't handle how many words need to be said without wanting to rip your ears off."

Tate pulled him aside. Ready to bat against him. He would hate being stuck in our house with the Bradbury women. "You are overreaching here. I am not going to stay at their house. They don't need that, and neither do I."

They were trying to keep their voices down and keep somewhat of a private conversation, but it wasn't doing much, so I happily eavesdropped. The rest of the girls and the two remaining Guardians were happy to avoid eye contact and sit peacefully while the others discussed.

"I hear you, but she is worried about that, and the others probably are too. We came here to protect them, which is what we will do," Seth tried to soften the state of their conversation and even lobbed Tate on the shoulder. "You already sneak off often enough. The boys aren't even surprised when you aren't around."

I could only wonder if he was talking about when Tate had snuck off to my house or if there were more times that Tate was nowhere to be found.

It didn't take any more persuasion from Seth for Tate to agree, but there was a different energy in the area after he did. That sixth sense that Grandma told me the humans had suddenly became clearer to me because I could feel something terrible would happen.

Seth took back over the group, starting the training how he originally wanted to. "Blair, Celeste, and Piper. Go with Huxley, and I will join you." He was choosing to separate those who were struggling with each other. Tension was high as the battle came closer. I don't think he wanted to deal with Penelope and Celeste going after each other again or Fabian and Piper exchanging any harsher words. "We are going to learn a few more spells. Then we will switch."

We all knew the program and went forward to our assigned positions. Huxley directed us to the left side of the field, telling us to spread out and stretch. He led us all to practice what we had learned the weeks before; keeping our skills ready to deploy at a moment's notice meant constant training. Celeste, Piper, and I used our magic to make weapons appear, made some targets, and even pulled a few chairs from the bleachers closer for the boys. The younger boys appreciated it, but the elder of the four rolled their eyes at our bravo.

Out of the corner of my eye, I could see Tate and Seth having yet another heated conversation. Whatever they were fighting about now was getting them just as animated as it had the first time; both seemed to be making their stances wider as they spoke, their faces deepening in color with each word they said.

"Blair. I want you to move that tree," Huxley shouted to get my attention back, pointing to one of the trees near the school and off the field. After his words with Piper, his usually calm exterior was gone. He was starting to look more like Tate, hard line around his mouth as his lips remained in a snarled expression. "Pull it out from the roots and lay it down at our feet."

I turned my attention to where he was pointing and thrust my hand out. I forced my magic to come together to one point, all to try and get the tree to come to me. It shifted at the roots, obviously trying to do what I wanted it to, but it refused to come to me. I thrust my hand forward once more, focusing all my magic on a single point, but again it didn't move.

Huxley came up to the side of my body. His chest lined up on my back, his arm extended beside mine until his hand cradled mine. "You will want to use your magic with the intent of destruction. You need to put your mind in that position. It might take a second since that is an entirely new way of magic. Now imagine taking your magic all the way down to the tip of the roots, following the grains of the tree. You need to think about extracting them from the ground. It's like pulling weeds; it won't come with you if you don't get it to the roots." It felt like I was doing something wrong, but I refrained from looking over at Tate to see if he was watching Huxley come in close to me and if it bothered him. Somehow it felt like I was cheating on him even if nothing was happening, now or with Tate. "Now imagine pulling it up, moving your hand at the same speed you want to take the tree. You want to be gentle, so you don't disrupt the soil; then, we can replant the tree when you are done."

I knew he was trying to be helpful, but half of me wondered if this was something I could do, especially as the additional shift of my hand resulted in no movement from the tree. Forcing my hand out, I tried again to focus and conduct my magic down to the roots as he told me to. At the back of my head, I could feel the stares of the rest of our group. Without looking, I could tell that Celeste was giving a disappointed look at my proximity to Huxley. She had a definite bias in favor of Tate.

"Stop messing around. You know that you can do this!" Tate came storming across the field, pushing Huxley away from me and grabbing my shoulders as if to claim me as his. It was almost primal. He looked over my shoulder to where Huxley had moved too and the expression on his face had the younger boy shaking in fear. "Stop indulging her. It's not going to get her anywhere."

"What do you mean 'coddling her?' I need help! I don't know what I'm doing." I knew better than to be sassy with him, it had not done well for me in the past, but something about him pulled it out of me. I almost wanted to tease him and continue to rile him up just to see what he would do next. I liked seeing him jealous. "He is taking the time to explain what I must do. Something that you have continuously failed to do."

I knew I couldn't do it, but I was desperate now that he was so aggressive and in my face. My hand shot out over his shoulder, and I used all of my magic to pull the tree up the roots to bring it down right behind him. It was close enough for the bark to hit the back of his legs. The dirt and mud from my sudden excavation came flying at us at the same speed, but I used my magic to make it only hit Tate, especially his arms and the back of his neck.

"You're right. I could do it."

Tate's face twitched as he tried to keep it as flat as possible despite how unhappy he was with me. I could hear the chuckles behind us. The remaining Guardians, Ninnie, and the other Bradbury women enjoyed the entertainment our back and forth brought to their day, especially now that I had bested him.

Taking the opportunity to walk away from Tate before he had time to react, I hurried over to Grace and Penelope. My sister reached over for a high five, a silent celebration for showing up Tate, something she had been trying to do since day one of this whole thing.

"You did so well!" Thankfully, Grace was willing to celebrate my little win as I did with hers. She and I rivaled for the title of most enthusiastic. "You *did* that. I can't believe that you did that! I am so proud of you."

"Me either, but it made me feel really good to stick it to him," I replied, not hiding my smile. Out of the corner of my eye, I watched Tate, trying to gauge his reaction now that he had gotten a second to breathe — not that anything I did would slow him down. I watched him pinch his fingers tightly together and bring a cloud out of nowhere, using the light rain it produced to wash the mud away from his arms.

"How did you do that?" I called over to him as I tried to get my hand to form the same shape as his, convinced that would facilitate the same magic with only the addition of thinking about large clouds filled with lots of water.

"Maybe if you did a little less talking and a little more watching, you could figure it out without your hand needing to be held," He snarked back at me, unwilling to take another second to teach me what he was doing.

Suddenly I understood what was happening and why I didn't fully comprehend what he was doing. I quickly realized, just by looking around the group, that no one else saw what I saw. Except for Penelope, and based on the expression on her face, she had picked up that something was fishy about the situation and how he responded.

The magic he was doing was supposed to be forgotten a long time ago. Why would they be going against the wishes of the Council and using it anyway?

The boys kept going without a care. Tate doing this magic didn't seem to bother them, so what other Council-forbidden practices were they teaching us? Tate didn't let the moment linger, only pointing to our strange interaction. He gestured for me to stand before him, focusing only on me. "Fine, you can do that, and that's great. Now let's go for something harder."

I was annoyed that he was making me take another turn before the other girls again, but I was ready to do anything if it meant showing him that I was capable. I would not let him be right, especially regarding his opinion of me. "*Fine,*" I bit the word out as aggressively as he had done. "Let us do that."

He pointed aggressively to the tree, "Put it back."

I reached out my hand, using my magic to pick the tree up and set it back in its place. "Done. What else do you have for me?"

"Now, I want you to do the same with the light pole." He was upping the stakes, just as I had hoped. I wanted to prove myself to him, even if it made me feel the need to question myself. "Don't blow a fuse. We don't want to trigger an alarm."

This was the first time that he had acknowledged the human justice system and that there was a real risk of something going wrong that would affect the peaceful world that we lived in. Nothing would go well if we were all crammed in a jail cell for the night.

I pushed my magic out of myself, forcing it across the field to the light pole he was talking about. The electricity felt familiar when it mixed with my magic, pulling through the lines until I got to the plug at the back wall. I pulled it from the socket and used my magic to bring it back to us until I held it in my hand. "Done."

My eyes didn't miss the slight look of pride cross his smug face as I handed the plug over to him. Tate was willing to let me have my success with that one. Telling me that he was surprised I did it with such ease. His smirk should have warned me that he had more coming for me. "You think you're funny?"

I gave him my version of his smirk, realizing that he was willing to play the game. "I think that you are underestimating my abilities."

"You can handle destruction, but you have signed up for a war and don't seem to understand that despite the constant reminders." He used his height to intimidate me further; knowing that the top of my head only went to the center of his chest, he stepped into my space until all I could do was strain my neck to see him. "Would you be able to kill someone if it meant your own life being saved?"

"Oh, of course, I can."

I didn't know what his magic was capable of, but the walls he suddenly erected around us were metal with no way out, which only showed how strong he was and what he could do with it. Despite the lack of doors or windows, it still had enough light for me to see him. "How about now?"

I felt a rush as my anxiety rose. My hand reached out to push on the walls, but they didn't budge. I knew that I would be able to breathe, even without access to the outside world, yet the walls were making me feel claustrophobic. "Tate, what is this?"

"This is you proving your point. You keep saying you can handle it, but I'm not sure you can." Tate rolled his shoulders back, straightening up like he was going into battle. "Now, let's up the stakes a little."

Tate snapped his fingers again, and a man appeared inside the cell walls this time. The shackles around his ankles barely touched his incredibly skinny legs, the same legs holding him up against the weight of the chains, although that wasn't the part that bothered me. His skin was sagging, showing a swift drop in weight; his eyes sunken so far that the bags overtook the darkness and shadows they produced.

"Tate, what is this? What is he doing here?" I could hear the bubble in my voice as the tears came to my eyes. Even without him saying anything, I somehow knew what he wanted from me. I felt the blood rush through me, and my hands clammed up and shook. "Who is he?"

"He is the object lesson." Tate's expression didn't change; he was just as stoic as ever. "You are going to kill him."

"I can't do that. Tate, you know that I can't do that." I couldn't believe him and what he was asking of me.

He reached into the waistband of his pants and handed me the weapon he kept there. It was the same dagger he had given me in training before, the only difference being that the handle was covered in a piece of pink fabric this time. He had taken the time to make the switch.

"Here is that pink dagger you asked for." His words were sadistic. He knew how much it would bother me, especially now that he had finally listened to my requests. "Now, you have to kill him."

"I can't do that!" I tried to hand him back the weapon, but he refused to take it from me. I pushed it against him, but he only shook his head.

"You keep saying that you can fight. I am asking you to prove it to me." He turned my shoulder until I was facing the man once more. I knew that Tate was forcing me to fully take the stranger in. The poor man's clothes were worn down to threads with enough holes to make me question if it could even be considered a shirt anymore, and it wasn't providing any warmth against the chill in the air. "All I am asking is for you to kill him," he said it like it was simple. He might have been trained to be a killer, but I wasn't.

"He has done nothing wrong, and he has done nothing against me. I can't hurt someone when they have done *nothing* wrong!" I could feel myself crying, but I couldn't tear my gaze away from the man who stared back at me with the same intensity. He didn't even realize that I held his life in my hands. I knew I was repeating myself, but my brain still refrained from processing Tate's words. "I can't kill him!"

Tate stood behind me, ducking his head down until it was in my ear. His closeness didn't bother me like it normally did. "What if he brought the Cabals here? What if he killed your mom?"

"I know that isn't true, though. I know that she is home with the girls. They are safe. I know that!" Even if I was saying those words, I was still very aware of how close I was to losing all control. It would only be seconds before I was sobbing. Although, my magic stayed low, it no longer threatened to escape me like it was doing before.

Tate let out a sickening chuckle like he found this situation amusing or, worse, enjoyable, especially regarding the pain he was causing me. "The girls. What if he was the man who killed the girls? What if I told you that he had his men get them? Sneak in the back door? Go upstairs to sedate your mom, kidnap the girls and hold them hostage. Then what would you be?"

I felt something come over me. My eyes blurred with red as my hand flew forward, only stopping when it was met with resistance. The knife sunk into the man, and I realized it was stuck when I tried to pull it back. The blade would not move; it was lodged inside of him.

I could hear the noise, but it took me a second before I realized I was the one screaming, not him. I was forcing myself to open my eyes back up, to see what I had done, and to be ready to live with that image and extreme regret for the rest of my life.

Instead of a man bleeding to death, there was a willow tree in his place with the blade sticking out. Even the shackles he had been wearing were gone, replaced by the fallen leaves of a weeping willow tree. The irony could only have been orchestrated by someone truly vial.

Now when the tears came pouring down, my chest rose and fell with rapid breaths. I wished to say I was only crying, but it was heartbreaking sobs. The noise echoed against the walls around me. The metal seemed like a worthy punishment for what I had done.

"I killed him! You made me kill him! He's dead," I looked down to realize I was still holding the dagger's hilt; I released my hand as if it was a snake that had bitten me, but that didn't replace the impression it left in my hand. "What is that laced with? What magic did you use to turn him into a tree?"

Tate reached over, grasped my shoulders tightly, and gave me a hard shake intending to bring me into focus, away from the stress of the situation, and get me to calm down. "Blair, you didn't kill him! The dagger wasn't infused with anything," He stared back at me, tightening his grip on my arms. "Get it together! You should be proud of yourself, not back down. You proved that you could do this!"

"I proved what? Proved that I am a monster? I know I killed him; he's gone!" I screamed at him. I was still seeing the knife in my hand, and I could only imagine the look on the man's face as if the same knife had penetrated his skin.

He shook me one more time to get my attention. "Blair! You didn't kill him! He is a character from an old pirate movie. It was all an illusion. I created him to see if you could do it." Tate leaned down so our faces were aligned. "The tree was always there. It was never a person. The girls are still safe at home."

"You're the monster! How could you do that to me?" I screamed at him. Raising my hands, I hit my fists as hard as I could against his chest while anger rang out of me. "How dare you make me think that I killed a defenseless man! You knew that would bother me."

"I also knew you would prove to yourself that you were strong enough to do this." I knew that he believed in me and what I could do, but that wasn't why it bothered me. Seeing that I could do something so awful and evil, even if it was an illusion, bothered me. Even for a split second, I found a piece of me willing to kill a man.

He could tell that our conversation was over. My fists on his chest only got more aggressive as he spoke. Tate raised his hands from where they sat on my shoulders, and in doing so, he brought the wall down around us bringing us back to where everyone was standing. None acknowledged our sudden addition to the field or that we had been gone for a few minutes.

Tate had proved his point, and I could see he felt better now that he controlled the situation. He directed us all back into the training, taking us through a few more of their newer exercises, and ending with the one that we first started with, having me put the light pole back in its place. The entire field had light, even if there was new darkness inside of me.

Even if it wasn't real, I still killed a man. That would stay with me forever.

I was still concerned about the man's death and what Tate had forced me to do, and it was affecting my abilities. I still felt sick over it, but I went forward up to the white line, throwing the spear as hard as I could at the target. I struggled yet again with getting it to land in the center like the Guardians wanted it to. Tate was frustrated enough by our lack of progress for the day, especially by my reaction to the illusion he had put me into, but it was Seth who snapped at me when I missed the target for what seemed to be the hundredth time.

"Will you use your magic?" His voice came out with a snarl that made me feel like a failure again. The two Guardians were not seeing my best qualities today. "You are playing it safe, and that is how you will end up dead. Now, knock that off and take this all the way, or get out of the way for someone else to do it. I will not have you be a dead weight."

To say that I moved forward out of spite wouldn't be far from the truth, but as I threw that spear, there was only one goal in mind. I wanted to show him I could do this, especially to show Tate, an onlooker not stepping in as Seth shouted in my face. So much for being my hero.

The spear left my hand and went flying through the air. It sank into the center of the target, but my accomplishment was not what made everyone stop. The shift in the earth made them freeze, the sound of thunder on a cloudless night.

Earthquakes weren't common in Salem, Massachusetts, but that was the lie we would tell anyone when they asked if we felt the earth shake that night. The noise was deafening, and the light that shot out of my hand lit the field more than the sun ever could have managed. There was even a line from my hands to the target where the grass was burned from the heat.

The look Seth and Tate gave each other scared me more than the power that left my body.

They almost looked afraid of me.

Chapter Ten

"I hate you!" She spit the words out at him and raised her chin in defiance of whatever he would respond with. She was not happy with him, not that she ever was. Their working relationship was a mess, constantly one step forward and three steps back. "I can't believe that you said that to her. No wonder she lost control of her magic with you in her face like that. Did you think shouting at her would give you the results you wanted?" Here came my big sister, Penelope, who was always ready to take on the world for me, even if it meant taking on the bully. The very bully that I suspected she had a slight crush on, especially if he kept looking at her in that way.

His smirk was there to taunt her further. He liked the games he could play with her. Seth knew Penelope was not one to be flustered and enjoyed getting that reaction out of her. "Why would you ever hate me? I am just lovely; everyone else thinks so. Haven't you learned by now; enemies make the best lovers?"

"Lovers?" She scoffed in response like the idea was so

far away from the truth. She was not thinking about their relationship in the same way that he was.

Seth came in closer, reaching for her hand until their fingers were intertwined. She didn't willingly hand it over, stretching her fingers to avoid his grasp. "Don't you know how it goes? Love and hate are four-letter words that can get confused quickly, especially when emotions are heightened. We might have to repopulate the earth."

Seth and Penelope continued to have an exciting way of interacting, and there was a part of it that I recognized. It was the same way that Tate and I walked in circles around each other. The temptation to push it further was always heavy in my mind.

"Don't you feel guilty? You did that!" Penelope was not going to let him distract her. She shouted at him and gestured to where I sat in the truck bed. They sat me there with a blanket wrapped tightly around my shoulders. After the illusion Tate put me into with the killing incident, I could not regain control of myself or my magic which had only turned me into more of a mess.

I don't remember what it was like to have Mom and Dad fight, but this was probably how it felt. It was strange to be sitting as an onlooker as they shouted about me, which made me feel guilty.

His eyes dropped to a glare right back to her. His intention of romancing her slipped into something else, and this wasn't the first time I had witnessed the flip in him. Their fire and ice was a bad combination, fueled back and forth at the risk of hurting the other.

"I don't have time to feel guilty, and neither does Blair. This is a war! We can't have her breaking down whenever there is a small problem, especially in her training." Seth was mad, but I didn't realize how angry he was until his face turned red. I wouldn't have said he had a temper when we first met, but it was present now. "I wonder which one will get you killed first, your loyalty or the stubbornness?" He was going for the kill, showing off the ice in his veins. He appeared to be waiting for the opportunity to strike with this very statement.

Despite everything, it came full circle back to this war; even when there was hope for something better, the chance at something between them would only remain frozen. No one would be getting anywhere in that realm if the boys kept circling back around to the fact that death was on the table. It put a real damper on the situation.

"You have got to be kidding me! You can't handle the concept that there is more to our days than this situation. We still have a life to live!" Penelope screamed in his direction, but it didn't do anything to change the expression on his face or calm the anger inside of him. She wasn't going to slow down now that she had gotten started. I was shocked that a fire hadn't started around us, something she had done before when she got mad enough. I was grateful she was saying the same things going through my mind, mainly because it seemed no one else was thinking of them. "We each must go home and spend time with our family. We must pretend that nothing is wrong when we go to work or walk into the store and act like everything is okay."

The number of times she moved her hips and rolled her eyes was enough to make us nauseous. She was aggressive in her position as my protector, but now her desire to continue the conversation had changed. Penelope was only going against Seth now because she wanted to.

"You are completely crazy!" He was just as mad as she was and had more control than she did, but calling a woman crazy would not set him up for success. He was preparing for war, and he might have just started one.

"Guess what? I have great news; I am not obligated to make sense to you!" Penelope threw her hands up in his direction, showing that she was done with him and the conversation.

My sister came stomping past me with a stern expression. I could see the fury in her veins. There was no sign of her slowing down until she was out of my eyesight, obviously choosing to walk off her anger all the way home. Seth was lucky he didn't have a car; she would have done something crazy, like cut the brake lines, if she had the chance.

Celeste had come up to the sidelines to watch the massacre in front of us, and I looped her into what I was seeing since she had missed the initial buildup and many of the exciting parts.

She leaned against the truck so she could take in the sight of Penelope walking away. We could almost hear the consistent stomping of Penelope's feet.

"I can't believe they haven't killed each other yet," Celeste seemed to be looking for a deeper meaning behind their argument instead of just taking it for the entertainment value like I was doing. "I guess knives were within arm's reach if they were tempted, so it must not have gone that far."

I was pleasantly surprised Penelope didn't turn around and just deck him, something she was known for regarding either of her sisters. I had enough bruises growing up to know better than to get into it with her when she was this mad.

"The two of you shared a room growing up. If she could handle that, I think she can handle anything," Celeste teased me. "It was a true testament to her self-control."

Celeste was obnoxiously clean; Penelope always managed to be organized like no one's business. Sadly, I was the only one left, thus deemed the messy one, which felt unfair now that we were all adults. "You make me sound like a pig in a mud stall," I whined.

She stretched her arms above her head, moving the muscles that had tightened during our workout. "It was close enough some days. Why do you think Mom finally stretched the house so you could have your room?"

"Because the only other option would be for you and Penelope to share, and she wouldn't be able to handle all the fighting the two of you would be doing. Today wasn't the first time you two were talking and it ended up in a nasty fight." It was supposed to be a joke, but there was some truth. Mom often stretched the house when the size got too small for us. We repeatedly begged her to do it when we were teenagers, but she only conceded when Penelope and I were at each other's throats, and she had gotten tired of it.

Celeste gave me a mocking smile. Instead of saying anything about it, she kept stretching. I could tell from the look in her eyes that Celeste was tired from our training. She had already voiced her excitement to go home and cuddle with her girls. Her yellow top was the same color as a highlighter, but I didn't think she would appreciate that comparison, so I kept my mouth quiet as she insulted me. Something that I internally gave myself credit for.

"I'm going to choose to believe what I want. I know the truth. After all, I was the second person used in the spell," Celeste retorted.

"Will you stretch the house so your girls can have their rooms?" I shifted the subject. Her girls loved sharing a room now, but how long would that last? Penelope and I loved it until the one day that it got to be too much. I think it is normal for sisters to hit that point. "Can our house stretch any further? I would think it hit its capacity."

She bobbed her head side to side with contemplation, lips pursed while she thought over her answer. "That's a five-year out plan, they won't be there for a while, and I can probably defer them for some time after that. Either way, future Celeste will have to worry about that one."

"Hopefully, future Celeste can handle that when it circles back around," I tried to get her to laugh. I turned my head in the direction our sister went in, my eyes tracking over to where Seth was standing. The previous redness in his face hadn't calmed down even after getting a second away from her to breathe. "Let's be honest; something is going on between them. We can all see it."

"Something is going on there, but I wouldn't say anything to her about it. You saw how badly it went for me," She pointed at the rip in her top, a product of her brawl with Penelope.

* * *

Tate tore into the building. His hand pushed the door so hard it swung open, barely missing the shelf on the opposite wall, and slammed just as loudly when it closed behind him. I could feel him coming before he got here, but the sound of the door still caused me to jump. I wasn't expecting him to be angry when he came in, or at the very least, not this angry.

"You are a brat! You do realize that, right?" He was annoyed with me. That was the only thing that felt normal, even if his presence in my life still wasn't. This war made our social group much more significant. He was on a rampage, his face redder as he stormed across the room.

"You are so inconsiderate to everyone around you. It's to the point where it can be considered dangerous to the rest of the group."

I was also annoyed with him, so it was more than fair that he wanted to pick a fight with me. I was ready to have it out with him, too. I had reached my max with him long before the illusion he had put me into, although that was a significant reason why I was mad today. Tate knew that would affect me and only did it to see if he could break me. It was almost like a game to him to see how far he could push me before he hurt me. Even I didn't know how much more I could take.

"First of all, I don't even know what you are talking about, and secondly, I hate to ask you again what you are doing here since I have become a broken record, but the tradition must stand," I threw my hand out to gesture to the originally locked door. "What are you doing in my shop? I've already closed. And don't you have somewhere better to be than here bothering me?"

Because this was becoming a habit of Tate's, we had gone through the shop to ensure all our security measures were in place. I realized this time, finally able to watch him do it, that he somehow managed to unlock the door from a few paces away. I couldn't figure out how he didn't need to touch the door to open it. Something my magic would not be able to do without a lot of additional training, and I doubt he would be willing to teach me right now.

"I came here to talk to you about why you are trying to set up Seth and Penelope. Having them fuel each other is not right and will only result in a mess. Your continuance to meddle in their business will only cause problems." His face was serious. Tate's eyebrows were pinched together so tight that the lines made an 'eleven' between his menacing eyes.

They only twitched once when he saw I was about to inter-rupt him. He rushed to finish his thought, "You realize why that will never work, right? They can't spend five minutes in the same room without being ready to rip each other apart, and that is on a good day when they are getting along."

"Now, you have got to be kidding me! I don't know what you are talking about, but if I did, I would tell you that you are wrong," I finally interjected.

He crossed his arms in defiance, looking down at me from his wide stance. I knew him well enough now to know that although he was mad, he liked that I was so much smaller than him, even if it was just so that he could intimi-date me.

"That doesn't make any sense at all, which further proves your desperation to cover the evidence of your actions," Tate's face was haughty. "You are trying to put them together. We can all see it, and it won't do them any good if they get involved with each other."

His argument wasn't going anywhere. I tried to keep myself as calm as possible, taking slow breaths, but that wasn't working well. There was only one other approach that I could think of: "I did no such thing; if I did, they know their limitations and what they can handle. I am not in charge of them, and neither are you. If either wanted to pursue something, it is well within their rights."

"I don't know what you are talking about," He flipped it back over to me, using my pause as an opportunity to step closer to me. "You do realize how insane you are acting? I came here to talk to you, and now you're acting dramatic."

What is with these Guardians thinking that they were allowed to call me crazy or dramatic? Did their school not teach them manners? Or at least what not to say to a woman?

I tried again to take a long deep breath. I realized that Tate would not let up even if I continued to disagree with him, which meant not biting back as much as I wanted to.

"I beg you to check yourself before you think it's okay to call me insane again." I wanted to applaud myself for my ability not to cry so far. I hated that when I got over-whelmed, I had that bad habit. "I hope you understand you were the one who found out this situation; no one else has expressed anything about this connection you are seeing. If it were a problem, then others would be seeing it."

"You can't turn this into a romance novel. There will be casualties if we aren't careful, and getting all these hearts involved is how you do that." I was ready to step in and question why he was using the word 'all' to describe only two parties, but he kept going. "What is with this family and not understanding our situation? You all have your heads in the clouds!"

"You have this assumption that I am some evil master-mind who is working on something behind the strings. Trust me, that is your area of expertise, not mine." There had been some sizzle between Seth and Penelope since the first day they interacted with each other, but I had done nothing to help or hinder their progress, and I would stand by that even if he was convinced otherwise. "I am not playing matchmaker with Seth and Penelope! I don't know how often I have to tell you I have no idea what you are talking about."

"You can't tell me that you didn't know that was what your sisters were fighting about last night," Tate said like there was no way I hadn't been lying to him. His ability to assume would only stand in his way if he wanted to have this conversation. "It doesn't matter if there is something there. They cannot entertain it."

I stepped out from behind the counter and threw my hands up in aggravation when I got near him. I realized that if he was going to make me mad, I would not be standing three feet away. I had gotten too much satisfaction out of hitting him yesterday not to allow myself to do it again, which just proved how much the Guardians were rubbing off on us. I would have never gotten satisfaction from hitting someone before they came to Salem; I wasn't Penelope.

I tried to ignore the smell of sweat that glazed his brow. It seemed like he had been on another run nearby. Tate's tight grey shirt was pulled taut along his muscles, and his short basketball shorts allowed me to peek at the tan muscles on his legs. I don't think I ever paid as much attention to anyone as I did to Tate until now.

"They are free to entertain anything they want," I sassed, "I might not have been putting them together, but I am happy to do so now that I know it will piss you off! You have no right to walk in here and tell me what I can and can't do."

Tate stepped back and away from me. He did not want to be on the other side of my disapproval now that I was expressing it so strongly. Not that he would be afraid of me, but I was grateful to see that he kept that in mind.

"Why are you so angry? I came here to have an open and honest conversation with you about a situation in our lives. Now, you are yelling at me," Tate said defensively.

"I'm only yelling because you frustrate me," I felt the desire to stomp my foot again, but I knew it would only have negative consequences, and this moment called for restraint. My words weren't helping me win this one, but I continued anyway, trying to show him how mature and rational I was. "You were the one who came in here aggressively, and you were mad at me first! *You* started yelling. This is all your fault!"

I tried so hard to enunciate and prove that he had started it all. There was only so much time before our next training, and I had a lot to do before then. I took my leave, walking away from the front of the shop and into the back room. Just because he was here did not mean I would go home any later than I had to. Tate could yell at me while I finished closing the store if he wanted. Aunt Mira had closed the store every day since the Guardians arrived, and I was finally taking my turn; I thought it would give me some time to calm my mind and get a second alone. It turns out I was wrong.

"You are the one causing the problem! I wouldn't be coming in here if you weren't throwing off the balance of the team," Tate grumbled. He seemed to have calmed down, even by a little. "You are to blame for that, although, Celeste has a big hand in it too."

He accepted the broom I silently offered him and started sweeping the left side of the room while he waited for my response. Somehow understanding that our conversation was only going to progress if he was willing to work with me.

"Are you *finally* calling us a team? I thought we were all just pawns in your game," I tried to highlight how irrational I thought he was being. I sprayed down the counter, wiping in swift circles while I spoke, careful not to mess with any of the piles the boys had put together. Their *war* room was a complete mess, but I didn't have the energy to deal with their reaction if anything got misplaced. I picked up a stray paper to wipe beneath it, and let out a grunt when I could only lift one or two of the more enormous piles out of my way to try and return them to their original place. "When were we promoted from our position as dirt under your feet?"

"You don't deserve to be considered a member of the team if you are trying to split it apart. I don't think that you understand that is what will happen if they get involved. It's not going to end well for anyone." He swept both sides of the room and approached me to continue our conversation. He stood before me, using his proximity to his advantage once more. It was a power game for him, and his size put him in the lead no matter what I did. "Their intensity must be aimed at the enemy, not each other. It would be best if you all learned that one too."

Intensity was probably not the best word, but he wasn't wrong. Statistically speaking, a distraction on the field would not do them any good, but neither wanted to die with regret. Regarding the two options, I knew a few people who would be willing to take their chances.

"Tate! As you can see, I am swamped! After I am done here, it doesn't mean my day is done like most people. After this, I have to follow you down to a football field where you are going to proceed to belittle me at every opportunity, usually by shouting in my face when I don't give you the results you want. And those are just the positives of the situation we have been placed in! While this has been a great chance to get to know you and your hatred of two people growing a real connection better, this conversation needs to come to a close. I will only politely ask you to leave my store once before I get ugly."

I was trying to stay as rational as possible since that was what he would respond the best to, although that would not work in the long run. Something about me burned up around him, so much that I didn't realize I was taking another step in his direction with every word. I was trying to intimidate him like he was constantly doing to me, crossing my arms to show how serious I was about the matter and shifting my weight on my hips to drive my point home. He took another step back, not allowing me to enter his space.

"Blair, don't test me right now," he slinked his body right into the cabinet. It was almost in slow motion as the bottle on the top shelf tipped, and the contents spilled.

"What is all of this?" He shouted back at me as the sparkling fluids poured onto his head. "Why is there glitter?"

I didn't know how I was supposed to tell him that it was the love potion that Aunt Mira and Grace had created the night before, and there were only a few seconds before it would start to go into effect. That would only make him madder than when he first showed up.

I ran to the cupboard and pulled out the stack of towels on the top shelf, throwing them in his general direction while I raced to the sink for water to try and wash the potion off of him before it had time to set into his skin.

"Tate! You have to hurry! We need to get it off," I yelled but he was still frozen in place. He didn't seem to have a care in the world, despite my frantic race around the room. "You have to take your shirt off, try to get the liquid off your body as fast as possible before it sets into your skin."

He reached up and started pulling off the shirt he was wearing, and I was relieved to see that the plain white tank top underneath seemed unaffected by the potion. I couldn't handle having Tate covered in a love potion *and* shirtless; that combination could only be deadly.

His eyes had started to glaze over in a way that meant I was running out of time, and the candle behind us wasn't helping.

Any candle burning by the light of a witch would

magnify the magic we wielded, and the intense, steady flame could only mean one thing; silly Grace had lit it before she left. She had claimed the back room smelt like boys, something she said with disdain.

It was inevitable; the spell was going to stick even if we tried to stop it.

"Tate, I don't think you are about to be very happy with me," I knew he wouldn't, but I was desperately trying to soften the blow. I could only guess how short of a window I had to explain what was about to happen before it did. "Tate, I need you to focus on my words because we don't have much time. A long time ago, there was a curse placed on my family. It meant for all of us to find a compelling love, which has proven to work for each generation that has come before us."

"Why are you talking about a curse?" I could see the light in his eyes shift with the potion, light and dark, as his body fought with the magic. It tried to control him, but his internal magic was fighting against it. "Blair, you aren't making any sense. I'm trying to figure out what you are saying. What does a curse have to do with body glitter?"

I only had a few seconds left before he fell under the love spell, although he didn't seem worried and kept interrupting me, which wasn't helping. There was not enough time to explain that it was not body glitter, even if that was the thing that he was the most focused on. He didn't even seem to register that he was soaking wet. I tried to move the towels over his arms, getting the small droplets that stayed there.

"My Aunt Mira has been trying to figure out how to break the curse by creating love potions since she got her magic. That's what this is. The last potion they created fell off the shelf and onto your head. Usually, they don't work, and she puts them on the top shelf, waiting to give them to humans. The problem is that I think this one will work on you — something rare when it comes to those with magic since we have so much more it has to go through to get to our hearts. Humans are much simpler." I ran my hand through my hair, trying to figure out how to get the words out without scaring him, not that I thought he was frightened easily. Tate was too logical for me to use any words that fell into any other category, and that was just a tiny part of the balancing act I was performing. "The first person that you see is who you will bond with. Our family has been blessed with extreme and powerful love, but our lovers must die once they have fulfilled their purpose. Any man who loves us is subjected to this fate. Only after we love them will we know if they are the one to break the curse."

No matter how often it was told that story did not improve. I had said everything so fast that I had to take a break to catch my breath.

All the words were tumbling out of my mouth without any grace between them, which wasn't helping the message. He reached his hand out for mine; the movements were slowed, which showed just how far the potion had taken to him and how unreachable he was going to be. "Blair, I don't mind being bonded to you."

"Tate, you have to understand. I'm telling you all this because this love potion has done more than bond us. It will make us love each other, and if it sticks, then you are subject to the curse." I felt a rush come over me as our hands intertwined.

This was it. This was the feeling that they had all talked about. My hands were suddenly clammy, my forehead broke into a slight sweat, and I could feel my breathing heavier. The joining of our souls was a rush that created tension in my body that suddenly released itself when he reached his other hand to caress my cheek.

His entire face was starting to change second by second, with his body coming to terms with what had just happened. Neither matched how he would have felt about me last week. A potion never brought love to the surface in a Bradbury witch, yet here we were.

Aunt Mira was going to *lose* her mind over this.

"You think that I am going to be overtaken by your curse? Things like that don't exist other than in fairy tales." As if witches didn't belong to the world of fairy tales, too. Tate played with a piece of my hair, incredibly gentle in a way I would have never been able to predict from such a soldier built for destruction. "You are beautiful. I have never said it to you, but you must know that."

"It does exist, and you must understand it and what will happen now." I couldn't fathom how he refused to believe in the powers of the curse when we were filled with magic. How could there be magic if there was no love? I tried to remain focused, but the way his fingers danced across the edge of my chin made me realize how close he was to falling away to this.

There was still something we could do to protect him; he just had to agree to it and, more importantly, not change his mind once he did since there was no reverse to the potion once it started. "There is so much you need to be told about before you start getting ideas. There are serious rami-fications that come with falling in love with a Bradbury woman that you need to know about before you-"

It was as if he knew what I was about to say, cutting me off before I could finish, "Kiss me." He was already doing it.

The hand on my chin traveled up the side of my face, diving deep into my hair as the other possessively reached out, grabbing my hip, and his lips forcefully landed on mine. I might have never been kissed before today, but I knew I would never have another kiss like that again.

His teeth came out, taking the opportunity to bite onto my lower lip when my mouth opened in surprise at how his other hand traced my neck. The hand on my hip flexed, Tate's fingers leaving impressions on the skin underneath. His lips released mine to almost growl at me. His voice was deep and husky, "Blair, I have wanted to do this since meeting you. We stood in this store, and you wore your sparkly little boots and were snarky right back at me."

His continued fascination with those boots made no sense. They had been a bold fashion choice I was not likely to make again, especially knowing how they stuck around in his mind even after I had hidden them in the back of my closet.

"Why didn't you do it then?" I'm not sure how I managed to get the words out, letting myself release him so I could get a chance to breathe. This only allowed him to start kissing down my neck, occasionally nibbling on my ear to make goosebumps come rushing down my arms. "Tate, wait."

I was being an idiot! Why did I interrupt his kissing to have a conversation? A conversation was the last thing necessary right now.

I must have sounded intense because he did stop his torturous kisses. Tate straightened back up and looked down at me. His eyes were still glazed over, but he did realize how important it was to stop, so that was a start. "Blair, why would you ever stop this? This is good." He pressed a kiss to my throat.

I tried to control the shivers that went down my spine. "Stop; I need to talk to you."

"This is better than good." Another kiss fell on my skin. "It's amazing." A third kiss came down on my jaw. "There has not been anything better since the invention of the world." Tate hadn't let up his hand on my hip, instead gripping me tighter. He was trying to prove his point, and I was ready to start listening to him; it was terrific to kiss him. He leaned down again to dance his lips against mine, soft enough that I leaned forward for more. His words dangerously danced out of his mouth at the same speed as his kisses. "Why would you ever want to stop this from happening?"

I had never seen this side of him, expressing himself so differently than he ever had before. It was like watching sunshine pour out of him with each word.

"Because you don't seem to understand what I am talking about. You are in so much danger now that this happened." It seemed too morbid to tell him now, but I needed to. It appeared that I had his death note, and he didn't seem to care.

Tate brushed his fingers through my hair, letting the strands keep me connected to him. Never had he been so physically expressive with me. It was something I could get used to.

"Blair, I don't care about whatever you're going to say. I am here; I finally get to have this moment with you. I am not going to let anything you say stop this now." He grabbed my hips, picked me up, and spun me around until I was firmly sitting on the counter. Somehow even with me on the counter, I still didn't manage to be taller than him. He continued to have the upper hand, using it against me by pressing his lips against mine. "I don't care. I have battled a million demons. I have passed by death thousands of times: escaping the hells of this world and the next. I would do that all again to get this moment with you."

"Tate. You don't understand what I am saying. What if we were talking about death? What if being with me meant that you were going to die? Then would it be worth it?" His head bobbed with each question, left to right. It was his way of showing that he was hearing me even when he wasn't listening.

He leaned in, returning to his position at the small of my neck and feathering the kisses back down until I ran out of visible skin, taking that opportunity to go up the opposite side. "Oh, I understand completely." He displayed his hands along my thighs, squeezing against them to prove his point. "I understand that you are going to be the death of me."

I reached for his neck, pulling him off me like one would draw a snail off the cement, leaving a wet mark in its place. "Tate!" His hand gripped me again, which set my mind off course again. "I need you to focus. Please!"

He finally gave up, stepping back with his hands up to prove that he would listen to me this time. His face fell to stone, almost returning to the man I knew before the love potion penetrated his skin. I realized how much I missed his aloof exterior; it was normal by comparison.

"Blair. You don't have to worry; I hear you. I am telling you that I don't care," He didn't let his exterior stop him from reaching out to tap my knee. "Whatever red flag you think you are giving me isn't going to stop me from going through with this."

There was so much about this that he didn't understand, but I knew that face. I had seen it enough times to know that anything I said wouldn't be listened to, even if I thought it to be necessary.

Once I got him willing to sit down alone for a second, I went into the store bathroom. I needed a moment without him now that his attention had turned from indifference to interest toward me. I closed the door tightly and even locked the door for extra security. It would only be seconds before he came after me, the effects of the curse and love potion being deadly even for a powerful Guardian trained against torture.

I looked into the mirror, deciding to talk to myself to hear it all out loud. I guess I was hoping that it would help it to make sense to my ears. Bounce the ideas off my reflection like I was having a conversation with another person. Aunt Mira swore it was the best way to understand how you felt, but she might just be crazy. The girl staring back at me looked just as flustered as I felt. "It's Tate. Never would I have thought it to be Tate. He's your person. Can you believe that?"

The noises coming from the other side of the door proved how real this all was. I could hear him shuffling papers and moving boxes. It took me a second to realize he was tidying their war room. He saw how the mess had bothered me and was trying to fix it, his actions softening my heart.

I paced from one end of the small bathroom to the other. Something about the rhythmic action made me feel better. I threw some cold water on my face, using the opportunity to reset myself before joining him.

He had finished his work, and I could see a big difference in the room. He knew where everything went, which helped make the chore easier. I was also aware that his quick movements were probably because he didn't want me to be looking at the papers they were working on.

Tate sat at the table, playing with a knife like the first

time I found him back here, even sitting in the same spot I had left him. It was almost déjà vu, his ability to be unpredictable but also a creature of habit.

"Blair, are you okay?" He was showing me genuine concern, setting the knife down and starting to stand up, but I quickly waved him off so that he would stay in place. "Will you at least come to sit with me? You look a little pale."

He was strangely calm now that he had gotten the opportunity to settle down. The potion had gone through him and passed the initial puppy love stages. It was interesting since I had never watched someone go through the potion before.

I did listen to him; it would waste time arguing with him any more than I have. I walked over to the table and sat, trying not to look surprised when he pulled a seat out for me. I would not have thought him to be a gentleman.

"What can I do?" He reached over, taking my hand in his, rubbing his thumb against my knuckles and calluses. "Do I need to beat someone up for you?"

He meant it to be a joke, mainly because he was discussing himself. There was only so much he could do to solve my problem. I did appreciate his initiative to solve all my issues now that our lives were joined together.

"You think you can beat yourself up for me? That might make me feel better." He only laughed back in my face, which did nothing to put me at ease. "You have to agree that this is a lot."

He smirked down at me once more, playing into his devilish side. It was a sharp difference, returning to who he was about thirty minutes ago. "You don't know what a lot is yet. Just wait until we have a few more go-arounds."

"Tate, I promise that I'm okay." It took a few tries, but I

finally convinced him I was alright, that the emotions had passed, and that no one needed to be beaten up. I got him to move by reminding him we had responsibilities and a place to be.

The walk to the field was even more painful than the one I had taken with Ninnie, although for a different reason. This time instead of the normal silence, I had Tate reaching over to hold my hand. No matter how often I swatted him away, he insisted that our fingers needed to be intertwined. "Tate, you have to stop. I *need* you to get it together. None of them can know about this."

"No one can know about what?" Even his voice was cute. My entire ability to keep control was slipping now that he had given me the attention I had been looking for since the day we met. I reached out, grabbed onto the sleeve of his coat, and pulled him back to me, yanking just hard enough so that he was standing in front of me.

"They can't know about us. That is too dangerous, and neither of us can take that risk right now." I realized that everything he said about Seth and Penelope was true for us, and now I could see that. I hated it when he was right. "We can't have them know about us. It's too soon, and there are things that we need to figure out before we let the others know what is going on."

Tate switched up the game, pulling me close and letting my back fall against his chest. Instead of yelling at me as he had done in the past, he was letting me lean on him. His muscles were addictive in the way they conformed against my body; all of him was addicting, if I was being honest with myself. "Tate, I think this might be overstepping. People can see us."

"I am being protective. You are overwhelmed, and I am trying to comfort you. Take care of yourself when you need it. That is my job." The love spell made him irrational, and it pained me to remember that it was not who he was or how he truly felt. Lying to myself that it was true made me feel better. It was as accurate as the illusion he had created for me, although this one would not slip away as quickly. We were stuck together until we fulfilled the curse.

He had sounded sincere, which almost caused my mind to glitch as it tried to decern what was true and not true. He was messing with the balance.

"No, you were acting something closer to possessive. Not the same thing."

He looked over my head, surveying how many people were watching, leaning down again to plant his lips against mine. "It's called being in love. That makes it the same thing."

Chapter Eleven

I wasn't sure if this was a Coven meeting or a family dinner. The group didn't change either way, so it was hard to tell, especially when Mom was the one to call us all together. It wasn't until she started talking that we would know what she was bringing us all together for.

My sisters seemed just as hesitant as I was when we came into the house to find our mom standing at the kitchen counter with our grandmother beside her. The two of them didn't seem all that happy to see us, despite their words, which only made me more nervous about why they called us all together.

"Girls, I'm glad you are home. We are just waiting for your Aunt Mira and your cousins, and then we can start eating. We have much to discuss before it gets too late, so why don't you take off to shower and change," Mom directed.

It was like a scene out of a horror film. All I was waiting for was for her to say something along the lines of "Come inside and take a seat" in an unsettling voice with the intent of murdering us before the night was over.

Celeste didn't seem as worried as me or Penelope, taking off upstairs to get her girls ready while Penelope and I went off to shower and change the way she directed us to. I did not want to get on her bad side, so I took the stairs two at a time, Penelope quick on my heels, probably thinking the same idea.

"Do you know what Mom wants to talk about?" Penelope asked me once we were out of earshot. She glanced over her shoulder to make sure no one was coming up behind us. "Or why she seems so tightly wound? When we left, she was in a good mood. It's like looking twenty-five years into Celeste's future."

I quickly shook my head back at her, looking back down the stairs to ensure Mom wasn't following behind us to overhear our conversation, which seemed like a quick way to get yelled at. "No, but I will tell you I hate it when she gets like this. It makes me sick to my stomach."

She got a little excited and waved her arms around to express it. "Yes! It makes me feel like a little kid again." She pointed off to where Celeste had gone. "I'm taking a page out of Celeste's book; I don't want to get on her bad side with this much of our day left."

Penelope and I split off, hurrying to shower and change before Mom came chasing after us.

"Hey, good looking," Tate had found his way through another locked door without us knowing. He was positioned across my bed, taking it further by casually crossing his ankles and throwing his hands behind his head. "What took you so long? I was showered and done before you made it down the street."

I closed the door and tossed my jacket onto the bed, reaching down to pet Jinx to avoid eye contact with him. A small part of me hoped he would go away if I ignored him. "Tate, what could you possibly be doing here?"

He watched me as I walked in circles around the room. I made quick work of putting my shoes and jacket away. I still needed to shower, but I couldn't force myself to walk away from him.

"Is it too bad that I wanted to spend time with you?" He was giving me a non-threatening smile that was doing the opposite. "I was trying hard to stay away from you before. Suddenly that doesn't seem as important now."

This love potion had flipped his personality, which made him chatty, something I hadn't seen before. I could only wonder if this was who he was before the Academy.

"Haven't you heard 'absence makes the heart grow fonder?'" I liked being around him, which was the confusing part. The further apart we were, the better his chance of living a long and happy life. That would not happen if he lounged on my bed with wet hair and tempting muscles. That combination made every romance movie make sense — no wonder the couples always kissed in the rain. The wet look was compelling. "Really, what are you doing here? I am about to have a family dinner, and you're not invited to that activity, so you best be going now."

"I'm not invited? What happened to my inclusion in your family? Isn't that what this love between us is all about? Blending and creating unity?" Tate got up from the bed and walked over to me, confidently crossing the room. Once we got close, he lowered his face to my neck, kissing it softly, even going as far as nibbling a little again. He knew from last time that it was my kryptonite.

His hand came thundering down beside my head, with the opposite hand falling onto my hip. "You can't deny that you want me here, Blair. The blush on your cheeks is giving you away."

"I am not blushing," I knew it was a lie. I could feel the heat radiating off my cheeks, and the color probably resembled a firetruck if the look Tate gave me was anything to go off of. "I'm flushed because we just finished working out. You ran us pretty hard tonight. Then I walked home and ran upstairs. Trust me when I say it has nothing to do with you being here."

"Blair. I have been trained to hear the fluttering wings of a fly from a mile away. Don't you think that I would be able to hear the rise and fall of your breath? Or the irregular pace of your heartbeat?" Tate used his lips against my neck to amplify my reactions to his presence. After finishing another line of kisses up my cheek, he placed the last one on my forehead. Pressing his head against mine, he smiled down at me. "Beautiful Blair, you don't understand what you do to me."

I tried not to let my reaction show any more than it already was by counting the seconds between each breath until I could feel my heart rate slowly begin its return to normal. Although, there was nothing I could do about the status of my burning cheeks.

"I want this moment. I truly do, but I also know that my family is expecting me. And they expect me to be clean, especially without the smells of our training. That can only happen if you get up and leave the room."

He let me go with a long glance up and down my body before going to the window and slipping out without another word. That bothered me more than if he had stayed with me.

The other Guardians had agreed that Tate being close to us was a good idea, and I knew he had listened to them.

But I was yet to see where he was staying and what being close meant. I wouldn't be surprised if he slipped back in later tonight to sleep at the foot of my bed.

"Blair! Hurry!" Penelope hit her fist against my door as she walked past it, which pulled me out of my pause. I hurried through a shower, using my magic to refresh my hair while I worked on getting the stink off my body. I threw my sweats on and went racing down the stairs. Jinx was on my heels the entire way, which gave me comfort.

My sisters quickly moved the food from the kitchen counter onto the dining room table. Most of the group was already there, so I went to my sisters and tried to join in before anyone commented on how long it took me to get downstairs. I used one last rush of magic to dry the last of my hair. "Sorry that took me so long. What can I help with?"

"Here, take this," Penelope handed me a large bowl filled to the brim with mashed potatoes and pushed me in the direction of the dining room. "Just go. Sit."

She was on edge, which didn't make me feel better about the situation. I knew we were all anxious about what we were waiting for, especially when I saw the solemn look on the rest of their faces. My cousins sat in their designated spots at the table. The aunts were at the end with Mom and Grandma, all rigid. There were empty spots for my sisters and me; I swept in and sat next to Grace. I did not want to end up in the seat beside Mom or Grandma. That seemed like a situation I would like to avoid at all costs.

Grace tried to hold back her chuckle, obviously having seen my actions and knowing why I moved as quickly as I did. She bumped her elbow against my arm to pull my attention to her. "Scared of them?"

I nodded, turning my head so only she could what I was

going to say. It would be best if they didn't overhear, "Always."

Mom started passing dinner around, moving dishes in a clockwise manner so that everyone got a chance to put food on their plates. I noticed that each person had the option of their favorite dish on the table; Grandma and Mom were trying to bribe us for whatever they had to talk to us about.

"Girls, we know that you have all been working hard, and we wanted to thank you for your efforts." That was not the only reason they cooked this meal, even if that was a small part. "You are all doing so much for this family, and we are all grateful," Mom kept talking, having everyone direct their attention to her and away from their plates. "We wanted to show you all how thankful we are."

All the moms and grandmas at the table nodded in agreement. They had all come together tonight with the same intention, obviously having a meeting of their own before collecting us.

My sister sat forward, taking a more significant part in the conversation. Penelope fidgeted with a napkin as she spoke, "There is a strength that we have all gotten to see in ourselves, and I think the Guardians are starting to see it too. Tate has seen it in Blair, especially today. Piper, did you see Tate showing maybe a little bit more attention to Blair today?"

Penelope had seen something on the field. I tried to get Tate to downplay how he was feeling, and that was what she was hinting at. She wanted me to talk about it and get more information. I knew she had already brought it up with Celeste; I could tell by how she avoided eye contact with me.

When I finally reached the point, I knew their reaction would only be bad, so I tried to butter up my way around it.

Penelope didn't know what she had opened with her baiting comment. She probably imagined that she had seen Tate and I having a crush on each other, teasing and flirting when we were near each other. There was no way that she knew what was going on.

"There has been a small development. Tonight, before we went to the field to train, I was closing the shop. Usually, Ninnie comes by to pick me up, but Tate Bishop came in to talk to me. He was mad when he came inside, resulting in an argument between us." I knew I was beating around the bush and taking my time to get there. "We went back and forth for a minute while I finished the chores. Our conversation was heated. I felt very backed into a corner, so I tried to stand up for myself. That resulted in him stepping back into the large cabinet in the back room."

Aunt Mira gave me a hesitant look, bracing herself for what I would say about her furniture, "Did he break it? I hope he didn't break it." She seemed to realize how inconsiderate that sounded and jumped back to amend it. "Is everyone okay? If needed, we can get a new one."

Shaking my head, I went on. "No. Everything is fine, but do you remember the love potion you and Grace made? It was on the top shelf. Walking into the cabinet caused it to tip over and spill on his head."

The collective gasps let me know that they were all worried about the results that would have left us with, all staring over at me in anticipation. The food on their plates long forgotten.

Celeste finally broke the silence by speaking up, "Did it work?"

"Yeah, that is why he was so enthralled with me." There was no better word for the way he was acting. He followed me everywhere with a slight smirk on his face.

They all went off in another round of gasps. This news was revolutionary, especially for Aunt Mira, who immediately exclaimed, "You're kidding me! What did he do after it set in?"

"He kissed me. That's when we found out that somehow the love potion did stick on him and latched itself onto me," I explained as calmly as possible, "You should have seen the way that he acted."

That was the part of the story that put them over the hill. Everyone at the table started furiously talking, the words flying out of their mouths with their hands waving.

"You have got to be kidding me!" Piper went off. The love and surprise that everyone else was radiating was very different from her expression. She almost seemed mad at the news. "You are the one who gets to fall in love? You are the one who gets the Guardian?" She got up from the table and went stomping down the stairs. Her mom, Cassandra, went flying after her to calm her down. Piper was made of the same fire Penelope was, and no one wanted to be the one it was directed at.

"I wasn't expecting that when I called us all together tonight," Mom mumbled as she moved things around on the table.

Grandma and Aunt Edna chuckled; both seemed to agree with her statement. Aunt Edna even went as far as to sing her praises to the ancestors for this match. Tate's love potion bonding him to me meant that we would always have the protection of the Guardians. We no longer needed Ninnie to ensure the Guardians stuck around.

"How do you feel about it?" Mom had a look of pride on her face even as she tried to hide it. She was excited about what this would mean for our family, especially me. "How does he feel about it?

Celeste had gone through the loss much better than Mom, already having hardened her heart for what was to come. I don't think she ever really let herself fall in love with the girls' father in the first place.

I took a bite of the potatoes on my plate, realizing that it would probably be my last bite for a long time now that we had started talking about this. Mom wasn't prone to letting significant conversations rest as Penelope did. "I am nervous about Tate. This will speed up his time of death, which he doesn't seem worried about. I tried to talk to him and explain what being with me meant, and he acted like it wasn't a big deal at all. I know he is strong and brave, but this is falling closer to stupid."

It seemed like my sisters were holding their breath as the conversation between my mom and me took place. That I understood, it was what I often did when Mom and Penelope got into it.

She circled the table and wrapped me up in a hug. Her joy came out with her words. Mom thought the situation I had found myself in was amusing; they all did. There was only so much we could do now that it had been done. "He isn't stupid. He's in love, and often that's even worse."

Aunt Mira lifted her cup in silent celebration to me, pumping her elbow against Penelope, pulling her into the joke she was about to deliver. "This is something to celebrate. You get to kiss a cute boy and do it as often as you wish," She then let out a long and heavy laugh, the irony of the situation falling onto her in fits. "Thank goodness I interrupted your kiss. You can't have a special moment like that in your mom's kitchen. That would have been a lame story to tell."

"I don't think anyone would care to hear this story." The only thing that would be heard louder than my words was the misery laced in my tone. As much appeal as this situation held, there was no way we could move forward with this. I had to find a cure for the potion to get him back to normal as soon as possible.

My comment was a mood killer; no one followed with any remarks. We returned to our meals, knowing there was nothing to do now. I could see the wheels turning in Aunt Mira's head; I could only hope she was thinking in the same direction I was.

Cassandra got Piper to calm down, and they returned to the table to finish our meal, although there was only silence now. I know that a large part of our group was taking this time to think about what Tate joining our Coven meant for this war, while the other part of the room was trying to stay silent, hoping that would help in not making Piper mad again.

I surveyed the rest of my Coven, taking in Aunt Edna's dark look. She was going deep into her mind. She had the gift of other senses, knowing what was coming in a similar way as Celeste. While my sister could only sense something was coming, our Aunt Edna was able to see a small glimpse into the future. Her eyes could see something more than what was in front of her. "There is magic in the night when the pumpkins glow by midnight. That is when we will ride."

Our brooms had sat in the closet for a long time. There wasn't much use for them when we all lived in the same little town, and planes weren't that great when it came to watching out for us. The pilots were surprised when they saw a teenage girl at the same height in the sky.

I could tell that it scared some and others seemed to let this news bring them higher. Those were the women who were ready for this war.

My sisters pulled me away from the group once the others went home. They wanted to talk about what they had seen on the field today and what I had brought to the family tonight. With my announcement, whatever the mothers had planned went out the window, and everyone left as fast as they could.

"When did you figure out the potion had fully set in?" Penelope held my hand tightly. I wasn't sure if it was supposed to be encouraging or if she was trying to keep me from running away.

Celeste maternally held onto my other hand and went in for more details. She was trying to be gentle, but it came out like a shark on the loose in bloody water. "Yeah, I was wondering that too. How did you figure out the potion overtook him?"

"How did you figure out it was no longer him?" Penelope went again when I paused longer than either one could handle.

"The way that he just leaned down to kiss me, not bothering to listen to me even after I told him about the curse." I was already emotional but knowing that it wasn't him was the part that hurt. Once the potion was off he would be back to normal.

"I wouldn't be so sure," Penelope wanted to believe that she knew something more than me, but I had spent enough time around Tate to realize he would not sway even if he were under the effects of a love potion.

"Even if I put my entire heart into this, no man has ever survived the curse," I tried not to think about what that meant for poor Tate.

Penelope raised her hand to rub the back of her neck. She didn't know what to say, and what she finally came out with was useless in the way of advice. "Good thing he is something more than a human man," She gave a morbid chuckle at the position I was in. "That will probably help his odds of survival."

She meant that to be a joke, but I was not laughing. It might have been a love potion that made this all happen, but the kiss sealed his fate of being affected by the curse of the Bradbury women. It was already working on him, and he was doomed.

With her comment, I decided it was time to go to bed. There was only so much I could take, and I had gone through enough 'end of the world' conversations today. I wasn't going to stick around while my sisters dragged me through another one.

I called Jinx, getting her to accompany me up the stairs where my bed sat empty. I made sure to leave my window unlocked, just in case Tate decided to come back.

He didn't.

* * *

Mom came down the stairs, forcing me to open my eyes from where I had been attempting to nap on the couch. It made me feel safer to sleep down here; I hoped the Keeper of the Dream would have a more challenging time getting to me if I wasn't in bed or avoided sleeping during regular night hours. I was desperate for any relief possible. "Aren't you supposed to be at work right now?"

I rolled over to face the ceiling and sighed, not bothering to look in her direction while the conversation continued. "I convinced Aunt Mira that I wasn't vital to the store operation today so I could catch up on some sleep."

"She believed that? I thought the store made you into the Three Musketeers. All for one and one for all?" Mom's comment made her laugh, but I stayed serious. She reached out and pressed the back of her hand to my forehead to see if I had a fever while assessing me for any illnesses or deformities. "Are you feeling sick? Do you feel like you have a fever? I can grab you some healing tea. It will probably help you feel better even if nothing is wrong."

"No, I'm not sick. I'm just tired." I was trying to figure out a way to tell her to leave me alone so I could go back to my nap, but there was no way she would walk away from me now that she was worried. "I got pulled into another Astral Projection last night. It really shook me up even when it was over. I was worried they were going to pull me back in all night. I'm trying to catch up before I meet the team for more training."

I was tempted to roll back into the couch fold, but she wouldn't let me now that she knew something was going on. "You got pulled into another one? It seems like this is on a nightly basis now." She pushed my shoulder to have me sit up, making room on the couch, and sat down next to me, not letting me get back to sleep like I desperately wanted to. "Have you gotten any sleep at all this week?"

"No, this is the third or fourth one they have pulled me into. I can hardly keep track. They are all running together at this point." I still didn't know who's controlling them. "They hide in the trees. Last night I tried to force them out. They didn't reveal their face, but they did send a snake out to eat me."

She let out a startled gasp, "They sent a snake to eat you?"

I had only shared the first one with anyone, and they had only gotten more aggressive. The Keeper of the Dream continued to come after me.

"That is low on my problem list. I have no time to sleep.

I have a job during the day and training when I get off work. I am completely exhausted at night and can't keep my eyes open, so I eventually fall asleep. That allows them to pull me into another Astral Projection." I ran my hand through my hair, pulling at the split ends in a rhythmic motion. "So, what do I do?"

"Why didn't you say anything sooner?" Mom pulled the hair I was playing with out of my hand and tucked it behind my ear. She hated when I pulled at the ends.

"What could anyone do to help me?"

"I can understand why you are falling apart right now. That is a lot to have on your mind." She placed her hand on my knee. Her head stayed forward, though, and only stared off into the distance. She was deeply thinking about something. "I wonder if there is a spell we could use to protect your mind from them. A protection spell would be to build the wall around your brain; when you sleep, it will be there."

I pointed to the stack of spell books on the coffee table. I had been studying all morning before finally deciding that sleep was needed. "Yeah, I've been looking for one. No luck so far, but I will keep looking. I need to find something soon, or I will go crazy from the lack of sleep."

She got a determined look on her face and quickly stood. Mom threw her hand down so I would put mine in hers. Then she proceeded to pull me behind her to the basement door. She was a woman on a mission; only a fool would get in her way.

"So, then we keep looking until we find one. There is a spell out there and we will find it."

Mom opened the basement to our magic room and quickly charmed the shelves to start sorting the books independently. I searched through the books stacked on the tables and the piles on the floor surrounding us. We needed to be better at putting them away when we were done with them, but there always seemed to be one more thing I wanted to reread before putting it back on the shelf.

We both went deep into our searches, only speaking up when we thought we had found a lead. "Would one for protection work if it's for a sacred space?" I called out to her while reading a spell from the book. The spell talked about protecting the place from any damage.

Her laugh echoed from where she was hidden behind another bookshelf. "I'm sorry, but I will say no to that one. You are very sacred to me, but that spell is reserved for a church or a temple or something along those lines. Your mind is neither."

Mom went through another shelf, using her magic to go through one book while her eyes went through another. The Guardians' influence had made us all fall more into our magic, and she was willing to use it freely now.

I sent my magic over to light the fireplace while I flipped through another large pile. I hadn't found spell that would work and felt discouraged that we wouldn't find an answer. My magic went through two more stacks of books, empty of any spells or charms that would help me find relief. We might have to create our own if we didn't find one before it was time for bed.

"Are you having any luck over there?" I called out to her. I wanted to know before I tackled the next pile.

"Not yet," Her voice rang out from behind another pile of books. "We will go to Aunt Mira's house and check her shelves if we can't find anything here."

That at least gave me a little hope that we could find an answer. I was desperate for some relief. "Do you think there would be any at Grace's house? I could ask her to look for us."

We both heard the doorbell ring. It interrupted us, but acted as a welcome break for me. Mom seemed determined to keep going, "Why don't you go get that? This shelf has some promising options I want to get through."

I agreed, taking the stairs two at a time to answer the door, ready to curse whoever chose to interrupt our search. "What are you doing here?"

Tate was at my front door, shockingly using the bell instead of just breaking in.

"I needed to check on you. You seemed off yesterday and weren't at the store today." His hand reached out, crossing the doorway, to caress mine. His thumb rubbed against mine in a way intended to be comforting but instead felt suffocating. He gave me a small smile, and his eyes softened. "Mira said that you just needed to rest, but I needed to see you for myself. I had to make sure you were okay."

His concern was almost unsettling. He always seemed hyperaware of me and how I felt long before our love potion.

"Why don't we take a seat and talk?" I pointed him to the swing on the front porch. I figured we wouldn't be interrupted by my mom if we stayed out there, and somehow it made me feel like I had more control over the situation. I could walk into the house and slam the door behind me if he said something that made me mad. Not that it would stop him from making his way inside behind me.

I decided to be vulnerable with him. I hoped he would give me some insight that his training had given him. I moved down the bench to get closer to him, hoping my voice wouldn't carry to anyone nearby since someone was always watching.

I fidgeted with the rings on my fingers only out of nervous habit. "Tate, remember how I told everyone I was put into an Astral Projection? They have only gotten worse."

"Wicked Witch, you can't fall victim to them. You are stronger than whoever they are and whatever they think they can do to you," Tate came closer, closer than he ever had before. Leaning down so that his mouth was against my ear, whispering into me as if he was afraid someone else would hear them. "Powerful people tell powerful lies. You need to be careful."

I couldn't tell if he was joking or not. "Victim? I have been holding my own for a while now without an issue. Excuse me for finally seeking help from those around me or expressing how hard this has been." I glared up at him, constantly annoyed that he belittled me and what I had gone through. He didn't seem to care, even if he was pretending that he did. "You might want to be careful."

Talking to Tate was a joke. His ego and self-assured attitude were always in the way. He had been permanently closed off since I met him, but it got worse every time we interacted. I hoped the connection would have fixed that and opened him up to being the Tate I was sometimes allowed to see, but that wasn't the case. As often as I saw his softness, the shift happened again, and he was back to being the jerk we all knew.

"You think you've been holding your own, but what if they are just waiting for you to be comfortable before they strike?" He said it almost to tease me, but I wasn't feeling it. His comment felt too real and too close to a threat to be comforting. "I think many things were waiting in the shadows, ready to strike. Or biding their time, waiting for you to reveal your strength."

It was eerie in a way that caused me to question him, and his mood seemed to flip. Tate could read me and was using that to his advantage now. Those two things were not a coincidence, which made me nervous.

"Tate. If anyone was hiding in the shadows, they would see I am prepared for their arrival." The Astral Projections proved someone was out there, and they knew I was preparing for them, even if they were against it. "I am ready for them. That is the truth; they will see it when they come."

"Yes, and they will also see a young strapping hero here to save the day and protect the damsel in distress from all the monsters. Especially if she wanted to kiss me in exchange for her protection and safety." He broke out in a grin, obviously trying to get me to lose the hostility in my voice and return to normal. He even went as far as to fake a yawn, using that as his excuse to place his arm around my shoulders, further pretending that we had a closeness I was not feeling. "I will always save you."

I was supposed to feel loved and safe in his arms, but the darkness inside of him continued to show more each day. He seemed more comfortable as he showed more personality each time we saw each other.

I didn't want to call him out on his comment and how it made me feel, but the words came out anyways. "You do understand why I struggle to believe that concept, right? Especially considering how you have acted."

He came closer to me, leaning his head down until his forehead was pressed against mine, a position that was starting to become very familiar. He was ready to bend down and kiss me when the opportunity arose.

"I am here; you have to believe that," He reached out, took my hand, and returned to the Tate I wanted to believe

I knew. "I'm right here by your side. No matter what else is true, you can know and believe that much."

The harsh lines on his hands felt right as they caressed mine. Even though I knew the love potion was being held over us, bringing the curse to the surface, and that was the only reason he loved me, I still let myself fall into the magic of it. If we were destined to fail, at least we would get the opportunity to love each other first.

There was only one thing left that we could do; light the candles and throw some salt.

The spell would be the real thing to cement the magic that would hopefully help me, but adding salt and candles couldn't hurt.

Grace was getting into the spirit, having gone around to all the party stores in Salem and purchased some commercialized black pointy hats that were the telltale sign of a witch. She loved it when we all practiced magic together and was overjoyed that was what we were doing tonight.

Mom would not rest until I was protected from the Astral Projections. She had looked through our entire spell room and any spell book our Coven had access to. She needed three other witches for the spell she found. The three witches had to be willing to share their magic with me, and while witches had become abundant in our little town, the catch was that they had to have pure intentions for my safety and my life. I asked my sisters and Grace to join in the spell. I knew they would do anything to protect me; they all loved and cared for me.

Mom would stand over us, as the leader of our group, and facilitate the spell while the other three witches stood around me, casting their magic onto my head. At the same time, it was my responsibility to empty my thoughts, letting their magic fall on me.

While Celeste put her kids to bed, Penelope and Grace prepared the room with as many candles as they could find and a large ring of salt. While I was sitting in a chair in the middle of a protection circle, I watched the hats on their heads bob as they moved and made the activities into an adventure — it was almost exciting. It has been a long time since we had done any spellcasting together.

Grace put a crown of flowers on my head, adding to the sense of whimsy, and placed a bouquet of my favorite black dahlias into my hands. She even went as far as to put a circle of spare petals around my feet.

Penelope walked around the room, placing the candles where the magic could bounce from one to another. Once Celeste came downstairs, she walked to where Mom held the spell book and worked on practicing the words of the spell so that she was ready to cast it on me when the clock struck midnight.

The intention was to cast the spell at the moment the Keeper of the Dream would normally drag me into their Astral Projection. The goal was to stop them in their tracks and hopefully give Mom a second to latch herself to their magic.

It made me feel guilty to be sitting there, letting all of them do the work to prepare me for the spell, but my preparation could confuse the magic since the intention was to have it protect me as if I was helpless. I sat silently in my seat.

The weather outside our house was loud; lightning struck and caused the room to almost shake with its power.

It was the *perfect* night for a protection spell.

The three pure-of-heart witches placed their hands in each other's, circled me, and began the spell in perfect unison.

A spell of safety here I cast
A word of might to hold her fast
A shield before her and behind
To right and left; protection bind
To her may no harm or ill whit come
By power of three my magic is from
With the sacred light around her
As above, so below, blessed be

I could feel each of their magic come into me, bonding me to them for my protection. Penelope offered me strength, Grace gave me her love, and Celeste presented me with her willpower. The combination of these three formidable witches' magic caused my body to rise from its chair, suspended in the air while it worked itself into me. Their magic each took a distinct color of red, green, and blue as it became a wind that encircled my body. Their power bonded itself to my skin as a form of armor until my entire body, inside and out, was covered in it; only then did their magic-infused wind release me and bring me back down to the same chair. I felt somehow lighter than I had before the spell.

None of us spoke; the witches around me released their hands and stepped out of the circle.

"How do you feel?" Mom asked in a tender voice as she approached our circle. She seemed in a good mood, having faith in the spell. Her hand came out to clasp mine, offering her strength to me in a different way than the other witches in the room had done.

I could only laugh at her question, something I realized had been hard to do for a while with that heaviness overtaking my body. "I feel so much better now. I had no idea how much my fear was holding me down."

The burden of the Astral Projections was gone, as was the threat of anyone else trying to come into my head, which left room in my mind to worry about the battle we were preparing for.

My three saviors brought me in for a group hug. It made me feel like I could take on the world. The bond of sisterhood could make anyone feel better.

Grace had decided to spend the night just as she would have done when we were kids, but this time we would not spend the night awake telling scary stories. We would be on watch for any Astral Projections coming for me. Her job was to wake up when I moved. The way that I moved in an Astral Projection was how I was currently moving in real life, so if I was hurt or killed in one, my body would end up the same way in the waking world.

Our group hurried to clean up the mess, sweeping up the salt from the floor and putting the half-used candles away in the cupboard. Mom gave us all a loving embrace, choosing to pray to the Goddess of Magic for our safety instead of going to bed like the rest of us were.

While my sisters did go to bed, Grace offered a different approach. She knew how terrified I was of sleep and the chance that the spell didn't work, so she suggested we sit up for a while to talk and watch movies, being willing to sit there with me until I crashed. She grabbed a bowl of snacks from the cupboard, trailing behind me while we walked upstairs.

"How about a romcom? Or we could do a regular comedy?" She plopped down on my bed, used her magic to turn the TV on, and started flipping through the movie options, suggesting some of her favorites. "I'm guessing no thrillers. We've had enough scary moments lately that I don't think we need to add to it."

We settled on a romantic comedy. Grace was overjoyed to be able to snack on junk food and talk about the boys. The protagonist was trying to win over the main girl, flirting with her despite being her best friend's brother and the problems that would cause them both.

Grace giggled, "He is adorable, not Fabian cute or matching Tate's level, but I see how he could be enjoyable to spend your afternoon with, especially if he ditches his shirt and shows off his muscles."

"Fabian! When did you start thinking Fabian was cute? I thought you believed the boys took up all our free time and were annoying." I hadn't been paying attention to the movie, but her comment brought me out of my head, which I think might have been her intention. "You hinted that you were digging on Seth last time we discussed the Guardians. Why the sudden switch to Fabian?"

She paused the movie, turning over on the bed so I had her full attention. She did not let the TV turn off when cute, shirtless boys were on. "I did think that he was cute. So, he is funny, charming, and has some flair when needed. Strong and capable, right? Getting the whole picture?"

I nodded along slowly, realizing that she was just getting started, and finally getting a glimpse at how much she had gone over this in her mind. It was almost like watching an actress practice their script from memory alone. "Okay, so what made the jump to Fabian so easy for you?"

"It is so obvious that Seth wants Penelope, and I don't want to have to fight my cousin for his attention. Not to mention how obvious it is that Penelope wants him too. They try to deny it, but it's there, and it's not going away. It's more than a cat-and-mouse game; it's tiger against tiger. I would rather not be the fool who gets in the middle of that." Somehow, this had turned into a group date in Grace's mind, with all of us getting paired off.

I couldn't help but agree with what she saw, "Yeah, those two seem to be intertwined."

"Now, three Guardians were remaining, all with desirable qualities and beautiful muscles to boot. The problem was of those three, one of them was Tate. I don't know if you know, but since the first day he came to Salem, he has always been yours, the curse bonding aside," She gave me a pointed look. "Neither one of you would have ever been able to look at anyone else since the moment he came here. You can't deny it. It's been written all over your face."

"Tate never saw me in that way, and he is only seeing me that way now because of a freak accident with *your* love potion," I explained as calmly as possible. "You could have had him. You still could if we find a way to break the love potion, and the curse would probably not affect him if he stayed away from me."

I tried to think back to the first day we met, how he treated me with incompetency, and that was when he was being nice. It had only gotten worse since then. There were a few small moments when he did treat me like someone he cared about, but it never lasted long. He was confused and had a habit of making me confused too.

Grace shook her head like I was saying something

ridiculous, which maybe I was. The lack of sleep was probably getting to me. "No, I could not! He was always yours and always will be. The love potion only accelerated the process of your bond," She gestured over her shoulder toward the stairs leading to the kitchen. "I wouldn't be surprised if he was walking inside your kitchen right now, waiting for you to come downstairs to get a minute with you."

I hadn't told anyone about the day he had been lying on my bed and didn't tell her now that he also had a history of coming in through the window when he wanted a moment with me.

I returned to the topic, "What narrowed it down between Huxley and Fabian?" The matching pair didn't differ much. Neither of the boys was that vocal, which might have been why Grace found them suitable as partners. "Or did you flip a coin? Put the names in a bowl, close your eyes, and then pick at random?"

She reached over and pushed against my shoulder, laughing the entire time. Her lighthearted nature helped this conversation continue without offense. "The other day, when Fabian got intense on the field, it blew me away! I had never seen that side of him before. Usually, he is calm or amusing, especially with the comments he makes under his breath." Grace explained quickly, showing how much thought she had put into her decision. "I thought that would be a positive in his favor, but I would rather not go against someone whenever I wanted something. Somehow, he became a mini-Tate during this."

"Yeah? That did that for you?" I tried to refrain from laughing at her, knowing that we all had things that got to us, and I was in no position to judge her for what piqued her interest. I hadn't seen his lighthearted nature as much as she had. My mind was usually preoccupied with Tate. "His intensity turned you off?"

Grace was a good sport, laughing harder at my questions and not bothering to get offended by the jokes. "Yes! It was different than when Seth or Tate got into our faces and yelled. When they do it, I feel like they are in charge. When Fabian did it, it only made me mad." She had a pinched expression on her face. "In my mind, we are on the same level. Where he doesn't have the authority to speak down to me."

"You might be a little messed up there. Most of us are fueled by love, not anger and aggression." I turned my attention back to the TV. "Tate's kind of mean to me through, and I can't stop thinking about him, so maybe I'm messed up like you are."

We both appreciated having the opportunity to chat about the boys we were surrounded by until we fell asleep, thankfully with no Astral Projections in sight.

Chapter Twelve

ord had come in from the Council, and our entire Coven sat down together to hear what they had to say. Ninnie and the Guardians joined us with anticipation. They were also hoping for answers from the Council about how they planned to deal with the Cabals. Grace and I were secretly hoping they were ready to discipline the Cabals and that they would handle the situation for us.

Mom graciously welcomed everyone, then opened the room with the truth spell. Grandma asked us all to sit together in the dining room so that everyone could hear the message from the Council when she was ready to read it. The Guardians sat utterly in silence. I think they were still hoping for this to turn into a fight. Tate and Seth were working towards the Council's Guard with Huxley and Fabian following behind them; this was their opportunity to prove themselves to the older boys.

Grandma was decked out in a festive dress, the florescent colors making her look more like a gypsy than a witch. She had dressed with flare for our guests as her wrists were lined with an overload of bangles that made a lot of noise when she moved her arms. It looked like she had gone shopping in Aunt Mira's closet instead of hers.

She sat at the head of the table and placed her weathered hands on the surface of her crystal ball. In an ominous tone, she read the words that came across the globe like one would read the headlines of a news article. "We, as the Council, are contacting the Bradbury Coven today. We have received word of the Cabals' impending arrival to the town of Salem, and the Council has decided to come to Salem only if the situation worsens and they contact any of your Coven members. We understand that the Cabals' influence will probably only continue for a short while. There is too much that cannot be predicted, and we hope they will see their ways and return to where they came from before we are forced to intervene." They had a very positive outlook on our chances. I could tell from the rest of the room that no one else agreed with their mindset. "We will keep tabs on the situation as developments are made and follow through. Word will be sent out if we decide to come to Salem."

"So, the Council isn't going to do *anything*?" Penelope's words cut through the tension, laced with anger that hadn't been there before. Her opinion that the Council was useless was reaffirmed now that they were unwilling to step in when we had a real problem. "Why would they bother to reach out to us if they weren't going to *do* anything? This is a joke and a complete waste of time."

She had a point; it did seem futile for them to say anything if nothing would come of it. Thankfully the nods from the rest of the room made it seem like they also agreed with her. We were all feeling somewhere between helpless and hopeless.

"What made them reach out now? Are they watching us, or did someone make contact with them?" Mom asked. She wrung her hands together in her lap to relieve her stress. The pinch between her eyebrows only got deeper each day while we waited for something to finally happen. If I asked her, the anticipation was the worst part. We were constantly looking over our shoulders to see if the other shoe dropped. Mom looked around the room and stared intensely at everyone, trying to decide if they had contacted the Council or if this was spontaneous. She also was hyper-aware of the traitor amongst the Council and if they had been the ones to share the news.

Everyone in the group seemed to shake their heads to announce they weren't the one who reached out.

Seth spoke up, being the spokesperson for the Guardians like always. "Before I left, I wrote to them and let them know what was going on. They told me they would have no part in this, and if we wanted it handled, we would have to handle it on our own." He gestured behind him to where the other Guardians stood with a confident smile across his face. "That is why we are here. We are 'handling' it."

"Is there something that I am missing?" Mom directed the second half of her questions only to the Guardians. She knew they were running their version of interference every day and that they would be the first to know if anything had changed. It was easy to see that it gave her peace knowing they were here looking after everything. Mom still kept tabs in every way she could, using her magic to ensure that all our barriers were in place over our houses, the store, and all our heads. She also was plagued with the knowledge that Celeste felt the Cabals' darkness coming closer every day. Because none of the Cabals had made contact with us, it was hard for her to track it exactly, so we had no idea how close they actually were to being here.

Tate stepped forward, not letting his hand leave its position on my shoulder. I liked that he wanted to be close to me. He came immediately to my side as soon as he walked in. This was one of those times when our connection felt right. It was something that I couldn't deny. "All information that we have has been shared."

Mom's face softened; she felt better once he spoke. She would still be nervous once they left the house. I don't think she would feel okay again until the Cabals were gone.

Grandma shushed the room again and continued reading from her crystal ball. The message was apparently not over, and our questions were interrupting her reading. "We, as the Council, understand that your Coven is coming together to fight back against the Cabals. We do not see them as a threat and suggest you back down before anyone else gets hurt. Engaging them in a fight will only discourage them from making the right decision, and we want them to learn and grow from this experience so that they will continue on a path toward making good decisions. We can only hope they will be able to learn this lesson before any other casualties occur."

"They are just expecting us to back down? Do they not care about our lives? The Cabals are dangerous and are coming here to kill us. That means we have to rise and fight against them, not back down in hopes that they 'learn their lesson' before it gets to that point." I was trying to remain as calm as possible, but the stress of the situation made me sick to my stomach in a way that happened so often lately I had almost gotten used to it.

The Council was acting as if we were in the wrong for preparing for a battle. We hadn't been the ones to start this, and if it hadn't been brought to Salem, then it would have been easy to ignore. Seth was standing beside Tate with Huxley and Fabian at his side, and the two older Guardians seemed to be conversing with their eyes. Surprisingly it was Fabian who spoke to the group and answered questions. I wondered if that would change who Grace had a crush on this week. His shy nature meant that none of us saw anything from him often. It seemed like he was slowly letting that fall. "The Council has no control over us being here, so we aren't a part of this message even if they know us to be here. They are only talking about you and what you are doing. It seems like they disagree with your decision to act in response to violence — which does align with their tendency to avoid aggressive situations when that is an option."

Tate tightened his grip on my shoulder to reassure me before he went on to reassure the rest of our group. "We aren't going to go anywhere, and as long as we are here, you will have protection. We promised to protect the witches of Salem, and we will do that even if the Council disagrees."

It didn't make sense why they were trying to damper the threat of the Cabals. It seemed to me that they were supporting them or even encouraging it. The only benefit of the Cabals coming here was that they would be allowed to take down our Coven. We were influential in numbers, and staying in Salem, our access to our ancestral magic was powerful. It would make sense if the Council decided to come after us. And ignoring the Cabals was a hands-off way of doing that.

I could see that Tate made a few of our Coven members feel better, although Ninnie was not one of them. She almost seemed more agitated now that we had gotten this answer from the Council. Although, she had been in a bad mood the entire day, so this was only adding to it. "What does that mean for Harriet? She was run out of her home when the Cabals killed her family. Not killing them will not bring back her family, and I understand that, but it will right many wrongs. I know it will bring some justice to her and her lost Coven. She deserves that?"

I think that she was grateful Harriet wasn't there; hearing the message from the Council and the way that it made her experience insignificant would have probably sent her further into her depressive state, which was something we were trying to avoid. She was too vulnerable for that as well.

Grandma shifted her hands on the crystal globe, trying to find any additional answers the Council might have sent. It was like she was reading deeper into their words. "They don't have that answer, but would come here if needed. They know best and will only do what is best for their people." My grandma was confident in our leaders, something I wish I could be. I was banking on being strong enough on my own, my magical skills, and a dagger to keep me alive. My Coven were going to sit together and converse themselves to death. The Council didn't seem to care if we made it out alive, and unless we got our training together, it might end that way.

"I don't know what the Council will do for her, but we will not turn our backs on her. She needs to be a part of a Coven and a family; we must do anything to ensure she feels that way." I felt confident in that decision, and with Tate's hand on my shoulder tightened, I knew I had his support.

* * *

Tate was anything but subtle. He had left a spell book on the shop counter, titled 'Unlocking your Full Magic.' It appeared to be a self-help book for witches. He had repeatedly advised me to stretch and strengthen my magic, which I was terrified of. I was caught between wanting to do that and the chance of failure. If I never tried, then there was no chance that I would fail. It was a terrible thing that I was strangely comforted by.

I waved my hand over the book cover to conceal it, then threw it under the counter so I could get to work. He might want me to study the book, but he was in the back room and wouldn't see my defiance. I also had to remind myself that I didn't have to do anything Tate told me.

Grace took care of stocking the front of the store while I manned the counter and any customers that might come in.

Today was one of the days when Penelope was allowed to help with their planning, which somehow made it worse. I hated that she got to be near him. It could have also been Penelope who planted the book on the counter for me to find. Penelope was not one to be subtle either, and she hadn't been quiet about how far behind Celeste and I were compared to her and how she thought we weren't doing enough to catch up.

They were deciding whether we would strike first or wait for the Cabals to come here. The Council's message pushed them toward wanting to seek out the Cabals to take them by surprise, something that none of us had discussed wanting to do, which was why Penelope was in there with them. She was acting almost as a spokesman for the rest of us. No matter what, the boys were going to do what they were going to do, but the addition of the Bradbury Coven was up to Penelope and if she thought the risk was worth putting ourselves on the frontline.

Grace and I wanted to press our ears against the door and listen to their conversation since neither of us wanted to meet the Cabals. Both of us were dying for the opportunity to tell them as much. The boys were hoping it would turn into a war while Penelope was trying to convince them that we could talk through anything. Although, it didn't take a genius to know that it was Mom who pushed the idea that we could negotiate first. She thought we could talk through anything if we had a willing audience. Penelope was always ready for the fight, and it was obvious she would be more appreciative of the fact the boys would push for it.

Aunt Mira went back and forth, not wanting to get into a fight but wanting this to be done. She would willingly send the boys in our place, but if Penelope got sent off, she would be less than enthusiastic about the plan. She ran in circles around the room, taking care of the store only to keep herself busy. I don't think she had finished a single task since she had walked in the door this morning, but she was working hard to appear like she had. Aunt Mira couldn't care less if any customers walked through the door — she was probably even more desperate than Grace or I were to press herself against the door at the chance of hearing what was being said.

The boys wouldn't be happy if they found anyone of us that way, which was probably how we managed to refrain. Only a fool would get on Tate's bad side. We all knew that once we did, there was no coming back, although I was starting to think that I was the exception to that. I was known for driving him crazy, but hadn't gotten any part of his wrath, yet.

The Guardians surprised us by taking frequent breaks, coming out into the storefront and willingly spending time with Aunt Mira, Grace, and me. While the others enjoyed time with my aunt and cousin, I liked to think that Tate orchestrated the breaks, that he couldn't keep his mind on his work — desperate for even a glance at me.

It was only in my mind because he barely came near me most of the time. Instead, he would grab some tea and walk back into the office to continue looking over their plans, leaving the others behind.

Penelope came bouncing out and surprised me by rushing me into a bear hug from behind, causing my eyes to separate from Tate's fleeting figure as he returned to their backroom. "Blair! They are listening to me. I am surprised they haven't kicked me out since I told Tate to be quiet more than a few times." That thought almost made her giggle out loud, starkly contrasting with her typically somber attitude toward the boys. "I think I have them almost convinced. Can you believe that?"

I had no idea what she had convinced them to do, but I knew that answer wouldn't be stopped by the Guardians coming out of the back office to spend time with us. They were going to decide whether she was in there or not. They just chose to listen to her when she was there, probably due to Seth enjoying her presence. He wasn't willing to admit it out loud, but we all saw it written clearly across his face. Seth enjoyed having her around him and not because she gave him an attitude she generally reserved for her dates. She also enjoyed being around him but would not admit it either. Penelope kept up the façade that she was only here for the meetings.

Huxley was taking a break only to his benefit, standing near Grace with a cocky grin while he flirted with her. He seemed to enjoy the reaction she was giving him, the former playboy getting back into the game. I saw her melting further into his side with every word he said. It was a wonder how we got any work done, especially with all their interruptions and so many boys struggling to keep their wandering eyes on the prize.

"I think I can convince them to give us a chance to make a change here and to take this on with eyes wide open," Penelope moved on. Not letting her body anywhere near Seth when he passed by, even if it meant stepping into my personal space. "You know what I'm saying?"

I didn't understand a single part of her sentence. When she got excited, her words started to run together like they were now. "Pen, you have to take a deep breath."

She mischievously smiled, glancing over her shoulder at the boys. "They want to go chasing after the Cabals, but I think I have convinced them to wait a week. I am hoping during that time we can get Harriet to share some more about what she went through. The more information we have, the better we can make a clear plan on their ascent."

"You say that like she's hiding something." I flipped between the receipt printer settings, not letting my sister's madness get in the way of my job and everything I had to do. "Weren't we supposed to have trust in people?"

"Mom doesn't seem to trust her anymore, which is good enough reason for me to be aware." Penelope wasn't taking that little knowledge for granted, nor did I.

* * *

There was a short list of things I would rather do than sit in the back garden with my family, although I would never have guessed there to be the additions of Guardians, Ninnie Walker, and Harriet. Although, the Guardians took their turns doing Grandma's bidding and were making it into quite a show, one that we could have sold tickets to.

"Idiots surround me," I growled the words out under my breath after correcting Fabian again that he didn't need to cut the bud off the flowering rose bush, especially since we wanted it to bloom before the season was over.

Grace bumped my hip with hers; her laugh rang out for everyone to hear. Even if she whispered, she meant every word, "But at least they are hot. It makes it a lot easier to spend your days with them."

She wasn't wrong about that. The shirtless Guardians were a wonder to the eyes. They all managed to have six-pack abs, and the sun was doing beautiful things to their tans. It was a wonder that we were getting anything done with that much testosterone nearby.

Harriet's presence was quick to ruin the experience.

Ninnie's mother had informed her that Harriet was to be attached to her hip. That meant that Ninnie's kind offer to help us get through some work meant Harriet was there too, and she wasn't quiet about how much she hated it. Harriet voiced how frustrated she was with the leftover bugs from the summer season, how they flew through the air, how the sun was coming down, the heat, and how long we had been outside. It seemed like every word that came out of her mouth was in the tone of a whine.

It was tough to remind myself that we had just the day before discussed taking her in and bringing her into our own. It did make me feel better that everyone else seemed just as annoyed with her as I was. Every time she opened her mouth, I could see everyone preparing their eyes for the roll that they would take.

"When can we be done here?" She refused to use her magic like the rest of us were doing to keep herself cool, claiming that the Cabals would track her magic if she was to use it freely. Tate graciously offered to cool her down with his magic, leaving himself defenseless against what could only be considered an unusually blistering heat for the beginning of September. "It's so hot. Why can't we just throw some grow magic on the leaves and get out of here?"

I wanted to snap, remind her that she wasn't asked to be here and that she wasn't exactly going to stay welcome if she kept up her bad attitude, but I knew that it would be playing into her game, so I restrained myself. Instead, I gently explained to her why we were not using magic to speed up the process. "We can't use magic on the plants to make them grow because when someone eats or drinks something we created here, they would be subject to growing or changing similarly. That's not something we could do to the humans in our town, especially if we want to stay under the radar."

Harriet's cross expression didn't change, nor did her attitude despite the magic my mom sent to help cool her the rest of the way. I realized that she would probably stay unhappy until we were back inside the house.

Grace and I shared an entertained look, equally choosing to ignore her complaining, and got back to work; we were using the last of the sunshine to work on our tans which meant tank tops and short shorts complete with matching flip-flops. I noticed how Tate looked down at me with fire beneath his eyes when he looked at my exposed skin. Grace wasn't subtle that she had taken notice of it too, her elbow knocked against my side. I also watched her try to show off her tan legs to Huxley, even going as far as to walk past him in a casual saunter that was indeed not casual at all. I knew her well enough to understand that she never did anything simple regarding boys. It was always profoundly thought over and almost methodical in the way she knew how to control their reaction.

My mind was trying to make sense of what was going through Huxley's head, but the way Seth smacked him upside the back of the head when his eyes followed after her took care of that question.

She was victorious in her pursuit, and Huxley was helpless.

We all continued working hard to finish the garden before the sun set. The boys made haste by creating holes in rows, and each of us girls followed behind them, dropping in the seeds. Grandma and Aunt Mira used their magic to moisten the ground.

Harriet had given up on even pretending to help us, sitting in a rocking chair up on the porch with a glass of lemonade that Mom had fixed, her shoes kicked off, and she seemed ridiculously carefree, like us working in front of her was just for her entertainment. I tried to act like her self-righteous attitude didn't bother me, but it was especially bothersome when she waved her hand in the air and asked me to get her a refill. "Blair, would you get me a refill of my drink? I am just positively parched." I hadn't heard more entitled words come outside of anyone's mouth. My right eye did a not-so-subtle twitch of frustration. "I would use my magic and do it myself, but we wouldn't want the Cabals to track me down. I would hate for them to track me to where we are so exposed here." It almost seemed like she implied that the little girls would be at risk.

My nieces weren't so much helping as they danced around outside in the garden. They were creating their own entertainment since Celeste had banned cartoons on the weekends. They danced around in their little fairy dresses with their sparkly wands outstretched to help any flower that looked wilted. Celeste sent her magic over to assist since neither girl had gotten hers yet.

My eyes bounced around our group, hoping that one of my sisters would see the desperation in my eyes and run to my rescue, but everyone else just seemed glad she hadn't singled them out and kept their eyes on the ground. I sat on top of the bucket I had been using and tried not to stomp my feet as I walked up the path. Traveling up the stairs, I barely slowed down as I took the cup from her hand. She's lucky that I didn't take her entire arm with me.

Filling her glass took no time at all. What took the longest was deciding whether I could justify spitting into it before I handed it back to her. My conscience advised me otherwise, so I grabbed a bendy straw from the bottom drawer, already planning to be my alibi if asked what took me so long. Quickly I moved down the same path, barely pausing as she reached for the glass. I didn't bother to say anything except for a curt, "You're welcome," as she thanked me for getting it for her. I restrained myself from pointing out that I didn't do anything a human couldn't have done since there was no point. It would be only disregarded. We were all doomed to wait on her hand and foot until she left and moved on. Mom would have our heads if we didn't. I returned to pick up my bucket, and moved closer to where Tate was, using him as a shield to control my bad attitude. If anyone was going to keep me in line, it would be him.

"I can't believe that you did it. I would have made her get it herself," He leaned in closer to me to whisper in my ear. The heat of his breath made my heart jump from my chest. I loved it when he was this close to me. "It would have been justified. No one would have blamed you."

Slowly and slyly, I turned to him with a fake smile. I knew there were eyes all around us, especially the susceptible eyes of my nieces. "Don't you know that it's better to be kind?"

"Kindness never looked as good on me as it does on you. Don't look at me like that. I'm trying here," Tate bit back at me after he saw the expression on my face. His deep eyes were already staring down into mine as if he could read every thought that went through my mind. "I am already putting my magic over her to cool her down. Is that not me being kind? Do I need to do more to win your approval?"

I tried not to be annoyed that he was doing something nice for her, especially since it was so rare for him to go outside of himself and help others. I knew he was doing it because he knew I valued that characteristic in people, but I didn't feel any less jealous. "Trust me. I am well aware of how you are helping her."

"Has the green in your eyes always been there?" Even a fool could see that he was not referring to the hazel color that I was born with, rather, he pointed toward the jealousy he could see I was struggling to deal with. I hated how we all continued to flip over ourselves to ensure Harriet had a good experience. It didn't seem fair to the rest of us who had to do the *flipping*. It didn't help how ungrateful she was to us.

Aunt Mira and Penelope stood to the left of me, talking in hushed tones that I was finally picking up now that Tate had stopped whispering to me. Once he stepped away from me, it let my brain have the space to intake other information, especially knowing that I should be paying attention to the two of them before they devised a sinister plan.

Aunt Mira got a deep look in her eyes as she watched a stray butterfly fly through our group. She was trying to get her attention off Harriet's lousy attitude and onto something brighter, a plan she created with Penelope's help. "W.B.

Yeats said it best, 'the world is full of magic things, patiently waiting for your senses to grow sharper.' It's a wonder that humans are so unaware of all that we do. Knowing what was happening in their town would shock them all."

It was a diversion, but she wasn't wrong. If humans even got the slightest idea of what was happening outside their world, there would be no way they could leave us alone; it would turn us all into a genie in a lamp. They would rub it until it shined like pure brass.

Penelope, the apparent mastermind behind the diversion, used that as her opportunity to slip away, making a brief comment over her shoulder about a music lesson that she had to give, which meant a video call in her bedroom since the boys had banned independent travel. The rest of us used her escape as our reminder to put our heads down and get to work. Our entire group hurried to go through the rest of the garden. We all started to disperse once the last plant was taken care of. Celeste took the girls inside to get them all cleaned up while Grandma, Aunt Mira, and Mom went into the kitchen to cook dinner as a thank-you to our group. The boys cleaned up the larger tools, which left Grace and me to take care of the rest.

I tried not to pay attention to Harriet as she came bouncing down the steps; feeling fulfilled from her break, she seemed to be getting up to help finish the job. She even went so far as to pick up a shovel and carry it to the shed, something I would have never guessed to happen.

Tate kissed my head and told me the Guardians would shower before dinner. They had done the most out of our group, and the sweat that dripped down their bodies proved it. Grace let her wagging tongue follow behind Huxley, landing her on the other side of the door and into the house.

She seemed to forget for a second that *he* was supposed to pursue *her*.

Slowly I realized that Harriet and I were the only two in our group still outside. She managed to avoid any actual work, even when she was standing out in the sun, but was suddenly determined to grab the remaining tools and drag them into the shed. I would be a fool to guess that her timing was not with a purpose. She was fraudulent in her grin; whatever she said would not be good. "Do you know why I struggle with you so much?"

It was a very bold thing to say out loud, especially since she was the one who was in the wrong, but we were alone, so what did she have to lose by being honest? If I told anyone what she said, she would only deny it, bat her eyes, and turn the conversation against me. "I assume it is because of my family?"

"No, you can keep them. They are too much to handle." That seemed a little unnecessary, even if sometimes it was true. "I struggle because you walk the earth with a power that echoes with each step you take. How could you have such a power and not use it?" She gave me a dark look that seemed more profound than her eyes. "I would kill for such a power."

I wouldn't put it past her, either. Something about how her eyes darkened made me think she could do that.

Chapter Thirteen

The road to hell is paved with good intentions, but that was not what was happening now.

Harriet was paving her road full of misery with the intention of causing us all to worry, and she was probably going to cause our ultimate destruction if she got her way. She might not care about us, but we cared about her, which constantly put us at a significant disadvantage. Especially now as Grace and I ran down the sidewalk chasing after her.

Harriet had joined us on the field, deciding after much groveling from Seth to give us a shot since our request was simple. We only wanted to teach her some self-defense so she could handle herself. None of us were expecting a lot from her in the ways of the battle when that day came, but we didn't want to leave her defenseless either. The last time she faced the Cabals, she survived by running and hiding until they vacated the area. That wouldn't work this time, they would not leave any survivors.

Even with us giving her the simplest instructions, she didn't last long.

Harriet stood on the field for only a few seconds longer than twenty minutes. I could have sworn she was timing it. Her face progressively got more annoyed at our antics before stomping her foot in classic Blair fashion and taking off toward the Walker household.

With a pointed look from Seth, Grace and I took off after her. She still didn't know Salem well enough to wander on her own, especially not having the training to defend herself against the creatures hiding in the shadows if they finally decided to show themselves. None of us were allowed to walk alone, especially at night. That was per the Guardian's request, not that Harriet would listen to that or even us as we called off after her.

We were just chasing after the sounds of her footsteps with how fast she was running down the street; she also didn't care that we were shouting after her in hopes of slowing her down.

Grace and I were a third of the way back to the Walker house when we first heard it.

It was the hissing noise that came with evil.

I quickly motioned with my hand for Grace to stay silent and tried not to give away that I knew they were there while I surveyed the space around us, hoping to see where it was coming from.

Magic shot out from the shade. The feeling of sharp shocks going up and through my legs caused me to come crashing to the ground. The electricity they sent through me caused my appendages to shake with a fury of movement. My flailing limbs barely missed Grace as I flew to the ground.

"Grace! Go!" I screamed as loud as I could after her, praying that she was faster than the thing that had gotten me. "Quick. You have to run!"

It was just the two of us on this path, and I was worried about what that would mean for her if there were more of them waiting to attack. Whoever this was had already downed me. If I found a way to keep them occupied, it would give her a chance to get out of here alive if she ran fast enough. I hoped Harriet was far enough away to be safe if there were more of them, and I hoped she was smart enough not to turn back around for us if she heard my screams.

I pulled my wand from where I had tucked it into my boot, using my magic to try to get my feet underneath me. Whoever it was that attacked us was a lot faster than I was. Their hand then shot out just as quickly as their magic had and latched onto my ankle, yanking me closer to them and stopping my escape.

"Not so fast there," They snarled as their other hand reached out for my leg, stopping my attempts to kick them away. "You aren't getting away that easily, you little Witch."

I jerked my body so aggressively that when the person tried to pull me closer, it flipped me from my belly to my back. This presented a tactical advantage so that I could finally see who it was that had me. His hood was covering the top of his face to conceal his identity, but the combination of our shaky movements caused it to slip back and reveal his face, and it was just as dark as his actions.

The man had a menacing look across his face; his skin darkened by the sun and dirt, with intricate tattoos creeping up the sides. The deep brown of his eyes stared back at me as his lips curled into a snarl, working as a team to intimidate me. He looked ready to growl at me or take a bite; either way, I was nervous about what he had planned.

Deciding to ditch the use of my magic, I reached instead

for the pink dagger that I now kept in my waistband. I finally felt ready for what they were going to do next.

When he reached out for me again, I dug the blade into his forearm like I had done to the man in the illusion. Instead of a tree that appeared the first time, the man beneath my knife screamed in pain. Sadly, the pain my weapon caused him didn't force his hand to release me like I needed it to.

My hand pulled back, quickly retrieving the knife, and went in for another spot on his body. I chose his left bicep, sinking it in, and started dragging the knife down the muscle, hoping to inflict the most pain I could so he would let go of me. Tate was right. It was helpful to carry a knife.

With blood pouring out of his arm, he let go and retreated from me. Thankfully, with my knife in hand, I still had a defense in case he decided to strike again. He reached over with his good arm, gripping the remains of his bloody arm together to keep it from continuing to lose blood. With his face scrunched together in pain, he growled again in my direction, "How dare you! Now I am going to kill you."

Taking his distraction as an opportunity to escape, I jumped to my feet, still facing the man. He didn't seem to be taking much care of his injury, instead staring me down. I could see that he was planning a new course of attack now that he knew I would fight back; even with the disadvantage the knife in his arm had brought, he seemed enthusiastic that I wouldn't make this easy. He liked the chase and the challenge I had presented him with.

I stood there holding the dagger in one hand and my wand in the other, ready to deploy whichever one was needed first. He reached out for me again. The stretching motion of his fingers seemed slower than I knew they were moving. My mind was working too hard to try and predict his movements before they happened. I could still feel the stinging feeling of his magic coursing through me; the electric shocks weren't going away.

A bright light shot out from behind me as the street-lamps reacted to the use of powerful magic. That same magic reached out and grabbed onto him in a fury of wind, pinning him against the brick wall behind us.

Grace didn't run away like I told her to; instead, she took his distraction as an opportunity to save me. She was the one using her magic to suspend him against the brick wall across from us, allowing me to fully stand up, regain control of my body, and let my magic join the conversation. I flashed her a grateful smile and surveyed the path around us. There didn't seem to be anyone else waiting for an opportunity to attack, but that didn't mean they weren't just around the corner. I could see that Grace was weary of the situation too; her eyes bounced around the path.

Raising my hand, I pressed my magic against him, letting the pressure hit his open wound so that the pain would hopefully make him give me the answers I sought. Something had snapped in me. Seeing the look in Grace's eyes reminded me of how vulnerable we were alone. I focused on my cousin, not the man, and the battle we were facing. Having the upper hand meant that I could finally catch my breath, reobtaining the ability to stand straight. Although that wasn't helping me have a clearer sense of what we would do next.

"Why were you waiting for us?" I moved forward with my interrogation, hoping that it would clear a path on what to do next. "Why did you attack us? How did you know we were going to be here?"

"I was sent here to capture you, Blair Bradbury. They want you, and if I don't get you first, hundreds more are coming for you. They all want your head." He pushed out his energy against us, trying to break our magic and the control it had over him. "Count your moments because they will come for you and be successful. You will not survive the descent of the Cabals." His magic was there, but it was weaker than anything Grace and I had on him, so he stayed pressed against the bricks. It was a temporary solution to a permanent problem. One of us wouldn't be able to hold him in place while the other ran for help, and I wouldn't want either of us to be left alone while the other did that anyway.

My mind refocused on his words, realizing that it was me he had come for. If I could distract him, then she could get the opportunity to run away. I used my magic to force open the wound on his arm, making him react further, and his screams of pain gave me the strength to keep going with my questioning. The harsh words Tate told me he had been trained in were suddenly the actions of my hands. I hated that I had to cause this man pain, even if he had been willing to do it to me first. I knew that if I didn't use pain as a reasoning device, then he would only regain his strength and come after us again. I couldn't risk that, not when I had Grace and the others to care for. Their lives were the only thing that mattered. "Now, tell me who is coming!"

"Are you dense? I just told you; the Cabals are coming for you, and there is nothing that you can do to stop it."

I desperately needed answers. That wasn't enough information, so I pushed against the man again. I was using my magic as an extension of myself; I focused on it heavily and forced it to be stronger than ever before. "Why are you here? Who wants me captured?"

He grinned back at me; the sharpness of his teeth almost seemed like their own weapons ready to deploy now that the rest of his body was out of the equation. The opportunity would be there if I took a step closer, so I took that step backward instead. I knew he had nothing to lose and would bite me if given a chance, but there was some relief in knowing it was only me he was focused on.

"I was sent here to get you and take you back to them. It doesn't matter what happened today or what you did to me," He spat out. "They know that you are here, and they are coming for you, Blair Bradbury. They will kill you as soon as they get the chance."

His words caused my body to react before I allowed it. The only thought going through my head was that if he escaped, he would only return stronger than ever before and with backup. His head dropped to the side as I pulled all of the magic from his body into my own. My desperation for answers was overloaded by fear from his ominous words and the fact that Grace and I were defenseless. The wound on his arm had lost too much blood for his body to handle, the lack of magic taking his life force from his body.

"You killed him!" Grace screamed out, tears falling down her face at what she had just seen — what I had just done to this man. Her loss of control caused his lifeless body to fall to the ground in a grueling slump. I could see that she wanted to check on him and make sure he was dead, but even his lifeless body was too scary for us to come near. "I can't believe you killed him! We must call the police and turn ourselves in before they come after us; that will only be worse. If we go now, then we can explain ourselves."

I realized I would have to be strong for both of us if we returned to our families or even our team. That would have to be our first stop, and the Guardians would know what to do. I gripped her shoulders tightly and gave her an aggressive shake, trying to pull her attention back to me before she could freak out more. "Grace, we can't call the police. He was a witch just like you, and he died because I stabbed him and then took all his magic. The human police won't be able to do anything to help him or his family, and they wouldn't be able to help us either." I tried to explain everything going through my head, the words I used to calm *myself* down. "We have to get back to Tate; he will know what to do and how to handle this."

Grace pulled herself together just enough to hold a tight grip on my hand, and the two of us started the walk back to the football field, both of us completely forgetting about Harriet and her possibly still being alone on the very same path we had just killed a man on.

Her body shook throughout the walk back, just as mine did. Our adrenaline was keeping us going, even if nothing else was. We looked twice at any shadow we passed, hoping to see something before anyone could attack us again. We quickly returned down the path and cleared the ridge that dropped down to where the football field sat. I felt relief fall over me when I saw our entire team standing there, especially the way Tate stood in the middle: tall, powerful, and extremely capable of handling everything.

I knew that if anyone else came here to attack us, at least we wouldn't be alone. The Guardians would be there to help us handle what had just happened. They could also deal with the body we just carelessly left behind.

Fabian and Ninnie saw us first, looking up from their training with the bow and arrows to see the rest of our slow walk back to the field. One of them must have made a noise to announce our sudden arrival because, slowly, everyone else turned or raised their heads to our approach.

Once he saw me standing there covered in a thick layer of mud and blood, Tate took off running in my direction. His feet moved so fast that they were almost a blur as he crossed the field. He stopped just inches before me and paused, almost afraid to touch me now that he was standing there. "Blair, what happened to you?"

The tears came out in thick trails down my cheeks. Now that I didn't have to be brave for Grace, my body was letting itself have the drop of adrenaline it had been searching for. I was always safe in his arms and didn't have to remind myself that he would care for me no matter what I asked.

"Tate. He's dead! I can't believe he's dead," I cried the words out as I tried to hold myself together with my hands, dropping the bloody wand into the overgrown grass at our feet. It hadn't been the thing to save me. "I killed him! He got me first, and then Grace stopped him so I could escape his arms. It was awful, and then I killed him. The man is dead, and it's all my fault."

The shock of the situation finally broke over, the sobs overtaking my body until I only made a series of noises that signaled my distress. Tate looked at my face, quietly looking over me to decide what to do next. "Blair, I need you to do something for me. I will teach you how to breathe like in the Academy before we go into a tactical situation. Take a deep breath in for four seconds, hold it for four seconds, and then exhale through your nose and mouth simultaneously. Do you think you can you do that for me?" I felt his hands slide down my arms until they landed in my hands, the tightening of his grip helping me go through the exercise. "When you see black, I need you to breath."

My breath came in and out the way he directed me to, and when I was done, I did it all over again, repeating the exercise until the darkness fell further away. I could finally see more than the dead man. I nodded with each breath, trying to remain as at peace as possible, although the tightening of my throat showed how close I was to crying again. How he looked down on me reminded me how strong I needed to be.

He still hadn't acknowledged what I said, so I repeated, "The man is dead, and I was the one who killed him."

"None of that matters right now. I don't care about any of it. I need you to look at me and talk to me." Tate reached out and moved the strand of hair covering my face. There was a slight scratch at my hairline that I knew had a little blood coming out of it based on how my hair was sticking to it. The way that I had fallen on the concrete probably meant that I had other cuts or scratches on my body, especially from when I dropped to my knees when his magic shot through my body. My hands were still shaking, and my breathing was labored. I realized that I was having a panic attack and was just starting to understand that he already knew that was where I was headed and was trying to stop it.

"Tate, I think I'm going to be sick."

His face danced in and out of focus as he spoke. The way he taught me to breathe did nothing in comparison to the calming sounds of his voice, although the combination was what made me stay in the moment. "Blair, I need you to talk to me and tell me you are okay. I can't move on or focus on anything you say until I *know* you are okay."

"I think so. I think I'm okay." That word felt empty, we had said it so many times within a few seconds that it had lost all meaning, even to my ears.

His hand didn't stop its search, and it followed a path down my body until it rested on my hip. His other hand checked the rest of my face for more scratches or cuts that his eyes might have missed when he went over me the previous times. "I'm glad that you are okay. You have no idea how badly you scared me." His lips came down onto my forehead, the fierceness of his kiss confirming how much my appearance had shaken him.

I nodded my head in response. The rest of our group stared at us from where they stood on the field, almost seeming nervous to come closer until Tate figured out the situation.

"The problem is that I don't understand what you are saying," Tate gave me a concerned look, much deeper than the one he had given me before, now that he was sure I could control my tears. "Now, I need you to take another deep, deep, and long breath." He raised his hand with my inhale and lowered it with my exhale, giving a visual of what he wanted me to do. "Then tell me what happened to you. Let's start with why you are covered in blood. I'm gathering that it's not all yours."

I did as he directed, finally able to get the breath back into my lungs, although that did nothing to stop the tears from continuing down my cheeks. At least this time, they were silent as they ran down their set path and collected under my chin. "We were running down the street after Harriet when someone's magic reached out and grabbed onto me. He sent a shock of electricity through my body, so I would lose control and hit the ground. It was a complete ambush; he was waiting for us. Somehow, he knew we were coming."

Out of the corner of my eye, I saw my sisters and cousin come closer with the other Guardians. Even Ninnie did the same, although her steps were more hesitant than the ones the others took. They had all held back, letting Tate take the lead until they knew we were okay. Piper went to her sister first, comforting her in the same way Tate was doing for me.

"We were just going down the path after Harriet. Then he shot his magic out at her. When she hit the ground, he grabbed onto her and wouldn't let go," Grace's voice shook, trying to combine the words into a coherent sentence. "We had been going after Harriet, but she went down a path that we weren't expecting, so we had to pick up the pace to keep up with her. Then he came out of the shadows and got to us. No matter what she did, he wouldn't let go of Blair. He was relentless," Grace jumped in to help me share the story, although neither of us made much sense in getting out the details they were looking for.

I knew we were both shaking with something that could only be pointed back to what we had gone through and would stay with us.

"How did you get away?" Tate looked down at the blood on my hands, the blood-stained wand, and the knife I desperately wanted to drop onto the grass. The shock I was going through wouldn't let my body let go of it, even as I concentrated on the action.

My knife was my only form of defense. Even now that I was with those I trusted most, my body was still on edge. From the look on his face, it was almost like he knew what had happened before I said anything, being able to piece together the broken parts of our story, especially from the way we both looked. I couldn't see myself, but Grace was covered in a spray of blood that likely happened when I stabbed the man or when she shot him into the wall.

I raised my shaking hand almost like I was presenting the knife to him; it was covered in a thick layer of the dead man's blood, matching the rest of my look. "I stabbed him! Then when he didn't let go of me, I stabbed him again. Tate, I dragged the knife down the muscle in his arm until he let go of me. I didn't know what else to do."

He pushed my hand out of the way, not caring what it looked like or what I had done with it. He didn't even care that the blade had been pointed at him in a defensive stance. Tate pulled me into a bone-crushing hug. His hand went up once more, and his fingers dove into my hair, pressing my head into the center of his chest, finally making me feel safe.

"You need to forget that and understand how good you did. I am so proud of you!" He rubbed my back with his other hand in a comforting manner that made me feel better, especially with how his arms seemed to make a cage around me. "Your survival instinct kicked in! That is some-thing to celebrate and be proud of. You protected yourself and Grace when it was your life or theirs. That is what all of our training has set you up for."

I didn't feel like the hero he was setting me up to be. I felt precisely who I was.

A murderer.

The girls huddled around and asked Grace more ques-tions, not wanting to interrupt the moment Tate and I were having. I couldn't tell if that was a relief or not. I was constantly stealing moments like this with Tate, waiting for the meaner version to return.

"I used my magic to pull him away from her, and it made it so she could stand up and add her magic too. Then between us, we could keep him in place while Blair tried to speak to him." Grace seemed to feel better than I did, taking the opportunity to share what had happened to us. Her body seemed to have stopped shaking, and she was breathing better, some of which made me feel at least a little okay about the situation. This was something that could break her, but it seemed like she was going to make it through it. Her life was the only thing that fueled me in those moments, and I realized that feeling would be the only thing that would keep me going. "He didn't tell us anything useful. Just let us know that someone was coming. They had sent him here to capture Blair and bring her back to the Cabals. They know that we are building an army."

My sisters had finally gotten tired of waiting for the moment between me and Tate to be over. Penelope made the first move of putting her hand through the gap to push Tate away and finally get to me. My sisters grabbed my shoulders and held me in a group hug while I cried over what I had gone through. Tate did reach through the mass and grab onto my hand, offering me support that I was missing when he was forced to step away.

"How did you finally get away?" Penelope asked us, and with those words, I felt sick again. I didn't know how I would explain what I had done now that my body had started to calm down. It was bad enough to tell Tate, but I knew he would understand. My sisters would try to understand, but they would also be clued into how dangerous I was.

Grace nodded at me, approving of me sharing the experience with everyone, which made me feel better about her wanting to run to the police since it seemed to have left her mind now that we had gotten back to the Guardians. I tightened my grip on Tate's hand and started talking. "When I pulled his magic from him, I realized that was what was keeping him alive. Without that, the cuts I made in his arm had lost too much blood for him to fight back or escape. Then he died. Right there in front of us in a slump on the ground."

The Guardians spoke alone momentarily and called the training to an end, deciding that Grace and I had gone through enough for one night. Huxley, Fabian, and Seth took off in the direction Grace and I pointed them in. They would take care of the man, whatever that meant, while Tate ensured we got home safely.

They all knew I would not do well if Tate was separated from me.

Grace and Piper were the closest, so we all walked to their house as a group. The two of them ran up the stairs and inside. Neither one of them turned around to look at us. Grace was still shaken up, and I think she was grateful not to go home alone. I was thankful for that too. There was relief in knowing my sisters would be with me when we got there, but I was more grateful that Tate held my hand the entire time. Since the second he met me on the field, he hadn't let go of me, and it didn't seem he would let it go anytime soon.

Ninnie's house was the furthest, but my sisters agreed to drop her off next knowing that when Tate dropped us off, I probably wasn't going to let him leave. He seemed just as desperate to stay with me as I was with him.

Tate was on a high level of defense; his eyes surveyed the path before us with his muscles tight. They were ready to deploy when needed. His mind was twitching with defense tactics. I could tell he was presenting his size in a way that would deter anyone from coming near. They would only see him as a threat, especially if they came close enough to see the look in his eyes. My sisters were the bravest, walking at the front with weapons, looking like the warriors we were all training to be. Ninnie held a knife too, but she had it differently. She stayed almost stitched to my side like I was to Tate's.

"Are you okay?" I asked her softly, repeating the question I had been asked multiple times since I rejoined the group. I hoped she felt close enough to me to share what was on her mind since it seemed like something more than the person who came after Grace and me.

She nodded and leaned closer to me so no one else would hear our conversation. "I haven't told anyone this, but I have felt darkness around me. Especially when I am at home. I am worried about Harriet and what she was exposed to, especially before she came to us. I can only imagine what she saw and how it would stay with someone."

I realized that might not have been how I would describe how I felt around her, but I had noticed that Harriet had a darkness inside her. A small part of me did think it was interesting how she took off down the same path that brought the man out, especially since it wasn't the fastest way to get to the Walker House or the way most people would go. It seemed too far outside of a coincidence, and it was something I had already planned on talking to Grace about once we had gotten some space from the situation. A clear head was the only way that we would be able to move forward and discern what the truth was.

There wasn't much I could do to help her or calm how she was feeling, but I extended the offer anyway, "Is there anything I can do to help you feel better?"

She shook her head quickly in the way of a response, looking down at the sides of the streets and deep into the shadows. It was almost as if she saw something there that the rest of us were missing. "If you would just keep an eye out for her? And maybe don't let your guard down when you are near her. I don't know what that darkness could mean for her or what it would mean for the rest of us if we continued to be near it."

Ninnie remained silent the rest of our walk to her house, not letting herself be vulnerable again like I wished she would. She flipped back and forth about as quickly as Tate did, which made it hard to know how they felt.

The wind picked up an unsettling chill and hit us all with it. I watched my sisters and Ninnie all shiver. I pulled Tate's jacket closer to my body; it had been his solution to my being covered in blood until we could get me into a shower and change of clothes. Tate was more than twice my size, so the jacket was as well, but it didn't do anything to help me now except cover me. I could still feel the man's dried blood sticking to my bare skin. That was the one thing I was desperate to get away from.

My sisters hugged Ninnie goodbye, displaying the newfound bond they had created with the Walker girl we barely knew. Then Ninnie did the same as Grace and Piper did, running up the stairs and into her house, although her door didn't shut behind her like my cousins did.

Mrs. Walker stepped out onto the porch and stared us all down with a sad expression, particularly Tate and me, where we were hidden behind the rest of the group. "Tate, Blair, I would like to speak with you. Alone if possible."

She phrased it like we had the option of refusing, but we both knew that we didn't have one. She wasn't going to let us leave. My sisters each gave me a confused look as Tate and I walked up the stairs of the Walker house. Neither one of them seemed to trust her either. Mrs. Walker had us step into her home, leaving my sisters sitting on the porch steps while we ducked inside and followed her to the dining room. The layout resembled my house, but the Walker's place somehow had a darker atmosphere.

All around me, I could feel the darkness that Ninnie had mentioned, and I flagged it in my mind as something to be concerned about, I could ask Tate about it later.

I saw Harriet standing in the kitchen and living room

doorway. It was apparent she had not been invited to participate in this conversation, but that she wouldn't miss what was said.

With Mrs. Walker's back to me, I raised my hand to cast a spell on my earring, bonding it to the ones my sisters wore outside. With this, they could hear everything that I heard. The downside of that being I could also hear the noises they made. I could only hope they would be as silent as possible while we were connected since there was no way to control the volume. I couldn't be sure we had a good connection until someone started talking, so we usually turned it on *before* going anywhere, but beggars could not be choosers. My only option was to wait and hope that if anything happened, they would be able to hear it and come rushing in to help.

"I imagine you are curious as to why I want a private meeting with you," Her voice trailed off. The tilt of her head toward the kitchen made it obvious she was anticipating listeners. I wasn't sure if she could see Harriet by the shadows of the wall. "It might come as a surprise to you, but the two of you and your influence are instrumental in the lives of those closest to me."

I wanted to catch Tate's eye and silently ask him if he knew Harriet was there listening, but his face was even more disengaged in the conversation than mine was. He stared ahead with a menacing look, choosing not to look directly at Mrs. Walker like she wanted him to.

"I can hear her. Can you?" Celeste's voice came out in a flurry in my ears. She was asking Penelope, who thankfully reminded her to be quiet so they could listen to the rest of our conversation.

I felt better knowing they were there and aware of what was being said. I took the opportunity to watch Tate and

Mrs. Walker, feeling confident that they didn't hear anything and that my face didn't give anything away either. I realized I needed to pay better attention to the conversation before me since my concentration was heavily set on keeping a blank expression on my face.

If I had learned anything from Tate, it was not to let others know what I was thinking; it gave them too much power — something he used against me often.

She presented us both with a seat by extending her arm formally. She was doing everything possible to separate herself from any emotion. Mrs. Walker sat at the opposite end of the table and folded her hands in front of us, making it feel like we were sitting across from an authority figure. "I'm glad you dropped Ninnie off; it presented this opportunity to be alone with you. I am hoping to have an open and honest conversation. Do you think that would be possible?"

It was patronizing how she talked down to us like we were children. I could see Tate's jaw twitching as he surveyed the situation. I bit my tongue to restrain myself from talking. "What do you want to discuss? I need to get the girls home before it gets any later," He almost spit the words out. Something about the situation bothered him more than he wanted either one of us to know.

Mrs. Walker didn't let Tate's impatient tone stop her; she had a mission in mind. "Harriet cannot handle the pressure you put on her to join your 'army.' You have no idea what she went through, and this is not something she can handle or add to her plate." Her voice went up a decibel with each word, further proving how strongly she felt about this. "It's bad enough that I can't convince Ninnie to back out of this nonsense. Now you are dragging Harriet into it as well."

I didn't think the quotations around 'army' were necessary, and it only pointed to how incapable she thought we were.

"We are not dragging either one of them into this. It is all within their rights to join the army we created, just as it is within your right to throw a fit like you are now." Tate countered with the intent of hurting her. He was not going forward with kid gloves on as I expected him to.

I could hear the sharp breath intake from one of my sisters. I made sure that the expression on my face matched the noise those in the room with me might have heard so that it didn't raise any red flags. I don't think Mrs. Walker would appreciate knowing my sisters were outside listening.

"Harriet is in a very vulnerable position. Can you even imagine what she went through? Being pursued and tortured in such a manner only to be left for dead," She said, implying we were completely heartless for not giving Harriet more grace.

Her response gave me pause; Ninnie said that Harriet had gotten away in just enough time. That she had somehow found it possible to hide until they were gone. Nothing was said about her being tortured and left for dead before she came to Salem.

I tilted my head in the direction of the hallway and saw the shadow of Harriet standing there. She was still hidden behind the wall and trying to be as silent and still as possible, hinting that maybe Mrs. Walked didn't know she was there like I thought.

The muscles in Tate's crossed arms were incredibly tight, more than when we were outside and vulnerable to an attack. I could see that he was trying to present himself as a threat, filling his chest with as much air as possible and holding his shoulders back. "I believe Harriet is an adult, and if she is looking for vengeance, then we are happy to have her join our forces." He shot his eyes off to the doorway when he heard the shifting of someone's weight. "That being said, no one in this room is pushing her to participate. She came to the field tonight to learn self-defense, which was her decision. Seth, *your nephew*, was the one who set that up and asked her to come. Neither Blair nor I had anything to do with that, so bringing the two of us here is pointless."

I wasn't sure I would blame Seth, but I was happy that there was no longer a crown of blame on my head, so I was willing to go along with whatever Tate had to say, especially if it would get us out of here. I tried to keep the corner of my eye trained on Harriet, my trust in her ever wavering, especially now that Mrs. Walker treated her like she was the weakest link in their family chain. I couldn't understand why Harriet would present herself so small if she had nothing to hide.

"Just imagine her situation. Even tonight, she ran home in a fury, saying you were screaming after her. I cannot believe you would be rude toward anyone; let alone someone you barely know." She raised her eyebrow and spoke in a condescending tone meant to belittle us further. I could see why Ninnie was so afraid of her.

This comment also caused me to pause. Her words did not match what I had been told before. "How long has she been home?"

Mrs. Walker didn't seem to have anything to hide, although the plainness of her face didn't change to show any indicators of how she felt. "She has been here just over two hours."

My mind moved faster than it ever had; the training from the boys made me sharper. We had run after her at 7:22; Grace had looked at her watch when we started running, joking that if she kept track of the time, then maybe the boys would go easier on us when we got back to them. When Grace and I returned to the team, it was 8:15. Tate had me keep track of the second hand on his watch to help regulate my breathing.

Even if Harriet had been the fastest runner in the world, there is no way that she could have been here for two hours. Where could she have gone in that time? The two stories did not match up.

"There is too much that you are asking of her. I implore you to take a step back and review it in your mind. What if that had happened to you? Then where would you be now?" Somehow, she was pleading with us with a straight face. The absence of emotion ruined the message she was trying so hard to convey.

My mind tried to flip the situation, imagining my mom or sister saying the same thing and what their faces would look like with those words or those emotions. The image it created was very different than the one on her face.

Tate was done, that message was loud and clear across his face. He stood up from the table, pushing against it to stand, and threw his hand down for me to put mine into. I was grateful he wasn't planning on leaving me there. "Mrs. Walker. As you have heard me say, we are not asking anything of her, and if she is saying otherwise, then that is a conversation that you need to go over with her, not us." He pushed the chair back in, treating her home with the same respect he treated me. "Do that first, and then we can return to our conversation."

The four of us walked back to our house in complete silence. My sisters seemed to relax a little now that there were fewer of us to look after, although their eyebrows were still pinched together like mine were.

Even if my sisters seemed to relax, Tate only gripped my hand tighter. The conversation with Mrs. Walker stressed him out even if he didn't say anything out loud. I hoped that once we were alone, he might be more willing to open up about what he was thinking and how he thought that conversation went, although our history did not point to that being true. There was a big chance he would only go silent again. I was under the impression that he did that only because he knew it would drive me crazy.

My sisters immediately ran up the stairs into the house just like everyone else had done. They might have been able to fake a level of calm before, but now that they were in the safety of their home, that was out the window.

I tried to relax, but there was still too much I was afraid of. My Guardian stayed outside with me, holding me tight. "Blair, you're going to be okay. Your bottom lip is quivering. Why are you going to cry?" Tate let go of my hand and put his arm around my shoulders, pulling our bodies closer together. It was probably the softest I had ever heard his tone be. "I'm here, and you will always be safe with me. Forget everything else and know that."

"I know, but now this is real. They want *me*! Tate, you don't understand it. He knew me by name." I tried to think back to the fight, the situation pacing in my mind almost like flipping through a thick stack of pictures. The man had only gone after me. He didn't even care that Grace was there or that he could get her. At first, I thought it was because I was on that side of the path. He had me down; if he had used his magic on her as he had done to me, he could have easily gotten us both. "Why are they coming after me? What is setting me apart from the rest of us?"

I let myself fall into him and find comfort in his strength. There was one thing that I knew for sure: Tate would handle the situation, especially when it got too over-whelming for me.

When we finally got inside and could tell her the entire story, Mom didn't do well with the news, which might have been why she allowed Tate to stay the night on my bedroom floor. She grabbed pillows and blankets to make a bed on the floor for him, which was a big step for her and put me and Tate in a new position within our relationship.

Although before we were allowed to go upstairs, Mom grilled me just as intensely as the Guardians had done. She cared less about what happened to the man and more about how I was feeling, asking me if I would be okay once the adrenaline fully settled down. She was already not doing well with the idea of us getting hurt, this only furthered her fears. All the Bradbury girls were grateful Tate was there just in case of any problems.

Tate closed the door behind us and laid his forehead against mine, letting his body almost engulf me with his arms coming down to my sides. Finally, he showed his full emotions, and how he felt for me only became stronger daily. The love potion was getting stronger each day it sunk into his skin. "Hell better lock their gates if I ever lost you," He kissed my lips gently without moving his body away from mine. The closeness of our bodies meant that I was encased in his warmth, which made part of tonight feel okay. "Blair, I don't think you understand what I feel for you or what lengths I would go to keep you safe."

I nodded back at him, completely understanding what he was saying because I felt the same way. Our bond was getting more complicated now that he was feeding into it. "That was an awful experience. I can't believe we made it out of there alive. If Grace left as I told her to, I would have died. Her bravery was what saved my life."

"Blair, you aren't giving yourself enough credit. You did it! Grace helped. I am not discrediting that because ultimately, she is what helped you get away. But your quick response was what saved your life. If you hadn't stabbed him, he would have taken that opportunity to take your magic. He would have relied on the physical touch as his anchor and pulled it from your body. I don't know how you managed to get back on your feet that quickly. I don't think you know what I would do if I lost you," He somehow managed to come even closer. The proximity and heat of his body were to blame for the flush that came to my cheeks. "You are amazing, and I will repeat it. I am so proud of you."

I wasn't proud of myself or Grace for what we had done. I had killed a man, and there was no coming back, even if Tate thought there was.

I was also trying not to think about the other Guardians and what 'take care of the body' meant, especially now that I knew all their training had prepared them for it.

Chapter Fourteen

The weight of what we went through held itself over me and Grace for weeks. I would have never described myself as depressed, but my mom and my sisters certainly did. Everyone was worried about the two of us. They were especially concerned about how that moment on the sidewalk had changed us, and, more than anything, they were all distraught over whether or not we would recover from it.

If Tate could help it, he never left my side. He had even taken up a permanent residence on the floor of my bedroom so that he could constantly be near me, which I would not have expected from the big tough Guardian. It made me feel good knowing he had a soft spot for me.

Even Aunt Mira had started treating us differently since the attack had happened. She had given Grace and me the easiest jobs at the store, trying to keep us sane by sticking to a simple routine. That meant restocking the store shelves with some new products she had just shipped in from Canada; even though we could use magic, she asked that we fill each one by hand.

Grace was doing better than I was, and while everyone was still concerned about her, most of them watched over me and ensured I was okay. They did this by piling on distractions whenever possible, which was probably why Ninnie had started to spend time at the store with us, although I knew better than to think that was the *only* reason she was there.

Ninnie's comment about Harriet and the darkness surrounding her stayed with me; even when I was in the deepest sorrows, that thought circled in my mind. It was something that I had also noticed when I was near her. I was worried that I felt it even more now, especially throughout the last few weeks since Harriet did make it a point to spend more time with us all.

The first time we were all together again, Harriet went in for a tight hug, whispering in my ear her apologies for what we had gone through and that it happened to coincide with her running away from our training team. It seemed almost like she realized how bad it looked on her end and that her influence on the matter was too quick to be blamed; I got the feeling she was trying to cover her tracks and shift the blame.

Ninnie did more than I expected when defending me against her roommate or keeping us separate. She stood beside me almost as a shield whenever Harriet was around, which opened the question as to how much she knew about Harriet and what she hadn't yet said to the rest of us. Ninnie was seeing more than us, especially how the show Harriet was willing to put on for those around her was so easy for her to flip on and off when she thought no one was watching.

"Ninnie, would you do me a favor and get me a glass of

water? I am just parched from all this work," Harriet asked Ninnie, putting out the straightforward request in a way that would be hard for her to refuse. We had been stacking the rest of our boxes on the shelf for the last hour, and we were taking our time getting items out of a large container and putting the contents onto its assigned shelf. "It seems to be hotter than normal in here. Is your air conditioning working?" She mumbled a few more complaints about the store's temperature, but I chose to ignore those to try and keep a happy attitude.

Ninnie nodded in agreement, rising from her position on the floor to go off to the backroom to get the water Harriet was politely asking for. If I were her, I would have said no or reminded Harriet that she could get her own.

Harriet gave us both a gentle smile, looking as non-threatening as ever until Ninnie crossed the corner, then she turned her body towards mine and turned up her charm. The soft expression quickly shifted to something else, something that showed just how quickly her brain was moving with the words, "How have you been? There seems to be a lot on your mind the last few days." She sounded sincere, but her smile was too broad, and her eyes seemed too trained on my face, like she was assessing me. "Is there anything that I can help you with?"

How dare she pretend not to know what was going on! She was well aware of the situation, acting like she didn't imply that she was so far above us that she was blissfully unaware of our problems.

"There has been a lot on my mind since that night, and a lot is happening in our world that has been out of my control. I imagine you can understand how hard that has been for me since you also have had many things happen out of your control." I tried to keep my voice as even as possible. I had to keep a level head about this if we would continue to have a rational conversation. Something in my body made me weary of being around her, similar to how the people in town would act around us. It wouldn't be that way if every word that came out of her mouth wasn't full of half-truths embedded between the lines and even more in the silences. "The situation the other night did shake me up and cause a lot of things to come into focus for me," I continued, "We are getting into a lot here, and this is only the beginning."

"Is that why you have decided to attach yourself to Ninnie? I would be aware of the company you keep." She warned.

I tried to keep the fake smile plastered on my face. It rivaled the one she had written across her own, both of us faking pleasantries to keep the conversation as light as possible. "I don't know what you are implying, but I think it's a good thing to have a friendship between us now that we spend much time together. We all need to support one another and have each other's backs if we make it through. I hoped you would support that plan after everything you have gone through and how everyone has stepped up."

"I guess you just don't know who she is." She looked down at me from the point of her upturned nose. I could not believe her ability to make me, and others, feel so small by simply being in the same room as us.

While I tried to rationalize the situation by reminding myself that only insecure people act out, it didn't help to know that I would need to remain pleasant as I would have to stay in her company for the foreseeable future.

"I know what kind of person she is. What I don't know is what kind of person you are," I spit out, shooting her down in the way I had been dying to do so since the moment she walked into the store today with her rotten attitude. Especially after what I had gone through the last few weeks and the small way I thought she was to blame. "I don't expect you to respect or appreciated any of us for protecting you and our families, but I will not warrant you speaking badly of Ninnie, especially after what she and her family has done for you."

Harriet didn't respond, looking back at me with her mouth open in shock when I finally told her I was done tolerating how she had been speaking to me since she got here. She silently returned to work, the chip on her shoulder ever prevalent after exchanging our harsh words. I tried to ignore how her bottom lip quivered, knowing that if I apologized, it would only tell her I was okay with how she had treated me and allow the behavior to continue.

Ninnie returned with a plastic water bottle for each of us and didn't acknowledge that there was tension in the air, which helped the three of us return to work without a problem. At least not one that we were willing to address, that might be the only way we would be able to get through our time together.

"Why don't we see if the boys want to do lunch after this?" I could tell that Ninnie stepping in was a way to separate us before any more words were lashed between us, especially now that she would be caught in the crossfire. "I know that they were too busy yesterday to stop for lunch; Seth and the boys were just famished when they returned to my house. Maybe we can get them to take a break today if we ask them nicely."

Aunt Mira was helping a customer at the front of the store, and Grace stood at the counter. The large smirk on my cousin's face showed how intently she had been listening to our conversation. She got a thrill hearing the words exchanged between Harriet and me. She especially seemed to enjoy how I talked back to her and was finally willing to put her in her place.

"I think that is just great. Blair, why don't you ask them? Maybe you can get Tate to concede. You get him to agree, and the rest will follow," Grace turned to the other girls and seemed to order them with her eyes to follow along without complaint. She could be scary when she wanted something to go her way, and this was no exception. "Ninnie, Harriet, and I will clean up this mess while you go ask."

There was a chance that Grace was creating a diversion, using Ninnie's idea as a chance to get me away from Harriet and tamper down the tension. More than that, there was a chance that she wanted her own opportunity to say the things sitting at the tip of her tongue and had just created the space to do so. I knew that she was also struggling with Harriet and how she could treat us, especially after the night of our battle with the mystery man. Grace also believed Harriet had something to do with it, even if she had no way to prove it. She was wise to be wary since the mystery man was the only thing that made sense from that night.

The door to the back room was shut, so I gave it a small, quiet knock, which seemed almost too soft for the loud noises I could hear on the other side of the door. The boys told us that only business was orchestrated behind that door, but I think they sometimes used their planning meet-ings to yell at each other since they weren't getting anywhere yelling at us. All of us girls desperately needed some tension relief, the incoming threat causing us to be a little overwhelmed. The boys were frustrated with us and what they considered a lack of progress.

They somehow managed to hear my knock because the door slowly opened, and Fabian's head peaked around the corner. He managed to keep the entry as closed as possible, not letting me see into what had become their back room and causing him to become a floating head. "Yeah? Are you okay?"

"We were wondering if you wanted to do lunch with us girls? We could go get something or be happy to bring something back here to eat together." I tried to look under where his head was floating. I hadn't cared about what they did in that back room until he was trying to keep it from me. Now it was like an itch that I couldn't reach, and I was desperate to scratch.

"Let me check. Wait here." Fabian threw his head back to talk to the other boys in the room. I approached the door, hoping to see what they were doing when it opened again, but he closed the door faster than I could joke about him needing to check with those in charge.

Tate's head popped around the corner to finish the conversation; our proximity forced me to take a hesitant step back. The flutter of butterflies that went through my abdomen was in a frenzy as his warm breath hit my cheek. "Yeah, you want to do lunch? Are you finally accepting my idea of us going on a date?"

Tate had kept the romance of our bond as a priority in his life since the attack. He had even shown up with a dozen red roses a few days ago for me to keep on my bedside table. Tate had made it his mission to convince me to go on a date and what a great adventure it would be. It was a way to distract me since the attack happened; he was working together with my sisters to 'fix' me.

However, there was an appeal to the two of us continuing our bond like we both wanted, but I also knew that the more we fed into it, the closer he potentially got to his death. He didn't seem to care about that part, even after I desperately tried to explain it to him, which only pointed to how potent the love potion was. He would have still been able to remain logical if it wasn't for it overtaking his mind.

As much as I appreciated his courting effort, I didn't know how to reciprocate it now that he acted on his feelings. It was hard to tell if his feelings would stay the same tomorrow since they constantly flipped back and forth; just trying to keep up made my head dizzy. I did get the opportunity to learn that when he wanted something, nothing would stand in his way.

I also understood that I was something he wanted, so any arguments I had would be worked against. He knew I wanted this, too, making it much harder to deny him. My brain started working, picking up cues from our interactions, and I quickly formulated a plan. While it seemed ridiculous, I decided to take the shot anyway, hoping the love potion would factor in and he would be more susceptible to letting me get my way. "Okay, I will agree to ditch the others if you do one thing for me."

Tate nodded quickly in agreement. I watched his face break into an enthusiastic smile. He liked it when he got his way, even when I put conditions on it. "I think I could agree to that. What is it that you want? Should I be worried?"

"We can go to lunch together. We can even call it a date if you want, but you must answer three questions for me in exchange." I tried to keep my request as simple as possible, hoping that would further motivate him to agree to the deal. It seemed easy enough, but I knew he would be on high alert throughout our lunch. I had to be as charming as possible if I was going to get what I wanted, so I came in just a little closer. "Can I get you to agree to that simple request? Please?"

He stared me down, obviously trying to tell if I was bluffing. His eyebrows pinched in disbelief, but his eyes glinted with something closer to mischief. "Deal. Should we shake or kiss to seal it?"

I went as high up on my toes as I could manage and pressed my lips firmly against his cheek, sweetening the deal even further if possible. "Kiss. With us, it is always sealed with a kiss."

I tried to remember that the Bradbury women had a talent for making men fall to their knees. For centuries we have been able to get them to do exactly what we wanted when we wanted them to. I also tried to remind myself that I had that skill within myself; I just had to figure out how to use it.

Tate was a talented Guardian, war strategist, and brave soldier. I had to remind myself that he was also just a man, and that alone gave me a tactical advantage over our conversations. However, that didn't stop my heart beating faster when he reached for my hand and clasped our fingers together.

He picked a small sandwich place just down the street from the Corner Shop. Grace expressed her annoyance that the original idea for lunch had turned into almost a date for Tate and me, but I knew she was also thrilled one of us was getting a Guardian. The sandwich shop was just far enough away to give us some private time together while we took the short walk. Tate ensured that my body was always the furthest from the street and that my jacket was zipped tightly before we left, showing me how much he cared about me without saying anything.

The two of us walked inside, and he stood behind me

while we ordered, acting almost like my bodyguard, with his eyes never staying in one place long enough to show he was staking out the room. I knew that he had already planned out the best route for escape and how many casualties we would have to go through to get out of there alive.

Tate carried our drinks while we found a table in the back of the room. He pulled out a chair for me, positioning my body so my back was facing the door, all with a tactical plan in mind. When he sat across from me, his eyes could be trained on anything that moved.

"What made you finally say yes to lunch?" He was gentle in his questioning, treating me with the same hesitation I was treating him. He smiled slightly as he grabbed my hand and started playing with the rings I had stacked on my fingers, moving them back and forth. "Not that I am going against your decision. I fully support you using me, even if I don't know why."

"You don't believe I wanted to spend time with you?" I tried to be casual about reaching across the table with my free hand and sipping my drink. The carbonation did nothing to stop my racing heart or settle my stomach like I needed it to. "Maybe I decided to fully dive into our connection? Why fight something that feels so right?"

It was something I had thought over a million times since he had decided to get closer to me.

His smirk called me out on my lie, but his words were gentler and loving. "I don't believe you, but I will take whatever I can get when it comes to time with you." Tate motioned as if he was about to tell me a secret and leaned closer, crossing the table into my personal space. "I'm not sure you understand your hold over me or how desperate I am to get even a second with you."

Tate's ability to go along with anything I said would

make these questions easier to answer than I thought. His stony exterior was gone, and in its place was a smile I didn't often see. "The hold I have over you? I am a prisoner to you."

"Have you as my prisoner? That sounds pretty good." If I were closer, he would have probably taken a bite of me.

"Oh, Tate, don't tempt me with a good time. I might ask you to keep good on your promise." I just had to keep him in this great headspace, so I winked at him. I hoped that it would send the same shiver up his spine that he did to me. I raised my hand in the air, snapping twice, and charmed our little corner so that no words we said would be heard by anyone walking or sitting nearby. The questions I needed answered couldn't be heard by humans.

"First, why did you come here? I can't imagine you are so close to Seth that you would follow him on any non-assigned mission, especially this strange one." I figured I would start small and work my way up to the more complex questions I was dying to ask. "There is no way your training prepared you for something like this."

Thankfully he seemed affected enough by my attempt to dazzle him that he did smile back at me and answer the question without any hesitation. "Seth presented me with the problem and was not quiet that he was looking for someone to accompany him. There was a thrill about it." He didn't lift his eyes from mine, instead deepening them further. The intensity made a shiver go through me from my head to my toes. "Think of it from my perspective for a second. A threat is coming to Salem, where a Coven of *only witches* lives. How are they supposed to take care of themselves? As far as the Guardians were concerned, you were off the record, which meant I would either be meeting a threat or finding a thrilling adventure. You can understand why that would be intriguing."

I knew that the excitement was the reason he signed up for it. He liked the chase even more than he enjoyed the catch, me included.

Quickly I moved on to my next question, knowing that I only had a short timeframe before he switched back to his customarily hardened personality. "Why did you pull me into that illusion? I know you had a hidden agenda behind it; you don't do anything without reason."

"I wanted to test you because you had proven extremely powerful on other occasions. You only had a few options to get out of it, so whichever you chose was going to show me something about you."

Despite his opinion, I hadn't seen any other options, but this wasn't the first time he played with our lives like a game. I pursed my lips and played along even though I couldn't believe what he was saying. "Interesting. And what did my reaction teach you? I didn't see any other option. There was nothing else I could do."

"You always had three options. One, shoot your magic out so that it would take down the walls. That would have made it so both of you could escape. Two, turn on me and hurt me to disrupt the scene and cause me to drop the illusion. Third, you could kill the man. You picked the one you felt most comfortable with." He dropped my hand and took a sip of his drink. It seemed like he was stalling, taking a break from answering the question to regain a sense of his thoughts and say the words without causing me to react. "Your reaction showed me that you still fall back to your human instincts, not feeling as confident in your magic as you need to be despite its strength. That shows a lot about you and how you will continue to fight all your battles, especially as we walk into what is considered a magic war."

"I did what you were telling me to do. That is completely different than me deciding on my own," I paused while the waitress set down our meal. She checked with both of us that it was satisfactory before moving on to the following table, thankfully not pausing long enough to catch what we were saying. "You knew I would listen to you and do whatever you said. Mind tricks are an unfair way to learn things about the people in your life, especially when you put someone in a vulnerable position."

"You didn't *have* to listen to me. You can't blame me; you were the one who made the decision. Now you have to live with it." He returned it to me like a parent would do to a misbehaving child. The cat-and-mouse game he played pulled me in just like it always did, even when I tried to control myself.

I tried not to let my anger overcome me; I hated that he felt he could talk to me in such a way. My cheeks were inflamed in a deep red. "You baited me, and you know it. You wanted me to do that! I would never do something like that unless it was necessary." I should have known he was going to flip it back onto me the first second he could. Even at his best, I still had a reason to worry about the devil he had inside of him. "I will not let this hang over my head when no real blood was spilled. It was all an illusion I couldn't get out of until I did what you asked," I tried to say it as confidently as possible to make myself believe it.

He gave me a quizzical look that made me second-guess my words and his intentions. "Do you think that is what happened? Or were you overwhelmed by the situation and followed my advice because you trusted my judgment?"

Tate was right, which was something that I hated. I did

trust him and let my actions show that I would mindlessly follow him anywhere. I silently promised myself that next time, I would not fall under his alluring spell and that I would make my own decisions.

My last question followed just as quickly, diverting the conversation to where I wanted it to go. "Why did all of you act so concerned when I threw that spear? Don't get me wrong, I was freaked out too, but I was only worried when you were worried. Which probably goes back to how I unthinkingly trust you and choose to follow your lead."

"Blair, I don't think you understand how powerful you are. I wasn't saying that before to flatter you. Seth and I both have been blown away by the power you hold." His entire personality flipped back to the stern soldier he was trained to be, and a stern expression accompanied his demeanor. "That was nothing we had ever seen before, especially from someone who had home-schooled training. You could not have learned that on your own unless it was ingrained into who you are. That says a lot about how capable your magic is."

That felt at least a little like a dig at my expense, especially with the air-quotations around 'home-schooled training,' but I wouldn't give him the satisfaction of responding to his statement.

I decided not to fall into his words this time and asked him directly instead of continuing to fish around. "Was it something to be concerned about?"

"You don't scare me, but your magic does," He winked, changing the narrative once more back to his carefree attitude. Tate Bishop could easily be confused with Dr. Jekyll and Mr. Hyde. "Don't worry; it won't keep me away from you. I am far too stuck on you to scare easily."

I liked the idea of him being stuck on me, mainly because I was just as stuck on him.

"Tate, I'm nervous about this fight. *I* don't know if I will be strong enough. I barely made it out alive the other night, and that was only because I had been willing to trade his life for my own." The look of his dead body slumped down on the cement stayed in my mind and wouldn't go anywhere. The nightmares I had constantly had since proved as much. "You have made it apparent that I am strong enough to do this and have the power."

Tate tightened my hand, willing me to stay in one place even if he had to keep me there. "I don't know how to tell you this, but when the boys returned for the body, it wasn't there."

My stomach was suddenly filled to the brim with the heaviest of rocks. "What do you mean they didn't find the body? Where would it have gone? He was dead!" Dead men can't walk away from the crime scene; any number of crime shows would have shown us if it had been even remotely possible. Somehow my stomach managed to twist even further, using the rocks as something to hold onto as it flipped over. "He told me that they were coming. He told me that they were coming for me! They are here."

"Blair, we know that they are coming. Why else have we been in constant preparation for them?" Tate didn't seem as worried as I did, not putting it together like I had. How he looked at me seemed like he was more concerned about me and how I seemed to be processing everything.

"The Cabals." I gasped as my mind realized what had happened. It was as if I had figured it out before, but I was only just now allowing myself to put it all together. "Before I took his magic, he had gotten some of mine. He gave up his magic so that he could control mine. Why else would he give up so easily?"

He became a Guardian in an instant. Tate's demeanor shifted again, his body tight and his jaw stiff. He didn't bother to let me finish my meal, instead grabbed his wallet, threw some money down on the table, and took me by the hand, pulling me along with him as he raced back to the others.

* * *

Tate and I were both on constant lookout as we returned to the store, getting them to close early, and went to my house. Actions needed to be taken, and they needed to be taken now, which was why Tate asked everyone to gather at my home. Gathering everyone together was easy; getting them to stay quiet while we talked to them was hard.

We had all spent a lot of time counseling each other the last few days. It felt like we were constantly planning our next steps without actually going through with them, until now. We all seemed to realize this was the last time we could do that without saying anything.

"They are coming. We have also realized they are coming fast and will hit hard." Tate stood at the head of the table like a general commanding his troops. He had me tucked into his side and used his size to cover me from everyone else's eyes at the table. I knew it was only temporary; he would have me explain what we had figured out to the group. I fidgeted with the chain of my amulet to distract my mind and calm myself down, it would only be seconds before he put me into the spotlight, which was my least favorite place to be. "Today, Blair figured out why the man wasn't there when you went to get him. We want to discuss it with you so that we can move forward and end this."

I could hear the eruption of shock from the group around us. That was something the Guardians had kept quiet from the more sensitive women until we had more information, especially information that would give them relief.

Mom looked ready to throw up at the news, "What do you mean he was gone?" She asked at the same time Aunt Mira questioned, "Where did he go?"

We didn't have answers to these questions, so I ignored them both and continued. It took a second for Tate's arm to release me so I could step forward, which made me realize how willing he would be to step back in front of me if needed. I let the eyes of our Coven bring me strength, and I felt a surge of confidence as I met the eyes of my sisters, cousins, aunts, mother, and grandmother. With their steady gazes, I knew we would make it through anything.

I took a deep breath to calm myself down and made my announcement. "This concerns the fight between Grace, me, and a strange man." With their affirming nods, I felt better knowing they were paying attention. The words somehow felt less stuck in the center of my throat when I felt Tate's hand reach out for mine. The tangle of our fingers helped my heart to stop racing. "It was a struggle, both of us fighting to leave there alive. While the boys trained us well, it was a surprise attack, and I could not do much to keep him from killing me."

I didn't want to say anything wrong about the boys' work preparing us for that moment, but I also knew that Grace and I were overwhelmed and not in the best head-space to fight. Against a trained killer, it was a wonder how we made it out alive, which was how I finally put it together that it was a setup, not just blind luck.

"We know this. Where are you going with this?" Piper seemed frustrated that we were talking again. She had voiced on multiple occasions that she was ready for some action.

"I promise I have a point and am getting to it." I hadn't realized I was on a time crunch, but now that I was, the words flew out of my mouth at an alarming rate in hopes of keeping her in a pleasant mood. Once she crossed over, there would be no coming back, and while she was unpleasant either way, one was better than another. "It was earlier today that I realized the man let me take his magic so they could use it to track me. He knew we would become linked that way, and I would return to our Coven. When I drained him of his magic, it took just a moment for his body to drop to the ground, and the loss of strength made his body slump there. This combination made him appear dead to me and Grace. But when the boys returned for his body, he wasn't there, and while the idea that he just stood up and walked away seems unlikely, it's not something that we are willing to rule out."

The pieces were still coming together in my mind, and my mouth had difficulty filtering out what I wanted to share with the group versus what I needed more time to review. I was getting stuck on the fact that the attackers knew we would go down that path, and it could only have been set up by Harriet, but she wasn't going to come until Seth asked her, so how could she set that up? Whoever attacked us had such a short window to make him appear 'dead' before those in his group needed to rescue him. They would have had to rehearse it, planning it down to the second to ensure all the parts came together perfectly, especially to have it cleaned up before the Guardians collected the body.

The Guardians all started to respond to my theory about being linked. I could only hope it was because they had begun to put it together, not just because they were mindlessly believing my words. I watched Fabian stand up from his seat and seem ready to pace the room while Huxley tensed his jaw and spoke up, "How would they have known you would go down that path?"

I was suddenly very grateful that Harriet and Ninnie hadn't been able to come to our house for this meeting since I was feeling confident about where the blame was to go. Still, by the look on Seth's face, he hadn't seemed to come full circle to that thought, so I braced myself for his reaction and if he would try to deflect the blame off of those he had initially come here to protect.

"Have they made contact since that day?" Seth asked instead, "Has anyone been approached or had any strange interactions we should have followed up on?" He chose not to acknowledge Huxley's question or even where my comments were headed, which didn't help me to know where his mind was.

Tate and I shook our heads in a synchronized fashion. He spearheaded this question like it had been directed to him. "They haven't made contact with us, but they are here. We know they are closing in."

Seth seemed to take all of this in turn. The veins in his jaw showed how reserved he continued to keep himself. "How can you know that? Blair would have no idea how to monitor for that unless you have shown her?" His eyebrow raised almost in an accusatory way towards Tate. He tightened his grip on my hand, but I declined to satisfy him with a response.

Celeste silently raised her hand to get the attention of the room. Her voice was quiet, but what she said held enough weight that everyone fell silent in anticipation. "I can feel them getting closer now that Blair has his magic." I hadn't considered that a possibility; I had a part of him inside me, and tracking could go both ways. "It's gotten stronger every day since she took it, and I can feel them nearby. I think they have decided when they are going to strike."

With her words, the war started.

Chapter Fifteen

It had been a while since I had been put into an Astral Projection, so long that I had almost forgotten what the forest looked like. The protection spell they placed over my head must have worn off if I was able to be brought here.

The Keeper of the Dream made me stand beside the stream like they always did, the water spray hitting my legs as it rushed past. I enjoyed seeing my black dahlia flowers as they lined the green grass. They were very different from the red roses Tate had brought me, with one meaning love and the other betrayal; it was no wonder which ones were supposed to soften my heart and which ones actually did.

I would say that the worst part was the silence that came while I patiently awaited my fate with the inability to turn my head. The Keeper of the Dream was in complete control over me. They were, yet again, freezing me in place with their magic. It was like they didn't trust me or something.

A slight buzzing noise broke out of the silence. It flew

around my head and calmed me down instead of making me more nervous, as they had probably intended. It also gave my eyes an excuse to focus on something small instead of the vast world they had created around me, which also calmed my racing heart. When the object of the buzzing noise came closer to me, I could see the delicate wings as if they had purposefully slowed down just for me to take in all of their beauty. The blue color seemed to have an iridescence, and the entire insect shimmered in the blistering sun.

"Did you know dragonflies have flown the earth for three hundred million years? In a way, they are a symbol of our ability to overcome trials and how we can adapt throughout time," Their voice startled me. They had me so focused on the dragonfly that the incoming sound of their voice caused my suspended body to jerk in surprise. The Keeper of the Dream sent a rush of a few hundred dragonflies out to me, making them fly in a circular pattern around my body after they quickly joined the original one in its flight path. I was surprised that the Keeper let the insect remain so calm, having them act in the way of something gentle, like a soft breeze, instead of the rush of a tornado like they could have. The Keeper of the Dream was in a more peaceful mood tonight than they usually were, which left me more unaware of what would happen next, even more ignorant than usual. "Dragonflies are also known to be Keepers of Dreams, especially in old legends. Isn't that a funny coincidence? I would have never thought to have something in common with such a beautiful and delicate creature."

A small part of me had given up on the search for who it was that controlled the Astral Projections. I was burning myself out by trying to make sense of everything they said or did. I knew it would be better if I just left it all to rest, but the larger part of me wanted to continue my search. In my mind, I kept note of the cadence in which the Keeper of the Dream spoke just now and how their words sounded so familiar, or at least the way they said them to me. It also felt familiar that they were pulling an interesting fact and blending it with something that could be considered mundane.

All of the words they were saying sounded closest to something Aunt Mira would say, and while she had been working on furthering her magic, I didn't entertain the thought that she was involved for long. I knew she was nowhere near this Astral Projection. She would never dabble with her magic into something so close to evil, especially something the Council had forbidden.

"Very funny." I could only move my eyes as I tried to pinpoint where they were since they had me in a tight hold. While I had such a small range of motion, I knew that if I moved them too quickly, they would retaliate in response, so I shifted them as slowly as I could. They did not trust their magic to hold me in place, so they tightened it against me once more, almost to ensure it was there. I tried to find the path their voice carried out to me, but they were far too deep in the treeline to be seen by the naked eye. I refrained from forcing my magic out for a more critical vantage point like I wanted to.

I would have good reason to believe it was the man from the other night if I hadn't taken his magic and left him unable to do such a thing. At least then it would make sense how he knew where to find me or how he could quickly track what we would be doing that night. However, it was obvious that the Keeper of the Dream cared about me, a characteristic that man didn't have. In some sick way, the Keeper of the Dream always tried to protect me. Whoever it was that continued to bring me here wanted to warn me of any dangers, and they seemed to take care of me in their way. They were always aware of what was coming next and quick to keep me from the dangers ahead. Somehow, I knew they wouldn't kill me, even if they threatened to. Those characteristics didn't match the interaction I had with that man or anyone who would have the same intentions as him, which again begged the question of who the Keeper of the Dream could be and what they were hoping to get out of these moments.

I could tell by the rhythmic tisk of their tongue, that they hadn't cared for my sarcastic response, but that didn't stop them from finishing their thought. I patiently listened as quietly as possible, hoping they would make sense once they were done. I knew from previous experiences that they would not give me my way, especially if I voiced what I wanted, so I just had to be patient and hope that they were willing to share extra details. "They say that the dragonfly can see all our intentions and true potential, which is why they choose to come close to some and seem to avoid others. Dragonflies also can inspire us to be creative, which might be why I have been able to create such a world. Most of all, dragonflies help us onto a path of enlightenment and discovery, which is why many witches cover their candles with drawings of dragonflies to aid their spell casting."

The Dream Keeper sent me one last dragonfly and let it land on my frozen, outstretched finger. They crystallized it in a flash, the wings folding over until it was a perfectly sized ring for my index finger.

I looked down at it in disbelief that the Keeper of the

Dream had created something so beautiful and wanted to leave it with me. It sparkled when the sun hit it, each detail of the insect perfectly preserved in a piece of jewelry on my body. "What is this?"

"Consider it a memento of our time together. I don't want you to look back at our moments with pain in your heart," Their voice carried out from the trees with a palpable sadness, an emotion I hadn't expected to hear from them. "I wish you could understand why I brought you here and what this time we have had together has meant to me. I am trying to help you, Blair. You do see that I don't want you to die, don't you?"

My eyes stayed on my dragonfly, and the way it was significantly colder than what felt typical for jewelry. It felt like the insect was frozen instead of like the crystal they turned it into, which was probably how it kept the colors so vibrant and the natural shimmer alive. My voice came out quietly but confidently as I responded to them, "I believe you."

I wasn't lying; I believed they wanted me to live in the same way that I knew they wouldn't kill me, even if they continued to threaten me. Somehow my soul knew the Keeper of the Dream even if I had never seen them with my eyes. In a way, we had created a complicated bond, one even more confusing than the one between Ninnie and me or even the one I had with Tate.

"So, you are a dragonfly then?" I called out to them, keeping my voice as soft as possible so that they would stay in the same mindset. It wouldn't take much to upset them, and I knew better than to do that if I wanted to get some answers. I hoped to understand what they were getting at and why they were bringing up an insect as a conversation starter, although it was better than the usual manner they called out to me.

Their laugh floated out louder than I would have expected. Joy was a strange emotion to hear from them. How odd it seemed to come quickly to them, like it was an emotion they were comfortable with and experienced often. "No, I am not the dragonfly," They chuckled, "*You* are."

"Me?"

"Yes, *you*. Don't sound so surprised; it makes more sense for it to be you than me. You embody the characteristics I just listed." Their voices continued to be light and carefree, much lighter than I had ever heard from them. A small part of me enjoyed being here with them when they were like this, which only pointed to how quickly Stockholm syndrome could set into a person and how easily it was to ignore when it did. "You seem to have a brilliant way of adapting to a situation and flourishing when needed. Something no one would have predicted from the baby of the Bradbury Coven. We all seemed to underestimate you. Every time we turn around, you show us another thing we had missed, and your ability to pick at those tiny details gives me some very long days. That is part of the reason why I haven't come to see you in such a long time."

I did appreciate that they saw that in me since I had seen it in myself. My character had changed a million times over the last few months in a way I would never have predicted. This wasn't the first time they had commented on my internal growth, showing how deeply they were watching me, which should have unsettled me; instead, it gave me something to rise to.

I liked that they were wrong about me.

"And what is the other reason?" I held onto their last comment, hoping it would give more information about their thought process and a deeper look into how their mind was in tune with mine. I needed to know what they were thinking more than I felt a need to fill my lungs with air, further pointing to my insanity and my desperate need for help.

Their voice rang out with even more emotion as they started to explain themselves, "Every time I come here, I realize how hard it is to contain myself around you and how much I seem to over share when we are alone. Being with you here feels like our place, somewhere we can speak and know each other without the bonds we are tied to."

My brain ran circles around their words while my hands tried to release from their magic with small, sharp movements. It would do no good to anger them; even if they were being gentle with me now, there was still the opportunity for them to flip back to the angry side. I was in no mood to be threatened tonight, but I did want to have control over my own body.

My voice came out quietly once more. I knew staying small and as gentle as possible would be my best tactic. "Why can't you talk to me? I would happily listen to anything you have to say. It's important to talk out the things that you are struggling with instead of keeping them internalized. It's not healthy to do it that way," I was trying to sweeten them up. How far had the Stockholm syndrome set into my body if I was trying to take care of my capture's heart, even after they offered it to me on a silver platter? I continued anyway, "I am here with you for a reason."

"I don't think you understand that being near you is infectious and does nothing good. I must remind myself to stay away from you and find the control to do just that," Their words came out with an almost hollow shudder, trying to contain their emotions since they had already shared too much. I knew this tactic well; it was the retreat. "It's hard not to fall in love with you, Blair. You have a way about you that only continues to pull me in even after I've convinced myself that you are bad for me."

How could they fall in love with me if this was the only part of me that they knew?

* * *

There were very few things I could have done differently to avoid being here, but that did not stop me from regretting my decision to sign up for this. I could only chalk it up to listening to my mother and how desperately she promoted a team effort between us all, how much Ninnie needed a friend, and how we all needed to do our part. Somehow, I let her influence my decisions, which is something I should know better than to do.

Ninnie had informed us that she was going through some boxes in their shed. The Walker family was making room for Harriet's things. They decided that when it was appropriate to return to her home, they would go to collect her items. Ninnie also told us she would be late for our nightly training if she even arrived. My foolish offer to help brought me here to the backyard of the Walker household, where the shed doors were opened wide and overflowing with boxes.

"I think it would be a good idea to go through this box first since it's one of the smaller ones, and I will grab one too. It shouldn't take that much time to get through them." Ninnie picked up a box that seemed almost twice her size and sat it at my feet as our starting point. I realized our minds thought differently about what a small box was, especially regarding our colossal task. "Then we can pick a wall and work through them that way."

Now that I was here, I realized how unsettled I was just near the Walker house. There was a race in my heart that prompted me to get this done as quickly as possible, especially when the swish of the curtain in the upstairs window let me know that someone was watching us. A chill went quickly down my spine. I didn't know if it was Harriet or Mrs. Walker, but either way, I was anxious to be so exposed. I kneeled in front of the box, pulled on the worn-down cardboard flaps, and started taking out the contents, setting them beside me to make a pile. Most of the box's contents were picture frames, most empty, but some had unpleasant portraits staring back at me with unhappy faces. "What do we want to save from this box? I think picture frames and pictures are the only things inside of it, but there might be more at the bottom."

She made a quizzical face, pausing while she thought over my question. "How about we start by first figuring out what is in the boxes? We can empty a few of them, and then we can decide if anything in it is worth saving or not. We will have to make a mess before we are successful." She pulled her box from the shelf and started pulling the items out. It was concerning that she didn't have a plan, mainly because she was determined to get this done today. "I can't imagine that my mom will want to keep most of this since it hasn't been opened in at least five years, and most of these people were dead for a few hundred years before that."

I believed that if she hadn't needed it for two years or more, then she probably wouldn't need it again, but I kept that comment to myself and continued working on emptying my box as quickly as I could. I put empty frames in one pile and the ones that had pictures in another. I realized the box Ninnie was going through had the exact same contents, so I used magic to blend them, trying to make this as easy as possible. I knew her mom didn't approve of anyone freely using their magic, especially out in the open like this. Still, desperate times called for desperate measures, and the rapid progression of my heart told me that this moment qualified.

"Is this all that you have to do today? Or is this the start of your to-do list?" I said it in a way that made it seem like there wasn't much to be done, even if there was. Even with us both taking on a box at this speed, it would still take a few hours to make it through one of the three heavily supplied walls of shelves.

Ninnie hurried through her box, making subsidized files that only she understood. "Yeah. Mom hopes that when we are finished, we can get Harriet's stuff from her house or what remains of it. Mom thinks having her stuff will make her feel better about being here with us." She repeated the explanation she had given us earlier, although it was full of emotion this time. "I'm not sure if it will work, but I hope so."

"Why is that?"

"I'm not sure she wants to be comfortable here," Ninnie bit her lip and did one more survey of our surrounding space, even furthering the idea that there were ears everywhere that she was worried about. "I've been noticing some things that have me concerned. It started small, but now I feel like everything she says is contradictory to what she said just the day before. At first, I thought it was a trauma response, but how could you forget the details in your life and then say it differently in the retelling?"

It seemed like she was seeing the things I was seeing. I thought that Grace and I were the only ones who thought something was off. A small part of me suspected she knew something, especially after the way she spoke about the night we were attacked. I decided to open the conversation slowly, allowing us both the opportunity to back out if we felt it was necessary.

"I think that darkness inside of her is something stronger, and sometimes I think she feeds into it instead of trying to take care of it, especially the more the rest of us train," Ninnie started speaking quickly as if there was a race to get the words out. I was surprised to hear her verbalize what I had observed in Harriet. I was also shocked that she was willing to say it so freely when there were potentially ears overhearing us. "At first, I thought it was because of some post-traumatic stress disorder and the effects following her because of what she saw. I hadn't seen anything close to what she was going through before, so who was I to judge her and how she chose to process it? But then I started seeing more. It almost seemed like she was walking a thin line between who she was supposed to be and who she is."

I realized that maybe I wasn't putting random pieces together, but instead, they were lining themselves up with the wish to be seen. "And if I told you I had seen that too? Then what would we do?"

"Then I would finally tell you that I am nervous." She took a deep breath, shaking her hands, and her bottom lip quivered. "I think that she is with them. Instead of running from the Cabals, I think she is a part of them and used their attack as her initiation, and they used that as a way to get into our lives."

"With them? What do you mean she could be with them?" That was further than I had ever thought, but I could see how she got there. "Why would she warn us they were coming if she was a part of them? They could have taken us by surprise if nothing was said. Wouldn't a surprise attack give them a greater chance of success? We wouldn't have the Guardians if she hadn't said anything."

Instead of responding, she let out a sharp gasp. I looked behind me to see what had surprised her and felt the earth around me tremble.

The man was alive! He was back, standing before us with the same menacing grin and a sizeable blood-stained blade pointed in our direction — the threat clear. "You're right. She is with us. What a smart little girl you are for finally figuring it out. I figured we had left you enough clues that it would be obvious, but you took your sweet time piecing it together."

He hadn't died like Grace and I thought that he had. It suddenly made sense why Seth and the boys couldn't find his body and why the timeline of Harriet getting back to the house was off.

The real surprise was who stood beside him, although it shouldn't have been. Harriet stepped out from behind his shadow wearing a matching look. Somehow, I hadn't seen this one coming. My hesitations about her would have never prepared me for her to be the villain. I would never have been able to predict who she was on the inside or what she was prepared to do to us after all that we had done for her. She was devilish in her smile. Ditching the weak exterior she had covered herself with since we met her, she came into her full power. "Ninnie. Blair. Thank you so much for laying this out for me. I would not have been this prepared without you and your desperate want to make me feel included. I thought my indifference would push you away, but instead, it made you so desperate for my approval that it brought you closer. It almost made me feel bad for you."

"Why are you doing this?" I was so impressed by

Ninnie's bravery in talking back to Harriet. I would not have been able to do that, even with how much anger surged through my body.

She gave her a look we had all seen before, still pretending to be a friend, but now that we knew what was hidden underneath; there was no going back. "I had to do it for my people. You understand that, right? The need to take care of what is yours. Is that not why you are building an army?"

"Do not pretend to be a meek little girl to me. I can see the vicious demon you are in your eyes!" Ninnie raised her hand to reveal a dagger, the matching one tucked away in the waistband of my pants, so I hurried to retrieve it, arming myself as well. I was ready to follow Ninnie into whatever she had planned next. "Don't come any closer, or I will have to hurt you."

"Hurt me? You think you can hurt me?" Harriet gave a haughty laugh in our direction, obviously not afraid of either of us or what we could do to her.

I realized something she didn't. "No, but I do think we will beat you."

"Carl has gotten the opportunity to learn of your magic, which was a surprise. You, little witch, have been holding out on us."

I realized with Tate that when I pulled the man's magic from him, it wasn't all of it. He let me take some so he could track me; the magic he had left in his body would constantly search for the magic he had lost.

The man, Carl, got a dark look in his eyes and started whispering a spell just low enough for us to miss the words. With his magic, they disappeared in a puff of black smoke like they were never there.

Ninnie hugged herself, holding herself together, "Have

you ever seen Hell in someone's eyes and loved them anyway?" This was not a conversation she wanted to be having with me. Still, a sort of sisterhood had grown between us throughout our time together, and we were forced to lean on each other. Especially now that we were the only two who understood this moment or knew what Harriet was like on the inside. I could only imagine the reaction of the rest of our group when we told them about this. "She lived in my house. She was around my family for so long that she had become a part of us. I had no idea she was capable of something like this. I thought she was just nervous, having PTSD from what she went through, and all of that mixed with depression to make her act so estranged."

They had been gone for a while, but neither Ninnie nor I had moved from our spots. We both anticipated that Harriet and the man would return to finish the job.

"You aren't the only one who felt something was wrong. Ever since that night we got attacked, I have been freaking out about how weird it was and how her running away led us straight to where that man was waiting." I realized right then that I had all the pieces together long before now. I didn't want to think of her as someone who could be evil, but if I had, maybe we could have prepared for this and taken care of it. "I have known about this and didn't do anything about it because I didn't want to paint her as the villain."

"Blair... we're friends, right? I mean, I would consider us to be friends." Ninnie spread her arms for me to fall into, knowing what I needed at that moment was a shoulder to cry on, and she was looking for one too.

"Worse. I think we've become closer to family," I mumbled into her shoulder. I would have never guessed that we would end up like this, but I was not going to do anything to risk that bond now that it was here. Ninnie Walker had somehow become my partner, and we had to have each other's backs until we got back to the rest of our team. "Never would I have thought it would be you and I."

We would have to join together to beat more than the Cabals; now, we had to defeat Harriet.

Chapter Sixteen

S uddenly all that we had trained for was here, and I didn't think we were as ready as we needed. Harriett exposing herself as a part of the Cabals was almost the same as someone firing a gun to start a race; the war had officially begun. Ninnie and I ran back to Aunt Mira's store as fast as we could and immediately got the boys involved. It took no time at all for them to spring into action. They directed everyone to meet at my house, where all the previous meetings had been. Each rushed off to start on their secret list of assignments they had prepared for.

"We will meet them here at nightfall," Seth began, "Harriet would be a fool not to come now that we know her position. While I would want to take them on in a surprise attack, we can't risk exposing ourselves to the humans by doing this during the daylight, especially right off the city path." Seth laid out a city map in front of us on the dining room table and pointed to a clearing on the south side of town, it was yet to be developed with houses but did have bike paths that were in constant use during the day. He had thought this over, and by the nodding of Tate's head, they were agreed. "We need to be ready for anything. She has seen all of our training. We are at a disadvantage."

"Why do you think they will go there? It's not like we can ask them to meet us there," Penelope was not arguing with him; instead, she was trying to understand his reasoning and seemed willing to listen to him. That alone was evidence that this might end the world as we know it.

"They will go there because we will be there. The Bradbury magic is a powerful source that they will be able to follow, and of course they will track Blair more specifically. The man will want the rest of his magic back now that he can get it, not to mention what the rest of us have to offer," Tate explained, motioning for the younger boys to join him. They both followed suit by nodding their heads in a synchronized pattern. "We would be a big win for them, much more than Harriet's Coven had been. You are Trial witches, which means that your magic has survived the worst thing to happen to our kind; then there is the impressive size of your Coven. Lastly, you have us boys. Their triumph would only be more impressive with each Guardian they take down," He asserted, "I don't feel good about Blair being used as a honing device."

"Tate, it's not like I will be out there alone." I laid my hand on top of the one hand he had laid on my hip. Touching him softly was sure to get him to pause and listen to what I said. I had learned that my words didn't always get him to do that. "You will be there to protect me if needed, and we will all be there to look after each other. You have trained us for this, have faith in your skills as a teacher."

The rugged look on his face didn't soften with my words like I wanted it to. They almost seemed to harden further with the pinch of his full eyebrows and the narrowing of his deep eyes. "Blair, I am not letting you be the bait for a war.

You are worth too much to me to risk losing you at the hand of a Cabal just because we need a way to lure them out here."

While I appreciated that, I also knew that there was no way I could stay out of this fight. Even though his feelings had grown, and he was more willing to share them with me, he was still harsher than I wanted him to be, which made the entire thing feel pointless.

"Tate, not once have you put me above the rest or changed any plans for my sake. Until that happens, what you are saying is just pretty words. Pretty words mean a lot on the surface, but they aren't going to get you anywhere with me if you don't follow them up with actions." I turned my body so our faces aligned and I could look at him in his eyes when I said what was coming next, hoping it would sink in. There I saw the love potion flittering back and forth as its effects started to wear off. "You don't get a say in what I agree to do, now or ever. So shut up and get out of my way."

It was the harshest I had ever spoken to him, and I immediately felt guilty. "Shouldn't I get a vote?" Tate muttered under his breath as he looked away from me. It didn't take a genius to know that this conversation was not over, and his dropping it now did not mean it would not spark up again later when we were alone.

Seth had let the two of us go at it for a second, probably to allow us to distract each other while he and Penelope got to look over the plans without Tate and I stepping in to interrupt. They were huddled together over the agenda, the other two Guardians standing on the other side of the table.

"They are coming for Blair first. If we position Tate and Blair in the middle of the field beside Penelope and me, it will allow our weaker teammates to be near the back, where they are least likely to get hurt and have a greater chance of getting out of this if necessary." Seth used his magic to create small, detailed figurines of each of us and positioned our tiny shapes on the map so the rest could visualize his words. He was still hoping this would stay civil, but that seemed unlikely. "Huxley and Fabian would stand here and there. That would allow them to cover the rear if someone decided to take us by surprise by coming up that way. I can't imagine that anyone would do that as they have already exposed their element of surprise. They are most likely going to take us on with a straightforward approach, but I would much rather have a plan in place."

Penelope used her magic to create some ugly wooden figurines to represent the Cabals and placed them on the path she felt they would most likely come down from. "If they come from here or over here, then we will have Huxley and Fabian facing them; that would be intimidating if we get there first."

"Would we want to get there first?" Piper asked from the side. She had been intently listening, choosing to step in beside Penelope. I think Piper was beginning to enjoy the idea of hitting someone. I was also hoping that she would channel some of the anger she was dealing with now that she knew about Harriet into taking down the Cabals. "Or would it be better to come up on them as a surprise attack?"

Fabian answered her before anyone else could, "Remember how we are going to force them to come there? That will be easier if we are there first so they can follow the magic."

Tate stepped away from me and up to the table, placing himself between the brothers. I let my body slink back to where Grace was standing. Being near her seemed like the safest place in the room now that Tate was unhappy with me. "Our training has taught us that the obvious opponent is the one they will go for, and we don't want to make this any easier for them. Intimidating would be if we-"

"The Council is coming," Aunt Edna spoke in a grave voice, getting louder from the corner. Her hands furiously went up and down the crystals lining her necklace chain. The repetition usually calmed her down, but not today. "They won't be here until after the Cabals have come. They are probably coming to dispose of whoever is left when you are done." She had been standing off to the side with my grandma, both observers of our situation since the Guardians took charge. I was surprised she was willing to speak up, knowing how she felt about the situation. Neither she nor Grandma would participate in the fight; they would stay with Mom and Aunt Mira to watch the little girls while we were at the battle.

Tate looked over at her with a surprised expression on his face. I didn't know if it was her prediction or if it was because she was willing to interrupt him mid-sentence. "How do you know that? What are you thinking?"

She exchanged a look with Grandma, knowing something the rest of us didn't. "They sent a new message this morning. They will be here when it is over to handle it. They have timed their arrival perfectly to be here when this is over, so their arrival time is subjective."

This would be the first time for many of us to interact with the Council, and by the expressions on their faces, this was upsetting news. No one wanted to risk being put in front of the Council, especially now that so many of us were against them coming. We were all losing faith in their ability to contain the situation.

I spoke up, "How will we know when they are here?"

"You will feel it when they are near," Aunt Edna's voice

shook in a way that made me nervous. I didn't know what else the Council said, but by the look she exchanged with Grandma, it seemed like maybe more passed through their message than they would share with us.

"Wouldn't it be easier to have them follow us to the Council?" Piper said in a way that hinted we were missing something circling through her mind. "Then we can hand it over to them. It would allow them to handle it and not force us to be the middleman."

An uproar of conversation flew out of the mouths of my Coven members with ideas for the battle and their opinions on the Council's arrival. No one was happy about them coming, but all for a different reason. Some felt their arrival was useless, others thought they were coming too early, but most felt they were too late. Huxley and Fabian were the most vocal about thinking they should have stayed away. They both felt that we could do this without their help. Huxley more so than his brother since he was the outspoken one, but Fabian nodded his head enthusiastically.

Grace spoke up, "What if we went against the Council? It doesn't seem like they are coming to help us. Forget about Blair being put out as bait. That seems to be what the Council is doing to us."

"How would we go against the Council?" Aunt Edna asked, shocked.

"I think that we observe them when they come. It seems as though they are hanging us out to dry." I tried to plan the words before they came out of my mouth, but that felt pointless as I watched the boy's eyes widen. "If it seems like they are going against us, then we will act."

Tate reentered the conversation slowly, "How do we act out against the Council?"

"It is too bold to want a revolution?" I was slightly

kidding; even suggesting something like that caused the rest of the room to erupt in gasps. Their noises only pushed me further. "There is something wrong with how they are treating this. Witches are killing other witches and stealing their magic, and our leaders are doing nothing to stop it. That is wrong! If the Cabals come here and the Council does nothing, we start doing something about it." I tried to gauge their reactions. "It is their responsibility to take care of their people, and if they aren't going to do that, we might need to find someone who will."

I could tell my suggestion bothered some. It wasn't every day that someone spoke of overtaking the Council. All of the witches in the circle seemed to be digesting the information, knowing that even saying it could get us in trouble.

The boys stepped away; they put their heads together for a minute, continuing their conversation about the Council away from the rest of us. Out of all of us, they were the ones who had the most to lose if any of this was heard.

Tate stepped away from the table, pulling me aside and steering my body into the foyer since everyone else was still in the dining room. He didn't think his input was necessary, especially if they were all talking over each other. His hand gripped my wrist tightly. "Blair, I am begging you. Do not be used as bait. I need you to hide in the background and stay as small as possible. Do not overexpose your magic; you are powerful, and they will try to take that away from you even more when they realize what you have. You must understand that if anyone finds out how powerful your magic is, they will try to take it away from you." While I knew he would want to talk about it, I didn't realize how fast he wanted to hash it out. I could tell by the pinching of his eyebrows that he was more worried than he wanted to appear.

I knew I should listen to him, take in his words and change my actions accordingly. I knew I should trust him enough to do that, but I didn't anymore. Before, when I pointed out that he hadn't *shown* me that he cared about me, it wasn't a bluff, even if it appeared that way. "I don't even understand what you are asking of me. How could I sit in the back and not give everything to this fight? It is my family on the line. I can't not give my all when those lives are at stake."

His eyes watered a little in the corners, and his grip tightened further; everything about his demeanor was different than it ever had been before. He was no longer telling me what to do. He was begging me. "Blair, I can't lose you, and if you do this, I will *lose* you. Don't do that to me."

"You won't lose me, especially if you trust that I can handle myself." With those parting words, I stormed off up the stairs, knowing that this would be the first night since the attack that I would be sleeping without him and knowing myself well enough to know I would regret that decision.

* * *

I was nervous waiting for them to show up. I wasn't the only one, though, my sisters all paced in tiny rapid footsteps, with my cousins nervously cracking their knuckles. Ninnie was the only one of us that was calm. I think it was her anger toward Harriet that was pushing her forward.

Tate reached over and clasped my hand in his. The calluses on his hand comforted me as they reminded me how strong he was. We were still fighting since neither of us had apologized, but I felt safe with him, and right now, that was what I was looking for. "You don't want to make a run for it? You know that I am still advocating for that plan."

"Not yet," I was still mad at his macho energy, and I would not let him get his way or make me feel bad about my decision to stay when that was obviously the right choice. "I'm ready for whatever they throw at us." It was a lie, but he didn't call me out on it like he usually did when I lied to him.

Aunt Edna wasn't wrong when she told us we would feel it when they came. Before they appeared through the trees, I could feel intense bad energy becoming stronger. It was the same energy that surrounded Harriet, although this intensity hit us with a magnitude that could knock someone off their feet if they weren't prepared.

There was only a small group, much smaller than I expected. They came forward and stood before us, still staying close together, almost to seem more significant than they were.

"We are here for the ancestral magic, and you are the only thing standing in our way," said one woman who stood at the point of their triangle. She seemed to be the leader of the Cabals and let her voice carry out to our group of warriors in hopes of putting a little fear into us; it was very theatrical, compelling. I watched Celeste shrink further to the back of the group where Grace and Piper stood, using them almost as shields. "I suggest you bow down and join us or step aside."

This is the first time it had been fully revealed what they had come for exactly, although it wasn't a surprise. They were pursuing power, and the next logical step was coming after the ancestors' magic. The magic of the fallen witches was still rich, and many believed they could harvest it from the earth. They were pooling the magic and using it against the Council for control over the witches.

Harriet was tucked into the side of the mass to be hidden, but that didn't stop all of our eyes from falling on her sly form. At least she was in a position of shame enough that she hung her head lower and avoided our eyes, tucking herself behind the man who attacked us, the one she called Chip. It seemed like they were familiar with each other like Tate and I were.

Seth was our spokesperson, stepping forward to talk to her while we remained behind the starting line. "Why are you here for the magic? You are powerful enough on your own, and your friend there would have never lost his magic if he didn't attack someone innocently passing by." He held out his hands casually, which I knew was fake. He was still trying to control the situation by using the lessons on body language that he had studied in the last few weeks. "We didn't come here for a fight and wish to avoid it if possible. How can we resolve this peacefully?"

I felt it was unnecessary to get the details, especially since that very man did not look apologetic for coming after me; instead, he almost seemed hungry because he continued to flash his teeth at me. Whether he was hungry for my death or a battle, I didn't know.

"We want it all." With her words, all those behind her took off toward us in something more than a run, each displaying a weapon or a wand that had been concealed behind their matching cape-like garments. They seemed theatrical and unnecessary, but it gave us an advantage over them because our standard leggings and running shoes uniform gave us a full range of motion.

Each of us had somehow managed to be paired off against each member of the Cabals once we caught up to them; since we were evenly matched, it made it into something resembling a fair fight.

It was no surprise that Harriet stood across from me with a knife in one hand and a wand in the other, with a rotten look on her face. She had never liked me, and now she had the opportunity to kill me. Like when she approached us in the Walker yard, she stood tall and was ready for the fight, which was a step up on me. I felt nowhere near prepared to hurt someone, let alone kill her. "I didn't think I would get away with it." She chuckled in a way that made me mad. How dare she act better than us! "You made it too easy. You and Ninnie were so willing to let me in, desperate to be my friend."

We were practically walking in circles around each other, one of us stepping closer while the other stepped back, barely missing one another when we swung a weapon at the other. It was a dangerous dance, each of us taking a turn to swipe at each other. "We made it easy? You are so heartless. We were trying to take care of you. We *did* care for you even if you never cared for us."

She swung her weapon near my head, and I barely ducked in time. I could hear the swish of the blade when it passed my ear. I tried to be faster than she was, coming forward while our bodies were still close. I abandoned using magic and approached her with a weapon, hoping she wouldn't see it coming. My trusted pink blade nicked the skin on the outside of her bicep and forced it to start bleeding down her arm. A small part of me was satisfied that she was the one who got hurt first; it meant that I was at least doing something right. Tate would be proud to know that I hit my mark first and that our hours of training were not pointless.

Some choice words flew out of her mouth as she

charged after me with a newfound rage. I was too focused on her actions to care about what she was saying as she used her magic to force my body to fly through the air. I pushed my magic beneath me to catch myself. There were only a few seconds to react before my body hit the grass, so I used the spell Seth taught us the first day and made a softer landing beneath myself in the form of a trampoline.

As soon as I got my feet back on the ground, I used my magic to force her body back and used another surge to move the trees on my side in a line between us to create a pseudo-barrier so that I could catch my breath. In our training, there were more pauses than what was happening now, and even with the added rush of magic to my lungs, I was still finding it hard to breathe. "Harriet, call this off. No harm has been done yet; it can still be turned around."

She pushed a tree out of the way and pressed her magic against my body to hold me in place while she walked closer. I knew she would kill me if she got close enough, so my only option was to move. My magic was stronger than hers, so I pushed mine harder against her until she was thrown off balance. I outstretched my hand and focused on her magic, pulling on it until it started to join mine.

Someone from the side of the field forced me to release Harriet's magic, making me lose the upper hand and restart our battle. I swiveled my head to watch each of my sisters in their battles. Celeste was holding her own while Penelope had already handled the witch she was facing off with and was hunting for another Cabal to take down.

Piper held a wand in one hand and a spear in the other as she charged across the field. Her hair flowed behind her head with a freedom of its own. At the same time, Grace seemed to be losing her battle judging by how the Cabal witch stood over her.

My eyes should have been focused on Harriet and what she would do next as she was in pursuit; instead, I found my attention being pulled to the left, where I watched Chip pick up a spear and throw it toward an unsuspecting Tate. He was facing off against two different members of the Cabals.

"No!" I screamed as my body raced across the field, using magic to push my burning legs faster to get to it before it hit its target. I used magic to force objects and even people out of my way. I didn't care where they ended up or who I was throwing.

There was too much field to cross before there would be any way I could stop the spear with my magic from where I had previously stood, so I forced my body to get to him.

Chip had used whatever magic he had left to charm the spear, and it was moving too fast for me to keep up; I suspected another Cabal was lending their magic to the spear. As I dove in front of it, all I could think about was my sisters and if they would make it out alive, and then only Tate was on my mind as I felt the spear pierce my sternum and go straight through my heart.

Chapter Seventeen

My eyes opened to the field they always brought me to. Standing next to the stream with the black dahlias surrounding my feet, there was peace. I could feel that they hadn't arrived yet; they had taken me here alone and were letting me take a moment to rest.

I knew I wasn't asleep like I had been before. My body was in an entirely different state of being. Instead of the Keeper of the Dream finding me sleeping in my bed, it was the battlefield where I had been struck down.

For a second, I could only question if this was death. Instead of walking amongst angels, perhaps as a witch, I was sentenced to a different ending, a combination of heaven and hell. The idea would be complicated, but all was possible.

Whoever it was that brought me here didn't have my body frozen as it had been in the past, so I looked around, knowing that this was different from any other time they had brought me here. It was only a matter of time before something happened and I would be frozen again.

I still thought it was an Astral Projection and acted in a way I always would. I knew that it would be better. Behind me, I could see that the stream went back for a long time until it looked like it started at a waterfall, the light casting off it to create the faintest of rainbows. At my feet, a dance of white butterflies went around the flowers, their lightness such a stark contrast to the dark color of the dahlias.

"You're not that easy to keep safe. You know that?" I hadn't felt the Keeper show up, so he made himself known. For the first time, he walked out of the trees, and suddenly all the earlier Astral Projections made sense, as did all the other interactions I had with him. He was always around when something terrible happened; he had tried to convince me that I couldn't fight this without giving me a real reason because he was with them! He was notorious for flipping between good and evil, and now I understood why. He was dangerous and disguised himself in a way that made me distracted. I wanted to pretend not to be surprised at his appearance, but the betrayal that crossed my face made that decision for me. I had never been able to disguise what I was feeling from him.

"Tate."

"I would apologize, but I doubt you would accept it now. I know how you must be feeling." He stepped forward with his hands raised in a non-threatening manner. "You have to understand why I am here and why, for lack of a better term, I did this to you." I knew that he was trying to be sincere. The way that he was looking at me would have shaken me to my core in the past, but suddenly I felt empty and somewhat heartless as I took in the disgusted feeling he had left me with. "I'm not the person you thought I was, as you can see."

He could give me no explanation or excuse that would make up for all he had done, and he knew that.

"You're right. You aren't the person I thought you were. Who preys on someone in such a way?" I took one last look at the rainbow, considering how delicate it was compared to the person who created it. He knew beauty and what would make me feel safe and used it against me. "You created this beautiful world with only the intention of hurting me. Did you bring me here to watch me? Scope me out so you knew the best way to hurt me?" I used my magic to whirl the winds around me, creating a defense against him with the sharpness of the leaves. I wished I had my knife; if I did, I would have gone after him, which would have done more damage than the leaves.

"Blair, I didn't have a choice."

"Don't tell me that you didn't have a choice! You have always had a choice. I know you would not let anyone force you to do anything you didn't want." I tried to watch his face for a reaction. I silently prayed that my words cut him a little. "What about the love potion? I know that it has gone past that. I know you felt it in that first kiss." I screamed at him, not letting myself be weak in front of him any longer.

Tate gave me a grin that was ominous in a way I wasn't expecting. This was not an expression I had seen from him before today, so it stopped me. "Blair, when you went to the bathroom, I took a potion to reverse the extent of your love potion." He watched my face intently for my reaction now that he had revealed yet another part of his betrayal. "I think it's a good thing. It made me realize that your feelings were real."

"You were aware the whole time!" I wanted to contain myself, knowing what my anger could do in this situation, but that wasn't possible. I could feel it bubbling inside me dangerously for both of us. He was fortunate I didn't have my knife on me. "You haven't been under the love potion since then? I thought it had just settled into your body, and you had come to terms with it."

"I'm not stupid. Of course I would always have something on me to reverse any potions or spells cast over me. Only a fool would spend this much time in the company of witches and not be prepared for such an occasion. All of you have something wicked up your sleeve, and my training has prepared for this."

With his words, I snapped my fingers to create a spark, flicking my wrist and shooting it toward the trees to make them to burn. He might have made this world for me, but I was going to destroy it for me too.

"You're right; you aren't stupid. But you are an idiot to think you can turn around and pretend we are okay."

"You were supposed to leave," His voice caught a little as the words came out. "I tried to keep you from finding out about this."

The forest around us caught fire and started to burn, the embers doing something to the color of his eyes that would have made my heart race in the past. Finally, I was unaffected. "Did you think that I would be willing to betray my Coven? My family! That's what I would be doing if I left them there alone. It's bad enough what happened to me. I could not imagine what would have happened to my family if I hadn't been there to distract Harriet." I could feel the heat of the embers as they sparked around me, somehow, they matched how I felt on the inside. "I thought you were on my side! I thought you were on my team."

"I was always on your team. All I have ever wanted is to protect you."

"So why did you do it? I imagine that you were a sleeper

agent sent by the Cabals. Were you with Harriet, or were you sent separately with the hopes that at least one of you would be able to make it through?"

Tate shook his head and again tried to come near me, resulting in me quickly stepping backward, splashing a foot into the stream, and taking out a few flowers. We both knew that if he wanted me, he would have been able to get to me, and if he didn't want to exert the effort, he could have frozen me in a place like he had all the times before. "I am impressed that you know the term. I was a sleeper agent, but not for the Cabals."

"Then who sent you here?" I don't know if my Coven could handle it if another set of vengeful witches came to Salem. "Are you leading a troop of traitors?"

He reached out to his bicep, raising his shirt sleeve and displaying a tattoo that a wizard must have done, since this was the first time I had seen it. He had kept it concealed with magic, but now he didn't care. "I am a member of the Council of Guardians."

I scoffed, "So, you are an *important sell-out*."

His face at least told me he still thought of me as funny. "Some might say that. I was sent back through the Academy, hoping to acquire a few more young men for the Council's Guard. Seth Walker going around trying to recruit soldiers to protect his Coven was a new thing that had not been done before, so my mission changed, and I was reassigned here. Becoming close to Seth was my cover, but getting as close to you as I have was never supposed to happen."

"You faked it all to get close to us?"

"When Seth was looking for a protection unit, it made it obvious that there was something more important here to protect than the ancestors' magic. That was when we learned of the Bradbury Coven. Your number of witches was a big surprise. You were smart to split your Coven, letting the magic divide itself into an individual line instead of following the lines from before. That was probably why you could get away with it for so long." He tried to walk near me, almost to the point of being able to touch me in the way that he had before, not caring that the fire was creeping toward him. "The Council wanted to know you first. Figure out who was strong because then they would take your magic."

I was desperate to wrap my mind around everything he was saying and go over every interaction we had, but the big realization was in front of my eyes. "That is why they wanted us to fight the Cabals. We get the Cabals' magic, and then they take ours, and they have it all. And all without having to work as hard for it." The Council was ready to end the Bradbury Coven.

"I tried to warn you that I would only destroy your world. I never thought that I would fall in love with you." As emotional as he could be, he reached out to me again, "I wished so many times that I could properly warn you, and if I could just take you out of the equation, this would have been easy. That was why I begged you not to fight today and not to overexpose your magic."

The bitter taste in my mouth was dangerous. I finally understood what I was willing to sacrifice for the sake of my family. I was willing to sacrifice the only person I had ever truly loved, which was the easiest decision of my life.

My magic pulled a tree from its roots and laid it between us to add distance when needed. Still, despite everything and the world he created burning around me, I knew that if he was willing to do all of this, he wouldn't hurt me, even if that was the only way for him to get what he wanted. Even now, I knew that a small part of him loved me, probably the only truth that had ever come out of his mouth.

I used the skills he had taught me to make a candle appear, using my magic to have it float beside me, and in a swift motion of my hand, I used the wind to light it. It would help me facilitate the magic to do what must be done. "I release you. I let you go. Let my heart be free of your binds on me."

Once again, he tried to come near me. He was trying to stop my spell from changing us. I knew he hoped that touching me would remind me of all the good moments we had shared, but I knew I would only see this moment and him walking out from the treeline. "Blair, please don't do this. I told you the truth because I need you to stay out of this to protect you."

The selfishness behind his words fueled me to keep going, using my magic in a way I never had before, screaming the words once more to intensify their power. "I release you! I let you go! Let my heart be free of the binds that you have on me!"

It was done in a flash, the link between us felt like the snipping of string, and it broke my heart to no longer be tied to him.

Our entire connection was severed, and there was no coming back from it. All the feelings from our union were gone. I knew what the only logical next step was.

I had to find a way to kill him.

That was the only way that I would be able to save my family from him. I didn't know if I would be strong enough to do it, but I would be the only one he would probably let close enough to do this.

"You are doing the right thing," His words came out of

nowhere, as if he knew what I was thinking. As much as I didn't want to believe him, something in his eyes told me that he was sincere and that despite everything he did, he loved me. "I know that you have to do this. It's the same reason why I had to do *this*," He gestured to the world around us, "We each have the role that we must play."

If it's the right thing, then why does it feel so wrong? No matter how hard I tried, I knew I would never return from this moment. There was no way my heart would ever be able to recover.

Tate gave me a look to let me know that he was serious. Even as I stared at him, I waited for devil horns to appear on his head in a way that would only confirm what I knew to be true. I don't know how I had never seen how far deep his evil side went, but now that all the puzzle pieces were coming together, I could see it. He warned, "Next time I tell you to leave this war, I will not be doing it with my words."

"I'm not going to leave! I have made myself clear." I didn't realize that I was still yelling, but I was. I wasn't sure that I could return to my calmness from before now that I knew the truth of his betrayals.

"I have warned you that this fight isn't for you. You must leave before they arrive. The faster you are, the better. They can't know you are a part of this." He reached again for me, but I was ready this time, pulling another tree out of the ground and adding it to the wall I was trying to create as a barrier between us. It was proving more efficient than the mental one I had learned to keep up since he continued to penetrate it anyway. "I am begging you to leave before you get hurt; you must understand why I need you to be safe."

"You are supposed to protect me, take care of me, and yet here you are bringing utter destruction to my world." I could feel my breath catch as I tried to keep myself from crying. "You're begging me to leave? Well, now I am begging you not to be a traitor."

"You have to go; you must run away from this." He had a misting over his eyes, an emotion I would have never thought him capable of after all of this. "You have to leave; I don't know what I will do next if you stay in this any longer. I won't be able to protect you if you continue to put yourself in the line of fire."

He walked back toward the trees, and I knew the Astral Projection was ending. He was going to leave me again. At least this time, I knew who it was doing the leaving.

I could see the world around me start to fade just as a black dahlia appeared at my feet, the symbol of betrayal and sadness staring back at me. He *knew* me and how hard this would hurt.

The Tate I fell in love with was back, the light in his eyes showing the person I desperately wanted him to be. He had joked once that he was the hero, and I think that is who he wanted to be. "I promised you, and I don't break promises." I could tell that he was holding himself back from reaching out to touch me once more, which I was grateful for. I couldn't stay strong if he felt me. "I am here, and I do want to protect you. That is all I've ever wanted to do."

I realized then that we would do terrible things to the people we love.

* * *

Magic pulled me back to the field where the fight had gone down. I was lying down in the grass, so I shot up quickly and frantically looked around, counting out those around me to ensure no one was missing. All the women who came with me to fight were sitting together on the green grass;

none looked like they had received much damage despite the mud and dried blood stained into their clothes. Huxley and Fabian were standing on high alert; their eyes moved from one side of the field to the other in a unified manner.

I used the remainder of my strength to stand and step toward the group. My hands rushed to my chest, where only a faint scar and dried blood sat. No longer was my chest punctured by the spear like it had been before I was put into the Astral Projection. Magic had been used to heal me, another forbidden magic that someone was using. "What happened?"

"You rushed forward to take the spear before it got to Tate. It punctured your chest, and the moment it hit you, it killed you. He froze those on the field and took you away in a flash. While we continued to fight, he somehow brought you back to life. He returned you in one piece." Ninnie explained gently like she was worried about freaking me out further with her words. She only confirmed something that I had been suspecting for a while. Tate was using dark magic; there was no other way that he would have been able to bring me back to life. The spy amongst the Council had to be him.

"When the fight was done, the Council's Guard showed up. They took the Cabals, and then Tate returned you before he joined them," Seth gave me the bullet points. It seemed like, out of everyone, he was the one who was hurt the most. His face fell now that he knew what Tate was hiding from him. As terrible as his betrayal was to me, Seth felt it even worse. "None of you have any reason to believe me, but I had no idea he was with the Council. He must have been with their Guard for a while."

"That doesn't matter now. He betrayed us and knew too much. He will go to the Council about what we know."

Herbs and Their Benefits

Aloe: luck, protectionCarnation: protection, strength

Chamomile: passion, sleepChrysanthemum: strength

Clover: wealth, successDandelion: divination

Heather: protection, luckHibiscus: love, lust

Holly: protectionHoneysuckle: wealth, spirit

Jasmine: wealth, loveLavender: peace, happiness

Lilac: exorcism. loveLily: healing

Marigold: protectionMyrtle: fertility

Poppy: love, sleep Rose: healing, love

Salt: protection, purificationPepper: banish spells, protection, warding

Cloves: prosperity, friendship, protectionRosemary: all-purpose herb, love/lust

Thyme: approval, money, purificationBasil: money, purification, love, protection

Mint: love, money, healingCinnamon: smoke cleansing, success, love

Bay: wishes, spell bags, psychic workGarlic: healing, protection

Family Tree & Character List

The Bradbury Family

Andromeda: Original Keeper of the Magic

Annabelle: Andromeda's daughter who caused the curse

Agatha: Blair's Grandmother, current Keeper of the Magic

Mira: Agatha's Daughter, Blair's Aunt

Endora: Agatha's Daughter, Mother of Blair

Steven: Father of Blair

Celeste: Endora and Steven's oldest daughter, Blair's Sister

Penelope: Endora and Steven's middle daughter, Blair's Sister

Blair: Endora and Steven's youngest daughter

Lucy: Celeste's daughter, Blair's niece

Kira: Celeste's daughter, Blair's niece

Edna: sister of Agatha, Blair's Great-Aunt

Cassandra: Edna's Daughter, Blair's First Cousin Once Removed

Grace: Cassandra's Daughter, Blair's Second Cousin

Piper: Cassandra's Daughter, Blair's Second Cousin

Walker Family

Mrs. Walker: Ninnie's Mother
Ninnie: Seth's Cousin
Seth: Guardian
Lydia: Mrs. Walker's Sister, Mother of Seth

The Guardians

Tate: Guardian
Huxley: Guardian, brother of Fabian
Fabian: Guardian, brother of Huxley

Inspiration for the Novel

Many people know there was a time when men, women, and children were accused of being witches. This period in our country was later called the Salem Witch Trials. This was a series of hearings and persecutions of people accused of witchcraft in colonial Massachusetts between February 1692 and May 1693. More than 200 people were charged, and according to The Boston Globe, 25 people were killed during the Witch Trials in Salem, "All 19 who were executed through a hanging died at Proctor's Ledge. Five others died in jail, and one was crushed to death."

The infamous Salem Witch Trials began during the spring of 1692, after a group of young girls in Salem Village, Massachusetts, claimed to be possessed by the devil and accused several local women of witchcraft. This was a time of significant religious influence, and those later accused of being a witch were considered cursed by the devil.

Bridget Bishop, the first colonist to be tried in the Salem Witch Trials, was found guilty of the practice of witchcraft. The law did not then use the principle of "innocent until proven guilty" – if someone made it to trial, the law presumed guilt. By 1711, colonial authorities pardoned some accused and compensated their families for what they had been put through.

Bridget Bishop was the first person executed during the Salem Witch Trials, killed by hanging on 10 June 1692 at 60 at the hand of the colony. The youngest victim of the Trials was 4-year-old Dorothy Good. She was accused and arrested, spending over seven months in jail. Her mother, Sarah Good, was also accused and was killed while her daughter sat in a cell. Another victim was Elizabeth Proctor who was also convicted and executed, although her execution sentence was postponed because she was pregnant.

In October 1692, Governor William Phips ended the special witchcraft court in Salem upon hearing that his wife was accused of witchcraft and ordered an end to the Trials.

* * *

My family often joked that we had a curse placed upon us, which was because the first daughter always got married, had a daughter, and then divorced. I, being the first daughter, was terrified of getting married and living in constant fear of the curse continuing. My husband thought it was hilarious and made regular jokes about the ramifications of the curse and how I wouldn't handle it well if our first child was a girl. My love of storytelling and the hilarity of my husband's jokes gave life to the Bradbury women and the Coven they have. After learning I was related to one of the women killed during the Salem Witch Trials, my story's end blossomed. All the words flew out of my fingers faster than I could control them, and with my husband's support, I had a book before my eyes!

I realized that there is a little magic in all of us, maybe that does come from those before us, and it's our job to keep it.

Meet your Author

Trena VanHoff has been telling stories since she was a kid. She always had a book to read and a notebook full of her own story ideas just waiting to be told. Currently, she is writing in her free time while working in the medical field. She lives with her husband and four dogs (yes, you read that right. They have four) in Utah, although she will always be a Cali girl at heart.

She hopes to make the bestseller list and dreams of finding her book on the shelves of Barnes and Noble. However, she will also tell you that she can't wait until her books have made it through the hands of twenty different people and end up with a broken spine, dog-eared pages, on the shelf of a thrift store for the next person to find, since that is where she has discovered many of her favorite novels.

She can be found drinking a diet Dr. Pepper or eating chips and salsa while reading a good book until she figures out an idea for her next book. Keep an eye out for it; it will be a good one!

Find her on Instagram and TikTok for book updates @trenavanhoffbooks

Or her website www.Trenavanhoffbooks.com

I would like to dedicate this book to the love of my life, my own Guardian. Peydun, you told me to sit down and write time after time, having more faith in my dream than I did at times. You are my forever hero, and I am so glad I get to live this amazing life with you.

My parents, thank you for your constant, unwavering support and for financing my expensive book habit growing up. You always supported me and this dream. I promise it was worth it!

To my own Coven of witches, the Wonderful Watts Women, thank you for teaching me beauty and grace can come with so much love for each other and a little sass when needed. You taught me that women are strongest when we work as a group and that any crime could be solved before dinner.

Thank you to all my amazing friends and unbelievable family for their support as I discovered who I was and how I wanted to share myself with the world! You have done so much for me, and I will never be able to repay you for that!

To the goofy group who spent Saturday nights sitting on my couch playing Dungeons and Dragons, thank you for letting me steal your words, stories, and quests for my book. I would not have known magic if not for you!

Thank you to all those who have supported my social media and for watching me talk about this book for over six months;

I imagine there were plenty of moments when it was annoying to see my face pop across your screen again. Thank you to everyone who read my book. You were so amazing to take time aside from your busy lives to support my dreams! The beautiful and incredible Alexa! I could not have asked for a better editor! You constantly blew me away with your attention to detail, and your encouragement kept me going. Thank you!

Thank you to my Heavenly Father for giving me the ability and chance to share stories with the world. The greatest blessings in my life have come from you.